D1519601

Prologue

Two men stood on top of the stone guard tower at the edge of the old highway, each of them wore thin armor made from mana beast hides, with a sword belted to their hips.

"Captain Hughes, it's been almost seven days since they went in. At this rate, the dungeon will soon spill over into our world," the younger man said, fidgeting with his sword holster, looking past the overgrown interstate. Nature had reclaimed the road ages ago, but spots of the old world still survived.

Tom ignored his lieutenant. They couldn't see the dungeon portal from the tower. All they could do was watch the flying mountain that hovered in the distance.

He fought the urge to fidget with his sword. There was nothing he could personally do now but watch and wait for the fate of the small town they protected.

But he knew what his lieutenant referenced. The nearby dungeon was the largest he'd ever seen, and if it spilled over, it would be a threat to the town behind him. But the level of the dungeon left few options. He had to rely on the Sect to deal with it.

No one in town was above a third-ring mage. Despite Tom's experience, he had trouble getting near the portal entrance.

"Captain, do you think it'll be okay?" Roger broke his thoughts. Tom turned towards Roger, realizing the kid was nearing the point of bolting and hiding in town. Not that that would save his life if the Sect failed.

Tom sighed inwardly. He had more riding on this than he cared to admit. He didn't want the Sect anywhere near him or Isaac. But he would need their strength to close a dungeon this large.

The city wouldn't survive if the portal spilled over. It would be a slaughter if the monsters in the dungeon crossed over. Even a fourth-rank mana beast could reduce the entire town to rubble.

Looking towards the floating mountain, he tried to get his emotions under control. Longing, anger and helplessness all broiled inside of him, fighting for dominance. He felt the weight of the responsibility he had for the city; all the while, he was unable to do anything about it. He took a deep breath and straightened his back.

They would have to rely on the Sect to protect them. The Sun and Moon Hall had been protecting Locksprings from threats like the portal since he was a kid. In return, the city was essentially indentured. The town's meager goods and any half-decent young mages disappeared down the greedy throat of the Sect to fuel their own conflicts.

Roger shook his arm, dragging him away from his thoughts. "Did you see that! The green flash."

He shook his head. "Roger, nothing happened."

"No. I saw it—it was a green flash. It came from over there and went towards the city." Roger was pointing frantically. "The city is a goner! We are all going to die!"

He couldn't be gentle, he knew this, but it didn't mean he liked having to do his duty as a commander. He grabbed his lieutenant by his collar roughly and easily lifted him off the ground with one arm. His three rings, each with their own mana beast, thrummed with power as he wound up his swing.

SMACK

A red welt formed on Roger's cheek.

"We will be okay. Even if a fourth-rank mana beast got out, they wouldn't be so fast that I couldn't see them. Maybe you saw some light flash from a spell, but it wasn't a mana beast."

Just then, something caught his attention, and they both turned. The floating mountain shifted, and the sky roared as it started displacing air. The Sect had cleared the dungeon and started moving away.

"It's over?" Roger finally stopped struggling with his words.

Tom put him down and patted his shoulder. He couldn't blame the man for being scared. The entire city had been on the edge of life and death, but that was the way it was now. Every moment was dangerous; that's why he helped protect Locksprings now.

"Come on, Roger. We need to get back and tell everyone the good news." Tom moved quickly, eager to get back to his son.

***

Isaac sat in his sandbox. The pristine greenery of the yard surrounded him, a stark contrast to the world outside Locksprings.

Packing the sand in his red bucket, Isaac ceremoniously flipped it over and deposited his newly made 'watch tower' in front of him.

Picking up his green figurine, he marched it over the landscape. "Ho! I am a guard of Locksprings! Isaac! Who goes there?!"

A blue figurine of a wolf beast came out and growled at the guard before it lunged to the tower.

"Too late! Beg my father for forgiveness!" The green figure stomped the beast into the sandpit.

"Can I join?" A soft hand dug another figure loose from the sand.

Isaac turned to see a pair of eyes so green he lost himself. He had never seen a woman so pretty before. He absently spoke aloud, "You're pretty."

She returned a soft smile, and he decided she could join the game.

"Sure, but you are a girl, so you should be in the back. Men fight up front to protect you." Isaac nodded at his own statement and reached to guide her figure behind his.

He arranged a few more figurines to stand with the wolf beast's blue figure.

An epic war ensued as Isaac directed the two figurines to defeat the mana beasts and climb a hill of sand in victory as the dungeon was closed. Isaac even had the soldiers go back home to their families after. Clapping, he turned to the woman.

"Hi, I'm Isaac." Brushing the sand off his small hand, he held it out like he'd been taught.

When he looked up, he was once again enraptured by the woman's green eyes again. They had talked during the entire game, but he'd never really looked at her again until now.

"I'm... a friend." The woman awkwardly held the boy's hand. "You aren't scared?"

It was then that Isaac noticed the shifting green form behind her. She saw his look and splayed her wings out.

3

When she spread her three pairs of wings, a dark shadow cast over Isaac. He leaned back and forth, taking in the new sight. She tensed, waiting for his reaction.

"Woah, you have wings... SO COOL." Isaac reached out before immediately pausing. "Can I touch them? Dad says you have to ask for permission before grabbing something."

"Yes, please." A green feathered wing dipped before Isaac. He immediately reached up and began stroking it.

"So soft," he exclaimed as he wrapped himself in the wing, covering as much of himself as he could. "Hey, do you want to be friends?" Peeling his eyes from her verdant wings, he looked back at her face.

"My home is gone, and people are looking for me. I can't stay... I would like to be your friend though." She smiled warmly at Isaac wrapped up in her wing. The boy didn't care. He stuck out his hand firmly and took hers.

"We are friends then! Best friends forever!" He linked their pinkies and held them tight. "Pinkie promise."

"Pinky promise?" She tilted her head at that.

"It means that I swear that we are friends. If I break the promise, I have to cut off my finger."

She looked at their intertwined little fingers in a different light. "Would you promise to protect me?"

"Of course, we are friends. That's what friends do, silly." Isaac puffed out his chest.

"Isaac!" A deep shout came from the house.

"If you pinky promise to eat this, we'll be best friends. I have to go away for a bit, but if you swallow this, I'll come back and we'll be inseparable." A sudden urgency flashed on her face.

A jewel so opalescent it seemed to give off a green light filled with gold motes appeared in her hand.

Isaac was so focused on it he didn't see the feathers starting to fall out of her wings. She held out the small finger on her other hand for the promise.

"I don't know... what is it?" Isaac was drawn to the shiny jewel in her hand.

"It'll protect both of us in the future. Please?" She had an urgency that was beyond the five-year-old Isaac, but she was his friend. He could trust her.

"It's a promise." Isaac joined their fingers, and she pushed the jewel past his lips urgently. It was large, but Isaac wasn't sure if he could swallow it.

"Isaac!" This time the voice was closer, and he turned away from the smiling angel to see his father storm into the backyard.

Tom looked relieved to see his kid in the sand.

Isaac still had the gem in his mouth and couldn't respond.

"Why didn't you answer me?" Reading Isaac's guilty face and puffed-out cheeks, Tom immediately followed up with, "Spit it out."

The stubborn boy shook his head and tried to swallow the lustrous gem. It was too big, and he grabbed his throat, opening his mouth but only managed a gag.

Tom flashed to his side and put a canteen of water to his boy's mouth. Why kids ate sand, he'd never understand. Water would help it go down though.

With the water helping, Isaac managed to swallow the gem. "Dad. Stop it. Don't do that in front of my friend." Isaac looked behind him for the winged woman but was only met with empty air.

"Oh, introduce me. What do they look like?" Tom teased with a cheeky grin.

"I swear she was just there!" Isaac said as he scanned the backyard.

"Oh, a girl. Was she cute?"

"The prettiest I've ever seen, dad! She had wings!"

"Ha, come on, buddy. Time to clean up. I had an excellent day. Let's go get pizza to celebrate. You can tell me all about your friend." Tom ushered Isaac back into the house.

Isaac couldn't help looking back, hoping to see his new friend.

Chapter 1

I rolled out of bed. I'd awoken from another dream about the imaginary friend I had as a child. I wasn't sure why the image of her stuck with me through the years or why I'd imagined myself eating what I now know was a mana beast core. I must have seen it in one of my dad's books when I was little or something.

Humans are unable to generate mana. Mana beast cores allow those that eat them to bind the mana beast and use its mana to step into the world of mages.

Actually, eating one as a kid would have killed me. Even now, I'm still working to prepare my body for my first mana beast.

It was light enough outside that I didn't need to find a candle to get around the house, though that meant I had less time to get to the academy.

I'd deal with being late if it came to that. First, I needed to wake up.

Yawning, I made my way downstairs to find the kitchen empty and the house quiet. A note sat by the coffee pot, my father's scrawled letters apparent.

I knew what it would say but read it anyway.

Isaac, I was called off to deal with a threat just outside the city. I'll be back in time for your evaluation.

Short and brief, that was my father's style. It didn't bother me; he'd been closed off since mom had passed.

My father spent more and more time protecting the city with each passing year, like he was trying to make up for her death.

I rinsed out a small mesh bag and filled it with dark, ground beans. Filling a black kettle with some water, I put it over the fireplace.

The beans had a bitter smell as they cooked. Harvested from the dungeons and cultivated for its caffeine, I'd read that the plant

6

was like the coffee beans used back when goods were traded far and wide across the world.

But all I needed was the quick caffeine hit, however that came.

The fireplace burned as it always had and always would. My father had come home once with an ever-burning fire, a look of pride on his face as he installed it. It was a magical item from dungeons; it would burn for hundreds of years before going out.

While the coffee was brewing, I couldn't help but check my chest in the hall mirror. They said you felt it when your first ring formed, but I still checked religiously.

It would be the sign that I'd formally stepped into the world of cultivation that I'd been eagerly anticipating my entire life.

Forming the first ring wasn't easy. It required a normal person, as we are all born, to slowly incorporate mana into their body through medicine and meditation. Breaking down the body through exercise, mana would slowly become a part of you until you had enough mana to form that first ring. Then, everything changed.

While still human, that first ring was like a metamorphosis, changing the person into a mage with endless potential and abilities, capable of soaring to the heavens.

I had high hopes mine would come before the final evaluation of the year. It had to; others had formed their first ring and gained their first mana beast the last few weeks. I refused to be left behind.

Running my hand across the unmarked skin of my chest, I couldn't help but feel a determination to succeed. Hands out in front, I started stepping through my sword forms.

I'd already planned out what kind of monster I would seal within my first ring. I would specialize in the neutral element metal, like my father.

It was a solid, stable way to use rings. I was just building my foundation for now.

The world would step to my beat one day.

My heart beat faster and the surge in my blood started to build up to a crescendo as I danced through footwork in the kitchen. Hitting my peak speed, the pressure in my blood feeling like it was about to burst, the kettle started squealing, breaking me from my fond dreams of the future.

Whatever was building inside of me dispersed. I shook my head and got back to my morning. It wasn't the first time I'd felt that rush.

I often felt the need to explode into motion and embrace the building tension that came with it, but I never quite hit the moment of complete satisfaction. I was always left wanting more, like an orgasm you just couldn't reach.

I sighed. I'd been dealing with that problem on a couple fronts. Hopefully, Kat and I would deepen our relationship and get there soon.

Scooping up the kettle from the fire, the warm wooden handle dispersed gentle warmth to my waking body. I slowly drank the liquid, enjoying the feel of the caffeine hitting my body as I prepared for more boring lessons.

I continued my daydreams as I got ready for school; I was so close. Soon, I could leave Locksprings for the first time in my life.

After graduating from the academy and receiving that first ring and mana beast, the world of cultivation opened up to you.

The Sun and Moon Hall was the only sect that had a presence in town. But they took so few, and it was usually just girls.

But that didn't matter. I'd likely end up among the many that just set off into the world to grow as a mage and explore all there is to see.

Locksprings was a small town. We got almost no visitors. The world had forgotten us since the dungeons opened up and flooded the world with mana.

I poured myself some coffee and started on my oatmeal. It was a simple breakfast, but what was important was my daily mana. It was more important than hurrying to class; I'd be late but getting mana into my system was more important.

In the cupboard, I pulled out a small wooden box and opened the lid. Inside, there was a fist-sized mana crystal and a file, one made of material from a dungeon.

My oats warming on the fire, I carefully held the crystal as I started filing off dust from the crystallized pure mana.

It was part of my daily ritual. I broke down my body through exercise and ingested a small quantity of pure mana. Eventually, my body would form its first ring.

Mana was a mutagen. It altered the human body.

Since the dungeon portals had appeared and started pouring mana into our world, everything had been changed by mana. Animals that strengthened with mana were called mana beasts, and humans could harness the change in a controlled process called cultivation.

Tempering my body with shavings of this mana crystal was how I would start on the path of cultivation.

They didn't teach why we all formed a circular seal on us called a ring, but they had taught us that pushing ourselves too hard too fast could end up just like the mana beasts, a feral creature obsessed with consuming mana.

Eyeing the now bubbling oatmeal, I figured a few more shavings wouldn't hurt and made a bit more dust before putting it back in the velvet-lined case.

It was one of the more precious things I owned; it literally held my future.

Scraping my bowl clean, I set the dishes to soak as I hurried out the door.

I was on my way to class when I saw Kat leaning against a stone wall. Her petite silhouette against the wall made a fantastic sight for any man. We'd been in class together for a long time and dating for about the past six months.

Kat's red locks fanned out behind her as she turned to see me. But the soberness on her face made my heart drop into the pit of my stomach.

I wanted to wrap her up in a hug and fix whatever was wrong. It sounded stupid, but Kat and I had felt like two halves of a whole since the beginning.

"Waiting for me, Kat?" It wouldn't be the first time, but something told me it might be the last. I felt my heart clench.

She shifted away from the wall and I got a better look at her. She was beautiful. Her curly crimson locks framed her heart-shaped face. She wore a fitted black V-neck with a flowing blue skirt. I reached her, brushing her cheek as I tucked a strand of her hair behind her ear. She'd always been so soft and sweet.

"Hi, Isaac." Just that had made her frown vanish for a second before whatever was on her mind weighed her back down.

"Let's head to school." I held out my arm for her to hook onto.

I left it dangling in the air as the world seemed to grow cold.

"I can't. Isaac, I'm leaving town. The Sun and Moon Hall has accepted me and will help my mother..." She trailed off, unable to meet my gaze.

Feeling like I was at the edge of a cliff, I wanted to scream and tell her that she should stay with me. This however, was the opportunity of a lifetime for Kat.

I took a deep breath and smiled warmly at her. "That's amazing, Kat! I'm so proud of you." I reached out and pulled her into a tight hug. She snuggled in, resting her head on my shoulder. I held myself together, the last thing I wanted was an ugly memory of us being her last.

"I asked if you could come too. I really did, Isaac." She leaned back, looking up at me with uncertainty dancing in her eyes, wanting to make sure I knew she had tried.

I believed her. Not for a second did I think she'd want to leave me behind. I smiled down at her and shrugged. "The Sun and Moon Hall just doesn't take many men. We both knew it was unlikely for me to ever make it there. Don't worry, I'll make a name in the world of mages in some other sect." I winked and gave her my best award-winning smile.

Her eyes warmed a bit and I could tell her spirits were up. "Good. I'll... wait for you. We always said we'd become top-tier mages and change the world for the better. I will always hold onto that."

The warmth in her eyes had kindled into a bonfire that I hoped would keep burning. Kat had ambition, and I knew the Sun and Moon Hall had always been a real path for her.

"Don't worry about me, Kat. This is a great opportunity for you, and we will be just fine. This doesn't change our plans at all."

She smiled so wide her eyes squinted and tilted her head back for a kiss.

I leaned down, claiming those soft lips. I deepened the kiss, reminding her of what we had together.

"I have to go, Isaac. But, one day, it'll be me and you against the world." Kat looked down, her hands lingering despite her words. She finally took a deep breath like she was about to plunge into icy water before turning and walking off.

I could see a tension in her shoulders as she walked away, each footstep heavy and forced.

Every few steps, she'd touch the vermilion bird hair clip I'd gotten her on our first date, ensuring she still had it.

After she left, I turned to head towards school, but I paused, knowing exactly where Kat was heading. The Sun and Moon Hall was well known, being the only sect that visited, but it was still incredibly secretive. I had yet to figure out where the Sun and Moon Hall held their presence in our town. I knew the Sect must have some place to recruit from and gather mages before taking them back to the Sect on the floating mountain.

They rarely took male disciples, but I figured, if I could be near their base, I could always casually meet and connect with those in the Sect.

I was making up reasons to follow her. I needed to turn around and let her go.

But... I had to make sure Kat was safe. There was still a lot of mystery around the Sect and who it took as a new recruit.

Decision made, I started walking in the direction Kat had gone.

She was walking through the city slowly when I spotted her again.

It was the early morning, and everyone was getting ready for the day. Her bright red hair stood out amidst the chaos of the morning bustle.

I took in all the pedestrians winding around the carts being pulled by horses or mana beasts. Buildings were patched up with whatever materials could be found around, but they still held a lot of their shape and old-world charm. The trimmings and decorative designs had been kept and replaced dozens of times to keep a bit of the old world alive. Locksprings had fared well since the dungeons appeared, but nobody had much extra wealth to throw around, making new buildings when they could patch up old ones in an endless cycle that made the buildings look a bit patchwork.

I followed Kat as she wound through the city towards the bustling bazaar, a different way than I'd gone before. She suddenly stopped on the street, pausing to stare at a dark black building with shaded windows.

After a moment's hesitation, she squared her shoulders and walked into the building.

A buxom lady, showing generous amounts of skin that would make any mother scowl, greeted Kat like an old friend. Even from a distance, I could smell the cheap perfume wafting out.

It didn't make sense. Why would Kat be here? Did the Sun and Moon Hall own the local brothel?

I leaned against the cool brick and watched as the lady welcomed a few men into her parlor. Eventually, I had no other explanation. I couldn't help wondering what kind of sect ran a brothel in town.

Turning, I bumped into someone. I went to apologize but stopped short when I saw who was standing in front of me. Aiden Hill stood there in the silver and gold robes of the Sun and Moon Hall.

I was surprised to see him here. Aiden had left Locksprings two years ago as one of the rare men to get accepted into the Sun and Moon Hall.

Aiden was a grade A asshole—one whom I'd butted heads with more than once over the past few years.

He had always acted like a spoiled rich kid in a town where everyone else worked hard and supported each other.

I still couldn't believe that he had been chosen for the Sect. He hadn't been the best fighter by a longshot.

There were several rumors around his acceptance into the Sun and Moon Hall that only made me lose respect for him even more.

He hadn't been strong enough to fight those his own age, so he had decided to come fight juniors in the academy before he left for the Sun and Moon Hall. We'd had some run-ins as a result, and Aiden hadn't loved the outcome.

"Isaac, right?" He followed where my eyes had been. "Listen, forget about Kat. Forget about all of them that join the Sect. Honestly, they are in a different world than you now. It's for the best." Aiden chuckled, bumping into me as he started to walk past.

I sighed. Bullies were so boring sometimes. "Feeling big after two years, Aiden? Come back for a rematch? I handed you your ass then. Happy to help reset that ego of yours again if you'd like."

I could feel that pulsing sensation again, my body priming for the potential fight.

Aidan's face started to turn red as he turned his body back towards me.

We'd gone a few rounds in the pit before he had formed his first ring. The fight was far from even then, and I knew he was replaying it in his head now.

I tilted my head, waiting for his response and assessed his strength.

By now, he probably was well on his way to his second ring. If he used his full force, I doubted my sword skill would matter for long.

But I wasn't one to stand down to a bully, and I certainly could get in some solid hits before he overpowered me. Maybe I could give that stiff face of his a few bruises to remember me by.

Aiden let his robe slip, showing off that his second ring was far from completion.

"Watch yourself. I could crush you like an ant. You aren't talking to a person. You are talking to a *mage*. Know your place before I put you in it." He spit a little at the end of his tirade.

I stood straight and stared him down. Raising an eyebrow slightly, I just smiled. Even if he attacked me, he'd never make it through the town after.

No one would put up with a mage attacking someone who hadn't even popped their first ring. That was a cardinal sin in today's world.

He huffed, seeing that he would not intimidate me. "See you later, and remember to forget about those that have left your pitiful world. Don't worry. I'll take care of Kat."

I watched him walk away for a moment before turning away to clear my head. I needed to burn off some steam and push myself harder. I picked up the pace and decided to get some exercise on the way into the academy.

The academy was a washed-out old college building sporting mismatched bricks. There'd been more to the college before, but the main building and the low built natatorium were all that remained.

There were only three classrooms, each built like small amphitheaters.

After my encounter with Aiden, I shook off my worries and headed to class. I had missed the first class, but I was able to slip into the second before it started.

Tossing down my bag, I sat down next to my two friends, Jonny and Steve, taking out a bit of my steam on the chair as I plopped down.

Steve was tall and lanky, like someone had stretched him a bit too much. But he had a tanned, tough exterior from working on his father's farm.

Jonny, on the other hand, was rounder. He blamed it on growing up in a restaurant. His coppery skin and black hair seemed to benefit him, however, as he seemed to have luck in chasing skirts.

Steve gave me his classic nod of recognition and continued to work on the pile of sticks before him. Steve had chosen to be an archer when we had decided on our specialties when we entered the academy.

As a result, he seemed to be perpetually making arrows. But I was pretty sure he was also selling them at his father's tack shop for some spare coin.

Jonny was more animated. "So, is today the big day?" He dropped his voice low like he was asking me for a secret.

Of course, I knew what he was talking about, but his antics made me smile. "No. Still no ring. It better come before this year's evaluation."

At this rate, I'd be the last in this year's class to get my first ring, and that would put me at a severe disadvantage.

Jonny had gotten his first ring a few weeks ago. He had already sealed a radiant peacock, a life mana beast. It wasn't really built for combat, but it was good at what it did, which was healing.

Steve had been the first of the trio to get his ring. He had absorbed the core of a gust horse. Both of them had obtained their first ring and bound a rank one mana beast to it.

Steve looked up, frowned slightly, and shrugged.

"Yeah, I know Steve. I just need to be patient."

I was thankful for his intervention, but I was just as anxious as Jonny. I already carried around the monster core I wanted to use, just waiting.

The Steel-Winged Swallow was a perfect fit for my swift and sharp sword style. It had tremendous boons for a mage; it was the

14

epitome of speed and focused on sharp piercing attacks. I was looking forward to dashing past monsters only to have them split open in my wake.

"I hear getting laid increases the chance of a ring forming the next day, something about how well you sleep after," Jonny said with a straight face, brushing away imaginary dust from his pants.

Steve and I had long learned Jonny's priority in life. He'd admitted more than once that his dream in life was to have a harem of beauties.

My thoughts flitted back to the brothel, causing me to frown.

"Jonny, that's ridiculous—there's no data to support that claim." Though I didn't have much force behind the denial.

"No data disproving it either," Steve tossed in his two cents without looking up from his pile of half-made arrows.

Jonny smiled wide. "See, Isaac? Steve agrees. I know a few ladies who'd be willing to help you out. Call it a birthday gift."

Before I could argue, Professor Locke entered the classroom and everyone's conversations subsided.

The professor was an older, well-fed man. I couldn't imagine him fighting monsters with a sword in hand. He was, however, old enough to lead the lessons. His crown of gray hair and wrinkles suggested he had made it to an older age than most.

After complaining to my father years ago about learning from a senile old man, I'd learned the man was a veteran mage who had formed his third ring, which had earned my respect.

Locke stood silently at the front of the room. He used his obvious irritation to silence the class.

He basked in the still moment before starting class with his classic phrase. "You are the newest generation—you have the opportunity to arm yourself with more knowledge than those before you. Learn well, and you and those you love may survive."

There was the unsaid inverse about what would happen if you didn't learn well.

I might not have believed it when I was younger, but now I was old enough to notice those a few years older than me heading out of the city.

Everyone tried not to make an enormous deal of it, but I noticed when some of their families suddenly became downtrodden or a mother's eyes were strained from crying. Every year, it seemed like more and more mages left while none returned.

"Now I know none of you can focus on my alluring tales with your evaluation around the corner. So rather than review monsters or herbs today, we'll go back over the basics of cultivation since so many of you are now forming your first rings." He picked up a piece of chalk and wrote as he continued his lecture.

"Humans have no source of mana generation, unlike mana beasts. However, once we form our first ring, humans are able to seal a mana beast and obtain the ability to generate mana. In reality, it's the mana beast creating the mana that we can then use. Can anyone tell me the elements of mana?"

A blonde at the front shot up her hand. I instantly recognized Michelle's form.

Responding before she was called on, she rattled off, "Earth, wind, water, fire, metal, life and void."

I rolled my eyes. Michelle and I weren't exactly on friendly terms. It was a long story, but we enjoyed taking opportunities in combat training to prove who was better.

"Very good." Locke continued.

Michelle glanced over her shoulder and winked at me, knowing I was annoyed with her antics.

The teacher cleared his throat, and Michelle snapped back to attention. "Mana, unfortunately, does not retain its pure form once it has passed through the dungeon portal, save for mana crystals that are mined within the dungeon. We cannot consume elemental mana safely. Thus, we must wait for our first ring to cultivate in earnest. I assume you all consumed some raw mana crystal with your breakfasts," he said, making his point. "Once you seal your first mana beast, you may use them as the furnace for your cultivation, so to speak."

Locke made eye contact with everyone in class. "But do beware. We all want to progress quickly, but some methods will damn you. Practicing corrupt techniques will lead to rapid growth, but also rapid loss of yourself. You will be killed for the good of the community should you be caught practicing corrupt magics."

The world was an enormous but incredibly dangerous place. Until you became a mage, it really wasn't smart to leave the city. Locksprings might as well have been an island.

Not far outside the city, there were mana beasts that had come from dungeons left open too long. Wild and deadly, they kept those without power confined together for survival.

Mages became corrupt because the power to be free was too tempting.

After that first ring, it was possible to go at it alone and travel outside the city if you were smart and avoided danger. But most people moved in small teams to have each other's backs and up their chance of survival.

In the end, most people joined a larger organization like a sect.

A mage needed to find dungeons suitable for their level of strength in order to progress. And, in a sect, stronger mages would take on the more challenging dungeons, doling out lower-ranked dungeons to lower-ranking members for a price.

I'd heard that a number of sects existed in the wilds past the city, but information didn't flow back to the city very well and not many mages ever returned.

I'd only heard rumors. But I already knew that, if there were options out there, I was going to find them. Cracking my neck, I casually rechecked my chest.

Jonny caught my look and flashed me a cheeky grin. Steve continued forming the arrow shafts and nodded. Wherever things went, we were a team and would stay together. The loss of Kat wouldn't break up this trio.

The class ticked by as Professor Locke continued describing the underlying principles of cultivation. Before long, the class was unbearable with the weight of anxiousness in the room as combat training approached.

Locke didn't hold us there unnecessarily. "Go, go. Practicals are next hour. Homework for today is to interview one current mage about dungeons."

Jonny nudged me, and I realized that, while I was lost in my thoughts of sects and my run in with Kat earlier, the class had mostly cleared out. We got up to head to our practicals.

Chapter 2

I split up from Jonny and Steve for practicals. Jonny went off to train with the other healers, and Steve went to go work with several other archers. I preferred a good sword fight, face to face with my opponent. And, after the morning I'd had, I could use one.

I ducked through an archway to the school's old natatorium. The academy had repurposed the forgotten college, turning the two full-length swimming pools into fighting pits.

A layer of packed earth with various large rocks and broken walls filled each of the large pits. The tiles that had once lined its walls were broken and shattered around the edge, colored with the crimson paint of those who'd lost their match previously.

Between the two pools, a weapons rack stood full of retired, blunted weapons. Among the weapons stood Rigel, their teacher for melee practicals.

Rigel was a man well past his prime, but still a force in the pit. His scarred and tanned skin showed his history with the sharp end of a weapon, but his skin sagged at his biceps where firm muscles had flexed previously. He had gray hair to match his age, but his eyes glimmered with life as he observed each of us entering.

I had respect for Rigel, one of the strongest mages in town.

The first time I saw him fighting, I almost thought he was some feral mana beast. But his soft heart eventually showed though as he beat us into shape with love.

He wanted us to survive and trained us hard so that we had a chance. It was his own form of love. I'd come to accept that.

I took up my usual spot in the class along the section between the two pits. I resisted the urge to jump into the pits for the fight. From this position, I could at least watch both if one got too boring.

Watching and learning was fine, but a guy needed to get in there and hone his reflexes if he wanted to become an expert.

Practice and experience were necessary to build the muscle memory needed to dodge and deliver hits.

The surrounding area filled up quickly with the other fighters in the class.

We had been fighting together for the last two years, ever since we began our path to cultivation together. Our paths, however, were as varied as could be. Cultivation as a mage could take any form under the sky.

Stretching out while I waited to get started, I could feel the hair on the back of my neck prickle. I smiled. There was only one hostile stare that felt that way.

Turning my head, I saw Michelle's hard gaze on me.

The blonde woman stood hands on her hips, shoulders back. I took a moment to admire the killer breasts that unfortunately were on such a frustrating person.

Our rivalry had really built over the past few years, but I had to admit, with honey blonde hair and a killer figure, she would be a catch for some guy willing to deal with her arrogance.

I smirked and cocked an eyebrow at her. She seemed like the perfect target for my pent-up frustration.

Her face flushed, and I could see the muscles along her jaw flex. I could tell this would be one of our better fights. She was as primed and ready as I was for a good fight.

At one point, I might have loosely called her a friend. I'd even thought that she liked me at one point. Johnny had talked me into asking her out, which had bombed. And, ever since then, our dynamic had been different.

I'd put up with the constant digs towards me, but when she started picking on Kat, I had to step in. After some verbal battles, we learned to deal with our issues mostly in the pit.

Part of me enjoyed our fights. They were exciting if nothing else.

We were both waiting for that first ring. Once we got them, we'd finally get some space from each other as we explored outside the city.

A booming clap rang out as Rigel got in front of the class. "Morning. I know we are all excited to graduate, but we can't slack now. If anything, you need to train even harder." He looked over the group, making eye contact with each of us. "To further motivate you all, I've brought the first years over to watch today."

Several younger faces peeked out from behind the gnarled old fighter.

In their first year, they knew enough about battle to approach the ring with wide eyes. They had two years of very intense work ahead of them to shape them into true fighters.

The level of training needed to go out and survive on your own among mana beasts, who wanted nothing more than to eat you for your residual traces of mana, changed everybody.

I'd seen it in all of my classmates, including myself. I wasn't the same person after that first time entering these pits.

The younger class chattered on as most of my classmates mimicked my stretching. I scanned the first years while I stretched, seeing if there were any interesting girls in the class.

I figured Kat and I were on pause now as she focused on the Sect. I still had strong feelings for her, but I shouldn't put my life on pause for her. One of the girls in the class would make a nice distraction.

Her going to a sect without me, or vice versa, had always been a lingering thought. I was still in love with Kat, even if she had left. We'd meet again—I was sure of it.

Rigel got everyone's attention again with a loud clap.

A couple of the first-year girls startled, and I realized they had been watching me stretch. One was still watching me, but I turned my attention to Rigel. I knew better than to let my head be too far out of the fight when in the pits.

The loose skin on Rigel's arms continued to sway as he finished another clap and began to speak. "All right, Lenard, Greggory, you two are up. Pick your opponents." Rigel always used people's full names, clinging to long-dead propriety.

Greg and Lenny stepped up to the weapons rack and picked their weapons. Greg now held a large two-handed sword and Lenny held a pair of daggers.

The two were comical opposites in their build, which matched their weapon choices. Greg was a mountain of a man while Lenny was a small scrappy guy. But each had learned how to use their size to their advantage in a fight.

I mentally checked off those weapons from my list of those available for when I would be called to fight. The rack wasn't refilled until the end of the class, so I'd end up with a limited choice as the class went on.

It forced us to practice with unfamiliar weapons and become more versatile fighters.

Lenny called out Anastasia's name. Knowing her preference, I guessed she'd pick a staff with metal braces at both ends. She was a logical choice for Lenny.

He'd been trying to match up against people who used longer reach weapons for the last month. I was excited to see if he'd improved at all.

Greg chose another giant of a man named Sebastian. Sebastian stepped up to the rack and started to pick up a round shield before looking back at the class. I knew he was asking Michelle for permission.

I didn't follow his gaze and give her the attention, but she must have shaken her head because he moved on to a larger tower shield.

Michelle had claimed the round shield early in the lessons. When anybody chose the shield before her, she would choose them the next day and make her feelings clear. She was possessive of that shield.

Occasionally, I'd pick it just to mess with her. She couldn't beat me into submission like poor Sebastian.

She'd once pinned Sebastian against the wall of the pit, speared his foot to the ground and used a shield to beat on his face. The healers came and fixed Sebastian up, but I thought his nose still looked a bit crooked from that day.

I chuckled, watching as my classmates descended to their pits and squared off.

Lenny and Ana's fight was off to a typical start. Ana was swinging her staff in low, wide half-attempts to hit him, taking advantage of the reach without exerting much energy.

The slow swings might seem innocent enough, but they could turn into a hard hit quickly if you stepped into the path. Ana continued her lazy swings like a taunt for Lenny.

Lenny probably had his ring now if he was challenging Ana.

Ana had gotten hers a few weeks ago, and he'd be crazy to take her on if he hadn't gotten his. But he was taking his time for now, slowly circling Ana.

Metal on metal from the other pit drew the whole class' attention.

I saw a thin line of blood flowing down Greg's forearm.

Sebastian must have blocked and gotten a small score back at Greg. Sebastian seemed to be going with a slow, defensive approach. He'd focus on small, continuous hits, slowly whittling down his opponent.

In response, Greg had shifted his approach to striking a hard blow. Heavy blood would speed up a fight, causing the bleeder to need to finish it before becoming too weak.

Greg recoiled from the attack and took a hard stance facing Sebastian. Both had already gotten their first ring and filled it with a mana beast, but the exchange earlier hadn't used that strength.

Greg surged forward, faster than before. I smiled. The speed of a first-ring mage was fast. I couldn't wait to get that extra boost.

Sebastian reacted as any tank would and positioned his shield. He aimed not only to block the hit, but also to redirect the force of the blow away from himself.

I watched as Sebastian readied the shield at a forty-five-degree angle from the incoming blade. However, I noticed that Greg wasn't putting his weight into the blow. Sebastian didn't seem to have noticed.

Greg swung fast at Sebastian's shield as expected. Sebastian countered, pushing the blade out and away. But Greg smiled as he firmly planted his weight on his back foot and used his force like a pendulum, spinning on his back heel hard enough to make a ripping noise, like he was tearing the very air as his sword passed.

As he spun, he hopped, and the air seemed to pull him along the undefended side of Sebastian.

Greg wasn't normally very agile given his size, but he'd picked a wind element mana beast. He hadn't shown much of what it could do yet, making the match even more interesting.

Sebastian didn't seem too concerned. He immediately stomped on the pit floor, causing a pillar of mud to shoot up behind him, catching Greg's whirlwind swing. The mud wasn't hard, but its upward momentum and thickness caught Greg's swing enough to pull its angle far above Sebastian's head.

Greg pulled back, abandoning his attack to get his sword clear of the mud. "What? Is that shield too heavy for you to turn around?"

"Nah, you just aren't worth looking at, you big ugly fuck," Sebastian chuckled, then he stepped up the fight by directly using his element with his mana. Using the mana in his body, Sebastian was manipulating the earth element.

Greg charged again with a wide overhead swing. He kept himself out of reach for Sebastian to retaliate and put his enhanced strength and speed into the blow.

Sebastian blocked as expected. The fight was becoming boring. Greg had tried and failed to finish this quickly, and Sebastian had the advantage of the elements to keep it relatively even. It would most likely devolve into a slugfest.

I pivoted to see what was going on in the other pit. Others followed my lead, changing back to watching Lenny's fight.

Ana had switched from her long lazy sweeps to shorter, more offensive swings. They were still probing attacks, but not as defensive as the earlier approach.

I respected the staff. Not only was its reach huge, but it could display an incredible range between offense and defense. But it still leaned more towards defensive fighting. And, in the end, I enjoyed a more dominant weapon.

Ana seemed to be shifting to be more offensive in order to force Lenny to attack. She took a step forward with each swing, pushing Lenny's back to a wall.

At some point here, Lenny would have to go on the offensive or he'd be stuck with his back against a wall, fighting someone with an enormous advantage in range.

He seemed to reach the same conclusion. Lenny flipped up one of his knives and caught it by the blade before a quick flick of his wrist sent it spinning right at Ana.

I'd expected a move, but not that one.

Ana managed to turn her staff into a spinning barrier in front of her fast enough to deflect the blade. A sharp ping echoed as the knife hit a metal brace.

Lenny had anticipated her move. As her staff went into the spinning barrier, Lenny covered the distance that her reach favored.

Ana kept the spinning barrier up, trying to assess Lenny's next move. She'd lost the advantage; she knew she needed to be smart.

Lenny's next strike glowed with mana and shot straight for her grip on the staff. She spun the staff to her side and pushed it forward like a spinning saw blade.

Lenny reacted well. He dove straight into the spinning staff, following his training over natural instinct.

The most dangerous part of the staff is the tip. By diving into it, he had to take a blow, but it was lessened from a direct hit and got him closer.

He stopped moving, his dagger glowing with a spell just before her chest, and Ana let the long staff spin off her hand to the floor of the pit. She had lost.

Martial techniques were a next-level combat move that required you to have gained your first ring. Its real power lay in the fact that the mana of the world assisted you in the attack. Lenny had overpowered Ana with that attack.

"You better at least take me somewhere nice for dinner." Ana pushed her face right in front of Lenny's, a small challenge in her eyes while a blush spread on her cheeks.

The room filled with stifled laughs as we realized there had been a bet in this fight. Lenny had clearly won a date but had taken a few hits to get it.

I went to give Lenny a hand out of the pit. "Well done, Len, even got a date out of it."

The thin fighter looked a bit nervous. "I gotta figure out where to take her now."

"Ask her if she can guess where you're taking her when you pick her up," I said, repeating some advice I'd heard from the guard house.

Lenny looked at me with a frown.

"Then tell her she guessed right and go there," I clarified.

"Oh!" Recognition lit up in Lenny's eyes. "Thanks, man."

I joined the mass of class that had pivoted back to the still going battle. The two enormous men were still hammering away at each other.

Most of the fighting stayed pretty standard since that's what we could train on before the first ring. 'This is where we hone ourselves on *how* to fight.' I could practically hear Rigel's voice in my head. But cultivation would progress us further with martial techniques.

Rigel clapped his hands and turned to Michelle, pointing to the empty pit. "You're up. Who's your sparring partner?"

I could see the haughty grin on her face as she scanned the crowd. I knew she had me in mind, but she enjoyed the moment of being the center of attention.

A few people turn their heads and shrank down, trying not to be picked. Hard to imagine them rushing into dungeons and fighting mana beasts if they were afraid of Michelle. I mockingly stifled a yawn as I stared her down.

Michelle pretended not to see it, but I knew she did by the small tick in her jaw. Finally, her eyes settled on me after a few more sweeps of the class. Her grin broadened, and she pointed to me with a curl of her finger in a come-get-me motion.

I noticed a few of the first-year girls leaning forward, so I gave them my most dashing smile before heading over to the weapons rack, walking past Michelle without a look.

I knew it would drive her crazy. Despite turning me down, she still acted like I'd jilted her years ago. I couldn't think of a thing I'd done wrong, besides listening to Jonny.

Sure enough, she stormed past me and didn't waste any time grabbing her weapons: a mace and a round shield.

I favored the longsword, and there was still one on the rack. It was far from its peak, beaten to near scrap iron. Picking it up, I took a moment to gather my thoughts and center myself before I headed into the pit.

My father had coached me early on how to use a sword style he had gotten from mom. He used it as well, and as much crap as I gave dad, he was one hell of a fighter and I respected what he'd taught me.

"You scared? Worried you won't be man enough after I beat you?" Michelle yelled from the edge of the pit.

I took my time turning towards her. "It almost sounds like your antsy for me to stick it in you."

Her face got so red it looked about ready to implode.

I strode over to her side by the pit, satisfied with my jab. I'd never lost to her before, but she did seem extra cocky today.

Locking eyes, we both slid down the side of the abandoned swimming pool to the packed earth below.

Michelle stomped the packed earth like a wild beast preparing for a charge. To the first years, it probably looked like impatience, but I knew she was making sure she had a flat area of ground to work with.

She didn't change her style much from battle to battle. She was a wall, a staunch bulwark that I had to beat down. She wouldn't be moving much outside the small circle she was preparing.

It was a limited fighting style that relied on an aggressive opponent. But she knew my fighting style as well.

I swung my sword in lazy circles, adjusting to the feel of the dinged-up sword. It was still well weighted, its center of gravity just a few inches above the hilt. It didn't slice through the air cleanly; it grated through the air in tune with its dented and chipped blade.

Once I was confident I understood how the blade would swing, I stepped up to Michelle and came at her with wild, wide swings.

She batted them to the side with her shield.

I wasn't putting enough weight behind the blows for her blocks to do much but give my blade a new direction. She didn't try to counter, knowing that the rebounded blade could meet her before she could get inside my range.

"Stop playing, love birds!" someone shouted from the crowd.

I chuckled. Our battle dance probably looked like flirting, lacking any brutal action, but it was just the start of our battle of wills. A few of the classmates shushed the shouter, knowing that things would heat up soon.

Michelle flushed at the comment, beating her mace on the shield in a challenge and scowling.

I swung low again, letting the weight of the sword carry the strike. She didn't even look but batted it aside, keeping her gaze wide, taking in every brief twitch of mine.

With a smile, I spun the sword with the force of her block. My wrist groaned at the strain of spinning the sword one-handed, but I didn't care as it spun itself back around and under the lip of her shield.

My blood was pumping again, the tension building inside me. But I didn't need it to beat Michelle.

I stomped down hard, redirecting the force of the strike into a thrust at her hip while positioning myself in front of her shield, using it to protect my chest from the mace.

Michelle had an enormous grin on her face. She seemed confident in a way I didn't understand.

We'd been in this position before and it came down to a struggle of strength. One that I won every time.

The gathered students cheered as we locked into a contest of strength. I could hear the girls chatter excitedly just as I could feel the dirt and sand shift under my boot.

Her grin broadened as she watched my confusion. Buffing me back with her shield, she hit me square in the chest.

Even braced for a struggle, she hit me hard enough to push me back, causing my thrust to end just short of her hip.

Readjusting while I figured out what had changed, I swung my sword in circles, readying for the next exchange.

I was stronger than her, or was I? She just somehow took a full press from me and shoved me back several feet. We'd spared enough for me to know that that wasn't in her typical capabilities.

Something was different, was she wearing some enchanted gear?

My body thrummed so fast it practically vibrated. This power wanted to be released, to crush Michelle.

Before I could really think about what was happening, she broke her pattern again and stepped out of her circle with a swing of her mace.

I swung and redirected the force of her swing away from my torso. It worked, but not without cost. It was like hitting a wall. The rebound on my hands was brutal and my fingers stung with the backlash that came through the sword.

The realization hit me.

She had gotten her first ring.

This was far from a fair match if that was the case. If it was true, she'd be able to overpower me easily. But it wasn't the case. She must be trying to make this look like a fair fight, like she beat me for once in this rivalry.

I shot her a knowing smile, giving the slightest mocking bow. I knew I could still win this, but I'd need to get her to make a few mistakes.

She was pissed and came at me with full shield charge. Her body was low and her center of gravity was directly behind the shield.

I feinted a strike at her shield, knowing it wouldn't dissuade her charge. When the sword made contact, I stiffened my arm and let the force of her charge ride up my shoulder and spin me to the side.

She didn't see it coming, and I enjoyed the look of shock as I carried the spin into a full two-handed swing at her back.

That must have scared her, because the next thing I saw was a wall like a spinning blue shell that caught my blade and tore it out of my hands, clattering against the pool wall.

She had just used a spell.

The crowd gasped. They'd seen the move and realized she'd gotten her first ring.

Michell spun angrily and smashed me upside the head faster than I could react.

I staggered back and rolled out of the way, barely missing her oncoming charge.

I didn't flag down Rigel. Nor did I call for help. In this moment, my blood practically sung as the momentum in me built to a peak that I just had to let it loose. I felt more alive than I had in ages.

It was like a beast had woken up in my blood after a long slumber, ready to feed. My blood pumped, and my body felt primed for battle.

I met her mace with my steel and the clash was hard enough to send dust flying. Amazingly, I held against her strength, maybe even beat her by a hair. I met her eyes head on, confidence radiating through me.

Michelle's eyes were wide as she realized I could match her strength for strength. She paused, unsure what to do.

Pushing her back, I came in again. Stroke after stroke left her back peddling.

Michelle raised her shield, and I felt the mana of the world gather around her before forming into another blue shield. I got a look at it this time. It was a dark blue tortoise shell of water mana.

I let loose a roar of frustration as I put my full force behind an overhead swing and shattered her little turtle shell.

It had felt almost offensive to the beast coursing through my blood. My blood was pulsing out of control. Coughing, I realized I was spitting up blood.

Michelle stood across from me, looking at the blood as I wiped my chin. "Shit. Stop. Stop right now—this is just practice." Her face had dropped the intense mask and was filled with what looked like genuine worry.

I pointed my sword and let my blood run free as I readied for another exchange. "Don't worry, I'll finish it soon."

"Fine, you win. Just stop!" Michelle threw her mace down.

I noticed then that her shield arm was hanging limp from when I had shattered her spell. Small rivulets of blood were running down her hand.

I smirked, realizing I had won again, even with her new abilities. Pain blossomed in my chest, catching me off guard. Stumbling to a knee, I coughed up another mouthful of blood. My body felt weak. I'd pushed it too far and the damage was catching up to me.

I wheezed again and started to cough. The world spun violently, and soon the floor was racing up to meet my face.

This was definitely going to leave a mark.

The world went dark as I realized I couldn't feel the rest of my body.

Chapter 3

I drifted through a void of darkness, feeling empty and lost.

It felt like something was missing, but I couldn't figure out what. It was at the edge of my consciousness, floating in and out.

I continued on through the shapeless reality, lost in mind and body.

A part of me knew this wasn't right.

Isaac.

A soft whisper floated through the void.

Was my name Isaac? I liked it.

Isaac, come back.

The voice spoke again, and I felt compelled to try to follow it.

Kicking my feet, I attempted to reorient myself toward the voice and swim. It felt good to have a goal, something to add some purpose.

Yes, Isaac. Come back.

A pin prick of light appeared in the distance.

That was enough. I pushed myself forward as fast as I could. The light grew until I could make out a green and gold circle.

The colors of life mana.

I must be getting healed. The thought came to me out of the ether.

Growing close, the circle became clearer. It was a ring, stylized with feathers.

It was my ring, but it was already occupied. I wasn't sure how I knew it, but it rang true.

A woman with an untouchable beauty looked at me from where she floated within the ring. Gold chains dripped off her like she was royalty of the highest order.

I paused. Woman might be the wrong word; really, she was more like an angel. A pair of large green wings fanned out from her back, and with a flap, she was directly in front of me.

Her gold hair floated out behind her as she stared into me with a pair of bright emerald eyes.

Isaac.

She spoke into my mind as she caressed my cheek, sending wave after tingling wave of life mana through my body.

"Where am I?"

The angel continued to run her hands over me, each pass making my body lighter. Her fingers ran through my hair, and I started to recall things.

Moments of my life with heightened emotion flashed before me.

The first time my father gave me a sword. He was so proud.

My mother's smile as she tucked me away one last time.

My first kiss with Kat hidden under the tree in front of my house.

Within them was the time when I was a child, when I saw... her before. My imaginary friend.

But what was she doing here, and how did I get here?

I'd been injured, hadn't I? Maybe this was part of death.

She kissed me, and I suddenly felt life bloom in my chest.

Sparks of mana bloomed in me as they raced throughout my body and mind. Streams of mana passed through my muscles and bones, strengthening me.

I pulled her soft body close, wanting to feel her with every fiber of my being. I wanted to feel more of this; it was like I was coming alive.

More voices entered the void now, hurried and frantic.

They were angry, but it was just hiding the grief as they ran out of options.

I could have sworn I heard Jonny crying. Pulling away, I looked around again.

The ring that the angel had come from was pulsing with more life mana than I had ever seen before. Veins of mana snaked out and disappeared into the darkness with each pulse.

She got my attention again and smiled as she pushed me backward.

I suddenly felt the bed beneath me. Then, after a moment of silence, I heard muffled voices arguing from behind the door.

"Do you realize what you've fucking done? If the captain's son doesn't wake up, the guard will gut you."

Definitely not a pleasant thing to wake up to.

I listened a moment longer, trying to figure out where I was.

Curling my fists, I felt scratchy thin sheets. I blinked, slowly adjusting to the bright light. I found myself on a bed with rails to keep me from falling out.

The room was... busy. Supplies and medicine were scattered about the floor, drawers were half-open with their contents spilling out.

I tried to turn to look at the other side of the room, but my neck instantly objected to any movement.

Hopefully, this place had some pain meds.

I crawled out of bed and stretched, satisfying a few of my vertebrae with pops.

One cabinet had a glass front, revealing glass bottles inside. I wandered over, hoping it might be some medicine. I could use some willow bark right about now.

Grabbing the handle, it didn't budge. But then I felt a surge of strength come from my chest, and I pulled again.

I opened the door... and the cabinet groaned and cracked as it came off the wall.

Jumping to the side, I barely dodged the falling cabinet and the glass bottles as they shattered all over the floor in a symphony of broken glass.

There was a moment of silence where I just stood there, holding the handle, before a commotion erupted outside the door.

The door flew open, and several people rushed inside shouting.

I dropped the cabinet door and held my hands up, unsure of what was going on.

"Impossible."

"He was hanging by a thread."

"Silence." An older woman stepped forward, breaking through the clamor. "Get out," she said to the doorway of people, and I heard the scuffle of boots beyond the door.

"Sit," she said, stepping into the room as the door clicked close. She slowly took in the room and the shattered cabinet. The old matron in healer's robes had an air of authority that everyone, myself included, respected.

"What's going on?" I asked. The last thing I remembered was the fight with Michelle, then the odd dream, and now this room.

She cleared her throat before stepping up and prodding me several times. Each time I could feel a faint burst of mana sweep through me like sonar.

"What is your mana beast?"

I shook my head. "I haven't formed my first ring." Unless...

Opening my robe, I got an enormous shock. My first ring!

I looked around for a moment trying to look for my Steel-Winged Swallow core before I did a double take. My ring was already filled with a gold and green wing, the edges stylized by two feathers.

No.

The old lady watched me. "So, you didn't have a ring before you... your accident."

"No, I didn't have my first ring when I... passed out." I couldn't help but scowl at the scratchy memories around the end of the fight.

"Hmm, odd." She poked me a few times before she got up and came back with a scalpel.

"Uh. What's that for?" I eyed the sharp implement.

"Give me your hand."

I did so, slightly unwillingly, but I doubted the healer would do more harm than she could quickly heal.

A sharp pain slashed across my open palm, and I pulled my hand back.

"Hey!"

She grabbed my hand and forced it open while we both watched.

The cut stitched itself back together right before my eyes. The wound closed only leaving a thin line of blood. "That's cool."

The old healer nodded to herself. "That must be a powerful life attribute mana beast for you to gain that grade of regeneration."

"Really?" I swallowed, wondering just how bad it had been.

"You came to me with hundreds of broken blood vessels. I did all I could, even exhausted one of our trainees. He seemed to know you." She shook her head. "We thought you were on death's door."

"Oh." That was all I could think of to say. They had thought I was as good as dead.

My bloodline, because that's what I realized it was, had forcibly strengthened my body to the point where I could compare to a first-ring mage.

Forcing my body to that point without mana to stabilize myself had caused a powerful backlash. Even with mana, I would be weak for a time, unless of course the healing properties from my ring were strong.

But... an ability that could bring me back from near death might be enough to balance using my bloodline.

She read me like a book. "No, don't count on this to bail you out again. From what I can tell, this healing wore out your mana beast."

"Okay, it's probably a terrible idea to rely too much on it. I would hate to become a never-ending buffet for some mana beast."

She visibly winced at that imagery. The old healer had probably seen some grim stuff.

"You seem in order, but please rest here for the night." She looked back at the doorway, which was now cracked open, packed with a number of younger healers and a few of the city guards I recognized.

"Did any of you tell my dad?" I asked one guard.

He gulped and looked at the other one. "N...no. None of us wanted to be the one to tell the captain."

I chuckled. "That's probably for the best." We would all be lucky if dad just killed Michelle.

The old healer got up and shooed the rest of the peanut gallery away as I leaned back into the scratchy sheets.

She looked back one last time before leaving. "Who knows, maybe you should thank that girl? Fighting her brought about whatever miraculous mana beast is in you now."

The door closed behind her, not giving me a chance to reply.

Resting in the bed, I struggled to process all I had learned. First, I had a bloodline, one my body couldn't handle. Second, I was a mage. I'd finally gotten my first ring. Granted, I had almost died to get here, but it was what I'd wanted.

The beast core I'd prepared was useless now. But I had a mana beast that I could never have imagined.

Tracing my first ring, I could hardly believe that I had a mana beast. And my imaginary friend was a bit less imaginary now. Her mark was in my skin.

But she could talk and had a mostly human form. Mana beasts didn't have a human form, nor were they intelligent enough for speech. What was she?

I sagged back into the bed, I really needed to have a conversation with her again and get some answers.

But my body disagreed, and I felt myself being dragged back to sleep.

***

I felt weightless, floating in my dreams. A warm pool soothed my aches and pains as something worked below my belt. I sighed, enjoying the bliss of the pool. I relaxed into the pool for what felt like ages.

I felt the water shift slightly as something slowly but surely started rubbing my stiff member, bringing it to attention.

I let out a shuddering moan. Opening my eyes, it took me a moment to understand what was happening. My head was still in the deep fog of sleep.

As the fog cleared, the sensation between my legs didn't stop. If anything, it got more intense.

I looked around, casting aside the dream. I was in an unlit room that smelled sterile, like a healer's office. The moonlight came in from a window and gave some view of the surrounding space.

There was a woman between my legs. I shuddered as she licked a long trail along my rapidly hardening member. "More," I groaned out.

She looked up and met my gaze. The moonlight cast a number of shadows, but her eyes were like radiant emeralds reflecting golden light. Like a prize jewel in the center of a dragon's horde. Her gaze engulfed my entire being, turning me inside out and gently filling me with warmth.

It was the woman from my dream, my mana beast. I pushed her off me, my cheeks burning with the sudden realization of the situation.

She sat back with a pout. "Please, Master, let me sooth you." Her emerald eyes bore deep into me, down to my soul.

"Let's take a step back." I shook my head, trying to keep my head clear. I couldn't believe the woman from when I was a kid was here... in my bed... begging to suck on me.

I let my eyes wander over her heavenly curves. Her face had a natural and soft beauty, making her seem like a jewel to protect. Her golden hair billowed around her frame, enhancing her curves and adding to the softness.

She smiled warmly as my eyes continued to rove over her. Shifting herself up slightly, she gave me a full view of the soft mounds of her chest, doing nothing to cover them. Leaning forward further, she traced a finger slowly up my leg and up my member, purring as she did so, and then licked her lips.

I swallowed hard, reminding myself that I wasn't an animal. "Could you please put on some clothes?" I needed to focus, and her naked body was making the blood rush away from my brain.

I cursed myself. I wasn't some horny teenager just hitting puberty. I needed to get myself under control. She had called me master and was some sort of mana beast. I refused to take advantage of her until I figured this thing out.

She ran her hands down her body, and a thin, green silk dress covered pieces of her. It was better, but she was still amazingly tempting.

From what I knew, her beast core, essentially her soul, was within me now. And that meant that she was a construct of pure mana at the moment. She must be able to control it enough to tweak her appearance at will.

"Okay. So, hi?" I'd never expected to have a mana beast that could talk. I had no idea how to talk to her. "So, what's your name?"

Her eyes crinkled as she laughed.

I tried to keep my eyes trained on her face as she laughed.

"We don't normally have names, Master. But, if you're willing, I think I'd like to be called... Aurora." Her mirth had vanished, replaced by a hesitant glance as she looked up at me.

"That's a beautiful name. Aurora, you are a mana beast, right?"

"Yes, I'm *your* mana beast." She nodded with a happy smile. "And I'm happy to help with your needs." She looked back down at my pelvis.

I shifted in the bed, instantly reminded that Aurora was still straddling me. And my body was having some involuntary reactions to her attention. I needed to shut this down, so I changed the subject. "Do you remember when I was a kid? We played in the sand together."

"Yes. After I escaped the dungeon and the mages, I was drawn to you." Aurora must have sensed my discomfort and shifted off of me, still sitting on the bed alongside me, with her legs tucked underneath her.

So she really was a mana beast. It was hard to believe until I looked at her wings again. If I remembered correctly from my childhood, she had more wings. I tilted my head, studying them.

"Master. Do you not like me? When you were with the other girls you wanted to…" She trailed off and made a circle with one hand, poking her other pointer finger through it.

"How do you know about…" I trailed off.

She bounced in my bed. "I've watched everything since you swallowed my core. I've been waiting for your body to be ready to accept me."

I pulled the cover up, all of a sudden feeling a bit violated. She'd seen everything, like a fly on the wall, for my entire life. "Everything?"

Aurora nodded, then scowled. "Some of it was fun to watch, but I hated being trapped during Michelle's stunt yesterday." She let out a growl that I could feel within my body, louder than Aurora had any right to be.

I knew that she wasn't just a simple mana beast. Being able to talk and appear mostly human wasn't normal. I had a sneaking suspicion that this wasn't her natural form, but I'd let her tell me more on her own time.

"I could have bailed on the fight and admitted defeat, but I'd wanted to push myself." While the fight with Michelle had ended with me in the healer's ward, I had hit a new level of abilities. "And, after all, you finally were able to become my first ring."

Aurora's scowl turned into a big grin. "I know! I finally get to be with my Isaac in the flesh." She pressed herself into me, her wings splaying out off the bed.

"Aurora, why did you decide to be my mana beast when I was just a child?" I couldn't figure out why I had been her best option.

"Easy. You smelled strong." She tried to wiggle her way closer, but there really wasn't any closer she could be.

"You bound yourself to me because I stank?" Now that was a new one.

I could feel her head shake against me. "No, silly. I didn't understand at first, but now I do. It was your bloodline. I could smell it on you. It calls to me. I can sense your dominance and can't help myself in submitting."

Before I could think much of it, she distracted me with kisses trailing up my neck before reaching my ear. "Please, Master," she whispered with a husky edge into my ear. Pressing into me, she again started stroking my member.

Fuck it. I pushed her down into the bed and claimed her lips.

My bloodline stirred at that and hummed like an eager puppy.

Aurora clawed at my hospital gown, looking for the tie in the back.

Suddenly, her head snapped to the door, and she let out an exasperated sigh. "I don't think they will react well to knowing about me," she scowled before vanishing into a trail of green lights that entered my chest.

Startled at the abruptness, I followed the trail and saw one of Aurora's green feathers neatly styled in my first ring.

I laid back down in bed conflicted, arranging the sheets to try to hide the obvious excitement I'd felt. I'd gotten myself covered just in time to see the old wrinkled healer from before waddling in, perched on an old gnarled cane.

Everything about her said feeble to the untrained eye, but I could tell she emitted a pressure that blanketed the entire room.

She noticed my hands still positioning the sheets. "Oh dear, I've seen it all before, don't be shy. Give an old woman a show. I'm Margret by the way, always nice to know someone's name before you get naked in front of them."

I felt my face flush at that. I didn't know how to respond; respectfully, I kept my mouth shut and tried not to be so tense.

Any thought that she might be feeble vanished as she held my arm in an iron vice of a grip.

I realized she was strong enough to crush my arm with just her grip. It felt like my arm was in the jaws of a beast rather than the hands of a gentle healer.

"Ah..." Margret frowned at my arm. "No... it can't be. There's just no way." She mumbled without a care for me as I grew more worried at each mumbled exclamation.

"Is everything okay?"

She took a breath before she continued. "Boy, your bloodline really did a number on you. It took all of my healing abilities just to stabilize you, then there is this miracle of your first ring."

She gave me a once over taking me in again. "Your body was a mess; you have an incredibly violent bloodline. You need to avoid using it. I doubt you'll get this lucky again."

"Why would my bloodline hurt me? It seemed to want to come out."

She gave me a blank stare. "If a wolf wanted into a sheep pen, would you let it in?"

"Of course not. But are you saying that my bloodline wants to hurt me?" That was a terrifying idea.

The old healer shook her head slowly, like she was gathering her thoughts. "Your bloodline wants to awaken, but it hasn't. You forced it to be active, and it was like a wild mana beast getting into the market. You had no control over it, and it made a mess of things, including your body. You are just damn lucky that your mana beast healed all of the remaining damage, or you would have been left with permanent injuries that no healer I know could help you with."

She gave me another questioning look like she could just draw the answers out of me.

I paused. Given the way she had hidden so quickly, I didn't think Aurora was ready to give away secrets, and it was often best not to give away too much about a mana beast. I tried to play dumb.

"Isn't that a magnificent thing that I'm not showing any signs of lasting injury? Personally, I am pretty happy with being healthy." I gave her my best smile.

She didn't laugh. Instead, the old woman gave me a hard stare. "Any idea what monster is in your first ring?"

"No idea," I lied, returning the stare. Best to keep the lies short and simple. I would take Aurora's desire seriously, especially while I had so many questions of my own.

She was a humanoid mana beast that could speak. That wasn't something I had ever heard of.

I was somewhat worried that I'd become some experiment for even having bonded with her. It had been ages since the portals had opened. I figured I would have heard of this if it was possible.

And then I'd gone and complicated all of this further by almost having sex with my sealed mana beast.

I had to resist the urge to plant my head in my hands. I definitely had some things to sort through, and I did not want to do that here under this woman's watch.

"If everything is alright, can I go home?" I asked.

She seemed to contemplate that, focusing on my arms again. Finally, she responded. "You are healthy, but do come back in a few days for a checkup."

"Of course," I lied again, moving to get out of bed and getting a look out the window. I doubted I'd actually come back unless I wound up needing healing again.

I could see the sun peeking up into the sky for a fresh day. I smiled. Today, I was finally on the path of cultivation. I knew what came next. I needed to start the Meridian Forging Stage, the cultivation of a mage's first ring.

Chapter 4

I was just leaving the hospital, moving quickly, when I ran into Professor Locke. He looked surprised to see me outside of the hospital room.

"I was just coming to see you, boy." Locke's gnarled hand clapped me on the shoulder. "You gave us all a big scare."

"Thanks, Locke." I smiled. Locke was a grumpy old man, but he always cared. His hand squeezed me, and his face turned grave.

Stepping back, he gave me an appraising gaze. "That bloodline you activated was something else. A bit too much for you to handle right now though. Say, do you know if your parents have shown any sign of that bloodline?"

I shook my head. I'd never heard anything from my father, and my mother died when I was young. "No, sir. Father hasn't said anything."

Locke nodded thinking. "Your mother never mentioned it?"

I barely felt the ache of loss at the mention of her. It had been so long. "No, but I was pretty young then."

"You know your mother was pretty elusive. What was her name again?" Locke asked it casually, but it had the undertone that felt like he was chronicling my lineage.

"Lilly. She wasn't that elusive. From what I remember, she was very lively." I felt the need to stand up for her.

Locke brushed that off. "Last name?"

I started to open my mouth and say my father's last name. But I wasn't actually sure if they were ever married. In the dangerous world we lived in, marriage was more fluid and more of a personal commitment than a big ceremony. But it did happen from time to time.

"I think she had my father's last name. Hughes. Why?"

Locke's demeanor shifted to a light-hearted old man. "Oh, nothing. Just my old brain trying to keep track of everyone in town. Habit to try, but there are almost too many of you guys to remember now." He shook his head, clearly feeling the tension and changing the topic.

"Boy, did you pop your first ring in the hospital?"

Best to tell the truth but keep it simple. "Yep! I just woke up with the ring."

"Well, congratulations are in order. You're a mage now." He slapped me on the shoulder hard enough to jar my bones.

"Do you have a mana beast picked out?"

I hesitated before answering. "Yep, already filled."

Locke rotated his hand and his spatial ring ejected a thin booklet that he caught in the other hand. "Here is the method to forge your meridians from the academy. I've been carrying it around since so many of you have been popping their rings."

He gave it to me like it was nothing, and it was to him. He probably handed these out so often it was boring by now. But I couldn't stop the excitement running through my body.

This book was the key to unlocking my path of cultivation. This was the first step to my life outside Locksprings.

I smiled and cupped my hands with a nod of my head. "Thanks."

Locke chuckled. "Already acting like a mage, eh? Glad you were somewhat paying attention when we talked about the hierarchy of mages. Just make sure you remember all you learned as you encounter them and keep doing your mental exercises."

I sighed. They'd drilled this into us so many times. Cultivating required both physical and mental fortitude; of course, cultivation had risks too. If you couldn't steel your resolve to take the step and follow it through to the end, death wasn't the worst thing to happen.

Yet another reason mages practiced corrupt techniques; they put much of the pressure on outside forces, bringing harm to other people to cultivate.

Holding the booklet close to my chest, I thanked Locke again before hurrying home.

There was so much to learn about the mana flowing through my body now.

I paused in my steps, realizing I had just the person to ask. I looked down at my chest. Aurora would have an understanding of cultivation; she was obviously more than just a general mana beast.

***

I reached our home, slamming the front door behind me as I made my way to the main room. I still wasn't used to my extra strength, but I was more concerned with answers.

I needed to bring Aurora out, but I didn't know how to do that. Cultivation was so… mystical and secretive.

"Aurora?" I asked the empty room in hope.

She responded, or at least that's how I was interpreting what felt like a nudge on my chest. I could feel the mana from her ring pulse, but instead of pulsing through my body, it reversed like it was pulsing into the air, vibrating around me and within me.

I held onto that feeling and imagined her coming out and standing in front of me.

It worked. The pulse grew, and I could feel my mana move. Aurora appeared before me clad in a simple, yet figure-hugging green dress that matched her wings.

She was distractingly beautiful; her delicious curves bringing my thoughts back to the previous night.

My hungry glare made her bite her lip and sashay up to me. I enjoyed her kiss for a moment; holding her just felt right.

But concern creeped into my mind as I shared the kiss with her. She was a mana beast. My mana beast. Was this forced by being bound to me? Moreover, she still wasn't telling me the full truth of everything.

The thoughts broke me from the moment, and I pulled back from Aurora. I used my hands on her shoulders to separate us. I decided that I could sort things out with her later; I needed to start cultivating.

I was thrilled to have a powerful mana beast, but then again, life mana wasn't particularly known for its combat potential.

"Aurora, how do I fight with life mana?"

Aurora smiled and bopped me on the nose, bouncing a little as she did it, shattering my serious demeanor. "I am aware of what's

43

happening when I'm in the ring. I've been watching your whole life." She put her hands on her hips and tilted her head.

"Don't worry. I'll make you strong enough to take Kat back." There was a possessive glint in her eyes as she said that. Then, the possessiveness left them, and she smiled once again. Her wings snapped out and a blade of life mana appeared in her hand.

My eyes were wide as I felt the blade of pure gold mana. It was sharp and savage, unlike the soft life mana I've seen before.

"See?" She watched with pride as I felt it, before letting the sword fade. She gave me a wide radiant smile.

I let out a heavy breath I had been holding. I'd been so worried on the way home that cultivating life mana would be a swift end to my cultivation.

"But first, I have been cooped up inside you for thirteen years!"

Aurora was like a whirlwind, going around the house touching and smelling everything like a child exploring the world. When she found the sandbox abandoned from my childhood, she just sat in it for a minute, happily running her hands through the sand.

"Oh! Let's spar." Aurora suddenly looked up.

***

Fighting Aurora had been eye-opening. She fought like a savage animal, with no regard for her body as long as she got the winning strike.

"Wow." I sat down with a thump. My body was still full of energy. "How am I not exhausted yet?"

Aurora giggled and cuddled up next to me. "Because you are overflowing with my life mana. You are constantly healing yourself." Her hands snaked over my shoulders, rubbing out any tension.

The scent of vanilla and spice wafted over to me, relaxing me to my core. I leaned into her, breathing in deeply and enjoying her scent.

I hadn't known this would be one of the side effects of life mana. All mana altered the body of a mage as they absorbed and refined mana. I knew earth mages grew tougher skin, and air mages became lighter and faster.

How much mana you were exposed to determined how strongly the effects would be. But I hadn't considered life mana effects before. Most mages started out with an element with more combat potential.

Aurora smiled and kissed my shoulder. She had been showing me affection in small ways all afternoon, but she was respectful of me when I told her I didn't want more right now.

It was almost like she couldn't help herself, which just made me more worried about her desire being forced.

"Enough play time though, I need to cultivate," I growled.

Aurora pouted, but then relented. "Come sit on the floor with me, and I'll help you. First, you need to harness my mana."

I plopped down and pulled her into my lap. I flipped open the booklet from Locke and leafed through it.

The book was a simple technique to form channels in a mage's body called meridians. They were how mana would flow through my body and could only be formed during the first ring.

Once you concentrated the mana in your body to the second ring, it was impossible to change your meridians without heaven defying medicines.

The book seemed overly simple compared to the rumors of cultivation. One read was all I needed to memorize the practice of forging meridians that it outlined.

Putting the book down, I started to draw mana from Aurora's ring.

"They taught you how to find your channels and flow the natural mana through your body already," Aurora stated, but I focused on what was happening in my body.

"Good. Now feel the fountain of mana coming from my ring." Aurora tapped my chest.

Concentrating on my body and mind, I entered a meditative state and viewed my inner world. It was hard to grasp with words. It was both within me, yet incomparably vast. Like a world unto itself within my body.

In this space, there was a clear and bright ring pouring out mana. The life mana coming from Aurora's ring was quickly dissipating into my body, but without focus.

"It's not flowing, just dispersing," I said aloud while trying to stay focused on my inner world.

"Correct. You learned the basics of meridian forging in class. Focus the mana coming out of my seal and use it to create a cycle." Aurora's voice penetrated my meditation.

Like cupping water from a spigot, I directed it down from my chest and through my body in what I could only describe as a bucket brigade of hands directing it each step of the way.

I sputtered and dribbled mana from the path, at times having to start back at the beginning. My mana flowed through each part of me, nourishing and bringing forth my potential with each pass.

My body bloomed with potential beyond a normal human where the mana flowed.

I kept at it until I managed a full cycle all the way back to Aurora's seal.

At that moment, I felt a sense of harmony. My mana stopped struggling and began to actually flow through the path I had carved for it.

"This was the simplest mana forging technique, simply looping through your body and creating a flow," Aurora said.

It sounded simple, but it was far more complex in execution than I had imagined.

The purpose of meridians was to provide a flow that would be constant throughout my body. Should you want to use mana to hit harder or jump higher, it would already be there. The flow of mana became a readily available resource for your body in times of need.

With mana throughout my body, I could carry foreign mana to Aurora's seal for her to feed upon and grow stronger. But there was always the risk of overloading your meridians. That was as good as a blood vessel bursting in your brain.

The reverse was possible. You could run your meridians dry. Though this would disrupt your flow and you could not use your mana temporarily, you'd be able to restart your mana through your meridians with some time.

I continued to cycle the mana, growing familiar with its circulation.

Coming out of my meditation, Aurora was asleep on the floor, and it had grown dark outside.

I stood up, stretching. I could feel the power contained in my body.

My stomach growled, and I realized I hadn't eaten all day. I wondered if Aurora could eat normal food. My cooking probably wasn't the best introduction.

Thinking of Aurora, I wanted to get to know her better. She'd spent thirteen years getting to know me, but I didn't know much about her. Maybe she'd like to see the city for herself.

"Aurora, want to go out to eat?" I asked, waking her.

Aurora's face went through a series of emotions but finally settled on sad. She looked down at her hands, fidgeting.

"What's wrong?" I pulled her up from the floor.

Aurora refused to look up. "I can't go out. People would realize." She flexed her wings to remind me of them. I had almost forgotten about them. I realized I had been thinking of her as my companion, not as a mana beast.

"I noticed you can change their size." She had a habit of enlarging them and wrapping them around me if I let her affection go too far.

Aurora smiled mischievously. "I could wrap you up in them again. You seemed to like them when you were a kid."

I cleared my throat. "Anyway, how small can you make your wings?"

A look of concentration came over her face. Aurora's wings slowly shrank until they were only about a foot long.

"That's as small as I can make them. It takes some concentration, so I couldn't fight like this." She made her best stern face, but it was short of being menacing.

I kissed her forehead and fished out one of my baggy coats for her. The night was cold enough this late in the fall that no one would think a woman odd for wearing a coat. "Here, put this on, then we can go out."

Aurora pulled on the surrounding coat, careful of her folded wings. She had a delicate smile and a blush as she snuggled herself into the coat. She pulled the collar up, breathing in my scent.

Her smile warmed me. I couldn't help thinking about how different my relationship with Aurora was than other mages would have with their mana beasts.

"Aurora, what was the dungeon like where you came from?"

"Big. Wide open oceans for me to swim in and a sky so clear you could see for miles when you soared. But the sky here is better. I like the stars."

"Did you have other mana beast… friends?" I struggled for the right word.

"No. There were two types of mana beasts in the dungeon with me. Those I ate and those that escaped." There was a flash of the wild predator beneath the woman.

I appreciated just how beautiful Aurora was with her gold spun hair and emerald eyes. But I knew in the end she was a mana beast.

That I was likely influencing her in some way through our bond meant she couldn't be anything more than an attractive companion.

I walked over and held open the door in invitation. She beamed and walked into the doorway, pausing when her face was just inches from mine. The fading light caught her eyes, and I was mesmerized for a second. I wasn't sure what it was about Aurora; I just felt connected to her. Then again, that might be the ring.

"You are stunning, Aurora," I said as her face lit up. "You'll make someone very happy."

She pouted at my ending but kept her thoughts to herself.

Too much was changing. Aurora was here in the present and I owed it to her to be a good mage, not chasing after a sect that didn't want me.

Aurora slipped her arm into mine, and we started down the sidewalk.

I suddenly became nervous. Aurora was stunningly beautiful, and no one had seen her before. The town was big enough that you didn't know everyone, but a beauty like Aurora would be memorable.

She seemed to sense my hesitation. "Isaac, we can go back. Or I can return to my ring." She rested her hand on my arm.

I could see she meant it. Aurora would give up this date to make me comfortable, but I knew she wanted to go out and experience the world.

She was just willing to sacrifice her freedom just because I was a bit anxious.

Grabbing her, I pulled her into me. "I want you to experience the town with me tonight. I can handle anything that comes up."

She gave me an upturned look, and I could see tears welling up in her eyes. She was scared.

I squeezed her tighter and kissed the top of her head to comfort her. It was just a walk through town, and it seemed to mean a lot to her.

Separating and taking a deep breath, I took Aurora around town. Aurora said she had been a ride-along my entire life, but she was wide-eyed taking in the city for the first time on her own.

It was the insignificant things that got her.

"Look at this one. It's so fierce." Aurora pulled another trinket from a shopkeeper's tray as we passed and held it up to me.

The old lady behind the counter gave us a warm smile. "That is a White Tiger, the pinnacle mana beast of the metal element. They say there's nothing sharper in the world than a claw of a White Tiger."

Aurora looked at it for a moment like she was trying to cement the image in her mind before picking up another one. "What's this one?"

"That is a Kun, the largest water element mana beast. It's said that when it outgrows the oceans, it takes to the sky."

Aurora turned to me. "I like that, kind of like mages. They seek greater pools every time they grow stronger too."

The shopkeeper's smile drooped when Aurora put the figurine down and turned to leave.

I quickly bought a bright green ribbon with gold birds on it. I thought it would go well with Aurora.

"Here, let me put this in your hair." I pulled Aurora back.

She spotted the ribbon and her eyes lit up.

The old lady smiled gratefully at me. "How about I do it for you?"

Aurora backed up to the counter and the old woman expertly threaded the ribbon through Aurora's hair in a braid that also tied her hair back.

My date squealed with delight as she checked it in the mirror, earning me a kiss.

The shopkeeper gave me a victorious smile as I paid her.

We wandered and made idle talk about the city and my time at school. I knew that Aurora could share my experiences, but she wanted to clarify a number of things. It quickly became clear that she really didn't understand humans.

The questions she asked reinforced that she really wasn't human, and her thoughts were more beast-like. She had spent the past ten minutes trying to understand the power dynamic in our town.

"So, this Mayor Hill only has two rings; he's in the Nascent Soul stage. And your father has his third ring, meaning he should be working on his immortal body. But the mayor tells your father what to do?" She tipped her head and asked me to explain it for maybe the fourth time.

I tried to explain it a different way. Voting had taken us down a bit of a rabbit hole. "Yes. That's just how it works. It's more about holding the popular opinion, being able to persuade people. They can't just destroy anybody who opposes them. They have to convince the masses they are right."

She shook her head, pausing to study a nearby shop window. "Huh, feels messy. Your father could just kill him and take over. Or even Locke from the academy could take him down. Even the Sun and Moon Hall could just make someone the mayor."

"What if they don't want to? They both seem more interested in developing mages and keeping the town safe than setting and enforcing rules. The Sun and Moon Hall wouldn't stoop so low to manage a small town."

She slowly nodded, something registering. "So it's like hens staying back to keep the eggs warm. You need some of your strong ones focused on protecting the weakest."

Nodding again in decision, she finished by saying, "But the mayor must still have some sort of strength to enforce what he wants. Maybe he's just backed by somebody bigger."

I paused. There could be something to Aurora's thought. The Sun and Moon Hall had favored Aiden, the mayor's son, when there had been far better mages the same age.

Feeling Aurora's grip tighten on my arm, I was pulled out of my thoughts to find what had startled her.

Chapter 5

It didn't take long to figure out what had made Aurora tense up.

Michelle was walking with Jonny and Steve. Michelle saw me a moment later and headed straight for us.

Jonny followed Michelle's line of sight, taking one look at Aurora and then wiggled his eyebrows, giving me a giant smile.

Steve just nodded 'hi'.

I sighed. I didn't want to deal with this. Whether Michelle was going to apologize or start something, Aurora was not likely to just let Michelle off the hook for landing me in the healer's ward. And we needed Aurora to keep a low profile.

"Let's go, Aurora." I held her hand and tried to pull her along, but she was rooted to the ground, staring directly at Michelle. I gave another light tug, and she jerked her hand from my grasp, crossing her arms and continuing to glare at Michelle in challenge.

The sweet, cuddly Aurora was gone. In her place was a bull about ready to charge. And Michelle didn't seem the least bit deterred in coming over to us.

I sighed. Clearly, just avoiding this wasn't going to happen. I stepped up next to Aurora as the other group approached, wrapping my arm around her shoulders. She stayed stiff but shifted slightly into me.

"Isaac," Michelle greeted me, walking in the group's front like she was in charge.

Jonny and Steve seemed to be taking their time behind her. They seemed as eager to avoid this as I was.

"Michelle," I said, letting the conversation die in a long awkward pause. If she wanted something, she could spit it out.

We stared, waiting for the other to make a move.

What neither of us expected was Aurora darting forward and the crisp smack of her hand on Michelle's cheek.

Michelle staggered, her face a frozen mask of surprise.

I felt Aurora's warm body slipping back under my arm, a small smile on her face.

Michelle recovered after a stumble and touched her hand to her face, looking up in disbelief and immediately sizing up Aurora. She probably hadn't pegged the girl with golden waves tied up in a green bow and wearing an oversized coat as a fighter.

"Oh, snap," Jonny helpfully commented, chuckling and sitting on a nearby ledge, pretending to eat popcorn.

I rolled my eyes at his antics, and then focused on trying to defuse this bomb. I got why Aurora was angry, but Michelle hadn't known about my bloodline. She'd just wanted a chance to best me.

Michelle didn't look away from Aurora, giving her a more serious once over after the slap.

"Who are you? I've never seen you before." Michelle's eyes stayed on Aurora's face. There was a challenge in her tone, but Aurora didn't seem to care one bit.

Aurora played with a strand of her hair, smiling and leaning into me. I felt the heat of a kiss on my cheek before she spoke. "Oh, I'm Aurora. Isaac's girlfriend."

She snuggled deeper against me, running her finger up my arm and shoulder, lightly playing with the hair at the base of my neck. Aurora was completely ignoring Michelle, and from the way Michelle's face was heating up, she was not a fan.

I tried to pacify Michelle with a smile. "So, uh, what are you three up to?" I ignored the hands that continued to wander my body.

Jonny finally helped break the silence. "Our plans don't seem nearly as interesting as yours. Nice to meet you, Aurora." He stepped past Michelle's icy form and held out a hand.

Aurora stopped her perusal of my body to look at his outstretched hand. When she looked up at me, I nodded my head encouragingly, and she stepped forward and shook his hand.

I used the moment to take her in. Even if that baggy coat hid her curves, her face was still a perfect ten, and I had to say I was a bit smug having her on my arm.

Michelle's nose flared as she blew out her annoyance at being ignored. "Look, I haven't seen you in the academy, so you won't understand all we're talking about. You may want to browse some of the pretty trinkets in the shops while we talk about cultivation."

"It's okay. I think she can keep up." I tried not to laugh. Michelle had no idea how well Aurora would follow our conversation.

"Fine. Whatever. What happened to Kat?" Michelle tried to appear disinterested, but I could tell she was waiting on the answer.

I didn't make her wait long. "The Sun and Moon Hall swept her away."

Michelle grew quieter. She knew what that meant. "Sorry to hear that. You two were... cute." A number of emotions flashed across her face that I couldn't interpret.

Pulling herself back together, she changed the subject. "You missed class today. We are supposed to make four-man teams for an exercise going out of town."

I eyed Jonny and Steve behind Michelle and knew where this was going. But I decided to play dumb to mess with her.

"Ah, cool. Thanks for letting me know." I let the silence hang.

Fidgeting, she glared at me, knowing I was trying to make her say she needed me. She nudged Jonny with her elbow instead.

Jonny started to speak, but Steve stomped on his foot keeping him out of the conversation.

Steve said nothing but put on his best innocent face.

Michelle turned her glare to Steve, who just looked upward.

She turned back to me and spoke through clenched teeth. "I think it would be great if the four of us made a team."

"Four-man team?" I pondered the idea. Grouping up for teams like that was common if you traveled long distances... or if you went in a dungeon. My eyes suddenly lit up. "Are we preparing to go into a dungeon?"

"Yes. We'll get paired with a veteran. We are going into a low-ranked dungeon for the assessment." Michelle couldn't suppress the smile forming as she said it. We all had waited for something like this.

I blinked several times, taking a moment to register what Michelle said. "Our final assessment is going into a dungeon this year?!" I struggled to keep my voice down. "But that's… insane." It was both awesome and crazy.

New mages had quite a few challenges to overcome. Many people expected newbies to crack on their first run. Dungeons were extremely dangerous and ridiculously lucrative.

It was why the Sun and Moon Hall was super selective of the first-ring candidates. First-rings were unproven, and the percentage that died in their first dungeon was high. The intensity was just too much for some people.

I knew I was ready to get into a dungeon, though. Jonny and Steve would have my back; we'd been preparing for this. We hadn't planned on me having life mana, but I knew they'd adapt with me.

I hadn't planned on teaming with Michelle, but I had to grudgingly admit she was probably the best defensive fighter in our class. She'd make a strong fourth.

Decision made, I looked up. Michelle was standing there with a raised brow and arms crossed, pushing her chest up. "Well?"

"Sure. I'll join you guys." I shrugged. "Training together tomorrow? I'm busy tonight." I leaned down and gave Aurora a peck on the cheek, making sure she knew I hadn't forgotten about our date. She squirmed happily along my side.

Michelle bristled, watching my display of affection with Aurora. "Of course, class tomorrow is changing to team combat. Come ready to fight, not flirt." She spat the last bit before turning and leaving. Steve and Jonny watched as she headed off.

Michelle was just so hot and cold. It was exhausting.

Jonny stepped forward towards Aurora. "So, how did you get to know a lug like Isaac? And do you have any sisters?" He flashed his pearly whites.

I felt a flash of worry. We hadn't really come up with a backstory for Aurora. I didn't think anybody would think she was a mana beast since even I'd never heard of anything like her, but they could figure out something was off.

Aurora matched Jonny's smile with one that showed off her dimples.

"I've heard all about you and Steve." Aurora nodded at each of them. "My Isaac has told me all about you two."

"My Isaac?" Jonny looked at me with a raised brow.

I grinned back. "Yep. Anyway, we were just going out for dinner." As I took in their faces, I realized they wanted to join us. Aurora must have realized it as well, because she asked them to join us.

"I'd love to meet you both rather than hearing all of Isaac's stories." Aurora beamed, and Jonny seemed to lose himself in her eyes.

Steve nudged him, a reminder that she was taken, and saving me the trouble of smacking him.

"Let's go to my family's restaurant." Jonny quickly pointed us towards his family's establishment.

I looked at Steve to see his opinion.

Steve just nodded his assent.

"That settles it. Lead on, Jonny," I said, and my friend leapt at the chance to lead Aurora and chat her up.

I resisted the urge to hover. Since Aurora had experienced my entire life, she knew Jonny just as well as I did.

"Where did she come from?" Steve asked, walking alongside me as we walked behind Aurora and Jonny.

I shrugged. "You know, around."

Steve gave me a skeptical look. I looked around, indicating I didn't want to discuss it further.

We walked in silence while Jonny asked Aurora about her entire life story before we even got to the restaurant.

The family restaurant was an old two-story building. The bottom level used to be a bar long ago. The large walnut bar was neatly polished but unattended. The oak seating clashed a bit, but it was what could be made using the local lumber.

Jonny's mother had done her best to create a warm space. She was often around, fussing over the customers. I understood she had never popped her first ring. It was rare for a person to not have a single mana beast bound to them.

Even those that didn't pursue cultivation often had formed their first ring. If for no other reason, it extended a person's life.

As soon as they walked through the door, the Persian woman wrapped each of us up in a motherly hug. Maaria stopped at Aurora and examined her for a second. "Well aren't you delightful! But so thin! We will work on that. Don't you worry. I've got lots of food here. So, which one of these hooligans dragged you out?"

Aurora blushed and gave me a side hug. "Isaac and I were going out on a date and ran into your son."

"My son interrupted your date?" She looked over at Jonny with a fierce glare that only mothers had.

I waved away her concern. "It's fine. I wanted to introduce her to them anyway. And what better way to show off for her than bring her here for some Persian food?"

I knew the way to Maaria's forgiveness was to complement her food. Maaria spent an inordinate amount of time trying to recreate authentic Persian food. She didn't have access to all the original spices in old recipes. She spent quite a bit of time testing new ingredients that came from dungeons and mixing them with what was available in the region.

Maaria grinned at the complement to her cooking and beckoned them to a quiet table in the corner.

At some point, I had realized that Maaria had been born after the dungeons appeared. There was no way that she had ever even had authentic Persian food, but I commended the effort to keep the culture alive.

Regardless, her food was delicious. That was probably what kept her business successful.

"Kababs?" Maaria asked after we were seated.

I nodded, hoping that Aurora would like it. We hadn't really gotten to discussing what mana beasts eat.

As Maaria stepped away, the barrage of questions started.

"So, this is new? You and Kat just ended, and I know you would never hide her from us. We're too delightful." Jonny took a giant bite of the bread on the table, motioning with it to Steve and himself.

"Of course. I was trying to make sure I sufficiently wooed her before I introduced her to you. But here we are. I guess I'll have to hope that my charm can still win out," I joked, stealing some of the bread for myself.

"Makes sense." Jonny nodded to himself. Steve stared dumbly at their friend, who was as charming as a camel.

"So, Aurora, what do you do? Do you have your ring yet? What element? How'd you two meet?" Jonny recovered from his first question with an onslaught that left Aurora looking like a deer in headlights.

56

Luckily, Aurora recovered. "I sew... I sew clothes. Isaac was at my stall in the market. I'm still saving up for a mana crystal to start cultivating, but I should have enough soon."

Jonny nodded, looking out the front restaurant window towards the markets. "Lucky find, Isaac, yeah... That's a good idea, go shopping for girls in the market."

I tried not to choke. Jonny really had a one-track mind. I could see the wheels turning in his brain. If I needed to find Jonny anytime soon, I now knew where to look.

At least Aurora's 'background' couldn't be easily investigated by Jonny. The stalls in the bazaar moved often, and the place was chaotic enough to make it hard to really find someone if you didn't coordinate beforehand. It was a smart backstory.

Jonny stayed interested in Aurora. "What kind of clothes do you make?"

"All kinds, dresses, shirts, martial robes," Aurora said. "How about you, Steve? How's the farm going?"

Steve shrugged. "One of our sows just had a litter, eight healthy new bacon machines," Steve chuckled.

"Do you have any mana beasts at the farm?" Aurora asked.

Steve shook his head. "Too hard to manage, not to mention they'd eat anything else we had on the farm. After that last time..." He trailed off, waiting to see if she'd take the bait.

Aurora appeased him, her eyes sparkling as she jumped in. "What happened"

I knew she'd heard the story before, but she was trying to build a connection with my friends. It was sweet. I sat back, knowing Steve was going to enjoy retelling it.

"So, my father got this great idea to bring in this pair of rank one mana beasts he had found. They didn't look like much, just two thin chickens. You see, my pa had this grand idea that they would mate. He then could make a farm out of them and eventually sell the meat and the cores for far more profit than a regular chicken."

"He had to know it wouldn't be so simple." Aurora leaned forward, chin in her hands.

"Of course, Pa's a stubborn ass, but he isn't stupid. He had a wrought-iron enclosure made for them. Spent so much time making sure it was rock solid that he didn't even blink to put them right next to the rest of the livestock."

Steve sighed and shook his head. "But they still managed to get loose. We lost eight pigs and two head of cattle. Those two little blue birds devoured them to the bone. But they were nice and plump when Pa cooked them the next night."

"After that, he learned his lesson and hasn't tried something like that again."

Jonny quickly jumped in with a dozen more questions. Steve's story seemed to have given him plenty of time to think them up. I gave Jonny a soft kick under the table when he'd go too far.

Aurora leaned into me, laughing and enjoying my friends. It felt really comfortable. She fit right into our dynamic, although I guess she'd had years of experiencing it.

Jonny's questions were interrupted when Maaria came back with four plates full of aromatic golden rice and seasoned hunks of meat barely clinging to the wooden spits.

"This smells amazing!" Aurora picked one of the kababs off the skewer and popped it in her mouth, moaning at her first taste.

I knew what that was like. Maaria's kebabs were to die for. "Try the next one in the sauce."

"Then rub it in the rice after it has the sauce," Jonny explained, expertly coating his meat in the tahini sauce and rice while keeping them on the skewer to keep his hands clean.

"Oh my. This is so good." Aurora smiled with her cheeks stuffed.

It brought warmth to me watching that smile. There was something innocent about her. I knew she was a powerful mana beast, but at this moment, she was just my Aurora, experiencing kebabs for the first time.

"So, you guys wanted to team up with Michelle?" I asked the question that had been on my mind.

"She's a really good fit," Jonny said with a stuffed mouth.

Steve nodded. "We could use someone to take the heat. That shield spell of hers is pretty strong."

It had taken a full-strength blow from my bloodline to shatter it, but she had likely also just started learning the spell.

Thinking of spells. "Hey Jonny, do you know if there are any life element offensive spells?"

He shook his head. "For the first ring, they are all healing spells. Life element gains some strength in the second ring when you use it with soul cultivation. But, for your question, there aren't any spells for the first ring at the academy.

"Fighting mana beasts is going to be a pain for me. More reason to get someone like Michelle in the group," he said looking down at his plate.

Jonny might be a handful, but he was a gentle soul at heart.

I waved it off. "That's what we are here for, Jonny. You just have to keep us in good repair."

My friend smiled and we all enjoyed the time together before we knew we'd be facing real combat in the near future.

Chapter 6

I woke up to a soft female body in my arms. Aurora was curled up into my side, and I took the moment to look at her in her sleep.

The angel was an enigma. I vaguely remembered gossip about a nearby dungeon before I'd met her. It had been strong enough to attract one of the floating mountains owned by some of the most powerful mages. I knew how mages measured power, but how to measure Aurora's power wasn't clear.

Aurora was likely a very powerful mana beast, and she'd proven that when she brought me back from nearly dying. But, despite all of that power, she'd willingly bound herself to me as a child. And now, here she was in my bed, completely defenseless.

I noticed a strand that had fallen in front of her face. Trying to keep from waking her, I nudged the strand out of the way.

"It's getting hard to keep laying still," Aurora whispered, starting to stretch her body against mine.

Laughing, I messed her hair. "Morning. You are cute when you sleep."

She smiled, shifting her body further against mine. "Cute enough that you'll give into me this morning?"

She batted her eyelashes and leaned forward to slowly kiss up my neck.

I groaned. I sorely wanted to dive into her, but there was still too much to unpack about our relationship.

"Your appeal is never what stops me, Aurora. Luckily, you are bound to me for the rest of my life as my mana beast, so we have time to make sure this is what we both want." I pulled her in and gave her a deep kiss to try to satiate her for the moment.

She sighed as I released her.

I had left out that I wasn't convinced this was entirely of her free will.

Aurora was in my life forever now. I didn't want to use her as a rebound; I had to make sure it was the right time.

"Oh! You have class today!" Aurora's wings snapped open and she floated off the bed. "I want to try to make breakfast before you have to go." She magically dressed herself in a green dress made of mana and was out the door in a flash.

I paused. Did Aurora even know how to cook?

I waited for a few moments, seeing if I smelled smoke. When I didn't hear any loud bangs, I figured she was figuring it out, and got out of bed to dress before wandering down into the kitchen.

I leaned against the doorframe, taking in the homely scene. Aurora had clearly figured out how to make eggs in the skillet without too much trouble.

She had changed her clothes again and was wearing nothing but a green apron. And somehow, she had made the eggs smell heavenly. I had to admit I was a bit surprised.

"The look on your face," Aurora laughed as she took me in. "What did you think? I'd make something that looked like black goop with poison symbols floating over it?"

I laughed and walked over, squeezing her side. That was exactly what I thought I'd be walking into.

Aurora rolled her eyes and nudged me towards the table with her hips. "Remember, I could see your life as you lived it. I can scramble some eggs." She gave me a stronger nudge when I hadn't moved very far. "Now sit down and wait. I've been excited to try something like this."

I accepted her invitation, and more than that, I found myself enjoying our banter and her affection. Keeping her at arm's length was proving challenging, but I still needed to slow things down.

"Thanks, Aurora. I sometimes forget that you have seen everything." I went to shoot her a smile, only to smile even bigger when I got a glimpse of her firm and naked behind, with only the strings of the apron covering her back. She was definitely comfortable in her skin.

"Make sure to thank me properly and practice circulating my mana through your body. I want us to get stronger. Although if you change your mind and want to thank me in other ways, I won't say no." She looked over her shoulder with a sultry glance before going back to the eggs.

I figured it couldn't hurt to do a bit of practice. I delved within myself and felt for the outpour of life mana coming from the ring on my chest. Letting everything else go, I channeled the energy and directed it to flow through my body. Like trenches dug in fields, I prepared the way, letting the stream fill them up and flow through all parts of my body.

It was easier this time. With every passing of mana, the trail was slowly worn away like paths through woods.

I lost myself as I retraced the pathways that Aurora had helped start, winding along the faint impressions of the previous path taken.

When I opened my eyes, Aurora was watching with a bright smile. "Sorry, you were doing so well. I didn't want to interrupt."

Looking at the eggs, I realized she had been waiting for a while. "Your eggs. I'm sorry, Aurora."

She'd been so excited to cook them and now they'd gone cold.

"No worries. I will make them again tomorrow." She shrugged. "Or maybe another day. We have a lifetime to choose from, but for now, you need to get going."

Aurora gave me a kiss that sent tingles through my body before she transformed into a stream of light that entered my first ring.

I looked down at my chest with a smile. Aurora would always be with me. I knew she was being patient with me.

She'd seen my relationship with Kat, so she knew we were close and was giving me some time. She probably didn't understand my concern over her free will as much, but that was something we'd just have to figure out as we went.

Inhaling the eggs, I hurried out the door to the academy.

Today would be my first day as a mage. I was filled with excitement at getting to practicals and using my new strength enhanced by the mana flowing through my body.

Stepping back into the academy, it felt different. Some younger students started whispering when they saw me. I knew some of them could feel the mana flowing in my body.

A popular girl a few years younger ran up and handed me a love letter.

I was popular before, but this was a different vibe. Maybe this comes with the first ring?

When I stepped into the lecture hall, everyone turned, and the air stilled like they were waiting for something. I paused. Something seemed off. My ring didn't seem like enough to have changed everything overnight.

Several of the gazes flicked back to Michelle, and I understood. They were waiting to see what would happen between us after she had knocked me onto my ass and into the hospital.

I didn't normally give into peer pressure, but I also wanted this. I wanted a rematch as much as the bystanders did.

After all, now we were on even footing.

"Hey, Michelle," I called down to the front row as I found the seats I, Steve and Jonny normally occupied and sat down. I didn't have to yell loudly as the entire room went silent, holding their breath.

Michelle focused on something in front of her and ignored me.

I smiled. I could feel Aurora's mana flowing through me. I couldn't believe the difference the first ring made in my body.

I couldn't help myself. Harnessing my mana, I took a deep breath.

"Michelle!" I put enough mana behind the shout that the windows rattled and the entire class jumped. I leaned backwards, I waited for her to respond.

She slammed her book hard enough that the old school desk groaned. "What?"

I could hear a bit of trepidation in her tone. She wasn't sure of herself anymore and seemed a bit shaken up.

"Rematch today?" I tilted my head, daring her with my eyes.

But before I could get her response, the doors opened and an angry Professor Locke stormed in. "Shut it. What twisted dungeon did you come from where you think it is acceptable to shout that loud? Now since you are all popping and getting your first rings, it's time to go over what happens between the first and second ring. That's where mages really differentiate the wheat from the chaff."

He wrote Meridian Forging up on the board before continuing.

I sat up a bit straighter. We were finally getting into the lessons I knew less about.

The process up to the first ring was about fortifying your body so it could handle mana, but now we were getting into how to cultivate as a mage.

"Who can tell me how we cultivate our bodies between the rings."

A girl next to Michelle shot her hand up into the air like it was a race, but the professor scanned the class, ignoring her. "How about it, Mr. Lakes?"

I could tell it took Steve a moment to realize that was him.

"After the first ring, the mage's body is still malleable to lay the foundation for how mana flows through the body. This is meridian forging." Steve's voice was a bit rusty.

"Very good. You can do this once you have a source of mana in your body, your mana beast. The next step is to ensure mana flows through your body correctly. Until you establish those flows, it is important not to use mana wildly, as it can cause damage in your body." The last point was said while he stared straight at me.

"As we let mana change us for cultivation, it is important that it stay controlled. Otherwise, you are at risk of letting mana control you like a corrupt mage."

I noticed he left out some important details about corrupt mages typically practicing techniques that caused their condition. But it was a repeated caution given to anybody pursuing cultivation.

"What other cultivation techniques can you use now?" Locke looked across the classroom for answers.

"Spells," someone blurted out.

Locke went with it. "Correct. Spells are a way to increase your strength. They combine your mana with that of the world for greater effect. Therefore, mages strive to create and perfect spells; once you've stepped into cultivation, they become the primary method of fighting. But where do techniques come from?" Locke asked, looking directly at me. "Mr. Hughes."

"Mana beasts. The base of spells is a mimicry of mana beasts, as they innately are connected to the mana of the world." As I answered, I suddenly realized that, given Aurora's power as a mana beast, she would likely have techniques I could try to copy.

My thoughts wandered away from Locke's class and to Aurora. I could feel her ring sending a steady stream of mana through my body. I decided to practice my meridian forging.

It was hard to focus and keep it flowing smoothly while also listening to class, but if I was supposed to do this during a fight, then I needed to practice.

Class went on as the professor droned on about various mana beasts and their weaknesses. To enter dungeons, he emphasized, ad nauseam, we had to know everything to take advantage of the environment we found ourselves in along with what to expect from each monster. A prepared dungeon team would know all of this.

I nodded absently, shifting to thinking about my next epic match with Michelle that was quickly approaching.

***

Michelle must have been having similar thoughts, because she snagged me before I could enter practicals.

"Look. I'm sorry about the other day. I just—" She sighed, shifting her foot and looking at the floor. "It was important to me to finally beat you." She raised her eyes up to mine slowly.

I shrugged, really not holding a grudge over it. "I could have called it off; I could have not forced myself that far. But you're a good opponent. I wanted to push myself."

She gave a small smile. "And here I thought you were going to give me a harder time about it." She started to reach out, but then shoved her hands into her pockets.

"Also, I'm sorry about Kat. I know she and I had our differences, but I saw that you guys had something. I know from personal experience that it's hard to see something you want getting pulled away from you like that."

"Thanks, I'm trying to turn it into motivation." I returned her smile, trying to decipher what she'd said.

We'd known each other for a while, but as far as I knew, she had dated no one. Heck, when I'd tried to ask her out, she'd tried to punch me. Talk about a clear answer.

65

When I looked up, Michelle had turned and was headed into class. Realizing the time, I headed through the doors as well.

Rigel stood with his arms crossed as we filed into combat training.

"We will move onto live practice here soon, but first," he turned his attention to me, "I think the whole campus heard that challenge. And it would be good for both of you to work it out in the ring."

I smirked and went to grab a longsword, ready to make sure Michelle knew she wasn't my match now.

Rigel stopped me before I jumped into the dried-up pool.

"Be careful. Even though you are both mages now, I don't want either of you to end up in the healer's ward again." He squeezed my arm a bit harder than needed for extra emphasis.

I gave him a nod and let my mana surge through me as I jumped down into the pool, making the eight-foot drop look like a casual step.

Michelle was ready on the other side with a mace and a buckler. Her face was a purposeful blank slate.

I gave her a nod. After the talk we had, some of the fire was gone from me.

But that didn't mean I wasn't ready to try out my new skills. I wanted to test myself against her again now that I had popped my ring. This time though, I'd hold my bloodline in check.

"Be clean, you two. I don't want to send anyone to the medic again. On my count. Three. Two. One."

Feeling the mana pump through my muscles, I kicked off the ground and flew at Michelle. I wanted to finish this, show myself and the rest of the class that I was back on my feet.

She reacted just as quickly, throwing up that blue tortoise shield.

I didn't have an offensive spell to punch through it. I only had my strengthened physical body.

I was ready to see how they matched up. Switching my sword over to my left hand, I drew mana to my arm and slammed a punch into her protective ability.

The crowd gasped before the room boomed like an orc war drum.

Michelle's technique cracked and flickered before stabilizing.

I stepped back before she could counter. The room had entered a shocked silence that rippled out from that strike.

Her spell was weakened, and I could break it with another strike. I felt high on the strength in my body; the power that came with being a mage was intoxicating.

Michelle was wide-eyed before she shifted her shoulder to me, ready for me to break the ability on the next hit.

My knuckles hurt, but I watched as the torn skin knit itself back together. Definitely a perk of life attributed mana.

Grinning, I appeared before the shell again and punched, shattering it and continuing forward this time.

Her buckler took the hit, and she rolled the strike away from her body to avoid taking the full force.

My bloodline sang for a release, but I pushed it down. I would not let it out in this fight.

More excited about testing my mana than using my sword, I dropped it and came in with another punch. It was weaker because my mana was already thinning in my meridians.

She blocked it and swung for my head with her mace. I didn't care. With the life mana flowing through me, my opponents would be put at a disadvantage if they wanted to trade blows.

With my right, I threw a wild haymaker that felt like it would tear the air.

Feeling the danger, she turned her strike into a duck, and she spun to get out of the way.

My fist went past her and into the side of the pool, shattering the tiles in a one-foot radius. It hurt, but nothing was broken.

Not wanting to let her off easy, I spun, using my left fist in a hammer strike that would pop her head like a melon.

I could see the fear in her eyes. She was currently flat-footed, with my wild fist closing in on her face.

It stopped a hair from her nose, and the force blew her hair backwards.

Rigel was there, his hand half-clasped on my elbow.

He would have been too late if I had finished that strike, and all three of us knew it. His brows were knit together in a scowl.

The veteran fixed me with a piercing gaze.

"Oh, come on. I wouldn't be so petty as to actually send my classmate to the medic," I said, giving Michelle a smile.

She didn't seem eager to return it, still looking rather startled.

The rest of the class seemed split.

"He could have really hurt her, too far."

"Oh My God. That was epic."

I paused a moment to ground myself and clear out the others in the class to meditate and ensure my meridians were primed once again with mana.

"Now, class." Rigel got everyone's attention. "We will split you up into teams of four for live exercises. You will be paired with a veteran and go through basic combat drills as a group this week. Remember, you need to be a team. Take this time to learn how to work together. Next week, we will go on a field trip."

That last bit stirred up the entire class. Whispers turned into a dull roar and the class practically vibrated from being told we would leave the city.

I knew that we would probably not go far or fight anything too difficult. I'd watched my father's guards keep the nearby area clear to protect the city and the farms. The further out you went, the more dangerous the mana beast became, and to try and protect someone else only made it that much more dangerous.

"All right, all right. Pipe down. I know you are all excited to die. So let's be clear: you listen to the veteran assigned to you. After this field trip, we have plans to send each and every one of you out on a supervised dungeon dive. If your assigned veteran doesn't feel your group is ready, I will not allow you to enter the dungeon. Let me repeat that. If your vet says you don't go, you do not go. Got it?"

I felt a lump form in my throat. Impressing this vet would be important. Dungeons were filled with opportunities and loot. If your luck was good enough, you could come out of one much more powerful than you'd gone in.

Murmurs not too distant from my thoughts sprang up around me.

"I get your excitement, but please remember all of those who graduated from this academy and disappeared after their first trip out. Take this seriously."

Rigel paused, looking over the group. No one spoke up. We all knew that many people disappeared after they graduated. But so much was unknown on what happened to them. I'd always figured they'd found some other sect or something.

"Most of those new graduates die in their first dungeon, and that's if they even make it to one. Some can't even get started because groups don't want to take a noob out into dungeons. Remember, you are all only half a step better than someone who hasn't even formed their first ring."

The room had sobered, and everyone was looking ashamed. What he said wasn't new, but he didn't say what happened to those who were not picked by a group. Most of them would end up working for my father.

The guards would take out a new recruit with several protectors. They'd have the recruit fight monsters one-on-one until they were banged up, desperate and scared.

Then, they'd bring the recruit back and reteach all of the core principles for survival and cultivation. It formed a strong brotherhood amongst the guards and taught most of the valuable lessons without getting them killed.

With this latest dungeon challenge, it seemed like the academy was trying something similar, but not quite as safe. With the number of students, this was probably as much support as they could give.

"Now get in your groups and meet your vet." Rigel waved behind him and a group of mages stepped out into the ring and lined up.

Just from the pressure I felt, I knew they were all second-ring mages.

People ran over to a posted sheet of paper and scurried away to line up perpendicular to the line of vets in small columns of four.

I didn't look at the sheet; I just followed Steve to stand with a man that looked vaguely familiar.

Michelle and Jonny lined up with us. Michelle pointedly looked anywhere but at me.

"All right, come with me, you guys," the man said, kicking up his spear from the ground into a showy twirl that gave off faint sparks. His mana must be fire, and being able to ignite the air with his raw mana was impressive, but showy. He gave a small bow to our polite oohs and ahs.

He led us out to a field where most of the other groups were gathering in their own huddles.

"Let's get introductions off the ground. I'm Zack. I've been dungeon diving for eight years. I've formed my second ring and use the fire element. My preferred weapon is the spear." He lifted the angry red weapon. "I believe the spear is the easiest weapon to use, but the hardest to master."

I went ahead and knocked out introductions. "I'm Isaac, this is Jonny, Steve and Michelle. Jonny is the healer, Michelle is the tank, and Steve and I are the two damage dealers. Steve is long range, and I'm short range."

"Good, good. I saw that fight. Wonderful show. But focusing on fighting with your first ring in life element?" Zack raised his brow.

"Yeah. It is a long story, but yes." There was no need to explain myself to him. I would just prove my power when we went out.

"All right. So, life, life, water and...?" He looked at Steve.

"Wind." Steve didn't mince words.

Zack nodded. "Balanced team... I guess. I want you all to get weapons ready for the field trip. We will train with sharp weapons. We need to make sure you are used to them before we go. They will assign us one of the pits at 2pm for the next three days. We go in with our chosen weapons. You three will fight me as if I'm a mana beast from a dungeon that requires coordination. I'll coach, and we will rinse and repeat until you guys are good enough for our team to survive the dungeon. Capice?"

We all nodded.

"Good. Let's have a bit of light sparing before we head out today. I'd like to understand where we are starting from." Zack had a gleam in his eye when he looked at me, like I was a new chew toy.

It wasn't the most comforting moment, but I was excited to get more practice in. Later, I'd get Aurora alone to see if she knew any spells for life mana.

Chapter 7

I closed the door to my house and slumped against it, sinking down to the floor.

With a bit of will, Aurora shot out of her ring to stand in front of me.

"Well, that was fun. Did you see her face? Ah, priceless."

"You have an interesting definition of fun," I mock scowled and pulled her down to me. Her soft body landed on me, and she pressed her chest to mine.

She took the offered physical contact and curled into me like a content kitten.

"Isaac, I want you to survive. So, you need to keep training," Aurora said into my chest. She knew me too well. If nothing else, I had the desire to keep pushing myself, despite being exhausted.

I thought about all I was likely to encounter when I left this town. Not only were mana beasts a threat, but often there was competition for dungeons. My thoughts flitted to the Sun and Moon Hall. I couldn't wait to reject them when I became a renowned mage.

I got the beautiful mana beast off me and jumped to my feet. If she was willing to train me more now, I was in. I could also pick her brain now about spells.

"Before we start, can you tell me more about spells?"

Aurora just winked. "I caught your change when Locke talked about techniques coming from mana beasts. I am not sure how to teach you them, but we can try." She sighed and looked me in the eyes. "The last thing I want is to lose you. I'll do everything I can to help keep you alive."

I gave her a reassuring smile. "Let's go in the backyard for training; it's a nice day."

I took a moment to appreciate her.

She had given her life over to five-year-old me and had watched over me my entire life. Now that she could play a part, she had done nothing but support me without asking for anything. She was a force of nature, and she was mine.

"Perfect." She clapped her hands and hurried outside before me, excited to train with me.

I stepped outside, noticing the abandoned sandbox. It reminded me of all those years ago when we had first met. My smile went away as my eyes moved on to my mother's grave.

My dad had spent a lot of time out here after she died. It had changed us both when she passed; not long after, my father set in on training me with the sword day in and day out.

Aurora had gone quiet, and I saw her looking between me and the grave. I pushed aside all the emotions building up to focus on training.

"So, what are we working on today?"

"Punching. You are terrible at punching."

I scoffed in half-surprise, half-disbelief, "What do you mean? Did you see those punches I threw at Michelle? I broke her shield!"

"Of course I did. Terrible, rotten, no good punches. Let me show you." Aurora took a fighting stance, with one fist chambered at her side. "I'll use the same amount of mana you used before."

Crossing my arms, I watched. I wanted to see what was so much better about her punch.

But that cockiness faded when she stepped forward. I could feel the life mana surge in her to a sharpened point.

There was an explosion of force through her entire body as her fist shot out faster that I could see. There was a pregnant pause in the world before the air boomed with the force of being displaced so rapidly.

It was the kind of force that made your body ache just imagining being struck by it.

"See?" Aurora said bouncing on her feet, making cute little boxing jabs in the air. It was easy to forget this beautiful bubbly angel was a lethal mana beast.

"Uh… no, not exactly. It looked like a normal punch, but I could feel your mana kinda spike before you punched. Tell me more about what you did to shape it."

"Yeah, it takes a bit to get used to it. First, you need to change your perspective on life energy. You seem to think of it as a soothing, calm light. But life is anything but calm. It's a raging maelstrom that stops at nothing to keep going. Life energy is as much a starving wolf finding a rabbit, knowing it must kill to keep on living, as it is the resting wolf in a cave recovering."

Aurora put one hand on my chest, reaching with the other hand to close my eyes.

"Instead of a flow, picture it as a surge that comes through you. You came closest to it when you threw that hammer fist at Michelle. Feel it again, and don't stop. Throw the energy along with your fist. This is a bit beyond your current cultivation, but if you can even touch it, I think I can teach you a technique. And it will help you in other ways."

I felt for the sense of life energy that she spoke of. Not the calm healing energy, but the wild, untamed wilderness that sought anything to survive.

Deep under my skin I could feel a raw, untamed edge to life mana. I grabbed hold of that and thrust my arm, using it as a vehicle for the energy.

I opened my eyes to the breeze of my fist as it struck with more force than I'd done earlier today. I might have broken Michelle's shield with my first attack if I'd done it this way.

"Yeah! That was better. Life is not just healing. It's growth—growth atop a thousand corpses."

My punch hadn't been as strong as Aurora's, but it was still stronger than my punches during the fight with Michelle. And I wanted more.

Closing my eyes, I reached deep again, looking for that ragged edge of life energy.

Life energy flowed peacefully like a gentle giant within me. But, if I dug deep, what sustained that gentle giant was brutal, savage and dominant.

The green and gold aura of life mana shifted, and the gold became a hungry beast killing to survive.

I pulled hard on that golden aspect of life mana and threw it with my fist. I felt it rip through the air and explode in the dirt. That was so much better.

I couldn't keep from grinning as I opened my eyes.

Taking in the damage, my grin shattered. "Oh no. No. No. I'm so sorry." I rushed to my mother's grave where I had just blown away the dirt. The beautiful ground my father kept pristine was now haphazard.

Aurora was by my side. "I'm so sorry. I didn't mean for this to happen." She froze as she looked at my mother's grave. "But..."

Seeing Aurora's confusion brought me out of my worried state. "What is it?"

"Isaac, this is your mother's grave, right? I mean, I saw you kiss the tombstone quite a few times."

"Yeah, it's my mom. My father brought her back after she died and buried her here." I remembered the ceremony. A bunch of the guards came, and we all dug the deep hole together. Or rather my father and the guards did. My 'help' didn't count for much at five years old.

"Isaac, I don't know what to tell you. Your mother isn't buried here. The bones are definitely a woman's, but she hadn't even formed her first ring." Aurora gazed at the ground.

The bones weren't visible, but both humans and mana beasts could sense mana as they grew in power. Aurora must be able to sense the bones.

"She's been dead a while. Maybe there isn't any energy left for you to sense." I couldn't keep an edge of hope out of my voice. If my mother wasn't buried there, did that mean my father had lied?

"I... I'm sorry Isaac. But even if she were dead a hundred years, if she had formed a ring, it would have left a faint signature deep in the remains. This woman was never a mage." Aurora squeezed my hand.

"Maybe..." I started as a dozen excuses and reasons passed through my head in an instant. Each was thrown out one after the other. My father would have been able to sense the same thing, yet he still brought back this corpse and buried it. He wanted everyone to think she was dead... but if she wasn't buried here, where was she?

I wanted to refute Aurora and say she was lying, but I knew she wouldn't do that. Instead, I stood there looking at the grave, fluctuating between anger and abandonment.

It was a lot to take in. Aurora dragged me back to the house, and we finished out the day quietly while I wondered where my mother was.

***

The next day, I met up with the rest of our group outside Jonny's family restaurant. We had agreed to go shopping for gear together.

I had taken some gold from an emergency stash that my dad kept. I hoped it would be enough for me to get some decent gear.

"Morning, Isaac." Michelle caught sight of me first. "Not bringing Aurora around to see the market?"

I'd been in a funk all morning after the previous night's discovery, but I couldn't help but smirk knowing that she'd be shocked at the actual answer.

"No, not this time. For now, we should check out the bazaar, maybe go take a peek in the Treasure Hall."

Michelle snorted at that. "The Treasure Hall is too rich for our blood. They trade in mana beast cores, not coins."

Michelle was right. Once you became a mage, gold lost its value, replaced by mana beast cores. They were how power was increased. We headed out from the restaurant, passing by the Sun and Moon Brothel.

I hid to the side, watching it as we passed.

"You okay?" Michelle asked, trying to figure out what had caught my attention. Her eyes found the brothel, and she scoffed, "No, come on. We are going to the bazaar. Men."

I caught Jonny looking at the brothel longingly.

"Come on. You don't need to stoop to a brothel, right, Jonny? You have too much swagger for that."

Jonny perked up at that and ignored the building. I was glad, keeping us moving forward and away from the brothel.

We rounded the corner to the bazaar proper. It was a sea of colored canvases shielding wares from the harsh sun. In the center of the colorful sea, a polished pillar jutted out. The Treasure Hall, which the bazaar had grown around, was the center of the city's marketplace.

As soon as we got to the edge of the bazaar, Jonny darted forward after something.

I looked at Steve and he nodded before turning to chase after our friend and make sure he kept out of trouble.

Michelle sighed, "Can't they be adults for once."

"They are just excited," I said, even though I agreed it was a bit embarrassing.

"Well, let's see what you buy."

"It probably would be faster just to do our own shopping and then regroup." I figured I'd give her an out. And it really would be faster.

"No, we are all a team."

I held my hands up in mock surrender. "Fine, fine. Let's help each other. What are you looking for?" We stepped further into the sea of tents.

"Mace, buckler or small shield, some chain armor," she said, rattling off her list.

"No heavy armor?" I asked, thinking that was the standard for tanks.

"I hate being clunky. You never see any of the mages wearing clunky armor. The goal is armor as heavy as you can get without being slowed down too much. So that's some chain mail."

"Oh... that makes sense. Speed is an important part of fighting."

"How about yourself? What are you looking for?" She paused from her perusal of nearby wares to look up at me.

"Longsword, leather armor, maybe a decent heart guard. Nothing clunky for sure." I chuckled at my joke. She didn't laugh.

A stall came up on our right that was all weapons, including maces and swords. Jackpot.

I stepped over and tried to get the merchant's attention. The middle-aged woman waved at me to check out her wares but didn't get up from her seat.

If she didn't mind... I picked up one of the polished longswords and held it out in one hand, feeling the balance.

The balance was a smidgen higher than I liked.

"That's a trash sword," Michelle said, soft enough that the merchant couldn't hear.

"Hmm?"

"That is a gray-tier weapon. Trash."

I focused on my mana and tried to sense the weapon. As soon as I did, I could see the gray aura. It was indeed a trash-tier weapon.

Trash-tier weapons were void of mana, which could harden the material. The normal tier had the barest amount of mana, but enough to improve the quality. Uncommon was the first tier that contained enough mana for the equipment to actually enhance the user, but it was unlikely I would buy something like that before I had beast cores to use as currency.

For now, it was best if I found some normal equipment to use. It might be pricier than the trash tier, but I could count on it to hold up against mana beasts unlike this gray equipment. It was worth it for a better chance at survival.

"Try this." Michelle pulled a dusty sword out of the pile.

I held it up and felt for the balance; it was a far heavier balance than I would normally pick, but that just meant it would hit harder. I would need to rely on my cultivation to make up for the loss in agility.

When I looked at this weapon using my mana, it radiated a clean white aura. It was a normal weapon.

"10 gold," the woman behind the display said, not even looking up from her book. I realized it was an old print of the light novel Light Lordy, some smutty lewd novel.

I handed over the 10 gold. Next to me, Michelle picked out a mace after touching a few and closing her eyes to sense their quality. She paid, and we headed off.

We were about to look for an armorer when the sound of crashing metal and shouts caught my attention.

Jonny's familiar voice called out and cut off, followed by more clanging.

I grabbed Michelle's hand, and we took off through the crowded bazaar before the most recent noise subsided.

I felt a jerk on my arm.

I looked back to see Michelle's blushing face as I pulled her through the crowd.

Her eyes were zoned in on where I was holding her hand, but I didn't have time to be delicate about it. My friends were in trouble.

The bazaar opened up as people had made room for the fight that had started. Bored men crowded around for entertainment.

In the center was Jonny trying to extract himself from a pile of armor.

Steve was standing between him and a red-faced Aiden. There was a pretty girl standing to the side looking bewildered. Her eyes were like a deer in headlights.

I suddenly understood what had happened. Jonny and Aiden had likely been trying to woo the same woman. I'm guessing Jonny won, given that Aiden had attacked.

"Aiden, I thought you'd be back in the Sun and Moon Hall. Or have they finally regretted letting you in?" I let go of Michelle and stepped out to help Jonny.

Aiden's head snapped in my direction, and I could feel his mana stir like a coiled snake about to strike. "Of course you'd come to defend this rat."

"Just trying to keep the bazaar peaceful," I said, wondering why the guard wasn't here yet. It was like they were actively avoiding this conflict.

"Well, your friend interfered with official Sun and Moon Hall business. I have every right to kill him."

The lack of guard made sense now. If he claimed he was on official business for the Sect, then no one would want to stop him. That was the power of the Sect in our town.

"We both know that is unnecessary. What Sect business are you doing here in the bazaar? I'm sure the Sect has nicer everything."

"I'm recruiting Sarah here." He waved to the petite girl next to him. "But while I'm at it, how about it, Michelle? Would you like to come to the Sun and Moon Hall?"

There was a pause as the crowd took in a collective breath waiting for her answer.

Not only me, but everyone present was surprised at that. The Sect was considered a higher social status in the town. No one turned down an opportunity with them. It was like ascending a mountain in a single stride.

"Not on your life." Michelle crossed her arms under her breasts. I realized I'd been holding my breath a bit.

Aiden's face grew red at being denied like that, especially publicly. "Fine. I still have to kill this offender." He pulled a sword out of thin air and sliced down at Jonny.

I was there in a flash, using my new blade to block him. "You can't really be this arrogant." I pushed his sword back, feeling my palm go numb. He was still in his meridian forging, but there was a stark difference between our strengths.

I realized that if I didn't tap into my bloodline, I wouldn't be able to fight him.

Aiden snorted, seeing my surprise. "Ha. Feel the difference between a real mage and livestock pretending to understand cultivation? Time to step aside."

I was tired of the entitled prick.

My bloodline stirred at the exchange, like a beast waking for a challenge. It coiled through my veins begging for a release.

I pushed it down as I blocked another strike from Aiden, making my hand ring.

"What? No snarky remarks this time?" Aiden stepped in a circle, looking for his next opening.

Not wanting to be on the defensive, I rushed him with a high overhead swing.

Aiden stepped back, and I felt the mana of the world surge towards him as he cast a spell.

His sword caught fire and pooled off his blade as he slashed until it formed a burning skull that shot forward.

My bloodline grew impatient at this, and I felt the surge of strength that came with it as I swung down with my full force, cleaving the burning skull in two and continuing forward to clash swords with Aiden.

I pushed my bloodline back down before it could run rampant and damage my body.

But the bit of power seemed to have done its part. Aiden stumbled back and coughed up a mouthful of blood as his sword dipped to the ground, as if his arm had lost all its strength.

Michelle and Steve were there with their weapons drawn. "If you press this, Aiden, we'll fight to the death." Her tone made it clear that she wasn't bluffing.

"Fine," Aiden huffed. "Come on, Sarah. Try not to wander this time. As a prospective disciple for the Sun and Moon Hall, I need to make sure you are presentable." Aiden led her away, clutching his injured arm.

"Bastard." I spat on the ground.

"You really just kicked a Sun and Moon Hall disciple's ass, didn't you," Steve said.

Michelle shook her head. "He's a nobody. Just an arrogant prick. I'm sure he's just putting on airs because he's at the bottom of the pecking order in the Sect."

"Think so?" I asked, helping Jonny up.

"You don't send anyone important to go pick up a woman for you," Michelle scoffed. "I think we have far bigger problems than Aiden."

"I'm going to head back. Th-Thanks for having my back," Jonny said looking down.

"Steve, can you walk him back?" I asked.

Jonny started to deny it before Steve cuffed him on the side of the head. "Let's go back. I want some kebabs."

The two headed out with the dispersing crowd. I turned back to Michelle. "Thanks for being ready to step in with me."

"I've been waiting for a reason to hit Aiden anyway." She brushed it off and started back through the market, looking for the rest of what we'd come for.

"I was surprised you didn't accept the invitation to the Sun and Moon Hall."

It was honestly the most surprising part of the entire exchange. It was most people's dream to join the Sun and Moon Hall. They were a fast pass to learning past the academy; otherwise, you were left fumbling on your own.

"Haven't you noticed? The girls never come back," Michelle said, quietly enough that only I could hear.

I tilted my head, trying to think of all of those that left and showed back up in town. I couldn't think of any girls coming back. I could think of a few of the men, but no women.

"I'm sure it's a coincidence. There has to be a few. They said Kat had potential and she was going into seclusion to cultivate quickly," I said with a bit of hope.

"No, my mothers have been keeping track for dozens of years. As a girl, it's something you notice. That, and it's always the pretty ones." She idled at a stall, looking over the figurines of mana beasts from myth without any real intention of buying one.

I could read where she was going. "You think something happens to them."

She shrugged. "I have no proof, just a gut feeling."

"Strong enough of a feeling you would turn that kind of chance down," I said.

I worried for Kat. If something odd was up, she'd be in danger.

Michelle seemed to sense my shift in mood. "She chose the Sun and Moon Hall over you. It was her choice to make, and she made it. She walked away from anything that wasn't the Sect."

I glared at her for that comment. "It is a fantastic opportunity. I don't begrudge her for taking it, even if it made us separate."

Michelle played with the baubles at the shop, looking away from me. "She could have done what I just did and refused them. Stick it out here and make something of it." She turned and looked me in the eyes. "She chose the Sect over you. You don't owe her anything, including so much of your thoughts."

"Kat has always had ambitions. I don't hate her for going to the Sect; she's always wanted to make the world a better place and to do that she needs to grow as a mage. Our paths are just different now."

I let what she said sink in. I refused to believe Kat didn't love me, but I knew she had gone in a different direction than myself. And whether I wanted to admit it or not, my heart was finding space for more than just Kat.

Chapter 8

Aurora stood; arms crossed. I had been training with the party every day for the last week and Aurora had been helping me grasp the savage aspect of life in the mornings and nights.

"You've made a lot of progress, but I think you need to face extreme danger to really tap into what it's like to be a starving beast fighting for its next meal." Aurora shrugged, uncrossing her arms to hang by her sides casually. "So, let me show you a spell you might be able to do later, since I may not get the chance before I'm able to come out again. Let's see if you can touch upon it."

I already knew she would have to remain in the ring for this trip. I trusted Jonny and Steve. And even Michelle, although to a lesser extent. But Zack and anyone we'd run into was an unknown, and neither I nor Aurora wanted to risk it.

"All right, let's see this." I smiled. I was curious given all the pomp Aurora had given this spell of hers over the last week. She continued to surprise me, so I was excited to see what she could do.

Aurora stepped back, creating some space between me and her. "Just so we're clear, I'm not going to actually hit anything. Just form the spell and dismiss it."

I nodded. She was being quite cautious.

Aurora's hand flexed into a wide fingered form like a claw, and she thrust it towards me. I could feel her mana flow through her in the pattern of a beast with six large wings that I immediately locked in my mind.

Her hand finished the thrust and suddenly the world grew dark as a four-toed talon appeared behind her. The form of this spell was so large I had to turn my head to see the entirety of it.

Pressure from the spell slammed into me, rooting me in place. There was no way to dodge the claw that filled the sky.

My entire vision was consumed by the image produced by this spell. I was sure I would die when the claw vanished. I looked over at Aurora and couldn't help but wonder more about her. She was bouncing up and down, pleased with my reaction. I was a bit too stunned to do much, causing her to laugh as she came over.

"It's time to head out, Isaac." She gently broke into my thoughts as she nuzzled in to steal one last moment of affection.

She'd toned down the full-frontal assault this last week, but she still took the physical contact that she could. And I wasn't complaining; it was comforting.

"Let's go." After one last squeeze, Aurora became a stream of light that entered my chest. I smiled to myself, realizing that, despite what I was walking into, I was calmer than I'd been in months. It all felt right.

The anxiety of waiting on my ring, the drama with Kat and the Sect, it finally all felt unimportant compared to what was ahead for me. Maybe even what was ahead for Aurora and me.

Heading towards the academy, I had a chance to think.

I had grown a ton this week, both physically and mentally. Although this last week had been brutal, Zack turned out to be a no holds barred asshole when we trained. Which I guess made sense when his life was also on the line.

And I learned why you didn't see people with multiple rings fight in the city.

I knew my father and the guards were strong, but until now, I had nothing to compare it to. Feeling the surge and strength and power from my first ring was intoxicating, but fighting Zack was humbling.

There were several two-ring guards that helped protect our city, and my father and his second were both third-ring cultivators. It was a solid force of power, but even then, it was still weak when compared to a sect.

A fight between me and Michelle in the city might damage the street. But if a pair of two-ring cultivators fought, it would likely level several square blocks.

I cringed thinking about what would happen if someone on the level of my father were to fight in the city. It likely wouldn't be standing.

As we prepared to leave the city, Zack reminded us that mana was more concentrated outside the city and we would feel it more strongly. The number of portals that had gone uncleared and inverted on our world caused mana to seep into the surroundings. It had strengthened not only the mana beasts, but the ground itself. It would take more to do damage than we were used to, so we didn't need to hold back.

"Alright, are we ready?" Rigel asked the gathered groups.

The students all nodded excitedly while the vets kept their calm and nodded somberly.

"Good. Now the goal is to go out and get experience." Rigel looked over all the students he had been teaching the last three years. "Do not be reckless. I don't want to lose any of you." It almost sounded like Rigel got a bit choked up at the end. "Best of luck."

I watched Rigel turn away, a bit of sadness touching his face. He knew he was sending us into danger and there would likely be some injuries.

A part of me knew we wouldn't all return, but I would do my best to survive and keep my team alive.

Normally, I'd be even more cocky with Aurora to help me, but she'd told me this morning that she wouldn't come out to help me. Even if I forced her out of the ring, she said I needed to learn the feeling of true life or death survival instinct to be stronger. I wasn't sure I believed she'd do nothing, but it was probably best not to find out.

We all shouldered our packs and followed Zack out of the city.

He didn't have a pack, but I noticed his spatial ring on his finger. The item was a common treasure, but the quality varied. It could contain anywhere from a few inches of storage space to enough space to fit a house.

"From here onward, you follow my instructions, got it? No question. I'm here to keep you all alive. You do as I say."

The four of us nodded, and Zack took off running. "Good. Now hurry," he shouted over his shoulder as he kept moving without looking back.

I didn't hesitate and rushed after him, letting my mana flow strengthen my legs as I ran.

It was amazing.

We'd run for exercise, but this was the first time I'd been able to run full out with the strength of my ring. The landscape shot past me as I chased Zack, a lighthearted joy spreading through me from the wind in my face as we ran with the morning sun at our back.

When we stopped half an hour later, we all were panting lightly, except for Steve. Wind element had the advantage of speed. He probably could have cranked his speed up a notch if he'd wanted.

Zack looked back at us. "Weapons at the ready from here forward. Be ready at all times."

I had my sword at my hip, so that wasn't a problem, but Steve had his bow on his back and Michelle her buckler.

Both of them got their weapons ready.

"Good. First lesson of this trip. Monsters can come at you any time. Guards up." He then stepped back from us as growls came from the woods beside us.

I realized he must have sensed these monsters and stopped so we would have a chance to fight.

The growls materialized into goblins as they pushed through the bushes towards us. While standing on two legs, they showed no sign of intelligence.

They were hunched over, feral creatures. Their dirty green skin was pulled taut over their muscles and bones. They had overly long arms that looked like they walked on their front knuckles like an ape. Unlike the friendly monkeys, these monsters radiated savagery with their sharp claws and saw-like teeth.

I watched as nearly a dozen stepped out of the bushes and started circling our group slowly.

"These are rank zero monsters. That means, during one-on-one combat, a non-cultivator can fight them. Don't embarrass me and die here," Zack said, leaning on his spear.

The goblins looked at Zack warily and moved to the side, away from him. They could feel that he was the strongest in the group.

But when he made no move to interfere, one of them bayed and gibbered at me.

When Zack made no motion to stop them, the rest joined in, taunting us.

But we held our formation. Michelle was up front, and I was to the side, with Jonny behind and between us. Steve was in the very back, protecting Jonny from any surprises and ready to use his bow to pick them off.

The leader of the goblins staggered forward, and Michelle was ready for the first attack.

Or so she thought. The goblin went from a stagger to a pounce in a blink of an eye. Her training saved her, her mace meeting the pouncing goblin before her mind had caught up.

It threw itself downward until it was nearly flat on the ground before surging forward with its maw of teeth like broken glass. Another new goblin lesson.

Michelle wasn't going to block in time.

I shifted out of position and thrust my sword through its neck before it latched onto her.

But that set off a chain reaction as the goblins now saw the center exposed. Their pack mentality identified Jonny as the weak one.

They rushed forward like starving animals towards Jonny.

My heart leapt into my throat. I'd broken the formation, and now Jonny was exposed.

Michelle was there. Her shield spell cut them off from Jonny.

Steve was firing arrows from the back, but the goblins moved erratically among the rest of the party, and I knew he was having trouble keeping up.

As the goblins continued circling, looking for weak points, I was separated from the rest of the team.

I was becoming overwhelmed. Missing one, hot pain lanced through my neck as I heard and felt the squish of teeth sinking into my shoulder.

I froze in panic for a moment before the goblin thrashed, bringing enough pain to knock me to my knees. I looked over towards my friends.

Michelle had blocked for Jonny, but there were too many. Michelle and Jonny were losing. Meanwhile, Steve was doing well fighting his own two goblins, but he wasn't going to be able to help Michelle and Jonny.

They would die.

Where was Zack? I looked around and found him buffing his nails against his chest as we all died, without a care in the world. What kind of sick shit was this?

I could feel every heartbeat like it was my last. Time had seemed to slow as I took in all that was happening around us. Jonny let out a scream.

Blood pounded against my skull. My plan to leave Locksprings and find a sect, to grow stronger as a mage... It was over, being cut short.

At that moment, on my knees, watching my friends being taken down, I knew the savage underside of life. I felt the primal fury to survive.

I knew it was what Aurora had been trying to get me to touch—the sharp edge of life forged on the corpses of thousands to survive.

My time was not up. I would survive. I would become a mage.

Reaching up, I flipped the goblin over me, ripping him off me but taking half my shoulder with him. With the adrenaline in my body, I barely felt it. I needed to survive, to live.

I poured life energy through myself as I swung at the goblin staring back at me in surprise, its mouth still full of my flesh.

He exploded in a shower of viscera.

The air shuddered as I took a mana-infused step, crossing a dozen feet to cut down the goblin attacking Jonny.

Everything seemed to slow as my blade blurred through the next goblin, turning him into mincemeat and reversing my blade to stab through the one behind me.

I lashed out with a hammer fist that shattered the skull of another as my sword swung back at the ready.

Surprise was registering on not only the remaining goblins, but the rest of my team.

But I wasn't going to let the goblins flee, swiftly severing head after head like they were child's play.

When the last goblin died, the world came crashing back into focus. I barely caught myself from falling over by stabbing my sword in the ground.

Clap. Clap. "Fuck, that was... fantastic." Zack walked over, acting like he'd just gone to some martial arts play.

"You ba—" I was cut off by my own stomach. Leaning over, I heaved out what was left of my lunch.

"Ah, yeah. That's what happens when the adrenaline crashes hard. You have to build a tolerance up to that. Sorry, bud, but still, that was fucking fantastic. What was that?"

I wiped my mouth and looked up, feeling pretty worn down. Everyone else looked as confused as Zack. "I'm not sure," I lied. My mana was in chaos, and I was having trouble circulating it properly.

"Well, that wasn't your bloodline. But be careful with it, whatever it is. It looks like it really wore you out." Zack shrugged like it was no big deal; cultivation took all sorts of forms.

"Based on where things were, if you hadn't tapped into whatever that was, you were probably all dead. Well, maybe not Steve, I bet he could have escaped after you all died."

Steve gave Zack a what-the-fuck stare. There was no way he'd abandon us.

I went to give him a smile when I registered Michelle coming at me like a charging bull. "We almost died because you broke formation."

I sighed. I was not taking her bullshit right now. "I was trying to save your life. I take thanks in the form of foot massages." I pulled myself up straight. I could feel the weakness in my legs, but I'd be damned if I showed it.

"You broke formation. I didn't need your help. We all almost died because of you."

"Calm your tits," Zack said, which earned a fiery look from Michelle. "Yes, he saved your life at risk to the party. I agree it was stupid, but honestly if he didn't help you, you were going down. Once you went down, they would have torn you to shreds. So yeah, he put the entire party at risk. But Isaac also just killed all of them practically by himself. So maybe give the dude a bit of credit."

Michelle spun away. I'd known her long enough to know this wasn't over. Her anger was like a banked fire. It was now lying in wait for the faintest fuel to reignite it into a blaze.

Aurora was so much simpler. Maybe it was because she was a beast, but she didn't hide her emotions.

"Well, our little fighter looks like he will be useless for a bit," Zack said, still acting like all of them almost dying was no big deal.

"Probably time to set up camp anyway. There is a stream a few miles away; we'll go slow for you."

I grit my teeth and tried to keep up with the rest of the group as we trudged through the forest far slower than we had run from the city.

Jonny had healed up everyone's physical injuries, but there was a fatigue that came from using mana that had us all moving slower.

Well, except for Zack. Since he hadn't lifted a finger to help, he moved through the woods like he was taking a casual stroll.

When we found a natural overhang on the side of a hill, I knew this was where we would camp.

Sure enough, Zack saw it and made a circle around it, looking for signs of habitation before coming back. "This is where we will make camp. A nice spot like this means that if something or someone comes at night, our backs stay protected."

"Couldn't someone bring this whole overhang down on us?" Jonny asked, looking at the rock suspiciously.

"Potentially. But remember that the land out here, including this stone, is much harder than what you have experienced in the city. It would take a powerful two-ring, or maybe even a three-ring cultivator, to collapse this shelf. And if one of those tried to kill us, we'd probably be screwed anyway." The mellowness with which he continued to talk about our deaths was concerning.

Zack waved his hand and a large tent stocked with amenities sprang out of his ring onto the ground.

"Cool. So, you guys should make camp, set up a watch schedule—ya know, the important things. I'll see you in the morning." With that, he disappeared into the tent, closing it behind him.

I looked back at the rest of the group. "Okay, so shift schedule. Michelle and Jonny take first watch, me and Steve will take second?" It was always best to watch in pairs to keep each other awake.

"Why do I have to be with Michelle?" Jonny whined, but a sharp glare from Michelle silenced him.

I set up my tent under the overhang while Jonny and Michelle found suitable logs to perch themselves on for the night watch.

There would be no campfire tonight. It was too likely to attract the wrong sort of attention. For food, we had packed dried trail bars of jerky and nuts glued together with honey.

As soon as I retreated into my tent, I could feel the tug from Aurora's ring. I had the tent enchanted for privacy, knowing she'd want to come out of her ring at some point during this trip.

I summoned her from the ring, and she was on top of me immediately.

Aurora showered kisses down on me, each one leaving a lingering tingle from her contact. "I was both so proud and so scared," she whispered, leaning down to tuck her face into my neck.

I could feel my neck growing damp.

"You said I needed to learn," I reminded, stroking her back softly. "And you were right. Look at what I was able to do."

"I know, but that was scary. I am bound to you forever, Isaac; I need you to grow stronger. But even if it was the right call, it felt like I was abandoning you. You forgive me, right?" She looked up with watery eyes.

"Of course, no forgiveness needed. If anything, you were a part of what helped me pull that off." I remembered what it had felt like after. "Will touching that aspect always throw my mana in turmoil?"

"No, it'll get easier with practice. I'm so proud of you for touching on it. But no more close calls like that again. If you were to die, I don't know what I'd do."

I looked down at my heartbroken mana beast. The fear and affection she was showing was sweet. She may be powerful in her own right, but she was entirely mine. I still didn't know how my ring affected her or our bond, but the connection between us was undeniable.

Grabbing her head, I tilted it back and kissed her, enjoying the surprise that lit up on her face before she closed her eyes and sank into me.

She pulled herself up to get more, her tongue flicking my teeth and exploring. The kiss deepened, and she began moving her hips back and forth, rubbing against me, causing me to stifle a moan.

I put my hands on her hips, encouraging the rocking as I sucked on her lips and let our tongues intertwine. Her hands moved up to cup the back of my neck as she pressed harder in her rocking, tipping her body back and moaning.

"Master," she whimpered.

It was like a string snapping me back to the present. I couldn't ignore the clear subservience or the uncertainty that came with it. But damn, it was getting harder to fight. I put my hands on her waist, stopping her.

She felt the change in me and pushed back, looking confused. "What's wrong. What did I do?"

"You did nothing wrong... I just don't understand why a powerful mana beast..." I gave her a dry look, letting her know I knew there was something more to her, "...would be so submissive to me. Do you really want this, or is this forced by the ring?"

She huffed out a sigh. "If I say it's not the ring, then it's still suspicious because you could think I'm only saying it because you want it. There's no way to convince you, so what am I supposed to do?" She sighed wistfully as she touched her swollen lips, drawing my attention.

There was the crux of the issue, and I didn't know how to get past it. One day, if I found out this was all forced upon Aurora and she didn't want any of it, I would be wrecked.

"Maybe tell me about what it's like being a mana beast in a ring? Help me understand our bond more."

Aurora looked thoughtful. "It's like being an observer mostly. I live in your inner world and can watch out of your spiritual sea."

"Where my mind touches my inner world. Can you see everything?"

"Yes, but not just see. I can hear too. But I don't get your thoughts or reasoning behind it. Sometimes you do really stupid things. Like when you were little, and you and Jonny tried to compete to see who could stick the most rocks up your noses," she laughed, shaking her head.

I had forgotten about that.

"I mean, seriously. Why? Not even the stupidest chick will stick a rock up their nose. Humans are weird." Aurora settled into my side.

"I mean, I don't think I can justify sticking a rock up my nose, but I will remind you that I won," I said, stroking her hair.

"Hah, yes. Clearly you were destined for greatness based on your nose rock prowess," she laughed, before the smile wilted a bit. "It was also scary. I picked an innocent kid who smelled like he was destined for great things. And I made a gamble, binding myself to you forever." Her eyes met mine.

I felt like, in that moment, we could see into the depths of each other's soul. I cupped her face in my hand, leaning closer. "I'll do my best not to disappoint you. If it makes a difference, I like to think you made a pretty good gamble. And I'll continue to work to try to reinforce that."

"Uh huh. And you're not biased in this at all." She dragged out the last word. "But I think so too. I've had over a decade to get to know you, Master. To love you."

"Yeah, and if I weren't an idiot, I'd be balls deep in you enjoying that love right now." I nudged her nose with mine.

"Yes, but instead, you are being putting-rocks-up-your-nose stupid right now." She gave an over exaggerated sigh, shaking her head back and forth before smiling and refocusing on me.

"But I'll wait again for you to realize that rocks don't belong up your nose, Master. After all, we are together for the rest of your life."

She got a wicked glint in her eye before continuing. "And I'm fairly confident it will only take you being balls deep in me once before I convince you it's a great idea. After all, I've had most of your life to learn what you like. In all aspects."

My mind started spinning from all the fantasies we could play out. But I was never going to get the sleep my body needed if I continued down that path.

"We need to get some sleep. It's hard to stay alive if I'm dead tired." I rolled over and put an arm around her, adjusting us to sleep. She gave in, pressing her body against mine. She fell asleep first, her face full of serene beauty.

I calmed my mind, using her restful state to help slow my breathing. I needed to sleep now. I would figure the rest out when I woke up.

Chapter 9

The next thing I knew, Jonny was poking me to get up for my turn at watch.

Luckily, Aurora had disappeared sometime between going to sleep and now, or I would be having a really awkward conversation with Jonny.

"Yeah, yeah, I'm up. Get some sleep, Jonny." I sat up and rubbed the grit out of my eyes. I felt far better than I had going to sleep, clearly my mana had done some work. I smiled at the thought of being a mage. The joy of it still hadn't worn off.

Fishing out my canteen and a trail bar, I found Steve already sitting on a stump.

"Want some?" I asked, breaking the bar in half and offering it.

Steve just shook his head and knocked his head back.

I handed him my canteen knowing what he meant.

"Thanks," Steve said, giving a meaningful enough look to indicate that it was for more than just the water.

"No big deal. We are out here together. A team."

"No really. You saved my life; you helped me survive. Now I see things differently." Steve looked out into the darkness wistfully.

I let my friend gather his thoughts. Steve didn't speak much, but occasionally, he would open up.

"You know, I never understood why my father stayed in town with his farm. I always wanted him to go out and get another ring, or bring back another horse. It sounded exciting. But it's not that exciting, is it? It's... terrifying." Steve took another slow sip of water. I understood what he was saying. A bit of our childhood naivety had left us all today.

"You aren't going back, are you?" I asked.

Steve shook his head. "Not yet. There are so many beautiful horses to see."

"Oh god. You really need a girlfriend. Soon we'll think you love horses a bit too much."

Steve's grin stretched to its limits. "Just make sure you knock before you come in the barn, Isaac."

I chuckled and rolled my eyes. He always took that joke a bit too far.

"I'm glad you aren't having second thoughts," I said.

He looked into the distance. "Michelle is in the worst shape mentally. She's shaken up. She looked haunted after watch."

"That bad? I thought she'd be too stubborn to let it get to her." I thought of the woman who had been a constant, annoying pain in my side for the past few years.

"More like too stubborn to tell herself she isn't in the right headspace for this. But she would never back out, not while you are out here being a badass."

I smirked at the complement. "I know we were rivals of sorts at school, but you think she would stick it out just to beat me?"

Steve gave me a 'you can't really be that dumb' look but a twig snapped, and we both went silent, paying attention to the dark night.

We waited, holding our breaths for another noise.

The forest continued on with sounds of insects and the rustle of the trees. Deep in the night, we couldn't see more than twenty feet out, but nothing moved and the sounds of the forest at night continued.

Nothing came, which was even more concerning. If it had been a passing animal, there should have been more sound than just a single twig.

Time stretched on, and I finally broke the silence. If something was out there, it wasn't showing itself. "I know you think she has a thing for me. But remember that time I tried to ask her out?"

Steve chuckled. He laughed for a solid minute, clearly remembering when she lured me in for a kiss then slapped me so hard my head spun.

I made sure to get her back for that later. And the constant competitiveness between us had begun.

We talked, or rather, I talked, and Steve nodded occasionally until the sun crawled back on the horizon.

As soon as the sun peeked through the trees, Zack woke up and we started the day.

"Where to?" I asked, shouldering my pack.

Zack looked around, taking his bearings. "We need to head another half a day's travel away from the city. Then we will be about the right distance to find some rank one mana beasts. We will give each of you a chance to fight one, and then we will see how you work as a team."

"Will there be any rank two beasts?" Jonny asked.

"Unlikely. They would need to be runts pushed out of their territory. Rank zero and one beasts essentially run amok, but when you get to rank two beasts, they absorb a large amount of the mana in their territory. They often fight to keep others out so they can keep absorbing mana and growing. Same goes as you get to rank three and four. The denser the mana, the stronger the monster that will make that place their home. Right now, the mana isn't dense enough to attract a rank two. It would have to have been weak enough to be pushed out by all the others."

"So we'd sense a difference in the mana before we stumbled into the territory of a strong monster?" I asked. This seemed like important information for staying alive.

"I figured they'd taught you this, but I guess you are all pretty freshly formed. But yes, as you get closer to your second ring and touch upon your nascent soul, you'll be able to sense mana. Right now, you can probably sense it in your body and maybe a few feet out. But as our bodies adjust to mana, they start to crave it and you will learn to sense it further out."

Zack stopped suddenly and held up his fist for us to stop.

A growl came from the bushes as a skin-and-bones wolf stepped out. Its fur was matted, and its ribs could be seen clearly through the layer of fur.

"Michelle, you are up. None of us will help. Once you kill the hungry wolf, we'll be on our way," Zack said.

I recalled the lessons on mana beasts and knew what this was. A hungry wolf was a creature that never seemed to leave its state of starvation.

As a rank zero, it didn't have a mana core or an element, but the wolf could eat for days and supposedly never become sated. It would fight like someone had kicked its survival instincts to one hundred and ten percent.

I gave Michelle a once over, and Steve was right. She was pushing herself hard. I was worried. Even after sleep, the fire that was always in her eyes had gone cold. She looked a bit like a zombie as she readied her weapons.

"Hey Michelle, I'm going to need you to destroy this hungry wolf. All the times I beat you will look less impressive if this thing can take you down," I said, taunting her.

"Fuck you." Michelle didn't take her eyes off the wolf, but I could see that fire in her eyes spark again as a small smirk spread on her face.

Stepping away from the rest of us, she circled the wolf.

"You are looking a lot better than I expected this morning," Zack said, turning away from Michelle to look at me, apparently already bored with the fight.

"Thanks. I guess all I needed was a good night's sleep." I kept my expression neutral and my eyes on Michelle.

Zack gave me an appraising look. "Uh huh. Just don't overuse whatever that was. Learn to rely on yourself, not some gimmick."

Michelle had engaged the wolf, but she was fighting too cautiously. She was trying to win the fight without taking damage, which was unlike her.

"Hey, hurry it up. We have a lot of ground to cover. Jonny will patch you up after you finish. Really, this is getting embarrassing." I tried to anger her. She needed to get out of her head.

"Shut it," she shouted over her shoulder, throwing a glare at me while she was at it.

The hungry wolf took that moment of distraction to charge.

But Michelle was better than that and caught its bite with her buckler before tossing the beast to the ground.

It didn't have a chance to react before she was on it, keeping it on the defensive with a flurry of blows with her mace.

She got a good hit on its head that made it wobble and fall.

"See, look at that, no problem." Michelle turned around to give me a full glare with hands on her hips.

But the wolf popped an eye back open, and I didn't have time to warn her before it lunged and sank its teeth into her ankle.

I tried to step forward, but Zack's hand was on my shoulder pinning me in place.

Michelle screamed and fell as the wolf threw its body weight to the side, taking her leg with it.

Rolling on the ground, she got herself facing the wolf and started bashing it with her mace until its skull was a pile of ground meat.

Zack stepped back, and Jonny rushed forward to heal her.

I couldn't stop staring at her leg as the puckered wound shrank and folded in on itself closing shut with a fresh pink scar.

The whole time, Michelle gave me a glare that said it was all my fault.

I snorted. If she couldn't understand that what I had done was for her benefit, that was on her. I was just happy that her eyes had held onto that fire once again.

We continued to travel, and only stopped once more where Zack forced Jonny to fight a rabbit beast. The poor guy had to heal himself so much before the rabbit finally dropped from exhaustion and Jonny managed to kill it.

But, true to his word after the half-day of travel, Zack stopped. "Alright, now we will cut from the road and go into the forest. You've gotten the basics of how this goes. It will be up to you four to lead now. You won't pass until each of you gets a one-on-one fight with a rank one and a fight that deserves the whole team's efforts."

I took that moment to step forward. "Alright, on me. We will head north."

Jonny and Steve stepped off the road with me without hesitation. I heard Michelle huff before she followed along.

The forest was quiet as we walked. By the road, the forest had been dense with small growth. It had seemed hard to pass through. But, as we continued, the trees got larger and further apart. Their canopies blocked the light to the forest floor. As a result, less and less ground cover was present as we delved deeper into the forest.

Animal tracks became clearer without the underbrush, and the forest came alive with crisscrossed old trails.

I shifted my vision up now that I didn't have to focus on keeping my feet untangled by the ground cover.

Zack was close by, but he kept himself far enough apart such that he wouldn't scare off any of the lower-level mana beasts. I would only catch glimpses of him through the trees.

Jonny shouted over to him, "Zack, will you warn us if we get too close to a stronger beast's territory?"

"Nope, but when you see me not wanting to go somewhere, that might just be a hint," he said with a laugh.

I knew on some level that Zack was enjoying this. Was this the callous attitude of a mage? Would we all care for each other just as little after we had years of cultivation under our belt? I felt some sympathy for him. Likely, he'd had hard lessons that had made him put up the walls.

I continued on, not wanting to think about it further and focused on the trees around me. They were strengthened by mana, so thick we'd struggle as a group to wrap around them.

It was darker in the forest, but it was still light enough to see by. After a while of not coming across any mana beasts, I was thinking we might need to change our strategy.

Almost as if in response to my thought, a low growl rumbled through the trees.

What sprawled out on the limb of a tree above us slinked like a cat, but I could see light reflect off glossy scales.

"Steve, I think this is yours." If my guess was correct, it was a lesser earth drake.

I closed my eyes and tried to feel for Steve's mana. I could feel it swirl around him like a faint wind as I heard the slight creak of his bow.

A moment later, the twang of his bow sounded, and I opened my eyes to watch the arrow blast off like a cannon. Unfortunately, it only took a chip out of the tree bark when the beast dodged.

The tree had barely taken damage. The world really was much sturdier this far out of the city.

We all stepped back from Steve and let him fight. The lesser drake jumped out of the tree, and I got a better look.

The mana beast was the size of a small horse. The drake was some convoluted mix of a lizard and a cat. I now understood why, after the dungeons, some people thought to name it after a wingless dragon.

It had a mostly feline body, but it was covered in earthy scales. Its face was shaped like a lizard, but its snout was square and full of sharp teeth dripping a dark liquid.

Lesser drakes were common and supposedly were some of the earlier monsters to mutate from the initial surges of mana into our world. Some say they came from house cats that were mutated by elemental mana.

As the drake came closer, Steve slung his bow over his back and pulled out a pair of daggers from his side.

While Steve had trained primarily as an archer, he had also spent countless hours working with daggers, knowing that he wouldn't always be able to keep distance between him and his opponents.

The lesser drake eyed the rest of us warily before darting at Steve. It was eager to get its kill.

Narrowly dodging the attack, Steve scored two long slashes down its flank before he poured mana into his legs and blasted away from the mana beast to get some room to work.

The lesser drake let out a feral whine and turned on him.

Steve already had his bow out. While still holding his daggers, he let loose two arrows. His ability to maneuver with all the weapons was impressive

The lesser drake dodged the first arrow only to move right into the second, which buried itself up to the feathers in its shoulder.

Between the gash on one side and the arrow in the other, the beast was drastically slowed.

I saw Steve put away his daggers confidently before he drew another arrow.

At this point, Steve had the lesser drake dead to rights, and it knew it. The lesser drake turned and tried to run.

Steve kept close, pelting it with arrows.

We all followed along as Steve finally brought it down.

I got close, wanting to see a rank one beast. We were taught in class about them, but seeing it for the first time was much different.

"Dig out its core, I'll store the body," Zack said.

Steve wasn't afraid of getting dirty and was quickly on his hands and knees carving out the back of the beast's skull. Once he could wedge his hand in, he pulled out a dirty yellow gem that glowed with inner light.

All beasts formed a core once they reached rank one, which many equated to a ring on a cultivator. The core was essentially crystallized mana. It could be used to try and bind the spirit of the beast to a cultivator and fill a ring, it could be fed to a beast within an existing ring, or it served as currency.

"Don't forget to absorb the chaotic mana," Michelle reminded Steve, who nodded as he sat down cross-legged and started to meditate.

Mana beasts would release a surge of mana on their death. That plus the tempering of one's mana through combat made for ideal conditions to cultivate. One couldn't cultivate in solitude; you had to experience combat and danger to progress.

I watched excitedly as Steve breathed deep and faintly glowed, absorbing the mana and starting his second ring.

"How does it feel?" Jonny asked, watching Steve stir.

"Tickles." Steve smiled at Jonny as Zack packed away the mana beast into his spatial ring. Steve would be able to sell the parts for some coin back home and use the mana beast core to cultivate once he found a safe spot.

I patted Steve on the shoulder in recognition of his success. We were one step closer to successfully completing this field trip.

Michelle took it upon herself to keep us moving. "Come on. We made a lot of noise. Let's move on before more potentially come looking."

I knew she was right. We needed to get away from the disturbance we caused.

"I'm eager to get my one-on-one fight. Let's get going guys." I hurried off in what I thought was the right direction and I saw Zack had stepped back again, trailing along out of the corner of my eye.

We didn't run into any more rank one mana beasts. We found a few rank zeros that we killed without trouble. Luckily, we still had plenty of time to complete the tasks for the field trip.

Finding an abandoned cave, I called a break for the day. We were all soaked and tired from fording a river.

The cave didn't have any recent tracks in the soft dirt outside and it was too early for anything to be in hibernation.

Michelle came out of the cave after checking it out for herself. "Yeah, the bones in there are too dry to be recent. There's no fresh fur or any other signs of habitation. I wonder why a perfectly good cave would be idle like this?"

I wanted to hush her. She was just asking for trouble.

"We haven't seen a whole lot of beasts. There just may not be enough to feed a predator that would take up roost in a cave like this," I thought out loud. "Either way, we should still be careful at night. Double watch again?"

"I call the second watch," Jonny said, a yawn eking out of him.

I rolled out my sleeping bag, not needing a tent in the cave, and gave Steve a questioning look.

"First with Michelle."

That left me on second with Jonny. Sounded like fun. I should have been hungry, but sleep felt more important. I was out like a light the second my head hit my bedroll.

***

A foot nudged me out of my sleep, and I woke, startled ready to fight.

"Your turn, sleeping beauty," Michelle said with a barely suppressed grin.

Yeah, she enjoyed that. I pulled myself together and waved her off. "I'm up, get some rest."

Grabbing a trail bar, I found Steve at the front of the cave and waved him off to go wake Jonny.

I found it odd how much I missed Aurora. I hadn't had a chance to call her out. She really had become part of my life if a single day without her showing up had brought my mood down.

Then again, it might be because I kept stopping myself from the feel of her soft body. I was getting pretty pent up.

"You okay, Isaac? You kind of had a perverted face on. Ah, you were thinking of that sweetheart Aurora you were hiding from us, weren't you?" Jonny said, walking up to take his post.

I chuckled awkwardly. "You caught me red-handed. I missed her last night." I felt both oddly relieved and embarrassed to say that out loud.

"Dude, just use her for motivation. If I had an angel like that waiting for me, nothing would stop me from getting back alive."

I almost choked with how close he got to reality with the angel comment. But I held it in and focused on the more important part of what he had said.

"You okay, Jonny?"

"I... I don't know if I can fight a rank one beast, Isaac." Jonny was looking down, drawing circles on the ground with his foot.

I wanted to tell him it would be okay, but I couldn't lie to my friend. "Look, if you can't, we'll intervene. In the worst case, we all go back alive. I would much rather have you alive than pass this without a friend."

"Thanks," Jonny said softly. "You know, I'm starting to understand why my mother is so happy. She never went through this since she never formed her ring. Ignorance is bliss, right?"

I gave Jonny the best pity-free smile I could muster, but the reality was that I could see him cracking too. I was starting to understand all the mental training they'd pushed on us at the academy.

But, if this occurred in a dungeon, it was deadly. There could be no room for hesitation with mana beasts around every corner.

"Jonny, do you still want to be a mage after this?"

"I... no, not really. I want to be a healer. I know that fighting is part of it... but I just want to help people."

I knew that Jonny grew up in a peaceful family. They were nothing like my father, but I needed my friend to pull through this.

"You know, you are most needed on the front line. That's where the big battles take place that could make or break a city in the long run. But, to do that, you need to be able to handle the front line."

"I know..." Jonny said and once again the ground had caught his attention.

"But?" I dragged out the word and let it linger.

Jonny looked up at me with a face of disappointment. "I didn't know it before this trip, but I just don't have that aggressiveness that you or Steve have. There's none of… you know… that umphf behind me when I fight."

He paused before continuing. "But I still want to explore the world, you know? There's just so much out there. We are just a small little island adrift in the world. What if just beyond what we know is an entirely different world? We'd never know it."

I looked out into the darkness hoping to find the same answer. I was filled with curiosity. The world could be filled with people who cultivated entirely differently for all I knew. Or maybe, there was a place that had truly found peace.

"I don't know what to say, Jonny. Maybe you could find a team that just needed healing, like a caravan that wanted a healer on staff. But the world isn't kind. If you can't fight back, it will eat you."

Jonny was about to respond when his head snapped up at a branch cracking.

I felt for my sword, hoping that it was just some creature passing through.

A plump, little, red-furred monkey wandered out of the bushes, walking on its knuckles.

Jonny let out a sigh of relief. "It's just a young monkey."

"Yeah, but Jonny, if I remember right, almost all primate beasts are social creatures and part of a pack."

I heard a sharp intake from Jonny, and I followed his line of sight.

One after another, pairs of eyes from red to gold were popping out in the night.

I hissed as I stood and blocked off the entrance to the cave. "Jonny, go wake the others. Quickly."

Chapter 10

This was bad. Even if these were rank zero mana beasts, their numbers were steadily climbing to the point where, even if Zack stepped in, this would get dicey.

I watched as what I now realized was a young red gorilla played on the ground while all the monkeys in the tree watched closely. They were not the same type of mana beast. It was like the ones in the trees were there to look after the baby. Knowing monsters also cared extra for their young, this could go badly very quickly.

We would have to make a run for it. I knew in my mind that fighting these numbers would not be a winning prospect.

I stood at the cave entrance, waiting for the monkeys to make the next move.

Luckily, they seemed content to watch the little one wander. I began to wonder if they weren't just watching over it. From my experience with Aurora, I'd learned there was more to mana beasts.

I heard the patter of feet as the rest of the group came and joined me.

Even Zack had come out. When he saw the little monkey, his face dropped.

"That's a baby flame-back gorilla."

I pointed up at the glowing eyes in the trees. "Those too?"

Zack followed where I was looking and dismissed them. "No, those are too weak to be flame-backs. A flame-back is a peak rank one, or a low rank two."

"Oh, shit," Jonny cursed.

It was time to be tactical.

"Jonny, Steve, go grab our packs. Zack, I assume we need to get out of here?"

"Yes. Go help them get ready. I'll stay up here."

I hurried back, and Michelle was on my heels. "Do you think we'll die?" she asked.

I paused. There was no time for this. "We will all die if we give up now. Get your stuff together. We need to get out of here." I was throwing all of my gear together. Luckily, we didn't have tents to take down.

Zack's things were all gone. I realized he must have packed them away in his spatial ring as soon as he woke up.

Gathering back at the front of the cave with the rest, I looked to Zack. "We are ready, let's go."

Gone was the casual Zack. His face was set in a hard gaze looking out into the night.

"Too late. We've been spotted. I want the four of you to go together. Head east, back toward Locksprings." A red spear appeared in his hands and he twirled it, letting off enough fire to light up the area for a moment.

There were hundreds of monkeys in the trees. They ranged from burnt yellow to blood red. But what worried me most were the two looming shapes just at the edge of the light.

They both stepped forward on their knuckles. These were the little one's parents. Full-grown, flame-back gorillas. They were hulking monstrosities of raw muscle. Each stood ten feet tall, hunched over on all fours. They were covered in dark red fur except for their chests and face, which were a dark sooty black.

Both gorillas' fur was patchy, like they'd just gotten out of a tussle. Still, even with them injured, I wasn't sure about Zack's chances.

"As soon as this starts. You all run," Zack said, falling into a combat stance.

We all started positioning ourselves to fight with him, but Zack cut us off, shaking his head. "This isn't your fight—you all need to escape. There won't be any heroics here."

I knew he was right, but it didn't make leaving him to the big fight any easier.

The flame-backs reared up to twice their initial height and bellowed in challenge while slamming their chest.

The world was suddenly bright as two huge bonfires lit up, giving the flame-backs their namesake.

Zack moved quickly, and there was a boom as he collided with the first mana beast.

I could feel the shock wave in my gut, but now wasn't the time.

We took off.

Jonny stumbled, and I grabbed his collar, bursting into a sprint.

The fight had started, and I could feel the ground shake from it behind me. Some of the smaller monkeys started falling out of the trees and giving chase to us as we ran.

A fireball flew over my shoulder and stuck to a tree like napalm.

"They will set this entire forest on fire," Michelle panted.

I didn't have time to respond as another monkey fell on top of me.

Letting go of Jonny, I drew my sword and cut through it in one stoke. These were rank zero beasts, and weaker than the goblins, but what they lacked in power they made up for in numbers.

Killing one must have been a trigger, because the night lit up as sticky fireballs flew in every direction.

"Michelle, shield us."

She grunted, but she threw up her blue shield and held it above us like an umbrella.

"Steve, take out any that get too close," I said, pouring more power into my legs.

A fireball slipped under Michelle's shield and landed on her leg. She stumbled to a knee, hissing in pain.

We didn't have room to slow down; I grabbed her and hoisted her in a princess carry. "Keep the shield up." I could feel that ragged edge of my life mana, and I let it pour into my legs.

"Isaac, remember that river we passed on the way here? I don't think a fire beast would cross it," Jonny said between breaths.

I nodded. He was right. It was wide enough that the monkeys couldn't use the trees to cross.

"It's not much further," Steve said, firing off another arrow.

Sure enough, the trees thinned, and the forest opened up to a wide river. The current churned the water into a white foam.

"Maybe we should head upriver and see if there is a calmer spot to cross?" Jonny stopped at the edge of the roaring river.

Steve didn't hesitate, grabbing Jonny and swiftly jumping along the rocks.

Despite the situation, I laughed. Damn, Steve had really been holding back his speed. And now poor Jonny was along for the ride. But now it was our turn. I hoisted Michelle up and held her tight as I followed.

"Issac, I can't..."

I was about to ask what, but her shield flickered out as she slumped in my arms.

As the shield faded, a fireball slammed into my back, and I slipped into the river.

The world spun as I tried to right myself and hold on to Michelle, keeping us both from drowning.

I burst to the surface, and Michelle was sputtering in my arms. At least the water had woken her.

The current pulled me under again, and I held my breath as the surface was peppered with fire.

We tumbled through the rapids. My bag tore, and I had to shrug it off before it strangled me.

I knew the monkeys were keeping pace at the side of the river because the balls of fire continued to follow us down the river.

I wasn't sure how long we tumbled through the rough rapids before the water became less volatile, but it hadn't been short.

Letting the current take us, the patches of fire slowly faded behind us.

I fought the river and got a breath of cool air that soothed my burning lungs. Michelle was there with me, taking big gulps of air.

We were still being pulled down the river at an alarming rate, but at least we had gotten out of the rapids and cleared the monkeys.

"We need to get out of the river." Michelle's teeth chattered.

In all the adrenaline, I hadn't noticed it, but my fingers and toes were numb.

The two of us kicked together and managed to slowly make our way to the shore. When we finally reached it, we hauled ourselves out of the river.

I stumbled to my feet, my entire body aching from our flight from the cave. Michelle was still lying on the ground, and she looked like she was barely conscious.

Pulling her to her feet, the two of us stumbled our way out of the open river. My feet still had very little feeling in them.

"What's t-that?" Michelle's teeth clacked together as she pointed at something metal that caught the moonlight.

I squinted through the darkness and saw what she was talking about. A metal object not much bigger than a person was tangled into the roots of a tree.

"Don't know. It must be from the old world." It seemed so wasteful to use so much precious resources for whatever it was meant to do.

Michelle stumbled over to it and started pulling at the metal object.

"What are you doing? We don't have time to waste. We need to find a spot to rest," I whispered over to her.

"This thing. I think we covered them in history class. It should open up. People used to practically live in these." As if answering her, there was a click and the sound of metal rubbing against itself.

I winced, looking around to see if the noise had attracted anything.

"There," Michelle said proudly. I couldn't really see inside it; it was too dark.

I felt the inside, and there was a torn lining. There wasn't much room if we were both to squeeze in there.

"You rest in there. I'll keep watch."

"No way. I'm freezing. Get in here with me."

I could use the warmth as well, so I unbelted my empty sheath; the sword was unfortunately lost somewhere in the river.

I got in beside her, our bodies pressed together. She reached up and pulled the noisy hatch back down.

After it clicked, it was eerily silent in the pod. With no light and no sound, I couldn't stop focusing on the press of our bodies together.

Maybe it was adrenaline from successfully escaping or just Michelle's soft body and her natural scent, but I started to feel a reaction below my belt.

Despite my best efforts, I could feel myself starting to poke into her stomach, and there was nothing I could do to stop it. I shifted uncomfortably, trying to find a way not to press it against her.

I waited for her to freak out or make a sarcastic comment.

All of a sudden, I felt Michelle's fingers brushing against my growing erection. Slowly, her fingers traced back and forth, before forming around it. I could hear her breath picking up as her fingers started teasing the head through my pants.

My blood continued rushing south. "Michelle, what are you doing? I'm trying to make it go away. Just give me a minute."

"Shh. I'm just warming my hands." She started to pump my now fully erect cock. "But I probably need to get closer for it to work better."

Then I felt her hand slipping down the waistband of my pants until her hand was back against my erection, but this time, there was no fabric getting in the way. Her body was pressed closer too, and I could feel the peaks of her nipples against my chest, firm in her excitement.

"I don't understand. You don't even like me," I said, trying to focus and think it through while my body was humming from her touch.

She leaned in and bit my shoulder. "You're such an idiot. You don't really think that, do you?" She stroked me a bit harder.

"Um, yeah. You tried to slap me when I asked you out. I'd say that's a pretty clear message." I tried to pull away from her, but there wasn't much space to move.

"Can't we get past that? God, one wrong move and friend-zoned forever!" She paused, realizing she had just yelled while we were trying to hide.

She shifted back to a whisper. "Look, I was just scared. I'd been crushing on you forever. And then you just point blank ask me out. I wasn't ready, and I freaked out."

She'd been so quiet I had a hard time hearing. But I calmed down and listened.

"Then, I was so embarrassed that I refused to come to class for two days. By that time, you were already with Kat, and I hated all of it so much. I was mad that I was so replaceable to you that you could be with Kat so quickly, and I was mad at myself for screwing it all up and pushing you away."

She started shaking, and I wasn't sure from the cold or the emotions. I did my best to hug her close.

"Look, I didn't know. But we can't change the past, only move forward. And you are definitely impossible to replace. I'd be far more exhausted if there were more than one of you to keep up with at the academy." I gave her a soft kiss on the head, stroking her hair to help keep her calm.

At my touch, she relaxed and then I felt her shift to look up at me. "Now that Kat is gone, is there room in your heart for me?"

"Kat's not really gone. Just... away for a while. But yes, our relationship is on hold, or done, or I don't know. I guess to be seen."

Michelle froze in my arms. "Okay, she's not gone. She's not here though. And you're man enough to handle more than one girl, anyway. I already saw you with Aurora."

I paused. "You're interested in being with Aurora and me? Like a harem?" They weren't that uncommon, but I hadn't really considered it before.

"Yep. Imagine Kat and I on our knees in front of you, letting you have your way with us. And I'm not against Aurora joining in too; she's hot. I'd be happy to have you watch as I went down on her." Michelle cupped my erection that had continued to grow.

The thought of the three of them together was appealing. And my body agreed with me. I was surprised that Michelle was interested in other girls, well, and me for that matter. I paused. Something Kat had said earlier made more sense.

"You've talked this over with Kat, haven't you?" I asked. Feeling her twitch was the confirmation that I needed.

Michelle fidgeted before finally whispering. "Yeah. I talked to her about it not long before she left, and I was making headway. But no, she didn't agree." Michelle slumped like she'd just lost hope.

"Huh. Well, I guess I'm glad all this happened and we got stuck in this thing together. Who knows how much longer it would have taken before we'd gotten here and started something?"

"Wait. Started something?" Michelle's voice pitched up.

"If you want to. You and Aurora have been knocking at the same door. Kat's not here, and who knows when I'll see her again. Sure, I'd love to have her back, but fuck, I can't put my whole life on hold for her," I said, a growl creeping into my voice. "She chose to leave. If she doesn't enjoy having to share me when we meet next, then that's fate."

I could feel Aurora pulsing in her seal, almost like she was cheering for my change of heart.

Michelle had leaned in, her breath softly hitting my neck. "So... how's this for a first date?" she asked, resuming her strokes.

"Perfect opportunity to get to know you better apparently."

She laughed with me, both of us caught up in the ridiculousness of this situation.

Then we heard a thud.

We both froze. Laughter stopped, and we didn't even dare to breathe.

Even as soundproof as the pod was, it couldn't stop the sound of whatever was stomping around outside. Each step resonated inside the pod.

We stayed silent, listening to each thundering step of the mana beast as it roamed the area. I was almost positive it was just outside, sniffing the pod at one point. But after waiting for what felt like an hour, the noise was gone, and we finally relaxed.

The moment from earlier was thoroughly snuffed out, and I was ready to crash from the tension.

Michelle rested her head on me and whispered, "I will rock your world *when* we get back."

I nodded at the sentiment that it wasn't an *if* but a *when* we got back.

A few moments later, she was snoring softly into my chest.

The whole dynamic of our relationship had just flipped on its head. It had all started from when she hid her feelings with aggression. Her and Kat had even talked about making this a larger relationship. I wondered why Kat had never told me about it as I drifted off to sleep.

***

The screech of metal startled me awake.

Michelle had a guilty expression as she continued to open the pod. "I really need to get out of here. I woke up with a cramp, and I need to walk it out."

I had to agree. We had closed ourselves in a tight space soaking wet and it had become stuffy in here. Hopefully, whatever had been thumping in the night was long gone by now.

Outside, the sun was up, and the forest was no longer quite as doom and gloom as it had been the night before. I crawled out of the pod and got a good look at the forest.

It was dense with greenery unlike the large trees we had been in yesterday. It felt like we were in a different part, but I also knew that terrain could change so suddenly there was practically a line.

"Look at those." Michelle pointed to a depression in the dirt that I didn't understand at first.

There were four of them in an arc, all arranged in front of an impression large enough for me to lie in.

"Holy... that's a footprint," I said, taking in the complete picture.

"Lizard footprint," Michelle corrected. "And one with two different limbs. See that one?" She pointed to another print. "Three toes on the front claws, five on the back."

Five? I looked again and noticed another depression opposite of the four I saw first.

"So, there was a giant lizard here." I looked back at the metal pod with a bit of thankfulness. The poor beaten up object from the old world had likely saved our lives last night.

"More like a dragon. It was far beyond rank one," Michelle said, walking to the river.

It might be the strongest mana beast Lockspring had seen if it really was a true dragon. But it wasn't worth worrying about something I couldn't even harm. We'd just have to do our best to avoid it.

My stomach growled loud enough to catch Michelle's attention. "Don't suppose you also know where our packs are?"

"I think we should wash up a bit and pray that some of our pack floated to the riverbank." She walked towards the water, stripping off her shirt as she walked.

I was suddenly very aware of her as a woman after our conversation.

I couldn't tear my eyes away as she continued to peel each piece of clothing off. She looked over her shoulder, making sure she had my attention. Then she turned to completely face me as she took off her bra and stepped backward into the water. Her chest bounced free from its confines, as she waded back into the river.

"Nope, don't think I see our pack," she said as she scrubbed at her clothes in the river, looking around as if she didn't just strip tease me.

"Pretty sure we lost them in the rapids," I said, stripping to join her.

But before I could, she waded out like a goddess, dripping wet in just her panties. "We need to make it quick so we can find the others." She gave me a peck on the cheek, as casually as if we'd been lovers for years. I caught a hint of blush on her face, the only sign that the gesture had made her nervous.

I was still a bit confused. Steve must have seen signs I'd missed, but I still swore she hadn't ever shown more than competitiveness towards me.

After last night and her confession, I saw it all in a different light. Slapping was still an odd reaction for being surprised, but I understood now that she'd challenged me because it was her main way of staying close to me after I'd started things with Kat.

It wasn't like she'd done anything unforgivable. There was the duel, but honestly, given the dangers of the last day, that felt like a drop in the ocean. I was also man enough to own up that the duel going as far as it had was partly my fault as well.

I hurried to rinse off in the river before we set off along it, trying to find our friends.

Not sure where we were, I thought it would be best to head back up the river and see if we couldn't pick up Steve and Jonny's trail at the rapids.

"So have you and Aurora... you know." Michelle made a lewd gesture.

I rolled my eyes. "No. I was still emotionally cock blocking myself. I didn't want to start anything till I wrapped my head around the deal with Kat. And..." I paused, not ready to share the part about her being my mana beast. "She hasn't been in a lot of relationships before. I want to make sure I am what she wants."

"Not even some light stuff? Come on. She's super hot."

I wanted to get off this topic. "Tell me something about you? What's your family like?"

She let out a whoosh of air. "Well, uh. My dad owns several small stores in town. He has two rings and is right on the edge of his third. My moms usually help around the shops with him."

"Moms, as in plural?" I couldn't hide my surprise.

"My dad likes collecting pretty things. Makes for a great merchant, but a not so attentive father, or even sometimes husband. But it's not like my moms were upset about it. We were our own little community. It was really supportive."

I didn't realize she came from a harem family. While not uncommon, they weren't the norm. But a two-ring mage probably could support a harem.

People accepted comfort and family where they could find it.

I went to ask another question, but she cut me off. "What about your family? I mean, everyone knows your dad is the guard captain."

"Well, my dad is as hard as his metal element. He really doesn't have much of a soft side," I said, putting an arm around Michelle as we walked.

"Your mom?"

"Gone in the big raid thirteen years ago." I stuttered a bit, leaving out that she might be out there somewhere. I was ready to take that one up with dad as soon as he returned.

"I'm so sorry. I... that must be hard." Michelle gave me a warm hug.

I shrugged, having long ago dealt with the loss. Although, Aurora's surprise that my mother wasn't buried in our backyard did open up a few fresh wounds. "It has been a long time, and it isn't like I'm unique in that. So many people have lost family to the world."

My stomach growled again. "Think we could find some food?"

She let out a light laugh. "Sure. We can get some beast meat. You've had some before?"

I nodded, remembering the time my father gave me some and didn't tell me. My body had rejected the influx of mana that came from eating mana beast meat. It burned in my stomach for hours before I could even fall asleep and let the rest pass.

Non-mages were not supposed to eat mana beast meat because their bodies couldn't handle the influx of mana. But, per usual, my father pushed me hard. But it sounded like Michelle had gone through it as well.

"Let's see if we can't find something to roast up," I said. We couldn't depend on our packs showing up, so mana beast it was.

Chapter 11

The biggest problem for getting meat was our lack of weapons. Michelle's had also been lost during the tumble wash through the river.

I decided to see if I could kill a rank zero beast if I found one alone.

Like answering my prayers, a growl came from the other side of the tree.

A hungry wolf prowled around the side of the tree to sniff us like we were a delicacy.

"Is there even enough meat to eat if we kill it?" Michelle asked, eyeing the scrawny mana beast.

"It's something. Though, I can't imagine it being tasty."

I squared off against the wolf, fists up. I focused inward and found that ragged edge of life mana. It came easier this time.

The world slowed as I watched the wolf.

Flashing to its side with a step, I dropped a fist into its side.

My punch slammed hard, rewarding me with the sound of cracking bones. The wolf was tossed several feet to the side.

But it would take more than one punch to bring it down.

"Wow, you really kicked the crap out of it," Michelle said, picking up a rock the size of her head.

The hungry wolf wobbled as it stood up, unwilling to give up its meal. It launched itself, mouth first at me.

I side-stepped it with ease and sent it flying over to my honey blonde partner.

It snarled at me, struggling to get up, but Michelle was there with a rock, and brained the hungry wolf.

"Tasty. Can't wait to cook that," I said looking at the mushed head.

"Honestly, that was easier than I was expecting," Michelle said, dragging the wolf by a limp leg. "You did that thing again, that bit you did with the goblins. But you don't look too bad."

I paused a moment, not sure if I should tell her. Ultimately, I decided that, if we were starting something, I wanted it founded on truths. "Yeah, Aurora calls it an aspect of life mana."

Michelle tilted her head as she broke a branch. "There are rare variants like lightning for air mana, but I've never heard of life mana used in offensive moves. They don't teach that in the academy. How does she know it? Don't tell me Aurora is really some old, wise monster or something."

I bent down to pick up some dry wood we could use for a fire, trying to figure out what to say. "No, well, she's pretty wise. She knows more about cultivation than Professor Locke."

"So Aurora isn't from Locksprings. I knew I'd have recognized that face if she had spent any time in town," Michelle said, not skipping a beat in adding to the pile of the soon to be cooking fire.

I cleared my throat. "I really don't know that much, Michelle. Yes, I suspect some things. But I haven't pried."

We continued to stack wood till we had enough to cook the hungry wolf.

"You trust her?" Michelle asked suddenly.

"With my life. She'd never do anything to harm me."

Michelle heard it in my voice and raised a brow. "Sounds like there's something there. Fine, let her keep her mysteries."

I joined her and helped spark the fire, bringing it to life with small curls of bark.

"So, what's the aspect of life?" Michelle asked.

"It's like a concentrated part of life mana. It's the wild, savage aspect of life, like a wolf hunting for its meal to stave off starvation."

My explanation brought a look at the hungry wolf from Michelle. "Sounds like pure survival instinct."

Survival aspect. I liked that.

"Probably. I think ice is an aspect of water." A few other possibilities went through my thoughts, but a look at Michelle said that more than that had come to her mind.

Michelle was lost in thought as we built the fire up and stacked cuts from the wolf around the fire to cook.

It didn't take us long. We cooked out some smaller cuts of the hungry wolf first. The meat was quite possibly the toughest I had ever had.

Hungry wolf was more like trying to eat soot flavored gum that had gone hard long ago. But it still was nourishment my stomach was happy for, and I felt the mana in the meat replenishing my reserves.

The larger pieces finished cooking as we ate.

"Remind me to bring a bag of spices next time we head out," Michelle said, chewing the tough meat, and making a face showing her disdain.

"Deal," I said. I was full enough to get moving. We needed to get going if we were to catch up with Steve and Jonny. With any luck, we'd also find Zack before long.

"Let's pack up some of this. Not sure how long we'll need it. Hopefully, never." I found a few leaves large enough to pack the cooked meat, smoking the leaves gently before using them to wrap the meat.

We set out at a slow pace, watching the river in hopes we'd be able to find our packs. If nothing else, some of our heavier gear should have settled in the bottom of the river.

A few miles up the river, I noticed a shine in the water.

"Hold up." I moved to the edge and looked in. I could see the straps of a pack waving in the stream, along with a metallic gleam.

Among them were my sword and her mace. We both beamed at each other. Our chances of survival were looking up.

"Yes! I got it," Michelle said, diving quickly into the water to retrieve them.

I did my duty and kept watch at the riverside, making sure nothing snuck up on her.

I got the added benefit of watching her resurface with her wet clothes sticking to her supple curves. She had a broad grin on as she held up my sword.

It would make everything so much easier. I hooked the full scabbard back into my belt.

"I don't suppose any of the food survived?" I eyed the soggy pack she had managed to find.

She tossed me the pack while she belted on her mace. Her buckler wasn't so lucky. It had probably floated down the river much further since it was made of wood.

The pack was unfortunately mostly empty, but a few things had survived. We had a canteen and an old lighter. The lighter would need to dry out, but it might still work.

"It's something," I said, feeling much better with my sword back on my hip.

Tossing everything back in the bag, I strapped it to my back. Michelle was in step with me as we continued down the river. I was surprised to find myself happy for her company. Things between us had changed drastically on this brief adventure, and I had a feeling that it would only keep changing.

I was glad that Aurora had given me the go-ahead feeling when Michelle had been opening up. It saved me from stressing out that she'd disapprove when I had the next chance to talk to her.

We spent most of the morning walking back up to the rapids. I could see burnt out trees on the other bank, so we must be close to where we had entered the water. It looked like the fire got out of hand from the monkeys, or possibly the fight between Zack and the flame-back gorillas.

Luckily, I didn't see much more than a few charred spots on this side of the river, and I had hopes that Steve and Jonny escaped the mana beasts to safety.

Maybe Michelle and I drew them away.

"We should leave a message," Michelle said, looking around for signs of our friends' trail.

"What do you mean?" I asked, watching Michelle look up and down the beach.

"Like make an arrow out of stones pointing the direction we are going. Zack might find it."

"Or someone with fewer scruples." There were not only corrupt mages that would kill you to cultivate but those who lived off banditry and would kill you for your possessions.

But we would have a better chance to reform the party. As I thought about Steve having to look out for himself and Jonny, the decision was pretty easy.

"Fine. Let's make an arrow pointing into the woods here." I gathered stones. I was growing more worried about my friends.

Michelle must have sensed my worry. "They will be okay. If nothing else, Steve is fast enough to run from most things."

I put my worry to the back of my mind and set back at the task of finding them.

It turned out we didn't have to go far. About a hundred yards from the bank, we caught a trail.

Looking at the boot prints, I was sure I had found a mage's trail, likely Steve's. The way it crashed through the brush looked like he was still being chased through.

"Come on. This way." I hurried after the trail with Michelle on my heels.

Crashing through the woods, the forest grew quiet as we disturbed the world with our passing.

Rounding a tree, we found the first body.

The arrow in its face gave me hope that Steve was still alive.

The bronze wolf was a rank one variant of the hungry wolf. If a hungry wolf was able to find a strong source of metal mana, it could form its beast core with the metal attributes.

Like humans, mana beasts also cultivated; though more often than not, their form of cultivation was raw consumption of mana to continue their growth. Beasts weren't afraid of consuming mana, and they only grew more savage with each cultivation. Their hunger for mana continuously increasing.

I cut out its beast core for Steve later. The corpse was too old for me to absorb mana from its death, and I didn't have time to cut it up, so I left the rest for scavengers.

Hurrying through the woods, we found two more bronze wolves, but this time they were alive.

Together, we dispatched them without trouble and continued following the clear trail. Clearly, they had been in a run for their lives, because it was not hard to follow them.

When we finally caught up to Steve and Jonny, we found them stranded up in a tree with four bronze wolves circling below. I was so relieved to see that they were okay. Motioning to Michelle, she nodded and we started approaching.

I was already drawing my sword before the wolves noticed. I attacked, hoping to catch them unawares.

But one managed to turn and meet my sword head on, literally catching my blade on the crown of his head.

My hands stung when the sword bounced off and my momentum was interrupted.

The wolf was dazed, but it bought time for the others to refocus.

Michelle clubbed one in the face before it got to me, but their bodies showed that they cultivated metal mana.

Their skin felt like it was reinforced with bronze.

"Isaac, remember the idiom about wolves?" Michelle said standing next to me.

I paused, unsure where she was going but annoyed at the interruption. But she continued on.

"Head like iron, spine like steel, but..."

"... waist like tofu," I finished for her, breaking into a grin. It was worth a shot.

Two of the wolves came at us, one each. But I ignored the one going after me.

Instead, we did a practiced move, one that required absolute faith in your partner.

We both side-stepped our own wolf and struck at the side of the other. If your partner didn't follow through with their attack, then it left your back wide open. This move was the ultimate form of trust.

True to the idiom, my sword sliced clean through right before the haunches.

Over my shoulder, I heard a solid snap of the other wolf. Knowing that Michelle put her full force into that, I felt a little bad for the now crippled wolf.

But the remaining two didn't give me time to be concerned. Unlike their friends, they showed some caution and circled us.

An arrow shot out of the tree and struck one. The other flinched and looked behind it.

Michelle and I didn't hesitate, launching a two-pronged attack in the wolf's moment of distraction. It didn't have a chance between our two attacks.

I could see a bit of competitiveness shine in Michelle's eyes, like she was about to argue over who actually killed it, but then her eyes snapped open and she threw her blue shield up behind me.

The last wolf bounced off the shield, limping with an arrow in its haunches.

Michelle's shield faded as soon as it absorbed the wolf's pounce.

I was on it, severing its spine before it could recover.

"Phew." I stepped back and looked around for any more surprises.

Michelle walked up to the one who's spine I had just severed and smashed its skull in for good measure.

"What? I learned my lesson from last time. Make sure they are dead. Mercy is not a kindness to yourself."

Steve and Jonny climbed down unsteadily from the tree, and I wrapped both idiots in a fierce hug. They both leaned heavily on me barely holding themselves up.

I saw Michelle standing awkwardly to the side, and I pulled her into the team hug.

I looked at Steve. "Why didn't you just take these guys out with arrows?"

Jonny was the one to answer. "While these guys were bad, they kept all the other lower-level ones away. So we waited, figuring we'd stand a better chance after I was able to recover my mana."

I nodded. Giving him a large pat on the back.

Michelle turned towards the downed wolves. "Let's cultivate these guys."

I didn't disagree, but someone needed to keep watch. I looked at Jonny and Steve.

"You guys go ahead. We were up all night. Our mana is too unstable to cultivate right now," Jonny said, slumping against the tree with a yawn.

I gave Steve an appraisal and saw that he wasn't much better.

Steve just nodded, pointing to his eyes then around them.

Michelle dragged me down to sit by the fresh wolf corpses. "Take their gift and cultivate with me."

Red ran up her cheeks in a hurry. I remembered that cultivation is what some of the guys back in Locksprings had started to say instead of sex.

I shot her a flirty wink before closing my eyes and focusing.

The mana was dense with the four rank one corpses.

I breathed in all of the mana that was rapidly decaying from them. It was like I was giving a target to the thin threads of mana leaking from their fresh bodies, leading into myself.

My body suddenly pulsed with the chaotic mana that was flooding my system.

Then, another target opened up near me and helped share the burden.

I focused on my inner world, bringing the chaotic mana on a shared trip with my existing mana as I cycled it through my body. Each pass carried more and more of the new foreign mana.

It churned and swelled, like it was trying to break out of me. It seemed almost unwilling to be tamed and used for my cultivation.

I could feel my body starting to heat up. I felt like a kettle about to blow, but instead of steam, it would be my insides.

Pushing down, I reigned in the foreign mana and tapered the stream, letting myself acclimate to it.

Every time the cycle passed by my first seal, I could feel some of it leave me, nourishing Aurora as well.

With time, the foreign mana started to feel like my own. It assimilated into the familiar energy that came from Aurora.

My breathing eased, and I opened the flow of chaotic mana once again, allowing the hostile mana to rush into my body.

This cycle continued until the flow trickled off and there was no more.

I opened my eyes to see the sun had only shifted maybe an hour in the sky. My clothes were drenched with sweat, but I felt great.

Fantastic even. I pulled my collar down and saw the start of a second seal growing from my first into what I knew would eventually be a second interlocking ring. When it completed, I could seal my second mana beast.

Michelle was next to me having a similar revelation, only her creamy breasts were on full display with her actions.

Looking up, she caught me looking and gave me a look like a cat who got the cream.

She would cause some trouble when we got back. I just knew it.

I half-expected a comment from Jonny, but he was so out of it even with his eyes open, he somehow missed our exchange. Not that I blamed him. A dead person looked better.

"You two will not be able to make it far. Think you can take a brief rest here before we head out?"

Jonny didn't even acknowledge me and just fell over counting sheep almost instantly.

Steve took a moment to get his bedroll under his head before nodding off himself.

Michelle and I stepped a dozen yards away to keep watch and not disturb them.

"Awe, they are so cute together," Michelle teased.

"I'm just glad they survived."

And I was. My understanding of the world of mages had drastically changed on this trip. It was a lifestyle of confronting death and surviving at every turn. There was no mercy in the wild.

At every turn, I would have to crush death to move forward. There was just no other option, no matter what form death took.

Michelle lay her head on my shoulder, and we watched after our friends as they slept.

"I think we head back from here. Locksprings should be back that way." I pointed east. "We should let Locke and Rigel know about what happened. They can get out here and search for Zack far faster than we could."

She nodded into my shoulder, and I got a whiff of her. She smelled like sweat and the iron tang of blood. But there was a sweet lavender and honey of her natural body scent.

I breathed in deep, feeling connected to her. We'd come out the other side of this hell together and that counted for something. If it wasn't for the danger of the situation, I would be all over her.

Turning her face up, I stole her sweet lips. Letting her know that I was past Kat and open for her.

Her soft body pressed into mine, and I let my hands wander from her hips to cup her full breasts. Lifting her up, I firmly sat her on my lap, letting her know exactly how I felt about her.

She bobbed her hips against my constrained erection as her kisses grew hungry, and she pulled away and fished it out of my pants.

"Holy shit, jackpot." She blushed, seeing the size of my cock for the first time.

"You felt it last night." I grinned as she trailed a finger from the head to the base.

"But seeing is believing," she cooed and licked her lips.

A gruff voice agreed with her. "It sure is sweetheart. Damn, what a lucky find."

I hurried to stuff myself back in my pants as I turned to look at the voice.

Three men stood not far from us. Two had bows leveled, with eyes that looked like they were used to death. The third had a scar over an eye and chewed on a cigar that had been overstuffed.

All three of them wore mottled dark brown clothing meant to blend into the woods. But Scar Face decided he was too good for a shirt and just wore a leather vest, which highlighted the two-and-a-half rings on his chest.

"I didn't mean to disturb you two." He gestured with a hand. "Please, by all means, take her clothes off."

That was meant for me, but no way in hell was I going to strip Michelle for them even if he could kill me.

My silence earned me a scowl.

"Boss, there are two more," the first archer who I dubbed Tweedle Dee called out.

Tweedle Dumb snickered, "I think they were supposed to be on lookout. The other two are asleep."

"Well," he paused, staring at the two idiots. "What are you waiting for? Go bag them. Three laborers and a woman for sale. Seeing really is believing." Scar Face gave me a predatory grin that sent chills through my spine.

"Four freshly popped mages. It took you until adulthood before you popped your first ring, didn't it? God, out here really is a shit hole."

I couldn't help myself. "What do you mean out here?"

"The frog in a well really doesn't know there's more to the sky, does he?" The man chuckled, and I wanted to ask more, but I felt a sharp pain in the back of my head before the world went dark.

Chapter 12

Pain. That's all I knew as I cracked open my eyes.

The light hurt, sounds hurt, everything hurt. I rolled over and dry heaved as my body tried to reject the fact that I was still living.

The sun was drooping through the afternoon sky outside tent flaps. I tried to get a better look but was stopped by the clink of chains as I tried to get to my feet.

Feeling my ankle, I found a cold metal clasp holding me tight.

I had not hurt this much since my father had taught me my first sword lesson.

Even when I'd woken up after fighting Michelle, my mana had helped replenish me.

I paused. As I tried to circulate my mana, it felt sluggish and unresponsive, like something was blocking it.

I'd never heard of something like this. Typically, you crippled someone if you wanted to prevent their mana use.

But I could feel that it was the cuff on my ankle that was somehow suppressing my mana. Studying it further, it had a number of small runes etched on it, marking it as some sort of enchanted item.

There was a class of mage that didn't fight but crafted items instead and performed other professions. I knew one of those mages must have made this.

I realized that, if these thugs had such elaborate gadgets, they weren't simple thugs. No back-alley gang would have something like this; enchanters were incredibly rare in Locksprings.

I looked around further. Steve and Jonny were laying in the tent with me, and as my eyes adjusted, I could see similar cuffs on their ankles tethered to the center pole. Michelle was nowhere in sight, which concerned me.

Who the hell were these guys? The guy that had knocked me out was a mid-tier two-ring mage judging by his rings. I would have thought he would be known in Locksprings with that level of cultivation.

Yet here he was, a kidnapper, or maybe slaver. Whatever he was, I wanted nothing to do with it.

Now I just needed to figure out a way to escape.

If I ran and the second-ring mage was able to chase after me, there was no way I would escape him.

I sighed and laid back down on the ground, wishing my headache away and trying to think.

It was quiet outside the tent, but I couldn't discount that there might be a lookout.

First things first, I needed to break out of these shackles.

One good thing about being the son of the guard captain was learning more than was healthy about jailing someone and, more importantly, how people could break out.

I examined the shackles, and indeed, they were similar enough to the ones my father had shown me.

I cast about the tent until I found a stick that felt hard enough to do the trick. I bent it a bit, or at least tried to. I was lucky these trees had been exposed to enough mana to be strong enough for this.

Stepping on the body of the lock, I angled the stick through the shank, using the other side as a counterpoint for leverage.

Locks often weren't strong in every direction. I applied pressure to force one end of the shank out the side of the lock.

The stick strained against the lock, but eventually, the end of the shank popped, and the face of the lock came loose enough for me to wiggle the lock free.

Instantly, Aurora's mana slammed into me like an overeager welcome home. I had to lay back down and concentrate on restoring the flow of mana through my meridians.

As my mana returned to its normal flow in my body, I could feel the itch of my minor scrapes healing and a soothing, blissful touch spread through my poor skull as my headache washed away.

Blinking and feeling a hundred times better, I re-evaluated my current predicament.

I had been quiet enough, but I held still listening for anyone outside the tent. Peeking out, I didn't see anyone, but I did take a moment to swipe a metal stake that kept one of the corners pinned down.

I moved over and shook Steve and Jonny awake.

Jonny groaned, "Not now, mom."

"Jonny, you need to wake up. We are in trouble."

He startled awake and opened his eyes, only to groan loud and grind the palms of his hands into his head.

"Quiet. Channel your inner world, Steve," I said, looking over at Steve, who was using his hand to filter the light and slowly increase how much reached his eyes.

While the two of them acclimated, I started with Steve's shackle, breaking it like I did mine.

Working with Jonny's, however, the lock must have been of poor quality, because instead of the small controlled break, the lock shattered, and his shackle and chain clanked and clattered with the sudden release.

We all held our breath, waiting for someone to shout an alarm or the thud of feet. But we heard nothing in the quiet camp.

Jonny, now released, was tending to himself and Steve. We were all going to need to be at our best to pull this off.

Watching Jonny heal Steve, I realized I needed to learn a spell to heal others; it could come in handy sometime to be able to heal other people.

Jonny and Steve were still adjusting, starting to stretch and get ready for a potential run.

"You guys ready?" I prodded them.

"Yeah. Where's Michelle?" Jonny asked.

I just shook my head. "I woke up here a few minutes before you guys. I don't know anything more, but we won't leave her behind."

"Of course." Jonny got to his feet and dusted himself off. He looked around the tent for a weapon, but our captors hadn't been so kind. All we had was the metal stake.

I walked over to the tent flap and stood, listening. When I didn't register anything nearby, I pulled back the tent flap and confirmed there wasn't any activity. The sun had maybe two hours of light left. If we were going to escape, we needed to do it now and hope that they wouldn't pursue us in the dark.

I slipped out with my friends on my heel.

The sturdy parade tents had debris built up along the sides, and the fire pit was overflowing with coals.

These guys had been here a while. What they did here, I had no idea. Nor did I want to stick around to find out.

Now that I was out of the tent, I could hear a soft male voice coming from the other side of the tents, but I couldn't make out what it was saying.

Right now, I wanted to find Michelle and get out. I crept around the campsite. The tents were large, but I hoped that it was a tent per mage and they just enjoyed the luxury.

Rounding the tent, I saw the owner of the voice standing in front of a caged Michelle.

My heart constricted. Michelle was hunched, shoulders so compressed they nearly grazed her ears. Her eyes were illuminated, but only by the deadened light of someone who'd long given up. I'd never seen her like this.

"—just promise and I'll let you go. You can even join the Earth Flame Sect with me." The man, maybe a year younger than me, seemed to be trying to convince Michelle to join his sect, one that I'd never heard of before.

I waited and watched the camp. The guy was distracted with Michelle and there didn't seem to be anyone else in camp. I wasn't sure where they all were, but this seemed like our best shot.

With his age, this guy wouldn't have his ring yet. The others must be out hunting mana beasts and left him home for his safety.

I turned back to my two friends, speaking quietly, "One guy, too young to be a mage. Let's be quick. Don't kill him, just knock him out, tie him up. Sound good?"

Getting nods from both of them, we darted around the tent together.

Our motion caught Michelle's attention as her head snapped to me.

The guy turned too.

It was the first time I had gotten a good look at the young man. He had on bright red robes with gold threaded into a burning mountain. They kind of reminded me of the Sun and Moon Hall disciples, but the color was all wrong.

The boy turned to us as realization dawned on his face, quickly turning into determination. "Not on my watch."

Before I could realize what was going on, my knee snapped and reversed itself courtesy of the kid's fist.

I was almost too stunned to feel the pain, but it crept up a moment later as I staggered to the side on one leg.

Luckily, I had Steve and Jonny here to distract him while my healing kicked in.

The reality of what had happened came a moment later when the red-robed disciple jumped back, and his robe opened a bit, showing his almost two rings.

This guy was a mage and at his second ring.

Together, we might be able to take him, but every minute we were here was another that the scarred, second-ring mage could come back and join in as well. I decided to try for negotiation.

"There's no need to fight. We'll just release our friend and be on our way."

"I'd hate to waste perfectly good slaves, but I can't say I'd hate to kill the man my future mistress has been so worried about. So, what's it gonna be? Slavery or death?" The kid fanned his robes and a pulse of scalding hot mana came from him.

The boy's body was nothing to be impressed about, except for his rings.

No, not rings. I looked closer. He had one fully formed red ring and a second that was almost complete. It was just missing the last bit. While I was looking, what he had said clicked.

Looking at Michelle, I raised a brow. "Mistress?"

She sagged and shook her head.

"I'll consider your decision made. Say goodbye to him, darling." The boy wound up a punch.

I decided I'd stalled enough. I wasn't about to let this twirp hit me again. I touched the savage edge of life mana and met his punch with everything I had.

Our fists met in a small rush of wind that shook our clothing. My knee ached from the exchange, but my self-healing kicked in to help.

Steve was behind him then, sending a punch for his head that he barely managed to block.

"Oh, you can't face me one-on-one like a man?" the brat shouted. He looked flustered, as if this was the first time he'd ever actually fought.

I hoped there wasn't anyone else nearby. He wasn't exactly being quiet. I ignored his baiting. We needed to finish this and move on, quickly.

My next fist came with the same power, and this time, he was forced to take it to his side in order to keep blocking Steve.

I expected his ribs to crack, but instead, it felt like I punched a brick. He was knocked to the side and stood up, wiping his mouth.

"I'll get you back for that. Do you even understand who I am? I am the scion of the Rhys family." His statement ended in a sneer, like it was supposed to mean something and I should be afraid. All I cared about was that he was distracted. When he finally turned, he did it right into Steve's knuckle sandwich.

The hit comically caved in the side of his face for a moment before blasting him off to the side.

Ouch. The rest of us drew in a sharp breath in sympathy.

"Guys! Get me out of here." Michelle had found her fire once again.

I spotted some nearby keys and snagged them. I tried the keys until one worked and gave her a hand out of the cage. "Do you know where our weapons are?" Rather than answer me, she took off into one of the tents.

The Rhys kid stumbled back, blood leaking from the corner of his lips. "You are all dead. To do this to me is to ask for worse than death. If you beg for my forgiveness, I might reconsider and make it quick."

"What?" Jonny said blinking. "So let me get this straight. We've almost killed you, yet we should be scared? And let you kill us?"

The brat smirked before shouting, "Flaming Lion Palm!" As he struck out with the heel of his hand, a phantom of a flaming lion surged out.

"Get back," I shouted, feeling the intense pressure from the spell. It felt far stronger than the spells I'd seen in Locksprings.

We all jumped back before the attack landed amid the campsite.

The image of a burning lion exploded on impact and several of the tents were blown away, along with their contents. As it all landed, I heard the welcome metallic clang of weapons.

"Michelle, find a weapon." I stared at the boy, who I needed to recognize wasn't really a boy. He was a mage and further along than the rest of us.

"Good. This would be boring if you died so quickly. I came out to experience the world." There was a giddy gleam in his eye, like this was all a game.

"I don't get it. One minute it's worth ending quickly and now it's worth continuing? You may want to get your brain checked."

The kid waved it off. "I enjoy inflicting a bit of pain. A servant's son once cut me during practice. You should have seen the fear his family all had, offering their son up to be executed. Dad let me kill him, and after I got my first taste of blood, I craved it every practice. I was untouchable."

Since he was in a talkative mood and clearly an idiot, I thought I'd see what else we could find out to up our chances. "Where is everybody else?"

"They're off catching me, my mana beast for my second ring. That stupid hick flame mage interrupted our hunt last night." He pointed off to a figure tangled in one of the tents that had been blown away by the technique.

Zack. He looked like he was in bad condition, but I could see the rise of his chest. There was relief as I realized we hadn't lost him.

My anger kicked up a notch. This spoiled brat came in here and trampled on our group for no reason other than that he wanted to have an adventure.

"Anyways." The boy flexed. "I'm bored. Let's end this." He tensed up like he was preparing for a big move. I could feel the mana of the world gather around him, but it was slow.

I wasn't about to just sit here and let him attack me. What an idiot.

Michelle tossed me my sword. "Sorry, kid. Don't know your family," I said with a finality as I cut his head clean off. The boy clearly had no real combat experience.

Might be due to killing his trainers when they injured him.

"Damn, you killed a kid," Jonny said.

I pulled what looked like a spatial ring off his body. There was no doubt in my mind that doing anything less than killing him would have ended in disaster. Based on the mana he had been drawing, that last one likely would have killed us. Kill or be killed.

Michelle snorted, tossing each of us our gear. "No, that was a monster in a kid's body. You should have heard the things he was 'promising' me when we got back."

"He say anything about this Rhys family?" I asked her as I searched another tent.

"They seemed like a big deal. He said they were in the Earth Flame Sect. Kid had one two-ring guard and a handful of one-rings, so he must be somebody. But that's a puzzle for another time. We need to go. I'm not sure when they will be back." Michelle looked anxiously over her shoulder.

Holding the tent aside, I recognized Zack. "Jonny over here."

Together, we freed him and patched him up, but he still wasn't waking.

"We need to go," Michelle hissed.

I looked at the surrounding tents. There could be more victims in them, but we couldn't do them any good if we were caught. I threw a prayer out for the rest of my classmates and refocused on our best course of action.

"Let's hurry back and warn the academy." I decided that the best thing we could do was get back and have the academy or the city send someone like Rigel or my father that could overpower a two-ring mage. I just hoped that they weren't killing any of the other groups.

Carrying Zack, I put the sun to my back, and we hurried east, hoping that Locksprings wasn't too far away.

We only got a few hours of travel in before it grew too dark to see.

I called for camp, and we were too tired for anything fancy. Luckily, Steve and Jonny had some trail bars left.

"Think they will find us?" Jonny asked, looking out into the night.

Steve shrugged. "Doesn't matter. Are you going to do anything different knowing that?"

Jonny looked to me to save him.

"Doesn't matter. We move forward all the same." There was no benefit to worrying about if they would catch us, just like there was no point in worrying about that kid's family. We were in survival mode; there was no looking back.

"Get some rest, Jonny. Michelle and I will take first watch."

"Some good that did us earlier," he grumbled back.

I shot him a glare, but I did feel a bit guilty.

The two of them settled into their sleeping bags while Michelle and I took up a post for watch. It felt a bit like deja vu.

"Sorry, no sex this time. You know, kidnapping and all." Michelle cringed a bit but shook her head like she was trying to shake it all away. "But, when we get back, you are mine."

I had no issue holding off. The last thing I needed was to get ambushed again.

"By the way, did that guy say anything else to you?"

She snorted. "That guy just walks up and declares me his concubine. Telling me everything is going to be okay. The guys there with him did whatever he said, though. He talked like his dad was some bigshot in this Earth Flame Sect. And I guess his dad must be powerful since he was calling the shots. But yeah, his group had been hunting those flame-back gorillas."

She paused thoughtfully for a moment. "Actually, by the way they said it, they may have been hunting the gorillas before we met up with them."

"That would make sense. The mana beasts shouldn't have been in that area from everything Zack said, but it starts to fit if they were fleeing with their young one."

"Poor gorillas, just trying to save their baby."

I gave her a flat stare. "Yes, and if we met them under normal circumstances, they would still try and eat us to absorb any mana in us."

She rolled her eyes. "Point. But still, I'm feeling oddly sympathetic to being hunted right about now."

"The only thing the world recognizes is power. Without that, it doesn't matter if you are a mage or a mana beast, you'll be hunted."

Michelle looked at me like she was seeing something new. "True, but don't lose yourself in the power, Isaac."

Looking over at Zack for a distraction, I hoped he would come to soon. We could really use his help.

The rest of the night went by without trouble before we changed watch. When Steve woke me peacefully, I sighed in relief.

Zack was still out cold. Jonny said he had tried to help him, but he would need to have the clinic look at him when we got back.

Heading off again, this time towards the sun, I had high hopes of getting back to town today. About midday, I started to see familiar landmarks.

Suddenly, a man stepped out from behind a tree.

I wasn't sure if it was Tweedle Dee or Tweedle Dumb, but one of the two archers from before stood in our way with his arms crossed.

"Damn, boss was right. You would make straight for the city." He smiled, and without wasting time, shot a burning arrow straight into the sky.

"Now please hold until boss comes." He redrew his bow, starting to sing a random tune.

Michelle growled, "We can take him."

"No." I handed Zack over to Steve. "I'll take him. You guys hurry ahead."

The archer eyed us. He knew he couldn't stop all of us. He was just buying time.

Michelle looked at me like I'd betrayed her.

I shrugged. "I have the best chance, and don't worry, I have an ace up my sleeve," I lied, hoping she wouldn't press. I wanted to see her safe.

But Michelle didn't even acknowledge what I'd said. Instead, she charged forward and swung for the goon.

He blocked with his bow, but at the last moment, she pivoted and darted around him running at full speed.

I wasn't going to let the archer get a shot on her, so I rushed him.

Steve and Jonny took off after Michelle, leaving me with the archer.

"Awe, your friends ran off and abandoned you," he sniffed as he blocked my attack. "Don't worry, I'll go get them after I'm done with you." He licked his lips like he was looking forward to eating them.

Before I could strike again, he shot off a barrage of arrows.

135

There were too many to dodge, and I felt the slice of two in my legs.

"Poor little birdy can't run no more?" he taunted, keeping his distance.

I let my life mana rush through my legs, pouring healing into the two wounds. They itched as the wounds pushed the arrows out.

But I just needed to distract him long enough for my mana to heal my legs.

"Why hunt us? Why are you guys even in these woods?"

"Boss said so." He shrugged.

"Boss said so," I repeated. "You know you can think for yourself."

"Naw, I don't want to die. I'm just a vassal to the Rhys family."

I needed to keep him talking, stalling was my best tactic to keep my friends alive.

"So, the Rhys family, who is that? The kid mentioned something about it."

The man looked at me like a hungry wolf would a piece of meat. "Hah. Yeah, I shouldn't kill you. Let the family have fun with you. You'll learn soon enough"

"Yeah yeah. So who are these Rhys people?" I asked again. I needed to keep him talking.

"My lords are one of the strongest families in the Earth Flame Sect. I can't believe this mana-less shithole doesn't even realize who their masters are."

"So educate me." I had had about enough of this bullshit. Maybe it would take the family down a notch when they found out their son had battled a one-ring and lost.

"Naw, no need to educate a dead man," a second voice sounded behind me.

I had both brothers now.

"Where are the rest?" Dee asked, stepping out of the woods and looking around.

"Not far, this one was putting on a show for me." Dum played with his bow.

"I'll—"

I smiled. They'd underestimated me, and now was my moment. My wound from the arrows was closed enough for me to move.

I was behind Dee, chopping for his neck before he knew it.

He managed to sway away from my blade and take a bloody wound to his shoulder.

"Idiot. I thought he was disabled."

"He was—took two arrows to the thighs." Dum was drawing his bow on me yet again.

This time, I knew I couldn't take the two of them on together. Dodging between trees, I used them for cover from their arrows.

"Don't just stand there, help me."

I smirked and tried to pour on speed, but the wounds on my leg split open.

I taunted them before darting into the trees again, "Hey idiots, did you know I was the one who killed the brat? Sliced his head clean off."

It didn't matter if my wounds wouldn't stay closed, I needed to push forward. I found myself once again harnessing life mana. I focused my mana to even greater heights as I took off into the woods.

I knew running through the woods would just take longer for anyone from the city to come to my aid, but I couldn't stand still with the Tweedle brothers.

A burning arrow barely missed my head and singed my shoulder, bringing me back to the task at hand.

"I got you," one of them said, jumping out from behind a tree in front of me.

Still drawing on that savage edge of life mana, I shot out a punch that cracked the air as it broke his arm. These two weren't as powerful as the Rhys kid. They were more on the level of first-ring mages back home.

The trees shuddered from the punch; we were close enough to the city that the surroundings weren't as durable.

I dodged right, heading back towards the city. If nothing else, I could hope to make my own way back. If I got close enough, maybe a city guard patrol would find me.

As I got closer, I spotted somebody. I paused, realizing it was the man with a scar, the second-ring mage.

Chapter 13

This was bad. Really bad.

I could have played with the twins for a while, but a second-ring mage was out of my league.

To make things worse, more mages showed up one after another until I was surrounded. Five first-ring mages and Scarface circled me. I was so screwed.

"Look what we have here." Scarface smirked, standing still. "You know you are dead right?"

A punch to my gut knocked the wind out of me. I hadn't even seen him move.

"You have caused me a lot of trouble. But don't worry, I'm here for interest." Scarface tossed me to the ground. "You see, I was supposed to protect the young master. Now that he is dead, I'm screwed. His family will butcher all of us. Probably even our families."

"That's sick," I wheezed.

"That's the new world. I'm not sure which of the Sun and Moon Hall's little projects you came from, but let me educate you on the world." He rolled me over with his boot.

"Might makes right, which makes the Rhys family right in this case." Scarface looked at me with pity. "And because I'm going to die when I return to the family, I'm going to make you also suffer so I can have a bit of enjoyment before my death."

"That makes no sense. This is for your sick pleasure?" I said with more strength, as I regained my ability to breath.

"No, to appease the Rhys family's anger, I'm going to torture you." He shrugged. "That way, they just cut my head off and are done with it. I really don't want to be burned alive for seven days." Fear flickered through his eyes at the mention of it.

"You could just run."

He laughed in my face at my suggestion. "No, I don't think I can. They would have known the moment that the young master died. Since I was sent with him, they likely have already put a bounty on my head. The more I run, the worse my death will be, and the more of my family that will die alongside me."

Looking at me with pity, he cut into my armpit. Pain blossomed.

My left arm flopped uselessly to my side, my tendon cut. But I refused to cry out and let him enjoy my pain.

I quickly realized I was still circulating my mana, and it started to itch as my tendon tried to reattach itself.

He watched as my wound rapidly healed before him, a bit of wariness entering his eyes as he shook his head. "That's just going to make this harder on yourself."

I just glared. At the same time, I could feel Aurora pushing on her seal wanting to come out.

I wanted to let her out, but I decided it was too dangerous. She certainly had some tricks up her sleeve, but she was made of my mana. That meant she couldn't fight a second-ring mage much better than I could.

If I let her out and she were killed, my ring would shatter, and I would regret it more than being cut to pieces here.

Scarface flicked his dagger back and forth. "If I were to keep cutting you, would you eventually stop healing just for it to all end? That sounds like an interesting experiment."

Aurora thumped hard from the inside of her ring.

I was pretty sure I could hold out, but Aurora seemed to disagree as that thought seemed to send her into a frenzy. I could barely hold her back from escaping her seal.

I didn't even know she could push this hard.

But it was too risky. I knew I'd take some heat from her later, but there was still another option.

My mana thrummed in my ears as I purposefully sped it up. Faster and faster it went while I continued dragging on the savage aspect of life mana. My bloodline stirred deep inside of me.

I threw a fist full of dirt in Scarfaces' eyes and kicked off the ground with the full force of my mana and bloodline working together. One of the twins was in my way and was met with a sword to the gut.

His eyes went wide as realization sunk into him at the fatal wound.

I didn't have time to recover my sword. I poured more mana into my legs, running as fast as I could.

It was different this time than when we had fought the goblins. I was more in control of the surge of strength. My bloodline felt more in control.

"After him! They will kill our families if we don't get revenge for the young master," Scarface called after me while trying to get the dirt out of his eyes.

I could hear shouts and people crashing through the woods behind me.

The spike of fear just made me push myself harder. The wounds in my legs reopened with vigor, painting my pants with fresh blood.

A woman suddenly appeared ahead of me swinging a large glaive into my path.

I threw my knees forward and dipped into a slide, like an extreme game of limbo.

The blade passed right over my nose, cleaving off a few stray hairs as I collided with her legs.

We both came down in a tumble, and I rolled myself on top, slamming a fist into her face with a satisfying crunch. It wouldn't kill her, but hopefully it would slow her down.

Her hands came up to block another attack, but I was focused on her glaive.

I spun off the ground with the bladed spear just in time to catch another attacker's sword.

He jumped back from the clash of weapons, taking a stance and slashing out with a beam of burning mana rolling at me from his sword.

Jumping clear of the spell, it soared past and left a burning scar on the trees behind me. I needed to finish this before the others caught up; I didn't have time to spend on this fight.

I swung wide to get him out of my way before letting go and sending the glaive spinning after him.

With some space between us, I didn't hesitate. I burst once again into an all-out sprint through the woods.

My mana surged through me as blood pumped in my ears. I could feel the strain my bloodline was putting on my body, but if it was anything like before, the moment I stopped, it would all come crashing down on me.

And right now, I didn't have the luxury of being exhausted. Carving more and more mana through my channels, I pushed my legs through physical limits I didn't even know existed.

Trees flew past until the sky opened up into a clearing.

I could sense another mage closing in on me. I turned, blocking his hit and shifting him into the oncoming path of another mage.

The mage's eyes went wide with surprise before a bloody hand punched out through his chest, and he coughed up a mouthful of blood.

Scarface was looking at me over the dead man's shoulder, burning hatred in his eyes. I had to admit, the glare paired with the scar really did quite the effect.

I hurried forward as Scarface pulled his hand out of the dead man.

"You can't run from me."

With my aspect and bloodline running at full steam, I swung, meeting his fist.

Scarface grinned, thinking I was done for.

But my arm held strong, and I managed to match his punch, ultimately only losing a bit of ground as I backpedaled.

Surprise flickered across Scarface's face before shifting back into a neutral look. "Doesn't matter. You won't be able to keep that up for long."

He came at me again. This time, I only managed to block and use the force to put some distance between us.

Turning again, I ran. He was right; I couldn't keep it up and needed to escape. I already felt my body beginning to break down from the use of my bloodline.

Meeting Scarface's fist had only made it far worse. I couldn't keep fighting him.

Once again, he was suddenly in front of me. He saw my surprise and laughed. "You haven't seen a movement spell before? Now I'm a bit curious what the Sun and Moon Hall is doing out here."

I dodged to the side and tried to run, but he was before me in a flash.

"You're done," Scarface said simply as he blocked my path.

I heard two more people crashing through the trees behind me. There was only one option now, and I just hoped it would work.

Remembering the attack that Aurora had used before we had left, I channeled my mana as I made a claw with my hand before thrusting it out at Scarface.

The world grew dim as a massive phantom hung in the air, too indistinct to make out just what it was, but its claw descended on Scarface and was large enough to envelop the other two mages.

I thought Scarface would run, but he seemed frozen in place by the spell. Finally, he recovered and blasted out with a fire spell of his own.

It did nothing to stop the massive claw from descending.

The world exploded as the ground cracked and tilted.

The pressure alone caused my veins to erupt and I started bleeding out of a dozen fresh wounds.

Scarface wasn't in any better condition with two huge cuts across his chest and one arm completely severed at the shoulder.

I didn't have time to gloat, because the ground started falling out beneath both of us.

Grass and dirt continued to disappear around a growing hole.

I tried to lunge free, but I was too tired to get far. The ground slipped out from underneath me, and I fell into the void with Scarface.

***

Again with the painful wake up. I really needed to stop getting knocked out. This was a bad habit to start.

I tried to sit up, but my body refused to comply. Everything hurt, and when I tried to circulate my mana to restore myself, it sputtered, and my mana refused to flow.

Focusing on my inner world, I saw that Aurora's seal was intact, but its connection to my meridians was shattered. In fact, all of my meridians were like shattered glass. I was cut off from Aurora's life mana, and with it, my ability to self-heal. Sighing, I looked around.

I was in some sort of cave, and a faint light was emanating from down the cave. It was enough to barely see by, allowing me a glance at what had broken my fall.

Shifting and rolling onto my shoulder, I saw the lumpy mattress I was laying on. There was a vague memory of shifting him during the fall to cushion me, and it was a good thing.

Scarface had seen better days, much much better days.

Reaching out with shaky hands, I tried to find a pulse, but his stiff clammy body told me what I needed to know.

I let out a shaky breath as I realized I'd killed again. It was… easier. But a part of me only became more worried at how easy it felt, how calm I was looking at his corpse.

For him to be cold meant I must have been out for a while.

I managed to drag myself off to his side.

Wondering if I could still summon Aurora, I pushed mana into her ring, and she appeared before me.

"Master." She looked like she was about to cry. She went to hug me then stopped, looking worried.

"Hurts, but I'm alive. Don't think I'm going to die." I fell into a fit of coughing. "Bring me to sit up on the wall?"

Aurora gingerly pushed and pulled me to an upright position on the wall. "You sure you're okay?"

I pushed my palm into the ground fighting the pain, just trying to get into a more comfortable position. "Yeah, but I need to take a break for a bit. Are you okay?"

She nodded, still hyper focused on all my wounds. I needed to distract her while I caught my breath.

"How about you check him for goodies? Maybe he has something to help," I said with a chuckle that only brought pain.

She looked back at the dead Scarface and the other one, not even sure if it was a man. She dug around both like she wasn't sure what to look for.

"Check the hands—they probably have spatial rings," I offered. It turned out I was right; she brought back two spatial rings.

I checked my pocket, and I was surprised to find that I'd managed to hang onto the young brat's as well. The other two rings were far plainer than this one.

There was a hope and a prayer that there would be something for healing in the spatial rings.

I dripped my blood on them, hoping that even if my mana wasn't flowing, that there would be enough mana for the binding.

They both flickered softly in the darkness as their contents appeared to me.

Aurora waited by my side patiently as I dug through their contents.

I looked in the brat's ring and cursed. What was a kid that rich doing trying to pick a fight for no reason? With the wealth in his ring, his family must give him everything he wanted.

He probably could fill a mansion with servants and concubines with what was in this ring alone. Stupid brat got himself and his men killed for nothing. I doubted all the mages could be so arrogant, or they would be a dying breed.

The inside of the ring was the size of a small home. It was mostly luxury items, like a full four poster bed, and gobs of clothes that were far too small for me.

I noticed there was a whole section of well-prepared dishes of food. The sight made my stomach growl in a reminder that it had been a while since I last ate.

Putting the rest aside, I pulled out a dish of rice with seasoned meat and peppers into my lap, feeling like pure luxury. I searched a moment more and found a pair of chopsticks.

I was eager to dig in, but after everything that happened, it all just seemed ridiculous. I clasped my hands and shot a wordless thank you up to whatever might be looking out for me.

My first attempt at trying to pick up the food failed because my hands shook too much.

"Wait." Aurora stopped me and held out her hands for the chopsticks. She fumbled with the unfamiliar tools before holding up a hunk of glistening rice and meat.

I took my first bite and thought I was going to drool all over the floor. It was certainly mana beast meat, as I felt the heaviness sit in my stomach and disperse through my broken channels, but it was far less chaotic than what I'd experienced before. I sniffed at it again and realized there were medicinal herbs in the dish as well. I smiled, wincing as even that muscle movement brought pain.

"Good?" Aurora asked.

I couldn't help but just stare at the dish for a moment. This guy was really rich. It was beyond what I'd seen in Locksprings. This was practically like eating medicine for every meal.

"This is so expensive. This whole dish is filled with herbs for cultivation and healing. Did that kid eat like this for every meal?"

Aurora sniffed the plate, her delicate nose wiggling. "Lots of herbs. I think even some crushed medicinal pills." She looked excited at the prospect of this helping me and sat at my side feeding me carefully.

The food helped more than just my hunger. I could feel the pain easing in my weary body as well. It wasn't healing me like my life mana would, but the medicinal effect dispersing through my body was soothing my aches and pains. It would heal me, but it would be over hours or days, not minutes.

Aurora pulled the now empty plate off my lap and set it aside before leaning softly against me.

"I wonder what other good stuff there is in these rings?"

Looking at the ring again, it had piles of equipment and cultivation resources that would be enough for me to push through to my second ring.

But what was even better was the small unassuming pile of thin books. Each detailed a spell on how to use mana outside of general strengthening. They were what made guilds strong and created legacies out of a strong mage.

Jackpot!

Then I found the true jackpot for helping me survive long enough to enjoy the spells—the sealed jars of medicinal pills. They might be able to help me recover even faster.

Pulling out the jars, I unfortunately didn't know what any of them did.

"I can help." Aurora picked up one of them and sniffed the contents. "This one is for drawing more mana to you." She put it down and picked up another.

"This one... I think it makes you... uh horny."

We both looked at each other. There was a bit of a gleam in Aurora's eyes as she bit her lips.

"Sorry, Aurora, I'm not in any condition right now."

"Right now," she repeated the only part she seemed to have heard. "But later?"

I sighed, realizing what I'd just done. But after the conversation with Michelle, I needed to have another one with Aurora. "Heal, then we can talk. But yes, Aurora. The short answer is yes."

Her eyes went wide, and she hurried to inspect the other two jars. "This one." She fished out a green pill that had complex swirls in it and held it up to my mouth.

I trusted her and let the pill slide between my lips, swallowing it whole.

It went to work immediately. I felt like I was in the healer's ward all of a sudden as life mana radiated out from my core.

Unfortunately, I didn't have functioning meridians to direct the healing, so instead, it just slowly worked on me from inside out.

"Much better," I said, sighing. It was already becoming easier to breathe. "It'll take some time, but I think I'll be able to walk here soon."

Aurora nodded excitedly, happy to have been some help.

I needed to assess the damage to my body and cultivation.

Diving back into my inner world, my body was a mess: eight broken ribs, both legs had hairline fractures, and my left shoulder was out of its socket.

My meridians were worse, like a glass plate that had been abandoned in the middle of a market. Completely and utterly unrecognizable shards.

"You hear anything, Aurora?" I asked, knowing she probably had better senses than I did.

She froze for a moment listening. "Nothing moving. There's water nearby though."

I looked up at the yawning abyss above me, not able to see a pin prick of light even. "I'm guessing that no one is going to try and jump down here. It didn't work out so well for either of these two."

Aurora giggled. "No, it did not, Master. I think you only survived because your bloodline was active. It makes your body quite sturdy."

I tucked away that fact, noting that I'd also landed on Scarface.

Squinting harder up, I discounted any attack from the remaining mages. If they had been able to come down and finish

147

hunting me, they already would have. So I put it out of my mind; I needed to focus on what was down here.

Looking around more, there wasn't much. The small light down the tunnel was really the only thing of note besides dull gray rocks.

The medicine was taking effect; I wondered if I'd be able to try and move. I wanted to explore.

"Help me up?" I asked.

Aurora braced her feet against mine and helped me to my feet before ducking her shoulder under my arm. She was small enough that I had to hunch over to put my weight on her.

"You sure you're okay, Master?"

"Sore, but I'm good with your help. Don't think I'll make much progress otherwise."

She beamed up at me. Aurora was so easy to please. She really just wanted to be a part of my life. She was happy to be out and exploring the world with me. I just hoped that it was of her own choice.

It was slow and painful going as I pulled myself along the craggy wall with Aurora on the other side. We made our way down the tunnel towards the light, leaning heavily on the wall. Even with some medicine to dull the pain, my legs were still barely keeping me up. I kept most of my weight on Aurora.

The tunnel quickly opened up to a larger chamber with a curved plant hanging over a clear space with a small pool. It was an idyllic resting spot amidst this cave.

Aurora gasped, "This is a dungeon."

I shook my head, knowing exactly what this was. "It's an abandoned dungeon; one that inverted on the world and its inhabitants left. It's only so well preserved because it's underground."

I looked around warily. Abandoned gave it a false sense of security. There were usually still monsters; a furnished cave made a great home for many mana beasts. But, from what I could see, it wasn't in a portal, and the original inhabitants would likely be long gone. Most importantly, I hoped the boss was gone.

Aurora sat me down next to the water with a satisfied smile. This place would be perfect to recuperate from the fall.

"Let me, Master." Aurora carefully helped me out of my clothes and used my tattered shirt like a rag.

She dipped the shirt in the water, marring the otherwise clean pool with a wisp of my blood. It slowly curled through the surface.

I lay on the side of the pool as Aurora carefully cleaned me.

She seemed content. I watched her serene, angelic face as she cared for my body, and once again, I felt putting-rocks-up-my-nose stupid for not pursuing something with her.

I put my hand on her thigh wordlessly and traced patterns on her soft skin. I didn't miss her jolt of surprise before she went back to cleaning me more diligently.

When she got below the belt, I rapidly came to the ready.

"Master." Aurora looked at me, biting her lip. "Do you have any bed in those rings?"

I remembered the large four poster bed. I smiled and answered her by summoning the large luxurious bed.

"You know, I'm feeling better, Aurora." I got to my feet with a small grunt of pain before sitting on the bed and patting it for her to join me.

"Clearly not fully better. Maybe it's best you don't exert yourself too much." She grinned as she got on her knees before me. Her warm breath was thrilling on my thighs.

I ran my hands through her hair and pulled her up to claim a kiss.

She reciprocated eagerly, deepening the kiss with heavy breaths.

When we finally broke the kiss, she looked unsure.

Knowing this was where I put a stop to it last time, I kissed her again briefly. "I'm done being stupid. I care for you deeply, Aurora, and I'd be a fool not to see your love. I don't need to overthink it, and it's between us, no one else." I caressed her face.

"I do love you, Master," she said, getting back on her knees. "Now relax and let me do the work. You're in no shape to exert yourself." Her hot breath made my cock twitch.

I felt a hand brush my balls as she leaned in to kiss the base. Slowly, she made her way up to the head.

She stopped just shy of the more sensitive skin and returned to the base for a long lick from base to tip.

149

I twitched and looped my fingers in her hair gently tugging her forward.

Aurora tisked back at me. "You made me wait so long, Master. I thought you'd want to take your time. What is it you want?" Aurora asked with a bit of mischievousness.

Her big eyes looked up at me, sweet with an edge of fierceness. I instinctively knew what she wanted, to be claimed.

"Suck it, Aurora. Now," I demanded.

She shuddered slightly and latched onto my root, working only half of it into her mouth.

I leaned back with a sigh of bliss as her mouth worked my sensitive head, her tongue doing laps on the ridge.

She looked up at me with caution.

"That's great, Aurora." I held her head to the current rhythm even if I wanted to explore the back of her throat.

Aurora became more eager, sliding my length deeper into her mouth, touching the back of her throat as her hand continued to play with my balls.

I tugged on her hair, urging her to take me deeper.

She looked up at me askance of what to do next.

"Swallow the head. I'm almost there."

She did it like a woman with a mission, and I felt her throat contract tightly on my head and pulse as she continued to try and swallow it.

I bucked and unloaded, painting the back of her throat.

She suckled on my member, milking the last of my seed out of my balls with firm fingers.

I enjoyed the sensation until she popped off with a wet smack of her lips.

"Thank you, Master." She licked at her lips.

Pulling her up to the bed, I kissed her tenderly as I let my hands wander her body until they cupped her tight butt and pulled her onto my lap.

She answered with gentle kisses winding up my chest.

I wasn't feeling patient though and pulled her up to my face, taking a moment to enjoy her beauty.

Aurora was stunning. Her eyes continued to draw me in as I traced her cheekbones and caressed her face, slowly thumbing her pouty lips, slightly swollen from sucking on me.

I cupped her face in my hands.

She rubbed her cheek into my hand and eagerly started kissing my thumb, trying to draw it into her mouth.

I let her have it, and she moaned happily as she slathered it in her saliva. I lost my focus, and she smiled before offering her lips.

I savored her soft, sweet lips. Our tongues intertwined as we lost ourselves in each other.

I had just enough presence of mind to continue to explore her body. Cupping her breasts, I realized they were more than a handful, and I needed both hands to cup and encourage them.

She moaned when I rolled her nipple, and I could taste her heady breath. Her hips bucked, and I could feel her wet heat grind on my thighs.

Grabbing her by the hips, I pulled her slit closer to my member, now fully recovered.

"Master, you are still injured. Let me."

She lifted her hips and guided me into her silken slit. She readied my cock, playing with her entrance to make sure it was ready. She never once let the passion die in her gaze.

I could feel her sticky nectar as she teased me into her.

"Stop playing," I growled.

She savored me a brief moment more before she took me into her silken heat.

Gasping, I was engulfed in bliss. It wasn't my first time, but it was beyond anything I'd felt before. Her sex gripped me like a glove made just for me.

I could feel myself bottom out as our thighs met. She was perfectly wrapped around me in a way that felt complete.

Breaking the kiss finally, I stared deep into her eyes and I realized I had a sense of completion. I knew this was right. She started grinding and any other thought took a backseat to the pleasure I was experiencing. I reveled in the joy of feeling myself move inside of her. Her long, languid strokes filled me with desire.

I explored her body, rolled her nipples, nibbled her collar, but she just slowly enjoyed me. I thrust up into her and was rewarded with a startled gasp as her wings snapped open, and her body convulsed around me.

She collapsed on me, and I slowly ground into her, extending her pleasure.

When she was spent, I slid out and switched positions, being careful with her wings.

Her eyes were still hazy, and she leaned into my touch as I admired the beauty below me. Her hair was splayed out along with her wings, and the generous swell of her breasts swayed with her heavy breathing.

Aurora was a divine beauty. She bit her lip and spread her legs, wanting more. She lifted her feet up around my back, encouraging me forward.

I lifted her hips and slid back in. We both sighed; it was like the world had returned to its rightful state.

She moaned and cupped her breasts as I started slowly.

"Faster, Master."

The name sent a tingle through me, and I obliged my little angel as I started thrusting with abandon.

Aurora twisted the bed sheets and arched her back, moaning loud enough for the world to hear. Her eyes locked with mine, and I saw nothing but pure adoration for me.

It was that moment of such intense love and trust that sent us both over the edge together.

I shuddered as I erupted deep inside of her, and her channel milked me for all I was worth. Torrents of pleasure rushed through me as mana shot from my ring. It cycled and rushed into Aurora only to spout back to my ring, creating a loop that only grew stronger with each pass.

It must have been doing the same to her, because her pitch continued to hike along with the rush of pleasure.

I was at the point where I thought I might burst when it finally cut off, and I slumped on top of her.

"That was…" I didn't even have words to define what had just happened. My mind was slowly collecting itself after… that.

"Master," she said, pulling my face back to focus on her. And it suddenly made sense. She was… my mana beast, we were connected in a way no one else would ever be.

"I love you, Aurora," I said softly.

She bit her lip and recovered, straddling me again. "I love you too, Master."

Chapter 14

I woke up much later. Despite my body's exhaustion, we'd managed to go for quite a while before we'd spent ourselves thoroughly.

Aurora lay next to me sleeping peacefully with a satisfied smile. The little sexpot had started to go wild after the first round.

Sitting up, I felt far better than I had yesterday. The medicinal pill had done its job well.

My stomach grumbled at all the energy I had used with Aurora. Pulling out another prepared dish, I sat in bed and obliged my growling stomach.

I'd need energy to figure out a way to leave this cave system. With my crippled ability to use mana, being stranded in this cave system was going to be tricky.

Any cave provides shelter and would attract mana beasts. We were lucky none had come upon us already.

I had to be careful with my current state. Even with the medicinal pill, I wouldn't be able to recover my meridians so easily. Bodily damage was easy to heal, but damage to cultivation was far harder to repair.

Letting my eyes wander the cave, I found myself frowning.

The water of the small pool was once again crystal clear, even after all the blood that Aurora had rinsed off in it.

Getting out of the bed, I heard Aurora stir. I tried to be quiet, but I wanted to see how the pool filtered out the blood.

Pricking my finger, I dripped a few drops in the pool before putting some pressure on it to stop the bleeding.

The blood became a small red cloud, swirling in the water. I watched how it moved, and little by little, it was drawn to the side of the pond where the plant was.

The plant seemed innocuous enough. Just a dark, big leaf shrub.

But I watched as the cloud of blood turned into a stream and was absorbed by the roots of the plant.

"What are you doing, Master?" Aurora asked.

"The pool—it's clear again. I wanted to see why. That plant seems to be absorbing my blood."

Aurora's eyes went wide as she looked at the plant. She hopped off the bed and lifted the leaves to reveal a small cluster of berries. "Master! This is a Thousand Year Bloodholly," Aurora squealed with joy.

I remembered the herb from class. "Bloodholly is just an ingredient for healing pills, isn't it? By itself, it helps with blood recovery. You can tell it from its poisonous cousin by..." Flipping over a leaf, I saw the telltale red leaf veins that meant it wasn't a poisoned herb.

"Yes, but this is a Thousand Year Bloodholly." She bounced excitedly. "Its energy might be enough to nurture your bloodline."

I pulled off a handful of the little blood red berries. "So I just—"

Aurora clamped onto my arm. "You can't do that! There's so much medicinal energy in those you'll explode if you eat them all at once."

Sheepishly, I tore off a leaf and put them down. "You're right. I just got excited."

"We should test with just one." She sat down beside me.

I plucked up one of the plump berries and popped it in my mouth. It was bitter and sticky, with an iron tang. Everything in me said to spit it out, but I forced myself to swallow.

As soon as it reached my gut, it exploded with medicinal energy, sending waves through my body.

The beast in my body that made up my bloodline woke up when it sensed the energy from the bloodholly. It flowed through my body, devouring the energy from the berry. Each time it flowed through a part of my body, it left behind a feeling of strength.

Feeding the bloodline was doing more than strengthening it. My entire body was being improved rapidly.

My bloodline grew sluggish, and I realized the bloodholly had been consumed. Quickly, I tossed another few into my mouth and swallowed without bothering to chew.

Once again, the cycle started. My bloodline swam through my veins, strengthening my body as it consumed the energy from the bloodholly.

I continued to focus on my bloodline while I ate berries. The pile seemed to never end, and I expected that was Aurora's doing. But I kept going. I wanted to continue to focus on my bloodline.

Watching it grow till it swelled in my veins, I wondered if it would eventually get too big.

Soon after that thought, my bloodline shifted and raced towards my heart. It wedged itself in my heart and began drilling into the walls of my heart.

I was knocked from my inner world and came out coughing up blood.

"Isaac!" Aurora was at my side in an instant. "What's wrong?"

I felt disoriented. It was intense being jarred out of my inner world by my own body, and I couldn't answer her beyond a shake of my head. "Give me a minute." I focused back on what was happening inside my body.

My bloodline was destroying my heart while at the same time shrinking, like it was using up itself in the process.

I continued to watch as pieces of the bloodline beast merged with my heart, slowly but steadily replacing my human heart with one of itself. Making a heart of my bloodline beast.

As the change continued, I felt myself come back from what felt like the brink of death. And I was slowly gaining strength until I started surpassing my previous self.

I was completely bewildered as my heart beat like a fierce drum and chased out my blood, replacing it with something stronger.

My body grew several inches in that moment as my muscles swelled and my organs gained new vitality.

I threw my head back and let out a primal roar that echoed through the cave as my blood pounded through me.

The sound died down as I came back to who I was.

Aurora was beside me; her eyes were dilated with lust as her nose twitched. "Your bloodline, it's stronger." She looked like she was about to jump me right then and there.

But as I looked down at myself, I was covered in blood. I had been bleeding out of every pore of my body.

"Let me rinse off before we do anything else, Aurora." I stood so fast my feet left the ground for a moment.

"Woah. I'm a lot stronger." I could feel the strength in me as I stepped into the pool to rinse off.

The bloodholly greedily drained the blood from the pool, and after the help it had just given me, I cut my finger and dripped a few drops of blood on it as thanks.

"Master." Aurora joined me in the pool and started helping me wash off all of the blood.

She took the finger I had just pricked and sucked on it.

I could feel her tongue lap at the opening before she stopped.

"Master, your body is so much stronger. You feel like a rank one mana beast." She pinched my skin to test it. "You could probably fight on par with one, even without your mana."

I certainly felt stronger. I also felt bigger. My six-foot frame had grown three inches and filled out with the growth of my bloodline.

But I didn't have anything to test my new strength out on. A part of me was even more excited to make it out of this cave, but I was sure there would be something for me to fight in here.

Looking through the rings again, I pulled out a longsword and a pair of leather pants. Unfortunately, everything else in the rings was either marked with the symbol of the sect or far too small for my enlarged frame.

"You sure you want to fight, Master? You have enough food. We could take a nice vacation down here." She patted the bed.

I raised an eyebrow, taking in my beauty, but I had to shake my head and watch hers sink a bit. While I was sorely tempted to spend days in bed with her, I needed to get back home. My friends and family were there, and clearly, there was more going on in the world than I knew.

"Later, Aurora, we have the rest of our lives together."

She pouted at me using those words back at her. Giving me a parting kiss on the cheek, she disappeared into my ring. I did some final packing before setting out for something to test myself on in this cave.

It didn't take long for me to find my first challenge in the abandoned dungeon. Not far from the light of the safe zone, goblins crouched, partially hidden by the stones of the cave.

I wouldn't have known they were there before, but apparently, my vision in the dark had improved significantly. It was likely another benefit of the strange transformation my body had undergone.

But there would be time to understand what happened later. For now, I needed to take on these goblins. And I had to admit, I was a bit excited.

The feral creatures had fantastic instincts. As soon as I showed aggression towards them, they abandoned their hiding spots.

I came in with a low swing for the first goblin, remembering the first fight with them.

It leapt back, taking a shallow score on its chest. It didn't commit to the same move that the previous goblins had tried.

Instead, the rest tried to circle me while corralling me with probing swings of their wicked looking claws.

But I had other ideas. Charging for the same goblin, I moved fast enough to take it by surprise and cut a sizable chunk out of its torso.

The others took the moment to attack my exposed back, but I was ready for that. I turned my swing into a wide arc that carried behind me.

There wasn't as much power in a swing that wide, but the feral goblins shrunk back out of fear of the blade.

Using the gap to my advantage, I backed out of the hole I had created in the goblins to put the wall to my back. Able to focus more on offense, I quickly cleaved through each of the goblins in turn.

Rank zero beasts weren't too much trouble for me. At this point, my body was something like a weak rank one mana beast. It would take more than a few goblins to drag me down.

I wiped the blood off the blade before continuing down the cave.

I decided to leave the goblin corpses. Even if I was able to circulate mana in my body now, it wasn't a safe place to cultivate. Instead, I needed to keep moving forward and try to find a way out of the cave system. If goblins were down here, there was likely an exit somewhere nearby.

I made my way after killing yet another pack of goblins. Turning the corner of one of the tunnels, the cave opened up to a much larger room.

A skittering noise stopped as I entered, catching my attention. I looked around, noticing a carapace gleaming behind a pile of rocks. Not wanting to let it jump on me, I picked up a rock the size of my head and hurled it at the creature.

The rock slammed into it, but it wasn't hard enough to do much more than get its attention. As it crawled out of its hiding spot, eyeing me up and down, I finally got a better look at it. It was a black scorpion twice my size.

It clacked its claws at me in annoyance but didn't come in to attack me.

I tried to keep my eyes on it while looking around the room, seeing if it had a friend lurking nearby or if it was just being cautious.

Leaning back on instinct, a barbed tail barely missed me as my question was answered.

I swung my sword in a weak upwards stroke that clanged off the segmented tail's exoskeleton.

Done pretending to be scared, the first scorpion stepped in to join the ambusher with a strike of its own.

I kicked off the ground, giving myself some room to fight. I knew that I would need more leverage in my swing to cut through their armor or manage to hit a chink in the plating.

They regrouped after their failed ambush, fanning out in front of me. Clicking their claws in an angry chatter, they seemed to make up their mind and press in on me, side by side.

I put my back into the next swing as one of their leading claws swiped towards me. I'd hoped that the blade would be able to penetrate, but their exoskeleton held. I had to dance out of the way of the follow-up stinger.

Given how they'd fought up until now, they were going to try to hit with their stinger next. Switching tactics, I put bets on their fighting remaining predictable.

Baiting another attack, I switched my grip and stabbed for the junction between plates on the stinger's head.

My sword bit deep into the gap, but the tail shot back with an angry squeal from the scorpion, pulling my sword with it.

I pulled another weapon out of the spatial ring. It was probably for the better; a spear would be more fitting for this fight. I stabbed at one of the eye spots on the other mana beast, but it jerked, causing my spear to just scrape against its carapace.

The follow-up stinger scraped against my forearms; I grabbed hold and pulled. I was hoping that I could out muscle the stupid mana beast.

But I was quite wrong. The scorpion flattened its body to the floor and whipped its tail back with strength and leverage far greater than mine.

I was thrown back behind the first scorpion, still clinging to its tail as the second tried to take advantage with its own stinger.

Grabbing the sword that was still stuck in its tail, I yanked and sent the barbed tip spinning to the cave floor.

It shrieked and went mad, trying to catch me in its pincers. The other scorpion stabbed again.

I managed to dodge the stinger, taking a claw to the shoulder in a harsh wound.

The scorpion's sting instead penetrated its friend's exoskeleton, causing it to thrash even more wildly as it refocused on freeing itself.

Summoning a large axe from the spatial ring, I put my full weight into a swing that cleaved several legs off the already injured scorpion.

The other was still trying to dislodge its tail when I applied the same force, cutting off several of its legs.

Finally, they were both heavily injured and frantically trying to recover.

I stepped back and held out the axe, ready for the next attack. But between their wounds and their panic, they both began to slow until their legs curled involuntarily inwards at their death.

Not keen to take any chances with their stingers still available, I took a few swings of the axe until I was sure they were dead. And, at that point, I was also about halfway to carving out their beast cores.

Sticky with their innards, the cores gleamed in the darkness. I couldn't do much more with the corpses without access to my mana, but I worried leaving them behind would just attract more trouble.

In the end, I couldn't do anything about it and left them.

Too tired to dare push myself further through the cave, I turned back to rest at a space I'd already cleared out.

The lightly glowing crystal and the big four poster bed was a sight for sore eyes. I decided it was likely getting late enough for me to have dinner and rest.

Aurora shot out of her ring as I settled down with a stew I had pulled from my spatial ring.

The stew smelled rich with medicinal properties. I could really get used to living like this. While I ate the soup, Aurora started going around me with a cloth, wiping all of the scorpion goop off me.

"I can wash after I finish," I offered, trying to get her to sit with me.

Aurora shook her head "Please, Master. Things like this make me happy." She rinsed off the rag and returned to wiping me.

"You sure?" I didn't mind being doted on, but it seemed one-sided. I made a note to myself to find a way to spoil Aurora in the future. She just smiled, ignoring my question and continuing her work. Sighing, I enjoyed the moment of peace.

***

I woke up to something soft tickling my nose.

Achoo!

Grabbing the offending tail, I heard a yelp and opened my eyes to see a small black fox.

"What are you doing, little guy?" I asked the fox, letting go of the tail. I noticed I had only been holding one of three tails.

It pulled its tail in close and gave me an angry glare. Then it started to sniff and groom its tail while still glowering like I had tainted it.

"Don't be like that." I dug through the spatial ring for a piece of meat as a peace offering.

The fox happily growled as it dove on the meat and tore it to bits. It gave me a chance to look at the little guy a bit closer. The first thing I noticed was that it was a girl, not a guy. She was only about as long as my forearm and was jet black with a single white foot and some white at the end of her tail. Finally, there was a pink spot on her forehead that looked like a blooming lotus.

"She's cute." Aurora scooped up the fox, who became submissive in Aurora's arms and snuggled in.

"It's still a mana beast even if it's cute," I reminded her.

Aurora stopped petting the fox and gave me a terrified look that shifted quickly to hurt.

"That's not what I meant, I... Shit. Look, I don't think I even consider you a mana beast anymore. You are different—you are Aurora." I spoke, realizing it as the truth as I said it.

"What if she can become like me?" Aurora said, comforting the fox who had tried to escape during the moment of tension.

I looked at the fox again. I'd never heard of a mana beast like it, but if Aurora said it could become like her, then I had to believe it.

"So she can transform into a human?"

"Not yet, silly. Mei here is only a third-rank mana beast," Aurora said, holding the fox up. "Do you like the name Mei?"

The fox yipped in response, wagging its three tails.

"Third-rank mana beast." My eyes were wide looking at the unassuming little fox. I swallowed, knowing that this little fox could have killed us both in our sleep without issue.

"Mei won't hurt, Master." Aurora narrowed her eyes at the fox, making the statement a command before turning back to me. The fox seemed to give a small nod.

"See? She'll behave herself." Aurora went back to petting the fox while swaying back and forth a bit.

I was dumbfounded as the little fox continued to watch me. "She can understand us?"

"Of course! Third-rank mana beasts are just as smart as humans." Aurora took the fox back to her chest and cuddled it.

I couldn't help but wonder what rank of beast Aurora was for a third-rank beast to let itself be coddled by her. If she was stronger than that fox, that meant that, all those years ago if she had wanted to harm Locksprings, she could have destroyed the whole town without a challenge.

Pushing those thoughts from my head, I left Aurora to play with the fox. I wanted to check on the goblin corpses to see if they attracted any unwanted attention.

I stepped out of the safety of the crystal light to find the goblin corpses picked clean. I sighed. It was exactly what I had been worried about; the bodies had attracted at least one mana beast.

Whatever it was, it had to be huge to eat a dozen goblins.

I looked over the remains to see if I could get a better understanding of what had enjoyed the snack.

But when I examined the remains, I saw that there were bite marks on the bones. Tiny little bite marks almost as small as...

Aurora had wandered over with Mei hanging in my peripheral.

Looking over at Mei, she stared back with a face full of innocence. Maybe she'd just gnawed on the bones afterwards?

"Did you eat the goblins?"

Mei tilted her head and made her large ears flop in a cute way.

"Oh, now you don't understand me?"

Her ears went back, and she sat down in guilt.

"Don't bully my little sister. What does it matter if she ate so much?" Aurora harrumphed, squishing Mei into her chest.

Glad to not have another unknown to deal with, I just pet Mei on the head and kept moving. When I got to the scorpions, they were also picked clean, leaving just the exoskeleton. I stuffed them into the spatial ring. It was starting to get hot, and I felt sweat bead on the back of my neck.

At least Mei seemed friendly. If she was some vicious mana beast, she could have attacked me in my sleep. Instead, she was nestled into Aurora's chest as we walked through the dungeon. I found myself a bit jealous of the bugger. I'd also rather spend my time nuzzled into her breasts instead of trudging through this dungeon.

We continued through the abandoned dungeon over the next few days with only a few small fights. Interestingly, none of the mana beasts tried to attack Mei and Aurora. In fact, they all seemed to avoid the pair.

Hacking apart a tangle of vines, I could smell the green of the forest. Never had the smell of the forest excited me so much. After spending four days underground in a cave with stagnant air, I enjoyed taking some deep breaths.

Mei chattered and jumped out of Aurora's arms as I saw daylight. But as she ran forward, the fox rebounded like she had slammed into an invisible wall.

Aurora picked up the now wailing fox. "Shhh. What is it?"

I walked up to where Mei had hit a barrier, about a hundred yards from the exit of the cave. But I didn't feel anything.

Waving my hands in front of me, I walked all the way to the exit of the cave only to turn back and see Aurora and Mei stuck back at the barrier.

"What did Mei say?" I asked my mana beast.

Aurora frowned. "She said that a woman came..." She paused to confirm something with Mei. "Maybe a dozen years ago and put a stone there. Mei hasn't been able to leave the cave since." Aurora pointed to a spot at the opening to the cave that was covered in moss and overgrowth.

I pulled off the greenery until a five-foot carved stone appeared.

Calling it a stone didn't give it enough credit. Etched into the surface was the most complex enchantment I had ever seen. The lines were so fluid; it almost looked like it was naturally formed.

"Can you see this, Aurora?" I shouted back at her.

"Yeah." Aurora eyes were wide. "That's a very powerful enchantment. It's blocking all mages and mana beasts above the second ring from..." She trailed off and looked around like she was following a line I couldn't see. "From passing. It's a very large area. I guarantee it includes Locksprings."

I looked back at the stone, wondering why it would be here.

"While enchantments are difficult to make, they are simple to destroy. If you break this, Mei could step out of the cave," Aurora said.

I paused, wondering if letting Mei out was the wisest decision. But I pushed that aside and decided to trust Aurora.

Pulling out an axe from my spatial ring, I swung at the stone, only to have my hands sting when the stone didn't give at all. The enchantment was still smooth and unbroken.

Grunting at the unexpected outcome, I let the axe rise over my head before bringing it down with the full force of my bloodline-enhanced body.

My hands stung, and this time, I could feel the wet warmth of my blood on the handle. The rebound had been hard enough to split my palms.

The stone stood completely unblemished, and I looked at the axe head to see that it was now warped with the two strikes. "What sort of stone is this?" I frowned at my axe.

"What's wrong, Master?" Aurora called out, still holding Mei behind the barrier.

"The stupid stone is harder than enchanted steel." I smacked it with my hand for emphasis.

But that caused a reaction, as I could feel the stone suck the blood from my palm.

"What the—" I started before the world turned white with a light so bright it nearly blinded me.

When I opened my eyes, I saw the light turn into a beam and race towards the sky until it hit the clouds, blowing a hole in the clouds before exploding and wiping a whole sky full of clouds away.

"That's..." Aurora said from my side, having managed to pass the barrier. She was looking up with me. "We should probably get going." Mei made a noise that sounded like agreement.

I pulled my eyes away from the sky to look at the stone as it cracked and fell to the ground in large slabs. I snatched up the face that contained the enchantment, guessing that it had some value.

But what really drew my eyes was the sword. An opalescent white sword had been encased in the stone. I pulled it out, watching the radiating dark gold glow that indicated it was an artifact-grade weapon.

Holding up the sword, the blade seemed almost to be made of a lustrous bone. The handle was made of the same bone, yet intricately carved with an image that appeared to be a different beast depending on what angle you tilted it.

"Master, we need to go," Aurora repeated with urgency at my side.

"Sure." I tossed the sword into my spatial ring before hurrying away. After removing the sword, the beam of light calmed down, but I knew it was a poor idea to be anywhere near where that stone had been.

Taking a deep breath of fresh air, I was reinvigorated to find my way back to Lockspring.

Chapter 15

Stepping out of the trees, I couldn't help but grin at the sight of home. The patchwork stone wall surrounding the city was like a giant welcome home sign in my mind. After wandering the forests outside for the last week, I was ready for getting back home.

I frowned when I saw the large number of people coming and going from the city. There was certainly far more activity through the gates than I'd seen before.

Mei struggled in Aurora's embrace.

"Stop fussing. I know." Aurora held out the fox to me.

Mei gave me a lick on the neck before Aurora pulled her back.

"What's that for?" I asked. It had taken us four days to find our way back to Locksprings since I'd somehow broken that formation stone. In that time, I'd become used to our little foxy companion.

"She's saying goodbye. Mei can't come into the city with us. Not to mention that she has some work to do." Aurora gave the fox a knowing look and it perked up, nodding excitedly.

I pet Mei, stroking the little pink flower mark on her forehead. Aurora had been secretive about coaching Mei. "Be safe."

Mei nuzzled my hand again before hopping out of Aurora's arms and sitting like she was going to see me off.

"You need to hide too, Aurora. There's a lot of people down there." I watched the steady stream of people heading into the city. I even noticed one person riding on what looked like a sword.

Blinking to make sure I was seeing things right, the image didn't change. Someone was actually on a sword that was hovering a foot off the ground. He was wearing robes like I'd seen on Sun and Moon Hall disciples, but they were a dark blue.

"All of these are different sects," I said, realizing it as I looked through all the different colored robes.

"Yes, Master. I think Locksprings has changed drastically since we left."

I walked down to the gate, casting one last look and finding Mei waiting, just a speck on the top of the hill. I waved goodbye before I stepped up to the guard.

The guard at the gate gave me an odd once over. It probably had to do with the fact that I wasn't even wearing a shirt. Many of the people coming and going gave me an odd look when they noticed I was only wearing pants, and ones that were clearly not my size. A few of their eyes flickered to my ornate spatial ring, and I could practically see the question marks float around their heads.

"Sir." The guard started to stop me. "Oh! Isaac?"

The guard's recognition caused a few others to turn my way.

"Holy crap, it is," said another. "Someone go tell the captain."

I raised my hand to stall him for a moment. "I'm going to go stop by the academy. Can you tell him to meet me there?"

They gave me an affirmative as I walked into Locksprings.

Plodding through the streets to the academy, the town had changed. The influx of visitors had brought new merchants with colorful stalls. The visitors came and went around town with a purpose that seemed to have woken up the sleepy city. A city that hadn't experienced much change in my lifetime.

Now it was like someone had shocked the city to life with all of these visitors with insignias on their bright clothes.

I hoped the academy would have some answers.

"—qualified." An angry voice came out of the academy doors ahead of me.

"You can shove your qualifications in the trash on your way out." I heard Rigel's rough voice.

"Insolent!" A man wearing flame red robes with the Earth Flame Sect symbol I had seen on the Rhys boy stepped out of the academy doors, and almost ran me over.

He swung his arm out to knock me out of his way, not giving me a second glance.

I stumbled back. I'd only been brushed by his hands, but it had felt like a mana beast had charged me.

167

The man in the bright robes seemed startled that his motion hadn't sent me flying and gave me an appraising look. "Excuse me."

I tried to walk around him, but he blocked my path.

"Young man." The guy, who didn't look more than a few years older than me, scowled like he was studying my face.

"I need to go in there," I said, not wanting to get caught up in whatever he had upset Rigel with. I shifted my hand to keep the ring out of view, in case he might recognize it.

My voice must have carried inside because Rigel came to my rescue. "Isaac? Isaac!"

Rigel shot out and wrapped me up in a hug before holding me out in appraisal. "Did you get taller?"

Looking down at him more than usual, I realized just how much I had gotten taller. The transformation of my bloodline with the bloodholly had been greater than I'd realized.

"I guess?" I'd figure that out later when I got home.

"What's happened to the city?" I asked, but a snort behind me cut off Rigel's response.

Rigel turned to the man in bright clothes, giving him a fake smile. "I apologize. This is one of my students that has returned from a trip into the wild. We can discuss things later."

The man from the Earth Flame Sect gave me one last appraising look before narrowing his eyes and walking away.

I had a fleeting concern he'd looked at me like he'd recognized me. That maybe my face was known from the encounter with the group in the woods.

"Come on in, Isaac." Rigel said, leading me inside by the shoulder.

"What's going on?" I asked again as soon as we moved to a worn office.

"Where do I start..." Rigel shook his head. "About a week ago, we all saw a large beam cut through the horizon."

I felt my hairs stand on end... that had to have been me cutting the enchantment.

"Anyways, after that, all of the guilds started showing up saying that a heavenly treasure had announced itself." Rigel shook his head like he didn't believe it.

"They also said that with the light, a seal had dropped from the area. Lots of powerful mages have been wandering around here ever since." He gave me a look that reeked of caution. "Would you happen to have any more light to shed on the situation. Did anything odd happen out there?"

"Nothing like that. I didn't even see this light." I kept a straight face.

Rigel simply nodded, not expecting anything.

"How about the rest of my team?" I couldn't help but be worried.

"They all made it back fine. Some trouble followed them. A 'Rhys Family' has come into town to call accounts," Rigel grunted.

"Your father showed up though and has been able to keep the peace so far. Speak of the devil..." Rigel looked out the door behind me.

My father strode in wearing the guard military uniform, a boiled mana beast hide, and an exaggerated saber at his side. His signature steely face was expressionless as he walked in the room.

I could feel him inspect me with his mana. It felt like razor blades brushing against my skin.

But he moved faster than I could follow and snatched my wrist. I could feel his mana scan my entire body from head to toe. His eye twitched, the only outward expression I'd seen in a long time.

"Who did this?" he asked.

"Tom, what's the matter?" Rigel was on his feet halfway to me before he snatched up my other wrist and I felt more invasive mana probe me. It was quite unpleasant to be searched by two different manas.

Rigel sucked in a cold breath. "Who wrecked your cultivation?"

I sighed and started from the beginning when we were attacked by the flame-back gorillas and our flight, then abducted by the Rhys family, and finally, I recounted our escape. I ended with a vague recollection of the abandoned dungeon, leaving out the stone and Mei.

My father's expression didn't change, but I could tell that he could see the gaps. He had been hunting down criminals in investigations for longer than I'd been alive. "That's all?"

"Pretty much. All the important things." I shrugged, looking my father in the eye, letting him know I'd say no more.

169

Rigel scratched his bald head. "That sounds like quite the adventure. Maybe we should try and explain this to the Rhys family?"

"No," my father said. "You've seen them all running around town like it's their own personal treasure trove. They are either injuring or recruiting all our young mages left and right."

Rigel let out an angry snort at that. "Each one of those sects wants to take over the academy."

"Is that a bad thing?" I asked. The sects each had massive resources that would dwarf Locksprings.

My father answered, "They do not have our best interests at heart. Several remarkable talents have been discovered in our city, along with treasures we had not been able to recognize. The sects are treating our city like a field to pick over and take the ripe fruits."

"Like what?" I asked.

Rigel's face became solemn. "Some of our young mages have gone missing. A few homes have been broken into and robbed."

I bristled instantly. "We can't let them just walk all over us." I found myself standing.

"Calm down son, there is nothing you can do currently about it." My father held up a hand to stop me.

"But—"

"Nothing you can do, boy. All these visitors? They would squash you like a bug. You thought the Rhys family was powerful? Guess again, boy. They are the trash of the whole group that's come here."

"Isaac?" a shout came from outside. I recognized Jonny's voice.

I took the excuse to leave. My father caught my arm as I headed past him and leaned in. "Settle your friends. You pack tonight."

I nodded. If my father was going to train me, I wasn't going to resist. The change in the city had caused a sudden profound desire for strength.

"Thank you both." I gave them a respectful nod. I paused and looked at my dad. "We need to talk soon, too. It's about mom." I watched his brow furrow in question, but not wanting to deal with it right now, I hurried out to meet Jonny.

170

Steve, Jonny and Michelle were there as I left the building.

Michelle threw herself on me as soon as I was out. Her kiss smothered me in promised passion. "Hi Stud."

I was relieved that she hadn't closed herself off again in the days I'd been gone. I held her up by her pert ass as she ground her hips into me. I sucked on her sweet lips.

"What the—" Jonny started before yelping as Steve hit him.

I could feel my cheeks heat up as Michelle jumped off and whirled on Jonny.

She suppressed her anger and smiled, which to be honest, made her even more terrifying. "We made up on the trip."

"Oh," Jonny stuttered. "But I thought that guy from the Earthen Bull Sect…"

I perked up at that, watching as Michelle silenced Jonny with a glare. "Yes, he has been pursuing me. But, honestly, it's been more like harassment."

Michelle turned back to me, looking apologetic. "Really, he's just been chasing after me. Totally one-sided."

"Michelle!" a booming voice shouted across the yard.

I turned and saw a man that looked like he was built like a bull rushing over towards us.

Michelle hid behind my back groaning and whispering, "That's him."

He seemed to sense something, and he slowed down when he saw me. "You must be Isaac." His brow furrowed. "You don't look so tough. But Michelle said, because of you, she couldn't be with me."

I looked over my shoulder at Michelle, who just shrugged helplessly.

"Yes, Michelle and I are in a relationship. So you have no further business with her. Get lost."

"Haha, good. I will crush you to bone dust and then she'll be free." The large man smiled, like that was the correct way to court a woman.

"Uh, she's not my property. You may want to revisit your logic there." It was hard to believe this idiot was so primitive.

"If she likes strong men, then the best way to show you are stronger is by killing those that she likes." He nodded to himself, like

171

he had just spoken a wise proverb. Clearly, this dude had hit his head a few too many times.

Michelle spoke up then, "You asshat. I'm not interested, and getting yourself beaten into a pulp isn't going to benefit anybody."

"Beaten to a pulp?" He looked at my rings before laughing. "Clearly, you don't understand my abilities, but I'd be happy to show you. And after I show you my battle abilities, I'll show you my bedroom ones." He cupped himself, jiggling himself while staring at Michelle.

I almost fell over. It was pretty clear why this guy wasn't having luck with ladies.

"I challenge you to a fight in the tournament." The brute stuck a finger out at me.

There was an intense urge to cut off the offending finger, but I held back. I still needed to heal my meridians before I got myself too deep into another fight.

"Tournament?" I asked.

He gave a deep bellied chuckle. "All of us youth from the sects are gathered. There will certainly be a tournament."

"When will it be?"

He looked stumped. "Umm... sometime." He nodded to himself. I couldn't believe this idiot, but at least I might have some time to recover.

"Great. I accept. Until then, will you leave Michelle be?"

"Haha! Sure. I look forward to crushing your bones to powder." The brute slapped me on the shoulder in what I assumed was supposed to be a friendly gesture, but it felt like a mountain had fallen on me. I barely remained standing. Well, that didn't bode well at the moment.

The brute left, and I refocused on my friends. The rest would have to wait.

I grabbed Michelle's hand and pulled her close for another kiss.

"So, what have I just signed myself up for?" I asked her and my two friends.

Jonny looked more than a little worried. "That guy is a late first ring mage."

"Late first ring?" I asked.

172

"The mages from the sects that have arrived divide the rings into three stages. Early, middle and late stages for each ring. Each being roughly a third of the next ring formation."

"So, we are all early first-ring mages?" I asked.

I saw hesitation in most of their faces.

"Well, you see, with the mana in the air increasing and the resources we got after we came back..." Michelle pulled her shirt aside to show the top of her breast. She was almost halfway to her second ring!

She hesitated. "But you must have improved on your way back, right?"

I winced and showed my ring. The green and gold luster was gone from my ring since my cultivation had been severed.

They all sucked in a cold breath on seeing it.

Steve just shook his head sadly.

"Why would you challenge Grant if you lost your cultivation?" Michelle's eyes were wild with worry. "Wait, no, I'll take your place. These sect guys would probably allow something like that. They are all about tradition. I just need to find the rule that lets me."

I shook my head. I was not about to let Michelle fight for me. Besides, my father wanted to train me, and he had seen my shattered cultivation. He likely had a plan to help.

"I'm going to go training with my father after today. I'll get patched back up. How about we explore the city for now?"

She sighed though. "I can't tempt you back to my place? Just for a night before you head away again?"

Looking down at her pleading eyes, it was so hard to let her down. And I was more than ready to fully explore her body. But I knew my duty. "My father doesn't really do rain checks. But don't worry, if he's going to train me, there's no need to worry that we won't have time after this supposed tournament.

She snuggled into my side, clearly not pleased but taking the time she could get.

"Dude. What the fuck happened out there?" Jonny looked back and forth at us, completely baffled.

Shrugging, I really didn't know. "We just sorta clicked."

"And a metric ton of self-denial blocked chemistry flooded out," Steve said, nodding like it all made sense.

"Anyways... how about lunch?"

It was unspoken that lunch would be at Jonny's family restaurant. That was where we always met up.

Jonny laughed. "Maybe after you get some clothes."

I had almost forgotten I wasn't wearing a shirt or shoes. "I'll meet you guys there in a bit."

"I'll come with. I need to talk to you." Michelle latched onto my arm before I could get very far.

"What do you want to talk about?" I asked, feeling good with Michelle on my arm.

We'd broken past our awkward past, and I'd finally shaken the reservations I had coming from the relationship with Kat. But we still had plenty to talk about. Aurora was one hundred percent on board with me having multiple partners. She had practically demanded it as a status of my strength. But it still felt like a touchy subject.

Michelle was staring at me. "Do you need to talk to Aurora?"

"Yeah, so about that. She's actually pretty encouraging when it comes to me..." I hesitated on the word; it felt odd to speak it aloud. "Starting a harem."

Michelle covered her mouth to stop some laughter. "You've been with her since we last talked?" Then her brows narrowed in thought. "But when would you have seen her?"

I started to spout an excuse, but I didn't want to lie. "It's complicated. Nothing bad, but yes, she finally wore me down." A smile snuck out of me at the thought of our time in the cave.

"Fine. I won't dig. But you better tell me at some point. She must be pretty amazing to get the stoic Stud to grin like that."

Rolling my eyes, we continued to walk arm in arm. "What was it you wanted to talk about again?"

She relented and let the topic shift. "My mothers are begging me to bring you to dinner."

"Meet the parents already?" I teased.

She blew a raspberry at that. "Sorta. I may have talked about you before. Now that there's a chance, my mothers are pretty persistent." She looked at me for a reaction and must have found it acceptable.

"Not much of a surprise that you were raised by persistent women," I laughed as she elbowed my side.

"Look, before you meet my mothers you need to know they are… a handful," she sighed. "They'll talk about sex."

"Is that such a big deal?"

She blew out another breath. "I'm pretty numb to it, but I don't want them to scare you away."

I kissed the back of her hand. "Look, after the talk in the woods, there's some pretty solid feelings forming. I'm interested in the beautiful, sexy and tough-as-nails woman beside me. I won't scare easily."

Her face went beet red at the compliments.

"It will be fine; I'm not going to run away from this." I squeezed her hand with the commitment. She really was a hell of a woman, and I'd be stupid not to see where this led. We were just in the early stages of whatever this would be.

I managed to get dressed and back to the restaurant without wasting too much time. Michelle had left me at my door with a kiss and two more confirmations that I'd hold to my promise for dinner with her parents.

"Hello, Isaac," Maaria greeted me as I entered the restaurant.

"Hi, Mrs. H." I waved to her and headed to our usual table.

Steve looked up from a book he was nose deep into. "Jonny went to go grab a notebook."

"Everything went okay when you got back?" I asked.

"Dad heard that there'd been some trouble. He was a bit shaken up but got better when he saw me in one piece." Steve turned to look across the restaurant.

Maaria was fussing over Jonny like an overprotective hen as he tried to make his way over to us.

"—what about your toothbrush? Maybe you need more food, you are still growing."

"Mom, I'm not going anywhere. I just want to go to the bazaar today," Jonny whirled on her.

"It's okay, Mrs. H; we'll look out for him." Not that it would entail much if we were really going to the bazaar.

"See." Jonny pointed at me like I was the final piece of evidence to crack the case.

Maaria gave up and walked away quietly.

Jonny plopped down on the seat next to Steve. "She's been like that since I got back. I'm a mage now. I don't need my mom fussing over me."

"She just worried about you, Jonny," I said, giving his bag a once over.

"What's in the bag?" Steve asked, peaking into it.

Jonny shrugged. "Stuff. I picked up a few things in our rush to get out of the camp. Want to see if I can sell any of it."

The three of us looked through the bag. It was mostly junk, but someone would buy the beast teeth and such.

I smirked and pulled off the red-crested ring on my finger and put it on the table for them both to see. "Look what I got from the brat."

"No way. Is that a spatial ring?" Jonny said a bit too loud in his excitement, and I caught the next table over turning for a look.

"Yes and keep it down." I slid the ring over to him to flip between his hands.

Steve was less impressed. "Looks recognizable, like that family of his might be able to identify it."

Taking it back from Jonny. "I know, which is why I'm just using it to bring all of this crap to the bazaar. Afterwards, I need to ditch it."

I thought about telling them about the older man from the Earth Flame sect, but I didn't want to worry them unnecessarily if it turned out to be nothing.

Steve gave me an appraising look but shrugged.

I smiled and held the ring again, summoning out a weapon and a few magical items onto the table. "We are going to make bank at the bazaar."

Jonny took a deep breath and sat back. I could see a bit of jealousy on his face.

"We all earned this, together. So we will split it."

"Michelle?" Steve asked.

"We'll keep a part for her, yeah."

Jonny was practically vibrating in his seat. "Let's freaking go." He must be excited to be ready to ditch a meal.

I laughed, also eager to get started. "Steve, you want lunch or bazaar?"

"The bazaar has mana beast meat," Steve said before looking back at Jonny. "No offense. Just focused on training."

Jonny waved it off. "Nah, we understand. Mom can't cut the beast meat, so she doesn't use it."

"It's settled. Let's head over to the bazaar then." I clapped my hands and stood up. I was eager to see how much I could make from all these items.

Getting down to the bazaar again, I took in the busy stall-lined streets.

It was where we had shopped before, but that was when we were untested mages. Now we had survived an adventure of life and death, and I didn't just have coin to spend, I had beast cores.

The center building that the entire market was built upon rose out of the awnings like a beacon.

I could see a small trickle of the bright colored clothing of the visitors from the sects coming and going from the Treasure Hall.

"Let's go to the Treasure Hall." I surprised myself looking at the pristine new age building. I now understood why it seemed different than all the old buildings of town. It was clearly made with stone gathered far outside the city. Likely, it was tough enough to support a fight between mages without issue.

Jonny gasped as we stepped up to the polished steps. A set of guards eyed us like we didn't belong.

But I pushed forward. They didn't know what I had.

The inside of the Treasure Hall was an opulent show of wealth. I half-wondered if the cases and pedestals were worth more than the items they held. The entire first floor of the hall was a maze of glass cases and frames holding magical items.

The mages from the sects casually strolled through the Treasure Hall, congregated in tight groups. If I guessed correctly, it was mostly a small leader showing off his wealth to his posse.

I had let Jonny out of my sight for a second, and he had his face pressed against the glass of a large staff with a blue aura.

"How can I help you, gentlemen?" A woman stepped up behind Jonny. She had an impatient tone. She clearly thought we didn't belong here.

Steve and Jonny gave me a glance, which caused the woman to recognize me as the leader of our little band.

She wore a silk dress with long, loose sleeves. It hung heavily on her frame and highlighted her subtle curves. She wasn't near as curvy as Aurora, but she held an elfin beauty with her wispy hair and thin frame. There was an unmistakable insignia of a sect on her chest. An artful gold coin. It made sense now that the Treasure Hall likely belonged to a sect.

Refocusing on me, she ignored my obvious appraisal. "Sir, do you have something you are looking for." The unspoken ask for us to leave if not rang out in her tone.

"I have a large quantity to sell, and then I would like to talk about using the profits to purchase a few things." Little did she know, I probably have more wealth on me than some of these colorful peacocks.

She gave a sickly, sweet fake smile. "Of course, please come this way. We have a room for appraisals. I shall send someone to work with you."

The woman never even gave me her name. I made a mental note for the future. Respect went both ways.

She gave me a frosty look when she opened the door for us.

"Thanks, we have a number of items to show. Should I just drop them here?" I pointed at the open stone floor in the room.

She gave me a sly smile. "Of course, let's see what you have."

Grinning, I flicked my hand and dumped all of the gear and cultivation resources I had collected from the spatial rings. It steadily filled the large space.

As the large pile formed, I took joy in watching her smile stiffen and then shatter.

"I hope this is enough for the private room. I have some more, but I don't want the pile to tip over and damage any of them."

Her eye twitched. "Of course. The appraiser will be here shortly."

She paused and remembered herself. "Would you like some tea?" She leaned over, gesturing to the kettle and letting her cleavage show.

"Sure. Jonny, Steve, this place is nice right?" I plopped down on the sofa.

They were both quiet as they sat down next to me.

"Thanks," I said, picking up my cup of tea. "Don't think I caught your name."

She gave me a thin smile. "Emera. I'm the hostess of this Treasure Hall. We welcome your patronage."

"Thank you for the tea, Emera."

She pulled up her dress as she stood and bowed on her way out. Her smile was stiff the whole time.

Jonny turned to me with a grin as the doors closed.

Chapter 16

As soon as the doors clicked shut, Jonny turned to me. "She's going to eat you alive, dude."

I laughed. "I just think she's bitter for treating us so poorly when we first arrived. Don't worry, she just wants a nice tip now."

"Maybe we shouldn't antagonize all of the sects?" Steve suggested.

I let out a deep breath. "Yeah, I got a bit full of myself there. All of these sects look down on us so much. I was eager for a win."

Jonny started pouring out the tea, filling the room with a nice relaxing aroma. "But it's not the Treasure Hall you are upset with, is it?"

"No. Right now we need to keep an eye on the Earth Flame Sect, and maybe the Sun and Moon Hall. The others haven't done anything to us." I sipped at the tea, its taste just as smooth as the smell.

"It isn't even the full Earth Flame Sect that we have an issue with. Just one brat," Steve said, enjoying his own tea.

I shook my head and looked at the ceiling. "I think the Earth Flame Sect will cause us trouble unless we find another sect to join."

"We can't do much about that now. Let's focus on getting ready for the dungeon." I smacked my leg for emphasis. "We are going to have lots of cores to spend today."

Steve relaxed and drank his tea, but Jonny couldn't stop fidgeting and looking at the doors, waiting for someone to come.

When they finally opened, an old man came through stroking his beard as he looked at the pile of materials and me like they were an equation that he couldn't solve.

"Appraiser Hermon," the old man said as he held his hand out for me.

I stood up. "Happy to meet you." I pumped his hand. "We got lucky recently. Hoped you'd be willing to buy?"

"The Hall will buy, but we must make sure we are getting a fair price for everything." His eyes gleamed with shrewdness.

"Of course. I brought all of this to the hall because your reputation precedes you. Please, take a look." I gestured to the materials I had set out before. I tried to dial down my aggressiveness after what Steve and Jonny said.

I stayed standing as Hermon picked up each piece, taking notes on a small pad and moving the piece to a new pile.

It took several hours for him to go through everything. When I had refreshed the original pile, he looked at me in utter shock.

"Well, this was more than we were expecting... The Hall in this small town may have some difficulty in finding enough beast cores to compensate you. I need a moment to confer for the final price." The old man hesitated and watched for my reaction.

"No worries, can I get a line of credit? We are looking at gearing up for our next trip."

Hermon looked ecstatic at the idea. "Of course. That can be arranged if you let me go get a card ready."

He darted out the door after swiping all of the items into his own spatial ring.

"Holy crap," Jonny finally let out when they were alone. "Dude was so excited—I wonder how much they are going to offer."

"Quite a bit," Steve said, looking at the closed door.

I nodded and sipped my cold tea. It was still fantastic tea. "It will be fair. They have a reputation to keep."

As if responding to me, the doors opened, and Emera stepped in with a card in hand. "We've accepted your materials for a value of eight thousand beast cores." She laid the card on the table with a soft apologetic smile, while her eyes tried to read me.

"Eight thousand. That sounds reasonable. We would like to shop with this. Can you show us your best?" I hoped that she'd get some sort of sales credit that would smooth my earlier attitude over.

Her smile was stiff again, but that didn't matter. She bowed and showed us around the hall, even taking us up to the second floor.

"What kind of items are you looking for?"

Looking at Jonny's bag, I asked. "Do you have some modest spatial rings?"

"Of course." Emera led us over to a corner of the second floor and showed us a jewelry case with a dozen or so rings.

"All of these are two square meter's worth of storage area." She opened the case and showed us the tray.

Jonny looked up at me hesitantly and I knew he was worried about the cost.

"And how much would they be?" I asked, seeing his hesitation.

"500 rank one beast cores a ring."

Jonny audibly swallowed. It was more wealth than any of us had ever seen.

Killing other people was really profitable, I thought to myself.

"Great, we will take three rings." I picked out one that had soft blue accents in it. It would match Michelle's eyes.

"Would you like that wrapped? I'm sure she will love it," Emera said.

Damn sharp saleswoman. I was suddenly a bit nervous that she could pick that out of my actions.

"Sure. But keep it small, I don't want to make a big deal of it."

She gave me a flirty wink. "Lucky girl."

Emera was really pulling out the saleswomen charm now that we had money to spend.

"What next?" she asked, producing a small box with a bow to me.

"Weapons?" Steve asked.

I thought about it and agreed. New weapons would be nice, but ultimately, a nice new sword was worthless against a second-ring mage.

"We can take a peek at weapons to see how much they cost, but I really want to see some of your cultivation resources," I said.

Jonny and Steve were busy looking at some of the weapons. Emera encouraged them to pick up the weapons and get a sense for the enhancements they provided.

"You look bored. Why don't you follow me?" Emera led me away with her to a less pompous area of the second floor. Everything was in cases or mana-infused vials.

"Cultivation pills are stored in either vials or treated cases to help preserve their medicinal value. Left out in the open, even some of the best pills in the world will become worthless."

Emera picked up a case that had been set aside from the rest and offered it to me.

I opened the case and was hit with a herbal aroma that seemed to instantly calm the mana within me, making it more pliant.

"Wow." I closed the case, worried that I would have to pay for the loss in value.

"That is only the display case. But it is a good example of the pills we have to offer. That was a Calming Pill. Mages often use them in dungeons when there are large quantities of chaotic mana to cultivate." She pointed to a few vials of pills.

"Then there are Focusing pills like these." She brushed over another case for me to pick up.

This one I breathed in the scent like an ocean breeze and the world lit up. I was able to focus and sense mana far outside my small range.

"The Focusing pill helps one absorb ambient mana from their surroundings. This pill has several advantages, from helping someone absorb ambient mana to increasing your ability to scout and find dangers." She brushed the case longingly. "The effects of this pill do wear off, but most find that their sense of mana improves permanently after use."

I couldn't help but be excited at that. Even if I could expand my mana sense a few feet, it would be a great help in preventing myself from getting ambushed.

"The last of the rank one pills is the Boiling Blood Pill." She held her hand on the case preventing me from picking it up. "The pill is a lifesaving pill, capable of drastically increasing your mana flow for a short period of time. But you will suffer a backlash after using it and be weakened for a time."

She shook her head. "Unfortunately, nothing is free in this world. It is a dangerous pill, but one that could save your life in a critical moment."

That was an interesting pill. Given the troubles we had, it might be worth it. But at the same time, would it really be enough? I didn't want to rely on such a dangerous pill to survive.

"I'll take five Calming pills and five Focusing pills." I made up my mind. I needed to increase my foundation. That was how I would protect myself in the future.

"Good choice. The Boiling Blood Pill is dangerous, and too many people use it to fight above their strengths rather than for emergencies," she said, packing up two vials of pills. "It's 50 cores a pill, for 500 total."

I kept my face calm, but whoever made these pills must be crazy rich. Using mana to craft was certainly lucrative. Waving my hand, I added them to the plain spatial ring I had.

"Would you like to see the weapons again?" Emera asked, walking a bit too close.

A sharp laugh interrupted my shopping. "Look at the hicks."

I looked over to see a young man about my age with sharp features. He kind of reminded me of the Rhys brat I had killed. It was obvious because he was standing silently while the crowd around him hemmed and hawed for his attention.

Then I realized his clothes were the same color, a symbol of a burning mountain on his chest. He was likely associated with the Rhys family.

The rest of the crowd following him laughed at Steve and Jonny like they were monkeys in a cage.

I grit my teeth. I would love nothing less than to teach these guys a lesson, but there wasn't much I could do in the Treasure Hall.

"Please, do respect other guests in our shop." Emera came to my friends' rescue.

"Che. You are just some banished shop girl. Someone from the Treasure Hall working here is basically banishment," one of the followers jeered.

I could see Emera's eye twitch. He must have struck a nerve, but he also hinted at the Treasure Hall being much larger than just this single shop.

"My Treasure Hall is a vast organization. Maybe the Earth Flame Sect could learn a thing or two from our discipline, Hank." Emera's happy face froze in place as she addressed the leader of the group.

A couple of Hank's crew jeered at Emera, but Hank himself stayed stoically silent, taking her in. When the lackey stepped forward, Hank reached out and stopped him.

This interaction was a wealth of knowledge for me. Apparently, the Treasure Hall must have enough power to contend with the Earth Flame Sect.

Hank turned to the man. "Now now. You know it is poor taste to insult those so far below your station." He eyed Steve and Jonny before dismissing them and turning back to Emera.

Steve looked like he was about to punch Hank in the face.

Hank turned back to Emera and offered a fake smile. "We'll just get back to our shopping."

"Do remember that any violence in a Treasure Hall will ban you and your family from entering any Treasure Hall in the future." Emera's voice was cold, with direct challenge. Hank simply nodded, not breaking eye contact.

Switching to a happier tone, she clapped. "How about we take up some of this aggression in a more appropriate Treasure Hall activity." She led us to the third floor. It was really crowded and almost looked more like a bar.

Both my group and Hank's followed along, more curious than anything else.

"What's this?" I asked.

"Bumpkin," Hank snorted before an older man lazing nearby spoke up.

"Treasure Betting. You see those rocks on stage?"

Now that I looked, the stage that felt like it should have a performer of some sort just had piles of rocks ranging from the size of a fist to being as big as a person.

"Those are rocks from excavations of dungeons. You never know if they contain a treasure or just empty dust. Experts at the game, like me, can tell when one of those has real treasure," the old man explained before raising his hand, and a woman dressed to show off her assets came to his table and leaned over.

"Yes?"

The old man pointed at one of the rocks. "That one."

"80 beast cores," the attendant said.

The man handed them over like they were nothing. I couldn't help feeling my scalp go numb at how much money would pass hands in this place every day.

The attendant picked up the stone and made a show of putting it carefully on the table on stage. She pulled out a chisel and hammer, cracking open the stone with a single strike.

Everyone watched as the stone opened up, and a gold trinket rolled out.

The attendant handed it over to an old man whom I had mistaken for one of the rocks up on stage.

The old man hummed to himself as he inspected the gold trinket.

"Certainly mana infused. No combat properties though. A calming aura around it would help improve cultivation though." The old man eyed the better. "90 beast cores to take it off your hand.

The man who had bet on the stone nodded and the attendant brought back his bet plus the additional ten beast cores he had earned.

I thought through the process. The Treasure Hall really benefited from this. If someone were to get nothing, the Treasure Hall was only out an old rock and walked away with some earnings. But, if there was something in the stone, the Treasure Hall could try and buy it at a fair price and likely resell it at a profit.

But there was always the chance you could strike rich, and that's what drew everyone here.

"Now that you've seen it, do you want to play?" Emera asked me and Hank.

"Sounds perfect." I wanted to bet; after everything that had happened, I was feeling lucky.

Hank didn't hesitate to add his two cents. "Of course, but I bet the bumpkin doesn't even have enough to play."

Emera looked at Hank dryly. "He has a suitable balance with the Treasure Hall."

Hank snorted and judged me like I was getting favored treatment. I rolled my eyes. He wasn't worth my time, but I smiled knowing he'd likely stroke out if he found out how I'd gotten the wealth

"With that settled, I want that one." I pointed at a smaller stone among those on the stage.

"Excellent choice," Emera said, waving an attendant to collect it.

Hank rolled his eyes before picking out the largest stone on stage. "How about we add some additional wager to this?"

"What were you thinking?"

"100 beast cores to whoever gets the more expensive prize," Hank sneered. I wanted to argue that he had a larger stone; therefore, the chance of it containing something was likely higher, but I still felt the breeze of luck on me. Probably not my wisest move, but I let him egg me on.

"Deal. Emera can you hold the bet for us?" I extended my card toward her, wanting to make sure a neutral third party held the bet so Hank couldn't renege. I didn't exactly have the best impression of the Rhys family.

Emera nodded to me before having an attendant bring Hank's rock on the table before mentioning the cost. "1200 beast cores."

I could see Hank wince but hide it quickly, smiling at his group as he casually handed over the cost.

With a nod from Emera, they both broke open the two rocks.

I was focused on Hank's, which had what looked like a beast core in it, before looking at mine with what also looked like a beast core.

"I guess we tied." I looked at Hank, who looked like he was about to have a blood vessel burst.

"Please give them to the appraiser. All beast cores are not equal," Hank said, the last part directed at me.

When the attendant picked up Hank's core, it crumbled to dust and gave him a practiced shake of her head.

My core, however, glowed brightly with blue mana.

Emera went to hand me the bet she had been holding when Hank blocked her. "It could still be trash. Maybe it is pulsing out its final burst of mana."

She relented, but the appraiser got up out of his seat to collect the beast core, which still glowed brightly.

"Hmmm, this appears to be a third-rank mana beast core."

My jaw nearly dropped. A second-rank beast core was worth a hundred first-rank cores. A third-rank beast core was worth a hundred second-rank cores. That meant that this core was worth ten thousand beast cores.

"It has lost some of its mana over the years, but I'll buy it for 9000 beast cores." He handled it delicately, pulling out a case to place it in.

"Can you tell what beast it came from?" I asked, knowing that it might have more value for someone to seal in their ring.

The appraiser shook his head. "It is very difficult to know what beast a core comes from. Even those who claim to know usually only do so because the person who harvested it sold it with records."

"Then I'll sell it." It would be incredibly difficult for me to absorb a third-rank beast core. I could do far better with a number of first-rank cores to purchase other goods or cultivate with.

"How about double or nothing?" Hank said from the side. "Loser pays the winners tab."

I looked at the nine thousand beast cores that Emera was about to hand me, and there was no way I was risking that. I'd have to be a fool.

And there was no reason to provoke him further and create more enemies.

"I'm sorry, but I think I'm out." I waved away Emera handing me the bet. "Let him take his bet back. I have enough luck to share."

That seemed to really set Hank off. "Are you looking down on me, bumpkin?" The rest of his crowd got agitated on his behalf. The face of the rather pretty woman with him turned venomous.

"Fine." I took the bet from Emera and left for the fourth floor with my friends in tow.

"Emera, can I ask an odd question?"

"Sure, but I think I know what it will be."

"Why are all these guys so arrogant? I mean, it's like there is no way but to offend them." It had been bugging me since I met Hank. They couldn't all be that way.

Emera shook her head. "It's a mix of things. They were all told by their families that they were heaven-born geniuses while being fed the best resources there are. At the same time, they wear that arrogance like armor. If he wins while having that arrogance, he'd be praised like a hero. But if he loses, he wears that arrogance in hopes of you being afraid of his family."

She paused and faced me. "They try to use their arrogance and their family because they are afraid."

I thought about that. Maybe it just wasn't effective against me because I didn't understand just how strong his family was?

"How strong is his family?"

"The Rhys family, and the Earth Flame Sect for that matter, isn't the strongest in the region by a long shot. Certainly, they are large enough to scare many individual cultivators, but all you did is cause him to lose some money. If he went back to his family to help get revenge, he'd be laughed out."

I swallowed deep because I had done far worse to the Rhys family. The spatial ring suddenly felt like it was going to burn a hole in my pocket.

"The Treasure Hall is discreet about sales, correct?" I asked, keeping the ring in my pocket.

"Of course." Emera's eyes narrowed in curiosity.

"Could I exchange this ring for a similar capacity spatial ring?" I handed over the ring I had gotten from the Rhys brat.

Emera's eyes held some mirth as she saw the ring. "I guess you and Hank were destined to be enemies. Does anyone know?"

"Yeah, he had some guards with him that got away."

"This ring could only have belonged to someone of their main family. No one will want to buy this, but I can take it off your hands."

I felt a loss to give it over for free, but then again, I didn't want to walk around with a glowing neon sign that I had killed someone from the Rhys family.

"Do you have any spells for sale?" I asked as we walked through the fourth floor that held sparse items, most of which were far outside my budget.

"We do, but as a friend, I'd suggest you join a sect and use their library," Emera said, pausing and opening a chest. "This is a simple first-tier spell, priced at 20,000 beast cores in this small town. Yet you could get this free at a sect."

"That's generous," I said.

Emera let out a small laugh. "Not really. In a sect, you work for them even though I said they were free. But still, it would only be a small one- or two-day mission to earn something like a first-ring spell."

"The Treasure Hall is a sect, correct?" I wanted to confirm my suspicion.

"Yes, the Treasure Hall is a sect. We set up a shop in every city. On both sides of the war."

"War?" I said surprised.

Her forehead creased as she tried to figure out if I was kidding. When she realized I wasn't, she slowly explained, "Yes, there is a war among mages. Though those present here only represent one side. It's honestly nothing for you to concern yourself with. As a first-ring mage, you mean nothing in the grand scheme of the war."

"Oh," I said, not being able to come up with anything else.

"Not in a bad way. I'm a second-ring mage and I still mean nothing in the face of the war. When sects fight, it isn't about how many mages you have. It is about how many peak experts you have. Always remember, sects are looking for the diamond in the rough that they can polish to a powerful mage. They have no interest in a legion of mediocrity."

"Thanks. I appreciate the advice."

"No problem. If I might give one more piece of advice?" She paused a moment, unsure if she should continue. "It's best you stay away from the Sun and Moon Hall."

"Why?" I already had a distaste for them because of Aiden, but Kat was there, and I had hopes to see her again.

But Emera didn't give me a straight answer. "We are neutral after all, but it's just a piece of advice." She dodged the question.

"I think Hank and his crew are gone by now," I said, having finished our second lap of the fourth floor.

"Very well. Would you like to settle up?" Emera said, sighing at seeing Jonny coming back empty-handed.

Emera brought us over to a vault where she gave me the remaining beast cores on our balance. I doled out the cores to my friends and kept mine and Michelle's shares to give her later.

"Best of luck," Emera said as we left.

I had a feeling we'd need it. While we might have gone shopping to arm ourselves, I felt like all we'd done was put ourselves in more danger.

Chapter 17

Despite the drama, we walked out of the Treasure Hall with bright smiles. Even though Jonny didn't get the shiny gear he wanted, he still kept looking at the ring on his finger in awe.

Unfortunately, I could feel someone watching us. "Jonny, stop looking at your spatial ring." I hissed hoping that we hadn't drawn unwanted attention.

Locksprings was pretty safe, but there were criminal elements anywhere there were people.

"What do you—"

Steve smacked Jonny upside the head. "Someone is watching you."

He clammed up really fast.

But it was too late.

I was yanked into an alley along with Steve and Jonny before I realized what was happening.

"Wha—" A fist slammed into my gut, catching me by surprise.

"Don't speak," a gruff voice said as hands wandered through my pockets until he saw my spatial ring.

"Got it?" a second thug wearing a mask asked.

I recognized Hank's voice.

Somehow knowing who it was gave me the confidence to slam my head back into the guy's face before he could get the ring off my finger.

Steve freed himself and gave the guy holding Jonny a right hook that snapped his head back. I caught Steve's eye and motioned for him to get Jonny out.

I swept someone's legs, then punched the masked Hank.

He staggered back, but there were more of them. One clocked me in the face, but instead of me screaming in pain, that guy ended up pulling his hand back and nursing it.

"Rick?" They paused seeing the unexpected reaction.

"Felt like I just punched a brick wall."

I took the moment to get up close to the one nursing his hand and chop him in the back of the head, sending him to the alley floor out cold.

The alley lit up with a red glow as one of them started to cast a fire spell.

Hank cut in again as the fire winked out. "Do you want to send up a flare for the guards? Idiot!"

I looked back to see Steve pulling Jonny clear of the situation and decided to let loose. This would be my first chance to see how my bloodline-improved body fared against cultivators from a sect.

"His friends are running. Just take him down. He's the one with all the money." Hank smiled, and I found myself mobbed by the six of Hank's gang that were still standing.

Fists and kicks rained down on me, but I just shrugged them off and pulled off one of the attackers to throw him at another.

"It's really like punching a freaking wall. He's not even using his mana."

"Freaky, bumpkin," another said, trying to tackle my legs, but I met his face with my knee, eliciting a satisfying crunch of his nose.

I just snorted at these fellows. Obviously, they wanted the betting money I'd earned in the Treasure Hall, but they hadn't expected my body to be iron. But to be fair, I hadn't really either. The amount of pain I was feeling given all the hits was amazing.

"Pin him down," Hank called, and they piled onto me.

Even being tougher than them, there wasn't much I could do when sheer numbers tried to lock me up. I couldn't overpower them without being able to move my limbs.

Mobbed as I was, they still didn't manage to do any serious damage. I tucked down, trying to get my center of gravity over my feet.

"Hold him, I'll get the ring." Hank was trying to pry my spatial ring out of my hand.

Luckily, I'd gotten into a position where I could push with my legs. In a heaving motion, I pushed up, knocking half my assailants off me.

The hand that Hank had and was trying to get the ring off of turned into a short punch.

He turned and took it on the shoulder, just in time for Steve and Jonny to come flying back into the fight.

Steve grabbed one of the attackers and rolled him into a chokehold while Jonny went about making sure those who were slow to get up stayed down.

I smirked at Hank as I engaged him in a fist fight. We both threw hard fists in a series of blocks and punches.

I realized, even if Hank was decent at martial arts, he was rusty. Like many mages, he relied on spells after earning his first ring.

All it took was one gap in his defenses and I managed to clip his chin, sending him dizzily to the ground.

"Let's go," Hank said, rolling away and to his feet.

Most of his group were out for the count, but those still able to run grabbed their friends.

Jonny gave me a look, and I nodded. We let them go. There wasn't much we could actually do unless we wanted to start killing.

There was a commotion from the edge of the street outside the alley as the muggers bolted out of the other end.

"You guys okay?" a guard I recognized as my father's second, Roger, asked, giving me a once over. I could feel the places I'd been hit swelling, the start of the welts and bruises that were forming.

"Yeah, just a scuffle among young mages. No real harm done," I said, brushing myself off. If anything, we made it out ahead of Hank's group.

"Do you want to report it?" Roger asked, examining us for serious injuries. He gave us a low-grade medicinal pill that would have us healed from minor scrapes in no time.

I shook my head. "No, I got it from here."

Roger nodded and waved his men off the alleyway entrance.

Jonny piped up after Roger had left. "Isaac, you should report them to your father."

"I don't think I will, Jonny. I don't want to start more trouble between their family and mine. And they were just after the money. While not okay, they weren't gunning for our lives." I couldn't help but feel gratitude for the new strength I'd developed.

I needed to build more. As a mage, if I couldn't defend my own wealth, there was no point in having it.

"Just like that?" Jonny asked. "We are just going to leave that be?"

"It won't end there regardless, Jonny. You saw how they attacked us when the guards weren't around. We just need to protect ourselves." I was already mentally preparing myself for what felt like the inevitable next fight with Hank.

Jonny shook his head at me, unable to understand why I was so casual after being mugged. But he also wasn't fully invested in the cultivation lifestyle. I'd known that the path I chose was dangerous, but it was all I'd ever wanted. I wasn't about to let Hank stop me.

We walked around town. Steve was still eating drum sticks he'd snagged from a vendor. He had spent no small sum on filling up his spatial ring with deep fried legs of some bird-like mana beast.

"Are you going to cultivate from now on by eating?" I joked. Mana beast meat did contain mana that could be circulated, but it wasn't a very efficient way to cultivate.

Steve grinned over his latest morsel. "Fun way to cultivate."

"Just hope none of those are from horses," Jonny said casually.

Steve looked at his food in horror. "No... horses don't have drumsticks," he said, convincing himself before biting in again.

Looking up, I realized we were outside the brothel I had seen Kat enter.

"We should head back." I didn't want to risk another encounter with Aiden, and I still didn't understand why the Sun and Moon Hall would run a brothel.

"Hi, boys," a soft voice said before we could get away.

I tried to keep going, but Jonny stopped and stared wide-eyed.

Fine.

Turning, I saw a deliciously buxom woman with bright blue hair and a silver dress that was barely hanging on by the thin straps.

Seeing that she had Jonny's attention, she bit her lip and blushed for him.

Two more women appeared from inside and tried to entice us.

"Do you want to come inside?" She hooked Jonny's hand without him agreeing, and he was led like a sheep into the brothel.

Sighing, I followed along. It wasn't that these women weren't beautiful, but I honestly would rather enjoy Aurora or maybe even get my first taste of Michelle right now.

A woman stepped up to Steve, who didn't even look up from his drumstick.

I barely managed to hold back a snicker as the sinfully curvy woman tried and failed to get Steve's attention.

She huffed and stayed by his side, clearly hoping he'd give her some attention after he finished. Unfortunately for her, I knew my rail thin friend was more interested in horses than women.

I realized that I had lost Jonny while I was distracted. Steve and I were now on a curved couch in the lounge.

And I had gained my own admirer. She had gold spun hair and a graceful body as she homed in on me from across the room.

"Hi, handsome," she said, sitting down close enough for her breasts to brush against my arm.

Steve looked her over briefly before returning to his drumstick.

"Hi..." I dragged it out, hoping for a name.

She shushed me. "No names here, handsome. What brings you in?"

Honestly, I'd been dragged in here by Jonny, but I was also curious about the Sun and Moon Hall.

The woman guided me back to the present with soft trailing touches along my arm and a warm softness against my side.

I made eye contact with her, and she bit her lip and blushed. It felt like her beauty was luring my soul away.

"Follow me." She wrapped a scarf around my shoulders and led me to a private room.

The sway of her hips and the curve of her lips promised sinful delights as she drew me to the bed in the room.

My large frame dwarfed her curvaceous body, but she was in control as she sat me down on the bed and sat on my lap.

The way she writhed and moved had me in a trance as my stiff member threatened to burst free of my pants.

I pinned her hips still and tasted her sweet lips.

She leaned into me, devouring my lips before a sense of her mana invaded my body. She was strong. At least a second-ring mage.

Her mana swam through me, but it returned like it had missed something.

I felt somewhat uncomfortable with her mana invading me. It felt like a venomous viper.

Then things changed.

She leaned back and blinked several times before looking at me in surprise, and then around the room.

"Wha?" Something must have occurred to her because she punched me hard enough to bounce my head off the bed.

Now I was as dazed as her, but she stood up and cast about the room blinking rapidly like she was trying to process what was happening.

"Where am I?"

I wasn't sure how she was going to react, but honesty seemed like the best policy when alone in a room with a confused second-ring mage. I raised my hands, showing her I meant no harm.

"Sun and Moon Hall's Brothel," I said.

"Brothel!" she said in a whispered shout. "I'm in a brothel?" Her eyes locked onto me and they looked gold, like a serpent's.

"Yes," I said, waiting for her reaction.

Her eyes seemed to pierce right through me. "You're telling the truth."

I nodded. "One of your associates drew my friend in here. I followed to try to keep him from being an idiot, and then you drew me into this room. I was mostly just curious about this place."

"Right. You're right. I brought you in here. But." She frowned, like she was struggling to recall the event.

"Are you okay? Anything I can do to help?" I asked. "I can go if I'm making you uncomfortable."

She seemed to be calming down, but she put herself between me and the door. "No. Just don't leave right now."

"Okay." I let the word drag out.

Not sure what else to do, I looked about the room. It was plain with a veneer of luxury. There were some personal odds and ends that signified this was where she likely slept too.

"You know your meridians are shattered, right?" she said, catching my attention again.

"Yep, going to fix that."

"I... I think that's why I've come to. I'm Narissa." Her eyes locked on me again. "You really are a treasure, you know that?"

"Thanks?" I wasn't sure how to take that.

She shook her head and pointed to her eyes. "No. I can detect treasures. Your body is a treasure."

"Okay, but that doesn't explain what just happened."

"But it does." She grinned. "Your broken meridians and the fact that I am identifying you as a treasure is keeping what they've done to me at bay, because I have no commands or orders about what to do with something that is both broken and valuable! Or what to do with a person who is also a treasure."

"So as long as I'm here with you, you don't have any orders? And you just do whatever they order you to?"

"Yes, the spell they put on me isn't forcing any actions."

That revelation startled me. She was being controlled. "Oh fuck. You are being controlled."

Narissa sighed, "Yes, that bastard. I never even saw it coming."

I wanted to ask more, but the door was knocked open as I felt something fall into my hand.

And there was Aiden Hall, standing in the frame glaring at me.

"Get the fuck out." Before he turned to Narissa. "You. Leave."

Her golden eyes were gone, replaced with a dull brown. Narissa was swaying in that hypnotic way again with a pleased smile plastered on her face.

Aiden let her out past him before turning to me with a big grin. "I just got some good news. Your precious Kat has become the Sect's new favorite. She's getting the full strength of the Sect behind her cultivation."

"Good. Can't wait to see her wipe the floor with your face." I stood to leave.

But Aiden's shit eating grin didn't fade one bit. "You think that, after all of the resources the Sect will give her, she'll deny the Headmaster's son? I know for a fact he's intent on wooing her."

"Not my business." I shrugged, and for the first time, I didn't feel a twinge of pain in my heart hearing about Kat. I was happy for her if it was what she wanted.

Aiden's smile faltered at his failed attempt to get under my skin. "Not even a little bit jealous?"

"Kat is a big girl. She can make her own decisions." I stepped up to him, waiting for him to move. "Why do you hate me so much, Aiden?"

"Huh?" That question made him look like he's just been slapped in the face. I waited.

He huffed. "You always have it easy. Getting everything, like picking up apples." Aiden's hostility melted away slowly. There was clearly some deep resentment and insecurity there.

"Aiden. My father trained me brutally since I was a child; nothing about that was easy. I had to work and claw my way to where I am now, just like you." I realized that what Aiden saw as 'natural talent' was really all the years my father had tried to help me survive this world. It had been his way of protecting me, and it had been hard.

But Aiden had only seen the output.

I looked Aiden in the eye. "Look, I don't think we'll be friends, but I'd be all for not continuing this nonsense. Think about it."

He paused before stepping back to make way for me. But while he was opening up, I decided to ask him a question.

"Is something wrong with the girls here?" I asked.

"No, just women from the Sect coming here to cultivate. A number of them practice dual cultivation. You know, where you need a partner." He wagged his eyebrows, telling me exactly how that partner was involved.

I watched him for any signs of falsehood. But if he was lying, he was the best damn liar I'd ever met. He didn't know what was happening to Narissa.

Nodding, I left, dragging Steve to pull Jonny out of the brothel. It had been an eventful trip.

I felt for Narissa. I wished I could break her free, but I wasn't about to be able to do that at my current strength. For now, we needed to steer clear of that brothel.

I had a feeling that Michelle was very right about the Sun and Moon Hall. There was a reason none of the girls came back.

Kat flicked at the edge of my mind, but I pushed it off. I couldn't do anything now, and it sounded like at least in the short term she was going to be pampered.

But all that fled when I opened the crinkled ball of paper.

Save me. Dungeon.

I let out a big sigh. I'd do it if I could.

***

I headed back to the house with slight dread at what my father had planned.

I opened the door to my father waiting at the table. He was dressed in dark robes like he was going on a stealth mission.

Yet he was waiting for me...

"Son, let's go out for a small trip," my father said, stepping up to me and grabbing me by the shoulder.

He sniffed. "Brothel?"

I could feel my cheeks flush. "Jonny got drawn into one."

"Good, it's nice to blow off some steam from time to time. Just don't overdo it."

Not having anything to say to that, I just went along with my father.

Traveling together had been quick. My father had led me to a waterfall just outside the city.

"So, you crippled your meridians?" my father asked me. But I knew he had already looked at my body and seen the damage.

"Yeah," I said looking down in shame. I wasn't sure if I'd be able to restore it.

"You also awakened your mother's bloodline." It was a statement, not a question. "Tell me the whole story."

I trusted my father more than anything and told him everything. Only this time, unlike with Rigel, I told him about everything, including Mei, Aurora and the stone tablet with a sword in it.

When I got to that part, he seemed to be curious about the sword.

I pulled it out, half-afraid it would shoot a beam of light into the sky. Luckily, it didn't.

My father held the sword reverently and turned over the sword, looking at the hilt.

"I can't believe she actually left this for you." My father ran a hand over the sword lovingly.

"She?" I asked.

"Your mother. This was her sword." He gave it back to me.

I looked at the sword made of polished bone. It had attracted the sects like flies just being unsealed from the stone. A sword capable of that, yet it was my mother's.

The wounds of losing her opened up fresh again. Just what wealth of life would I have had if she was still in mine?

"Dad, you don't talk about her much. Where is she?"

My father looked up with a flicker of surprise, before it settled into sadness. "I should have guessed you'd figure out eventually. But the answer is... I don't know."

He sighed and looked off into the distance. "She came into my life in a storm. I was out on patrol as a simple guard at the time. She was heavily injured, and it was a miracle she was still alive. I brought her back and nursed her to health."

"She's from outside the city," I said, realizing now the significance of that.

"I think she's from much further away than that son. She helped me cultivate quickly. Without her, I wouldn't be the force I am within the city." He shook his head.

"But I'm getting ahead of myself. After she recovered physically, she still had to recover her cultivation. During that time, we had you." He paused, choking up before continuing. "Today, we will start the method your mother used to recover from crippled meridians."

"Tell me more about mom." I was more interested in hearing about her than training. If this sword was my mother's, that means she made that enchanted stone tablet. She had made a seal strong enough to block mages greater than the third ring.

Just how powerful was my mother?

Those thoughts stopped with my father's abrupt, "No."

I wanted to fight him then and there. I had a right to know more about my mother.

"Can I see your spatial ring?" my father asked, changing the topic. I sighed and handed it over.

He put it in his pocket.

"Dad, what are you doing?" Was he just taking away the ring?

"Training starts now." He pushed me under the force of the waterfall.

It crushed me, sending me on my hands and knees. I could barely hold myself.

It didn't last long before I fell flat on the rock. I felt like I was being slammed by a thousand hammers.

"What are you doing?" I shouted through the roar of water.

"Training," my father said simply. "We need to break you down, break your limits. Truth is, you can't heal the damage to your meridians."

"Then what?" If we weren't healing my meridians, then what were we doing?

"The only way is to completely grind them to dust, so you can start over again."

"Mom did this too?" I asked.

He nodded. "And far worse. The stories of her family's training would put anything you've seen to shame. She would say 'a mercy to oneself is no mercy at all'. Training must be tough in order to survive."

What he said sparked something in me. It was almost like I could picture my mother in the same position years ago. I pushed with everything I had to get up.

Fighting against the waterfall seemed like an impossible task. It wasn't a small curtain of water; it was a roaring waterfall that pressed me to the rock below.

But I refused to give up. If this is what it took, then I'd bear with the pain the same way my mother did. I'd walk in her footsteps and recover my cultivation.

The real pain started when my skin became raw and started splitting under the force of the waterfall. The pressure threatened to bend my spine, but I would rather break than bend.

Even my enhanced strength from awakening my bloodline was nothing before the persistent power of nature. Eventually, I passed out from the pain and woke up in a pit of liquid.

"What's going on?" I pulled out my hand; it was sticky and smelt like medicine from the dark liquid in the pit. My arms itched.

"It's a medicinal bath." My father was about ten feet away, barbecuing a large hunk of meat.

"What's in it? It really itches." I started scratching, but it just wasn't helping, like I couldn't quite reach the itch.

"Why don't you summon your mana beast? I'm curious to see her."

Aurora appeared at the edge of the pit. "Hi," she said awkwardly.

"Well, aren't you a darling? I hope my son hasn't treated you poorly." My father seemed completely unconcerned that she was a humanoid mana beast.

"No, not at all. It's a pleasure to be bound to Isaac," she said, tucking her dress under her and sitting down next to the fire.

They started chatting, but I was distracted by just how itchy I'd become. "Dad, what's in this bath? I'm so damn itchy."

Aurora turned and sniffed at the liquid before recoiling in shock. "That's poison! What are you doing?"

My father put out an arm to stop her from dragging me out. "Sometimes there's not much difference between poison and medicine. Yes, that's a poison to dissolve someone's meridians, but in this case, that's exactly what he needs."

I sucked in a breath, realizing just what was happening in my body as I looked into my inner world. Sure enough, the 'medicinal' effect of the bath was seeping in and clearing away my shattered meridians.

Looking back out at my father, I gritted my teeth and made a decision. "I can take more. It only itches."

He raised a brow but didn't say anything, directly producing a vial of powder. "It doesn't take much." He warned Aurora as she took the vial.

I nodded to my lovely mana beast. She sprinkled just a bit into the pool, letting me stir it in with my arms. The itching increased to pinpricks; it was uncomfortable, like being bitten by a thousand ants. But this was nothing if it helped be back on the path of cultivation.

Not wanting to wait, I pulled the poison into my inner world and began circulating it as I had when I forged my meridians.

I pushed through, gritting my teeth as the pain built and built until I passed out from my first lesson on breaking down my meridians so I could reform them.

Chapter 18

It had been three days at the waterfall. The intensity had increased significantly with each day. Aurora had ended up deciding to hide in her ring, saying it was too hard to watch. My father remained by my side, pushing me through his steady presence.

At first, my father had started sending sand and gravel down the waterfall to hammer out my body, but now we were up to fist-sized chunks of rock.

I grit my teeth as my bones cracked from the hammering of stones coming down the waterfall.

This was ridiculous. He was going to kill me.

My body was much tougher than it had been a few days ago, but it was not a happy experience. It felt like every bone had been broken and re-forged at this point, and every muscle was bruised beyond recognition. I'd grown a new appreciation for muscles I hadn't realized I had before.

But I continued to let the waterfall temper my body. I had already grown enough in strength to sit up straight in the torrent.

When the stones finally stopped coming, I opened my eyes and found my father before me.

He looked at me with pride. "You did good. Only someone with a bloodline like your mother's could withstand that."

"Now we need to get you used to this new body."

I didn't wait for him to attack. I burst out of the waterfall with a punch to his chest.

He blocked me and grabbed my elbow, tossing me to the shore.

Ducking into a roll, I gathered the momentum of the toss and came back up ready to fight.

My father was already before me, sending his own punch. I could feel that he wasn't using more mana than a first-ring cultivator.

I still barely managed to divert his fist by swinging in with my own.

"Good, now try and use your bloodline."

He sent another fist, this one stronger than the last.

I crossed my arms and took the blow, stumbling back a few steps.

"Again," he shouted, not giving me a chance to recover.

I matched his punch with one of my own, trying to eke out all the power in my body, but it didn't come. I was knocked back again.

A fist rapidly grew in my vision before I could stabilize myself. This one had more force than the previous two.

Badump

I felt my blood surge and my body swelled with strength.

"HA!" I shouted as I met his fist again, this time not giving ground.

We descended into a flurry of punches and kicks. Each attack of his was growing steadily stronger, pushing my new speed and strength to its limits.

My attack finally made it through his blocks and landed on his chest. It felt like I had just punched a steel wall, but it called an end to the exercise.

"Fantastic. By the end there, I was using the strength of a late first-ring cultivator," my father exclaimed. But it seemed like he wasn't just talking about my strength. He was impressed with the power of my mother's bloodline.

"That means with my mana, I might be able to take on second-ring cultivators?" I asked, somewhat amazed myself.

"Unfortunately, second-ring cultivators have control over their nascent soul—that's a step you won't easily cross. Not to mention they will have stronger spells and likely better equipment."

I sighed. I guess I really was a bumpkin. Even if I was physically stronger, a fist will still lose out against a sword.

"Now we need to work on your mana." He placed a hand on my chest, and I felt his sharp metal mana searching inside my body like razor blades.

"Your meridians are completely gone; you can restart your Meridian Forging."

"Yes!" I couldn't help but shout for joy.

"Now you must carve back out your meridians and start the process of advancing your first ring. You must completely temper your meridians before you fill your second ring." My father gave me a stern look.

"This is your foundation of your cultivation. Rushing it is completely useless. Nourish your meridians until they can take no more before focusing on advancing to the second ring. If your foundation is weak, your path in cultivation will crumble."

He handed me back my spatial ring and continued. "It would be best for you to join a sect and practice their techniques." He paused, a brief look of sadness crossing his face.

I could feel my father pulling away.

"You don't need me for this next part." He quickly turned away and looked at the horizon.

Something felt off. "What do you mean?"

My father looked back at me, sighing. "Going through this with you, doing what I did with your mom. All of this has just made me want to set off and look for your mother."

"But you said you weren't sure where she was."

"Yes, the journey will be long. I can feel that there will be many opportunities to grow along the way."

"So, you're leaving?" I wasn't sad. If anything, I was proud that, when the opportunity finally came for my father to hunt down my mother came, he took it.

I wasn't the son of a coward; he would chase after what was his.

"Good luck. Go find mom."

He smirked. "I will. You don't need me anymore; it's time to spread your wings, Isaac. Do what you want with the house. Oh, and the sword. Your mother said it was an heirloom of her family. Apparently, it's pretty important. Don't show it off before you are strong enough to protect it."

We had one last meal together in companionable silence. I understood how hard this was for him. But, at the same time, now that mages could leave Locksprings, he also needed to spread his wings.

It was a silent goodbye. I told myself it was just a parting, not a goodbye. I could tell my father was a bit choked up but determined.

When he was finally out of sight, I turned back towards town. I had my own path to walk. One my father had spent his entire life preparing me for.

It wasn't too long into the way back before three bronze wolves found me.

I pulled out a sword from my spatial ring.

"Sorry, pups, but I need to test out my new strength." I had to forcibly cycled mana through myself, getting ready for the fight.

The wolves didn't even acknowledge my apology before they lunged. Their movements seemed much slower than the past.

Easily sidestepping all three of them, my sword flashed, and the leader of the group split in two with a spray of blood.

The other two turned and froze, seeing their companion dead so quickly.

I flashed forward, slicing through the air, sending two more wolf heads into the air.

Grinning, I took my loot and kept on towards town.

***

I closed the door behind me, stepping back into my home. It felt like a lifetime ago that I left here for the trip outside the city.

My father was gone then too, but the house suddenly felt quieter.

Knowing we wouldn't be disturbed, I summoned Aurora from my first ring.

She tackled me as she appeared, and I held her as we both slumped to the floor.

"Welcome back," I said, feeling the emotion in my voice. I hadn't realized just how much I had missed her these last few days.

She shook, and I could feel my shirt quickly getting wet.

I drew her closer and combed through her hair with my fingers. "It's okay. It's okay, Aurora."

She raised her head to look at me. Those emerald green eyes sparkled with tears. "It was so awful. I had to watch as you nearly

207

died time and time again!" She sniffed. "And I couldn't even kill anybody!"

"I'm a mage, Aurora. I'll have to fight life and death battles."

She put on a stern face that did nothing to diminish her beauty. But then she broke into another round of tears that tugged at my heart.

If roles were reversed, I knew I'd be a mess watching Aurora become injured repeatedly.

Scooping her up into a princess carry, I had to be careful of her wings, but luckily, she was even lighter than she looked.

I laid her in bed, and she curled around me.

"I love you, Isaac." Her admission caught me off guard, and when I didn't respond, she got nervous. "You don't have to say it back. But watching you the last few weeks... I... I don't know what I'd do if I lost you."

Aurora sat up, and I kissed her tenderly.

Heat blossomed from our lips as we melted into each other. Her lips tasted like lavender and mint. I pushed her down, deepening the kisses, wanting more.

I let my tongue explore her mouth slowly as we learned each other's bodies once again.

When we finally broke the kiss, I looked into her eyes. "It's crazy. I've barely known you, Aurora, but I love you too."

Her eyes watered with happy tears. "I've been with you your whole life. It's not crazy."

Then her nose wrinkled. "But you are filthy. How about we take a bath?"

"Aurora, about Michelle..." I hesitated on how to bring this up best.

But the corner of her eyes crinkled with mirth. "Yes, and Kat. You are a busy man."

I chuckled. "Yes. I just wanted to make sure you were okay with it?"

She bobbed her head and just replied, "Yep, I approve of both of them. But if they hurt you, they disappear from this world." She said the last in a chipper tone that sent shivers down my spine.

"Master, I expect lots and lots of women in your bed. That's a sign of strength. And my master will be strong."

I looked at her a bit blank. I hadn't expected her to want even more women. "More than three women? You really want that?"

She nodded. "I want your other rings to be filled with lovely women that will be my sisters. Like Mei. She'll be a great addition."

"Mei? The little fox?" I frowned, wondering what she knew. "Something you want to tell me about Mei?"

Aurora giggled. "She's close to being able to take a human form. Mei is going to be so pretty."

"Really? How does that work."

Aurora started to speak, but then snapped her mouth shut. "It's just, when mana beasts grow strong enough, we can take human form. Just not quite human." She wiggled her wings for emphasis.

"Now hush and let me take care of you." Aurora shooed me off to the bath and took care of the bed and clothes.

She was gentle as she took the washcloth and slowly scrubbed every inch of me with tenderness. There was no lust as she washed me, just pure adoration.

In the end, I must have been exhausted, because as soon as I touched the bed, I was out like a light.

***

Last night had been filled with tender affection from Aurora.

But this morning, it was time to get back to class. This was the final one before we went to our first dungeon.

Stepping in, many in the class turned to me, watching.

For what, I had no idea. But when Michelle turned around, clearly having worked hard on herself today, I had an inkling.

Waving at her, she smiled so bright it lit up the room.

She stood up and many in the class focused on her. It was certainly hard not to.

Michelle had put her hair up in a bun with a few ringlets falling down, framing her beautiful face. Her blue eyes were matched by a low-cut silken shirt that fought to keep her chest pressed together. Her pale breasts were a mouthwatering display of flesh. She picked up her stuff and pressed them to her chest, making her cleavage even deeper, before strutting over to me and dropping her books on my desk. Then she leaned in for a kiss.

It was hot and heavy as she pressed her soft skin to me. I responded and pried open her mouth, sucking on her tongue.

The class erupted in whispers and laughs as she broke the kiss off.

"What was that?" I asked, not at all disappointed.

She blushed all the way down to her chest. "My moms have been… encouraging me to be aggressive the last few days. I hope you don't mind." She took the seat next to me.

"No, not at all," I said, feeling fingers trace my inner thigh.

Jonny and Steve joined us on the other side and shrugged like it was natural.

Class was about to start. The teacher walked in and stared at Michelle's empty front row seat before finding her next to me sitting contently.

"Well, I must say. I'm happy you both finally worked it out."

I kept my head high and fought back the burning in my cheeks as the entire class jabbered along with his comment.

Michelle kept herself sitting tall with a big smile on her face, like she was planting her flag.

I let out a breath. "So, your mom encouraged this?" I said before the class started.

"Yes, my other mothers too. Said to make sure I hooked you. How am I doing?" Her fingers continued to play with the inside of my thigh.

"Pretty good honestly. Want to play hooky?" I said, half-joking.

"My place or yours?"

"Mine, dad is out." Her fingers trailed over my stiff member.

"Great, your place to study after class."

"After—"

The teacher cleared his throat and looked at me. "Time to get started if you are done." His tone made it more of a statement than a question.

I gave him my best smile and kept my mouth shut, though Michelle's fingers were still playing to their own beat under the table. She really was going to kill me.

Trying to distract myself from Michelle, I took a look at the class. A number of seats that were previously filled were now empty.

In the pit of my stomach, I knew they didn't just miss class today. These were the costs of our previous exercise.

"Now. I want to congratulate all of those that managed to make it back here," the teacher said solemnly. "Some of your groups will get shuffled around, but all of your veterans said you would be worth taking into the dungeon."

I couldn't help but wonder, looking at each of the empty seats, what had gotten each of them. Were the others killed by mana beasts or by our new visitors in town?

I barely paid attention for the rest of class. None of what he said seemed important. Rhys family, the strength of my father, Kat leaving the city for somewhere I supposedly couldn't follow.

It's all tied together. This new world brought about by the portals only cared about strength.

And there was something or somewhere much stronger than what I observed in Locksprings. I needed to explore the sects in the area. They would help me unlock what was needed to better explore.

"Stud." Michelle got my attention. "Class is over. You were really spaced out."

I got up. We needed to head to combat training now, which would likely just be a gathering to explain heading off for the finals.

"Do you think we really are frogs in a well?"

She looked startled at my question. "Those guys really got to you, didn't they?"

"Yeah, but you've seen all of the sects. We are behind, Michelle. That guy was younger than both of us and had almost finished his second ring."

"We can't do anything about the past, Stud, just push forward." She shrugged, rubbing my shoulder with her hand.

Seeing her hand reminded me, and I flipped my hand over, producing the small box I'd prepared.

She took it with a big smile and pulled the bow apart before opening it and seeing the small ring box. "Isaac…" She hesitated.

It took me a moment to realize what was up, and I could feel my cheeks heat up. "Open it. It's from our earnings. I pulled a spatial ring off those guys and sold what was inside it at the Treasure Hall."

She looked both relieved and disappointed before opening the box to see the spatial ring I had picked out.

"It's beautiful, thank you."

But I could see she didn't quite realize what it was. "Bind it to you."

There was a flicker of confusion before her eyes went wide with excitement, and she did as I asked. "No way." She looked up from the ring and pulled me in for a short kiss before staring back at her ring.

"There was a lot in their spatial ring. We all have a spatial ring now. I thought it would make everything much simpler." I remembered she had a share of beast cores too.

I transferred them from my spatial ring to hers. "These are for you too."

She played with her ring to stuff them away. It was pretty fun to make things appear and disappear with a spatial ring.

"Come on. We don't want to be too late for combat training," I said, grabbing her hand and pulling her along.

She practically skipped along holding my hand. "You know, if you want to explore outside Locksprings, I'll be there with you."

"Yeah?" I asked. We didn't know what would be beyond the small piece of the world we knew. I mean, there were maps of the world, but since the apocalypse, our world had shrunken down to the small area around Locksprings.

"Sure. I feel like you are going to outgrow Locksprings. I won't be what keeps you here. And I want to see more of the world too." She squeezed my hand.

I felt my ring thump in approval from Aurora too.

"Okay, so after the dungeon, we set off." I could feel the conviction in my voice. I was happy that Michelle had decided to come with me.

Chapter 19

I had been correct. The time for combat training had been more of a meeting than class. We all gathered around the pits and reformed groups. It almost felt like normal life again, besides the missing classmates.

We were one of the few groups to not need any change. I was thankful for that, but by the time that the new groups had been formed, we were interrupted.

An old man walked in swishing a horsetail whisk. His robes were split half gold, half silver—the Sun and Moon Hall. Another dozen men in various sect robes followed him in.

"Excuse us." The old man waved his whisk.

I could see Rigel growing red in the face as all these representatives from the sects intruded on our meeting. "We can meet after I've finished with the students."

"Oh, that's quite alright. I would love to introduce ourselves to your students," the old man said with a sly smile.

"Get out!" Rigel said before disappearing from his spot.

He reappeared in front of the old man, frozen in place, his fist firmly caught by the old man.

While it was surprising that he had blocked Rigel, what was even more terrifying was that he did it without disturbing the surroundings. Blocking someone with equal force was one thing, completely suppressing Rigel's attack was another.

I swallowed, and it sounded loud in a room quiet enough to hear a pin drop.

The old man's wrist shook, and Rigel arched gracefully back to the exact spot he had been at before. "Where was I? Oh yes, we would like to introduce ourselves. The lovely people behind me are from various sects. I'm sure many of you have met our younger generations in the last few weeks."

"We have taken an interest in you youngsters and have been asking your staff here to help facilitate some recruiting."

My eyes narrowed. Something wasn't quite right. Why would these sects be interested in Locksprings? From everything I'd come to understand, the mana here was limited, and we'd developed slowly compared to the mages outside.

But many of the people around me weren't so skeptical. There were excited whispers about all the things they had seen from the sect members that had been in town.

The room was filled with gossip, from seeing large, tamed mana beasts to cultivation techniques and spells that shocked the people of Locksprings to the core.

I realized that this moment had been planned for longer than a few days. We had been shown all these things to draw interest.

"Shut up," Rigel snapped at all of us. "What they are failing to tell you—" He cast a wary look at the man with the whisk, but when he didn't move to stop Rigel, he continued.

"What they are failing to tell you is that those of you raised here are unique. With how little mana there is in Locksprings, most of you have essentially no impurities in your mana."

The old man nodded along with Rigel. "What he says is correct. Without a ring, the human body absorbs natural mana from the food they eat. This leaves behind residue of many types of mana that seep into a mage's foundations. Many powerful families raise their children off specially cultivated foods, so they can have a more stable foundation."

So that was it. Because of the unique environment, even though we had a late start, we had higher potential. It made sense why these sects would want to pick up talent here.

Another man with gray robes stepped up and nodded to all of us gathered in the pits. "We would of course welcome you all with open arms. But, to get there, a bit of competition has sprung up amongst us.

"The fairest way to decide would really be to let all of you choose which sect to go to. But you know nothing about us, and we obviously want to evaluate you further. So, in the grand tradition of mages, we wish to hold a simple competition in town tomorrow to get to know each other better."

He cupped his hands and bowed to the old man before stepping back into the crowd of old men.

I noted his gray robes for later. If the man with the whisk was the head of this crowd, then the other man to speak must be comparable. Otherwise, I doubted he would have had the chance to speak out.

If they were competing for our choice, they'd also compete with each other for attention.

Rigel stepped forward. "That's enough for today. We have two days before our trip to the dungeons. As long as you show up fit for a dungeon, what you do between now and then is none of my concern."

I could see the sect representatives smiling in their victory. Even if Rigel had the authority here, they held the strength to back their interests. They turned and walked out the door.

Rigel paused, looking like he was debating saying more before he clapped and dismissed the class. Promising Jonny and Steve I would meet up with them tomorrow, I headed home with Michelle in tow.

This moment between Michelle and I had been simmering for years. And after the stolen moments outside town, we'd become a full out boil.

Part of me wanted to say this was too fast, but we'd both accepted a dangerous path. Why not make the most of the current moment together?

I'd never know when the end was coming, and it could come unexpectedly in the world of mages and mana beasts.

All of a sudden, a large body blocked my path, breaking me from my thoughts. The brute that had been after Michelle before was back.

Grant cupped his hands and nodded to Michelle. "I've come to offer you a spot in my Earthen Monastery." He acted as if I didn't exist, and I could feel my blood pump as if my bloodline was offended.

He didn't really beat around the bush, but Michelle just clung closer to me and waited.

I smiled. "Thank you, Grant, but we have other plans."

His slab of a face twitched. "I wasn't talking to you."

"Oh, my mistake. Well, we have plans already if you'd just step aside." Motioning to the side, I tried to give him the out. My bloodline was already starting to warm up, sensing the potential conflict.

"Nah. Michelle is coming with me, and there's not really anything you can do to stop me." Grant moved fast for his massive frame. His punch was fast, but it was nothing compared to my father.

My hand grabbed his fists like a vice. My bloodline beast roared like a dragon coming out of its lair once more to assert its claim. As strength surged through me, I clenched, and Grant's hand spurted blood as it turned into a mangled mess.

He howled, completely caught off guard by my strength.

I grabbed his shoulder and slammed him down to his knees in front of me. "She is not going with you. She is with me. It's pretty simple. Try to remember your manners next time." I pushed him down a bit extra, emphasizing the point.

Michelle overcame her shock and gave me some space, but a cocky grin had split across her face. She hadn't seen me fight since my father had helped me fix my meridians.

"Make him kowtow," someone in the crowd shouted.

I hadn't noticed the gathering crowd until then, and I didn't know what a kowtow was. But whatever it was, I could see a look of fear on Grant's face when he heard that.

"What's a kowtow?" I asked Michelle.

"Kneeling on the ground and bowing your head to the floor. It would be the ultimate show of subservience. You make him kowtow and I doubt he'd have the face to come back."

I certainly didn't want him to come back, but I also didn't want to evolve into a bully. "Look, agree to leave us alone, and we can both walk away from here with our honor intact." My bloodline was roaring and ready, but I had just enough control to give him one more chance.

In response, the asshat tried to shove up and attack me. I was so done with this. I looked over to make sure Michelle was good before focusing back on Grant and letting my anger flow.

I pushed down on his shoulder to force him into what Michelle had described.

Increasing the pressure on Grant, his mana blasted out as he fought me like a cornered beast. He was certainly a creature of brute strength.

Too bad for him. With my bloodline, I was a match for his strength. Circulating my own mana, I pushed down on his shoulder harder.

He fell to his hands, and I heard his elbows creak as he tried to keep his chest off the ground.

"Holy shit! He's actually forcing one of those Earthen Pigs to kowtow."

That stirred up the crowd, and I could feel more eyes on me as I slowly pushed Grants head to the ground.

"Aaarg!" Grant roared and his mana flared in a final push to stop it, but it was too late.

I pushed his forehead to the ground with a thump that rang of finality as his body went limp and he passed out in the street.

"Who is that?"

"I think it's a local."

"Damn, he managed to force Grant to a kowtow. That's crazy. I thought all these guys were weak."

"Just because he can beat Grant with brute force doesn't mean he's a good fighter."

The crowd started gossiping loudly around me.

I took a few breaths and let the high that my bloodline had given me fade. It was like a content puppy, settling back down in my heart.

The crazy thing was I could have sworn it had grown even stronger during that exchange.

"Let's go somewhere quieter." I pulled Michelle after me.

"That was pretty hot," she said after we had cleared the crowd.

"I'm not really sure what came over me," I said honestly. Part of me wanted to blame my bloodline for going crazy. But I knew that, even without it, I was feeling hot headed by his provocation.

Michelle just held my arm tighter. "I think it's more about how mana changes us, as we cultivate. Not just our bodies, but our mind and mindset. It was fair for you to put him in his place after the way he acted."

"You would think they know better than that. It's not so easy to tell someone's strength." I shook my head. If they all acted like this, Locksprings was about to become a powder keg.

"I think the younger generation from the sects are like second-rank beasts establishing their territories, pushing out competition and establishing their resources," Michelle reflected.

I had to think on that. Was mana really changing my mentality to be more like a mana beast? Or was it just natural behavior of everything in the animal kingdom, humans included, to lay stake to what was needed to survive. Since the dungeons appeared, power was more essential to survival.

***

Getting inside my house, Michelle was impatiently undressing me with her eyes.

"Want a tour?" I teased her.

"Of the bedroom," she said, tugging on my hand.

But I didn't want to jump straight to the bedroom. "Maybe I'll make dinner. Hungry?"

Michelle got on her knees and gazed up at me. "Isaac Hughes. Don't play stupid."

I could feel Aurora echo her statement in my chest. I internally rolled my eyes. This was likely not the last time I was going to be outvoted by these two.

Leaning down, I kissed her deeply, and apparently, that was the permission she needed to start on my pants.

When my half-hard cock flopped out as she pulled my pants down, she cooed to it, "You're a big boy."

Her encouragement had an immediate effect, and I started to noticeably grow in her hands as she gave it a testing lick on the head. My final willpower dissolved. Dinner could wait for the beautiful woman on her knees before me.

I twitched hard as she dragged her nails across my balls, sending a tingle up my spine.

"Remember what I told you?" she said with a smirk as she took my member in her wet mouth.

It was hard to forget when she had said she'd rock my world when we got back. I guess time was due.

Her fingers continued to tease my balls as she eased my cock further into her mouth, adding soft licks along the underside.

I braced myself on the table as she took me deeper. Her tongue starting to dance and wrap around the sensitive head.

She grabbed one of my hands and put it on the back of her head.

I took the signal and started rocking myself into her mouth.

Michelle looked up at me with her bright blue eyes, half-lidded in pleasure, and moaned. The moan added slight vibrations around my cock.

I could hear a wet squish as I realized her other hand had disappeared into her own pants.

She held eye contact with me as she bobbed on my dick, taking it deeper.

When I reached her throat I paused, waiting to make sure she was okay. She smiled a smidge, grabbing my ass and encouraging me to push deeper.

I could feel her throat open up and swallow the head of my cock.

"Mfph," she started moaning on my cock, sending tingles down to my balls in a way that I knew would finish me soon.

She squeezed my legs, and I started to thrust again, this time slowly savoring her warm throat. I wasn't going to last long, and I tapped her head letting her know.

Devouring my cock, she bottomed out, her nose in my pelvis when I grunted and released my seed, painting the back of her throat.

"Fuck. That was good," I said, starting to pull out.

But she sealed her lips around me and started licking my over sensitive head. My legs almost gave out at the sensation.

"Too much. That's too much," I groaned, not putting any effort in pulling back.

She smiled around my cock and kept at it as my cock regained its hardness and she redoubled her efforts on me.

I could barely stand as my muscles started spasming and my vision spotted.

The buildup to a second orgasm was overwhelming to the point of almost being painful. But I wanted the release so damn bad.

She had asked for it. I grabbed the back of her head and started thrusting into her welcoming mouth.

Her body shuddered in her own orgasm as a sticky hand left her pants. Her eyes were filled with raw lust, and I drove myself into her throat. Her moans finally pushed me over that second peak, another rush tearing through me.

I threw my head back and groaned loud as the second orgasm ripped itself out of me, filling my vision with spots and nearly bringing me to my knees.

Half-collapsing on top of Michelle, I flooded myself with life mana, restoring strength to my legs.

Michelle gave me a satisfied grin. "Dinner now?"

I just chuckled at her and threw her over my shoulder. "Of a kind. Where did you... uh learn that trick."

She gave a throaty chuckle. "Multiple moms remember? Harem moms really like to talk about sex, I have been... well educated."

I'd have to think more about that later.

For now, I was tossing her onto my bed and closing the door.

I pulled her up and gave her a passionate kiss before tossing my shirt aside and peeling off her pants.

She tossed her bra aside in time for me to come back up and suckle on her pert breasts. They were just a bit more than I could cup; my finger sank into her soft breasts. Her nipples were hardened to a pinpoint on her pink aureoles.

"Not too rough, they are sensitive." She pressed my face into her soft chest.

I nipped at them playfully as my hand crawled down between her legs and felt her hairless slit.

The inside of her thighs was sticky with her arousal. I let my hand play with her, softly touching, feeling for what she liked.

A soft brush of her lower lips caused her to gasp my name.

"Please, put it in."

But I wasn't done exploring her body. I left her breasts to cool in the air as I kissed my way down her flat stomach to taste her.

My tongue made slow work peeling back her lips and dipping in, languidly lapping at her insides.

Her hands were restless on my head, tugging and pulling me, begging for more.

I let myself wander from each lip, distributing my attention before teasing her pearl with a single flick.

She gasped and her legs tightened like a vice pushing me forward for more. I put my hands on her knees and pushed her legs back apart, opening her for me. "You only get more if you stay put and let me enjoy you."

I cupped her ass and dined between her legs, eliciting gasps and moans.

I could feel that she was almost there, but then she started pushing me away. "No, stop. I want you in me. I want to cum on your cock. Please."

Fuck, I couldn't deny that. Pushing off her, I towered over her, enjoying the raw hunger in her eyes. I could see the impatience. "I want it rough now. Fuck me, Stud."

I pulled her hips to the edge of the bed and drove myself into her velvet heat.

It took a moment for her to loosen up enough that I could get myself all the way in, but when I bottomed out, she let out a ragged gasp. "Yes. I'm good. I need you."

Throwing caution to the wind, I pumped into her with my full strength. She was also a mage and could handle it.

Her back arched, lifting her off the bed as I rushed headlong into our shared pleasure.

She bounced on the bed to the rhythm, her breasts a sinful wave of flesh with each thrust.

I cradled her with one arm while dipping my finger into her slit for her pearl, which seemed to elicit unintelligible words from her. They seemed to end in mention of her coming, which was more of a moan than a word.

It didn't take much for her to slip over the edge, and I could feel myself cum with her as her silken love massaged me over my own cliff.

We both collapsed onto the bed, and I let my life mana restore my body.

Sighing in contentment, Michelle propped herself up in bed and looked around the room. "Pin me against the door next." She looked back at me, smiling wickedly.

It was a good thing I had life mana. I went to get up to carry her to the door, but I was pushed back down. Michelle was quickly on top of me, using her mouth to bring me back to the ready.

Chapter 20

Waking up, I saw Michelle's toned behind disappearing into her pants.

"Morning." She noticed I was awake and gave me a quick kiss. "Mind if I make breakfast?"

"You make breakfast too? Score." I rolled out of bed with a stretch. "Want help? If not, I'm going to go wash up."

"Nah, I'm good. Just don't let my food get cold." She tried to scowl, but it just came out like a cute pout.

"Wouldn't dream of it."

I barely dozed last night; Michelle had been insatiable. Luckily, like most mages, I found myself needing less sleep as I grew stronger—a break to meditate at lunch and I'd be golden.

Stepping into the bathroom, I felt Aurora thump hard against her seal with impatience, making me smile.

I let her out, a bit worried she would regret me having a relationship with Michelle.

But boy was I wrong. She kissed me deeply, tasting Michelle off my lips.

I turned on the shower before Aurora could start talking, not quite sure if I should tell Michelle about her.

"How are you, Aurora?" I checked the water temperature.

"Great! You were so great last night." She held my hand and kissed it a few times. She really seemed excited about my time with Michelle.

I hadn't been expecting that emphatic of a reaction. I was a bit at a loss.

She giggled into her hand. "You are going to be a very powerful mage, Master. It is only natural that you will have many women. Some will stay, some will go. But I hope you plan to keep Michelle around. I really like her."

Reaching out to the shower, it was warm, and I stepped in, Aurora following me.

"I'll wash you."

"No funny business. I can't let the food get cold. And it feels weird with Michelle out there and her not knowing." I emphasized it by waiting for her response, making sure she understood that I was serious.

"I'd never disrespect my harem sister like that," Aurora said, nodding.

"Harem sister?" I raised a brow, and Aurora started soaping up her hands.

"Yeah, or I can just call her my sister? I mean, we are both in your harem, and she said her mothers call each other sisters. Of course, she doesn't know it yet... but maybe we can tell her soon."

"You want to tell her already?" I asked, getting started on my hair.

"Master, she's been in love with you for a few years. If it didn't fade then, I don't think it will fade in the future."

I opened my mouth to protest, but she just put a soapy finger to my lips to stop me.

"Don't worry about it too much. Just enjoy your time with her."

"Thanks." I knew Aurora had been with me my whole life, but she could have turned out any of a dozen ways. I was lucky that she had become so caring and thoughtful.

"Now we need to talk about the dungeon." Aurora's voice grew serious. "I won't be able to fight in the dungeon, nor this competition. I can't let any of these sect elders see me."

"What will they do?" I raised my brow.

Aurora gave me a peck on the cheek. "They will be incredibly jealous of you, maybe even kill you. But they certainly will try and find a way to extract me from your ring."

"There are other humanoid mana beasts?" I knew that might be possible, but the way she said all of it made me realize these sects would recognize her value.

"Yes, I know there are. Though, I haven't met any. But I doubt there are many attached to a single-ring mage." She gave me a tug of my manhood.

"No funny business," I reminded her, trying to look stern.

Aurora pouted before winking and hopping out of the shower, grabbing a towel to dry me off.

"I can dry myself off," I said, grabbing for the towel.

She pulled it away and got down on her knees, starting at my feet and gently drying me off inch by inch. "No, I enjoy this. I might seem weird, but remember," she pointed to herself, "not human. Not really. When I'm inside your ring, I watch. That's all I can do— watch you do everything. Sometimes you struggle, sometimes it's the little things. I just want to reach out and help. I hate that all I can do is watch."

She looked up at me, her emerald eyes slightly wet with tears. It pulled at my heartstrings.

"So when we are alone, please let me do the small things." She continued to dry me off, leaving occasional kisses. I didn't have the heart to tell her to stop again.

I pulled her up and held her for a long loving kiss. "I love you, Aurora."

Aurora had seen me at my best and worst almost the entirety of my life. I was falling for her quickly. She knew me completely, and that had a level of trust in me that was undeniable. I still lingered on the idea of her free will, but I would do my best to make her life worth living. After all, we were joined together body and soul for the rest of our lives. If I let the doubt poison our relationship, it would be my fault.

She blushed and looked up at me with dazzling eyes. "I love you too, Isaac."

"Now let me finish so you can get to your warm breakfast." She focused with a determined expression and hurried about drying me.

Finishing, she gave me one last peck on the cheek before vanishing into her ring. I touched the mark on my chest lovingly and could feel a warm pulse from her in return.

***

"You look happy," Michelle said, starting to plate pancakes as I came downstairs.

I sniffed my way over to her. "Blueberry?" I hugged her from behind, feeling a little weird that I'd just spent time with Aurora. I needed to tell Michelle about Aurora soon.

She slapped away my hand with a spatula. "Yes, but you have to wait. I'm making the plates pretty."

I leaned on the counter and watched as she quartered a strawberry and focused on drizzling syrup in patterns on the two stacks of golden and blue spotted pancakes.

"There," she said, picking up both the plates and carrying them to the table.

I grabbed the bottle of syrup and brought it with me.

"No. You are not going to drown my hard work in syrup." Michelle snatched the syrup out of my hand, jumping out of the way as I went to grab it back.

"Aren't pancakes just a vehicle for me to eat syrup?" I feinted to the side before diving forward and tackling her to the ground, ending up on top of her. She squirmed a bit under me, but I knew she wasn't really putting up a fight.

As I went to grab the syrup, she chucked it across the room and grabbed my face, pulling me in for a kiss.

As we pulled apart, she kept hold of my face. "Just try the pancakes first. I put a little cinnamon sugar in them." I took in the importance in her eyes, so I nodded. Standing up, I helped her up and we went over to the table.

She watched me as I cut out a section of the pancakes and eyed it suspiciously.

Popping it in my mouth, I was amazed. It was delicious! She had put more than just cinnamon in them. I got hints of vanilla and lemon that mixed with the blue berries in a delicious pop.

They were really good, even with minimal syrup. I took a second bite without adding more syrup, and her grin was so wide she nearly broke her face.

"You look far too happy," I teased.

"Just lesson number two from my mothers. Lesson one was the cock. Lesson two was the stomach." She winked before starting in on her own stack.

I wasn't complaining. If she really was this good of a cook all the time, I would eat well. And I'd enjoy it while I could. We were heading back out into the woods soon, and she wouldn't have more than a campfire to use.

The spatial ring I gave her caught a bit of light, and I suddenly had a great idea.

"We still have today and tomorrow before we need to head out, right?" I asked.

"Yeah, but I need to head back home and pack. You can't keep me in bed for the next two days." She looked at the ring with a smile. "You have no idea how much easier this thing is going to make packing."

I had been thinking similarly. "My dad is leaving Locksprings. I'm going to take what I want from the house. I was thinking... we could work up the food that's left before we head out, and we could also take all the spices."

A look dawned on her face. "Oh. Oh! No trail bars!"

"Yup," I said, cutting more of the delicious pancakes. "How about I come help you pack after breakfast, and you come back to help me make some food?"

She had an excited grin on her face. "No better way to a man's heart than through his stomach," she quoted someone, probably one of her mothers.

I watched her pause for a moment, a sad look coming over her face.

Replaying the conversation, I assumed the look was from needing to leave her mothers for a while. "It's alright. We can come back and see them in a bit. But first, we need to get stronger and improve our cultivation."

"Yeah," she agreed with a muted nod. "Can you come help me pack and meet them? Maybe have dinner with them after the competition today?"

Meet the parents already? It had been quick, but I realized I did feel comfortable with it. I nodded and hoped they would go easy on me. Maybe multiple mothers would work in my favor. One had to like me, right?

Smiling to myself, I got up and started packing my things. I managed to grab quite a few things before we headed over to Michelle's parents.

As we walked up to her house, I took it in. The place was huge. She said her father did well as a merchant despite the scant visitors, but she may have undersold it.

I wanted to knock, wondering if a butler would open the door, but Michelle marched right on in the front door.

Following, I felt a bit out of place in the grand entrance, which had a chandelier and spiral staircase.

In the room next to the entranceway sat a petite brunette reading on a couch.

The gorgeous woman looked up and saw Michelle, smiling. As her eyes shifted to me, they went wide.

"Michelle. Now where have you been all night?" It sounded like she was trying to scold her, but it came out as a half-laugh.

"Hi, mom." Michelle ducked her head to hide her blushing.

The woman looked like she could be Michelle's older sister.

"This must be Isaac." The woman glided across the entranceway to size me up.

"Mom, we just came to pack for the trip." Michelle had wanted me to meet them, but she seemed to be trying to escape. Was this mother the embarrassing one?

Her mother turned and called into the house. "Michelle is home, with a friend." The way she said friend was filled with double meanings.

I heard something fall and the pitter patter of someone running.

A buxom blonde that had to be Michelle's actual mother stepped into the entranceway, smoothing down her shirt like she hadn't just been running. "My dear."

She gave Michelle a hug and then the brunette mother after making sure Michelle was still in one piece before turning to me.

"What a cutie," she said eying me like a piece of meat.

I admittedly puffed out my chest a smidge, and I took the chance to get a better look at her mom. Michelle's mother was fit and curvy. Her curves still proudly fought gravity.

"Could you stare a bit harder?" Michelle laughed, nudging me in the side.

"No no, it's okay. Please get a preview of what Michelle will be like in the future." The blonde mom glided her hands over her hip up to her chest, showing off how thin her hips were before catching her chest and squeezing while turning and wiggling her hips to show off her figure.

"Mom!" Michelle's face went beet red, and she tried to hide in her hands.

"What? We like Isaac, remember? Isaac, what do you think, Michelle will still be pretty for a long time?" she said it like she was fishing for compliments. Mages could live a long time, and many of the women fought to keep their youthful looks.

"I think Michelle is beautiful," I said, not sure what was safe.

But it didn't seem to help as Michelle got even redder. I hadn't realized that was possible.

She grabbed my hand and pulled me past her mothers, escaping up the stairs.

"I warned you," she said, sighing as she closed her bedroom door.

"All good. Parents are embarrassing." I walked up, wrapping my arms around her and pulling her into a hug.

"You have no idea, they are so... open. Too much information is not a thing here." Michelle squirmed out of my embrace and walked towards the closet. She started waving her hands about in it, taking an assortment of clothes into her spatial ring.

"So the blonde is your mom mom?"

"Yes, she is the one who gave birth to me. Rachel has brown hair, and Raven who you did not meet, thank god, has black hair," Michelle said it as she packed in a flurry.

"Why don't you want me to meet Raven?" I twiddled my thumbs, sitting on her bed.

"She would probably try to demonstrate how to please you better with you in the room."

I couldn't see her face, but I could tell there was an eye roll in there. I chuckled. I couldn't pretend I hadn't enjoyed all of the previous lessons she must have had from Raven.

Michelle made quick work of her room, snatching up most of her closet and her bathroom essentials.

"Okay, I think I am about done," Michelle announced, and I peeked into her closet. It was nearly bare.

"I know it's a spatial ring, but it wasn't that big, was it?" I eyed the closet size.

She gave me a flat look. "I am a master at packing." I decided I shouldn't let her get a good look inside my spatial ring.

I noticed Michelle start to eye her bed. It did look inviting, but I was not about to give her moms more fodder. Walking over, I gave her a kiss, and held her hand as we headed towards her door.

Michelle tugged my arm, pulling me back before I opened the door. "I think I've had about all I can take. Help me escape?"

Her eyes held a plea I couldn't ignore. "Sure."

Despite being quiet, Michelle's mom stopped us on our way out.

"Leaving already? You're just here to collect your things?" Her mom's voice held a bit of hurt.

"No, just with the spatial ring—it made sense to put my belongings in it." Michelle didn't quite answer the question, clearly picking up on her mom's sadness.

Her mother sniffled. "You're leaving me after one night with him? He must be fantastic in bed."

I nearly fell over hearing Michelle's mom say that.

"It's not like that. We are preparing to head out, but it will be a few days." I tried to alleviate some of the stress.

Michelle's mom perked up. "Goodie. You two go have fun and come back for dinner!" She nodded happily, walking away before Michelle could object.

Michelle practically dragged me out. "You've done it now. We have to come back and... and..."

"And?"

"God the things my mothers will say at dinner." Michelle hid her face. "They really have no shame."

I chuckled. Her mothers were lively, and a part of me envied how close she clearly was to all of them.

"It'll be fine. I mean, what could be more shameless than last night when you—"

"You dare say that in public and I'll never do it again."

I knew the threat was mostly a joke, but I shut my mouth because I could feel a kernel of truth.

We settled into a comfortable pace, walking through the city. And I took a moment to appreciate the beauty walking next to me.

We had already grown a lot closer in the time since I'd been back. We'd even agreed to travel together indefinitely. I was committed to both her and Aurora, two beautiful, intense women.

And they had both indicated interest in more partners. How another woman would fit into our trio I couldn't guess, but I figured I'd just see what happened.

Coming up to a junction in the road, I directed us toward the site that would be the competition later today. The competition was only open to first-ring mages, and I wanted to get a feel for the sects.

The sign-up area was crowded. We got in the long line.

A martial stage I had never seen before stood in the middle of the city, with half of a stadium surrounding it.

"Didn't there used to be houses here?" Michelle asked, confused.

"Pretty sure there were. But... how did they make this so fast?" I looked at the polished stone stadium and the bright white martial stage set in the center like the crown jewel.

"I bet all the materials are mana infused, so we don't destroy them." Michelle was also stunned by the display.

"Hello, you two. Are you locals joining the tournament?" A man in blue robes stepped up to the two of us.

"My Mountain Sea Gate is offering some low-level spells and martial arts to those we see a good future in." He smiled wide enough that his cheeks partially hid his eyes.

Michelle and I exchanged a look. While he was offering techniques without expressly saying there was a cost, it would be poor form to take the techniques and not join his sect later.

"Thank you for your kind offer," I said, neither asking for it nor denying. It was becoming trickier to work with their customs, but if I could avoid annoying all of them, that would be best.

I was probably on the Earth Flame Sect's must-kill list and had also offended Grant's sect.

It was all starting to become complicated, and we would likely need to join a sect for not only their resources but the protection to have a chance to cultivate.

I assumed with the Mountain Sea Gate coming before the tournament, they were likely weaker than the rest and trying to lock people in before the stronger sects could get to them. Given my and

Michelle's status in Locksprings before the sects came, I thought we'd have a decent chance at impressing the best.

Michelle had said something to the man while I was thinking, and he politely bowed off without handing anything over.

"Not interested?" I asked.

"Not if it doesn't include you," she said, and I felt a moment of warmth.

"Do you know enough about the sects to have an idea which one you'd want to join?" Since I'd spent a lot of my time training with my father since being back, I was a bit clueless on what all of these sects were about.

Michelle pointed to someone in the same gold and silver robes as the old man who had interrupted our class. "That's the Sun and Moon Hall. They are still the top dogs here, but... they say..." She blushed.

"They say what?" I played dumb to mess with her, but I knew what she was going to say

"They cultivate during sex." She lowered her voice so the other people in line wouldn't hear us.

My smile dropped as I thought about what I'd learned in the brothel. I needed Michelle to know so that she would protect herself. "Michelle, they harm the women to increase the men's cultivation."

"What?" She pulled back, shocked.

I pulled her close and whispered about what I had learned and seen.

"That's terrible." She looked pale. "We have to save her."

I smiled that Michelle's first thought was to go up against a sect to save Narissa.

I pulled her close and kissed her forehead. "I know, I want to too, but first we need to grow stronger or it won't be more than throwing ourselves on a sword."

She nodded and looked back over at the registration tables. There was a good representation of all the sects around the stadium.

"Teal robes over there, that's the Treasure Hall; Red is the Earth Flame sect... led by the Rhys family. They aren't anywhere near as strong as the Sun and Moon Hall, but people say the Sun and Moon Hall backs them."

She continued looking around. "That dried up mustard stain color is the Earthen Palace where Grant is from. They are one of the lower-tier sects here."

She was turning her head looking for one more before she finally pointed out someone walking by in another direction. "Them, they are the Ferrymen. The grayish blue robes. The Ferrymen are an odd one; they don't seem to be doing much recruiting or show much outright power, yet all of the other sects give the Ferrymen respect."

That was interesting. "What else do you know about them?"

"They seem to have fewer members than the rest," Michelle added.

But as I looked around at the various sects and then at the Ferrymen, there was a stark difference. Everyone else wore jewelry or had ornate stitching on their sect robes. The Ferrymen were... drab.

It was that simplicity that drew me to them. They seemed focused on cultivation, far more than many of the other sects putting on airs.

"Have you heard anything bad about the Ferrymen?" I asked her, still watching the crowd and hoping to see another member.

"No, like I said, people respect them—"

"People don't respect them for nothing. These sects only respect strength," I said, a bit of a hard edge sneaking into my tone.

I kept watch on the crowd and the members of each sect, watching how they interacted with each other. I eventually divided them into three tiers. The Sun and Moon Hall and Ferrymen seemed to be in the top tier. The Earth Flame Sect, Treasure Hall and Thousand Blossom Valley took the second tier. The rest, while present in my mind, were on the third tier and not where I wanted to end up.

The line finally ended, and we stepped up to a table manned by someone from the Thousand Blossom Valley. She was a thin woman, but I had learned from Michelle that they were all very dangerous women training in poison arts. If I hadn't known better, I would have called her a cute girl next door type.

"Would you like to register for the martial competition? We'll have to check your cultivation before you can challenge someone," she said almost robotically, clearly having said it many times before.

"Yes, we'd both like to sign up."

"Great. Sign here and let me take your bone age and cultivation levels." The woman gave us a form before holding her palm up for our hand.

I realized this was more than just a tournament to see our skills—they were using it to collect ages and cultivation status to further enhance their knowledge of us.

We each took our turn as she used her mana to sense our ages. Inspecting bones using mana was the best way to know someone's true age. Mages often used spells or resources to look younger.

"Now that you've registered, you should know there are prizes beyond showing off to a sect." She handed me a pamphlet and waved forward the next in line.

I took it and walked away with Michelle. "There are some good things in this, but ultimately, it doesn't seem like much compared to what we could probably get if we were to join a sect."

"Of course, they wouldn't give away the good things," Michelle huffed. "It really does seem like it is all about drawing us into one of their organizations."

The pamphlet was almost like a bounty list; the sects had put rewards for defeating their own people.

I shrugged, agreeing. These sects were essentially training grounds where they used competition to filter out the best and brightest to focus their resources on. It didn't surprise me one bit that they were looking for mages that could beat their current disciples.

"Looks like we have a few hours before we have to be back for the group stage. Want to snag lunch?"

Michelle hooked her arm in mine. "Lead on."

The diner was rowdy as more and more people from the sects filtered in. Based on all the conversations, they were coming for two things. Many had come for the competition, with more than a few of these people having ongoing rivalries. The other draw was food untainted with mana, apparently a valuable commodity for mage families.

Lunch was going well until Hank Rhys caught my eye across the room. I saw the moment of recognition as he puffed up like a fish. Sighing, I turned back to my meal, hoping he'd deflate and chill.

233

But I had no such luck. I heard him start to rally those with him to get up.

Michelle turned, and her body went rigid when she saw the brewing commotion. "We can't fight here; we'd destroy the place."

"I don't think he cares about that." I narrowed my eyes at him in warning.

The diner grew quiet as both the mages and locals waited to see what was about to happen, sensing the growing conflict.

As soon as he got close, he kicked over our table, causing an uproar in the diner. There were no words, just violence.

The kitchen door banged open and a red-faced older man came out yelling. "There will be no fighting here."

Hank gave one of his group a wave forward and they jumped out to strike the owner.

I knew that the owner wasn't even a mage, so I threw my butter knife to intercept the attack and try to protect him.

It happened faster than the shop keeper could register, and the attacker backed off as a knife buried itself in the wall next to him.

"You would attack someone who hasn't even stepped into cultivation?" I said loud enough to get attention even outside the diner. "Completely shameless. Is this what the representatives of the Earth Flame Sect are about? Bullying the weak?" I figured a little public shaming might do the trick and protect the diner.

The crowd around me took the bait. It was like they were hit with an electric shock as they came to life, cursing and scolding the Earth Flame Sect. Food even started flying at Hank's group. I braced in case of a fight and waited for him to make his decision. My blood pumped loudly in my ears.

"I will kill you and yours." Hank puffed up his chest with the threat.

"You can try. How about we work this out in the competition? Unless you're afraid of me taking you down publicly"

"Cherish your life till then," he sputtered before he abruptly turned and rushed out, his group struggling to keep up.

Michelle tugged on my arm to get my attention. "Are you going to make an enemy out of everyone?"

I took her point. "I think the ship has long sailed with the Rhys family. I'm pretty sure he suspects that I killed his relative."

"That's fine, but I think we need to find some allies. Soon. You're strong, but we need some support," Michelle said, turning our table back up right.

The diner owner had come to his senses by now and came over to us. "This is the third time today that a fight has started. Are all of these people barbarians? Isaac, can you ask your father to get me a guard, please?"

I went to say yes, only to remember my father was gone. But, given the state of things, I thought it wouldn't go over well to spread that. "Yeah, I'll ask Tom when I see him later. But it might be worth it to get a second-ring mage to stay here. Maybe give him some free food? These guys only recognize strength."

"Ridiculous. Why can't they just be civilized?" The restaurant owner fussed with the edge of the table that had a fresh chip in it. "Which sect was it again? I'll make them pay for a new table."

I shook my head, knowing that wouldn't be a good way to go about this. They wouldn't be willing to pay and would probably laugh him out if he went to demand reparations for a damaged table.

Before I could say anything, a soft voice spoke up from a nearby table. "You probably don't want to do that. Here, if it's a big deal, let me help make up for all the intrusions we've caused."

Chapter 21

A woman in bright green robes with purple accents handed the owner a beast core. In the present economy, that was worth far more than a table was worth.

The man snatched it away and hurried back to the kitchen with only a simple thank you.

I turned to her. "Thanks, you didn't have to do that. I'm Isaac by the way."

She shrugged. "It was an effortless gesture and it probably made his day. I'm Celina from the Thousand Blossoms Valley." She extended her hand.

I managed to keep my reaction in check as I shook her hand. But a part of me was afraid that it would turn black with poison when I took it back, remembering what Michelle had said about their poison specialty. But nothing happened.

She hid her mouth as she laughed. "Oh, the look on your face. No, I don't go around poisoning everyone. Only those that deserve it." She ended the statement with a wink.

I scratched the back of my head. My reaction clearly hadn't been as subtle as I thought.

"Hi, I'm Michelle. Gosh, you are stunning.?" She shook Celina's hands while batting her eyelashes a bit. She looked back at me. "Isn't she stunning?"

It was still odd having a woman I was dating checking out other women, but it did make me take another look at Celina. She had a thinner frame, more of a waspish body than my curvy Michelle. Her hair had looked black at first, but as I looked more carefully, it had a purple sheen where light hit it right.

Her face was a bit exotic, with high brows and cheekbones that almost made her seem a bit wicked. But her plump lower lip balanced it out and gave her a pout that took away the menace.

As I looked up, I met her eyes. There was an intellect and curiosity in them that held me.

"I think he approves." Celina chuckled with Michelle, giving her a wide grin.

I cleared my throat, feeling almost like a third wheel as I looked between the two.

"Why don't you come with us? We were just heading to the arena. You could join us there?" Michelle said sweetly. Celina had been sitting alone, and it looked like she was done.

Celina laughed, and looked me in the eye, a sparkle in them. "Yeah, people don't always like to sit with the scary poison girl." She wiggled her fingers in emphasis.

"You don't seem so bad." I played it off casually, but she had already seen me be cautious at shaking her hand. It seemed like basic self-preservation to be more hesitant around such a subtle attack. It also was counterintuitive to her beauty. Usually, poisonous things in the world are bright in warning, but her beauty softened her and pulled you in.

As we walked to the stage, the girls chatted. A question surfaced in my mind, so when their conversation lulled, I jumped in. "Celina, why do the sects incite so much fighting among first-ring mages?"

"It's like making a Gu."

"Gu?"

"Oh right. Sorry, that's common knowledge in my sect. So, you make a rank one Gu by putting a hundred poisonous insects in a sealed jar. The last one surviving becomes a rank one Gu, a poisonous mana beast. Guess how you get a rank two Gu?"

"Put a hundred rank one Gu in a sealed jar?"

"Got it in one. But how many rank one Gu do you think a second-rank Gu can kill?"

"Probably more than a hundred?"

"Thousands. It is the same for the sects. A second-ring mage is far more valuable than dozens of first-ring mages that might die in the process," Celina said with such a casual air. "But don't worry, I'll be the surviving Gu." She added a little extra skip to her step, like talking about the death of a bunch of peers was totally normal practice. I'd thought things were savage before this, I couldn't imagine growing up as she must have.

237

It all seemed so heartless. "But why go through it all?"

"You get the power to do what you want."

"But don't you just go back into the next jar each time?"

"Yes and no. Each jar gets bigger and lasts longer. Some don't make it into the next jar and find other uses. Most importantly, if I lose the drive to push forward, someone will always come step on me." A glimmer of pain hid in her eyes when she said that. "We all need something to drive us forward. What's yours?"

"That's easy. I want to protect those I care about." I stepped closer to Michelle, putting my arm around her.

My mother and father were out there somewhere, each in their own struggles. If I were to help them, I needed to become stronger. And both Aurora and Michelle were incredible women. The sects would try to come for them, and if I wasn't strong enough, I wouldn't be able to defend them.

Celina studied us, a sadness in her eye. "That's a noble reason. I want revenge." The sadness in her eyes left, as a bitterness swept into them. She paused and went quiet, lost in her thoughts. She didn't seem interested in talking about it more, so I left her to her thoughts.

"What about you, Michelle? What are you fighting for?" I looked down at her.

She blushed. "I just want to stay strong enough to keep your ego in check. It's gonna be a full-time job." She leaned up, nuzzling my cheek with her nose. I lifted my head away in mock annoyance. When I looked back, I caught Celina watching us. There was some confusion in her face; it was like she was trying to figure out a puzzle she didn't have all the pieces to put together.

The stadium was getting busier by the second as we approached. The crowds funneled in, unperturbed by the press of bodies. Those that were higher cultivation simply jumped to the top of the stadium.

I watched with awe at their strength. The walls had to be four stories high, and some of these people jumped it like they were stepping over a stone.

"Those are third-ring or higher," Celina said, seeing my interest. "They are elders or sect leads from the closer branches. My sect leader is a third-ring mage; she still hasn't formed her immortal body for the fourth ring."

It was a casual comment, but something I put in the back of my mind. I had no idea what an immortal body was.

We went through the entrance and up the stairs, but when we got to the seats, my jaw dropped.

A number of fights were occurring among the younger generation over the first few rows of seats.

When I looked, the elders of each sect were all surrounded by people of the same robes sitting calmly in their spots, but there were plenty of people fighting for spots.

"Are they going to kill someone for a seat?" Michelle asked.

I shook my head. "None of them seem to be actually trying to kill the other. Injure, yes, but not kill."

Celina spoke up. "They are mostly probing each other before the tournament. Sizing each other up. It's the lower ranks in each sect starting the fights, so others in their sect can evaluate them."

I watched them again after Celina's comment, and the behavior made more sense. Those sitting calmly were trying to act casual, but they were closely watching each fight.

"Hey, you." Someone came up to me as we looked for seats.

"Not interested, go away." I didn't even turn around.

He apparently didn't care. I could feel the punch coming and turned around, ready to fight.

In a flash, Celina was inside his guard with a needle stabbed into his neck. His veins were rapidly turning black from the site where she had struck.

His eyes went wide with fear as he aborted his attack and ran away, clutching his neck. There were others waiting in the wings ready to fight too, but they all seemed to think better of it and gave us, or Celina rather, a wide berth.

"Is he going to die from that?" I asked, sitting down on a vacant seat.

"I'm sure someone will give him a detoxification pill. It shouldn't be too hard to get rid of a low-grade poison like that." She shrugged, her gaze roaming the stadium. I couldn't believe how casual it was to her.

I was starting to really understand how callous the world of mages was. It only reinforced that my own strength was paramount—that would be the difference between being crippled or doing the crippling.

Once all of the fighting over seats quieted down, a gathering of elders from the sects came down to the stage.

I recognized a number of sects: the Sun and Moon Hall, The Earth Flame Sect, Mountain Sea Gate, even a young-looking woman wearing the same robes as Celina. She must be an elder from the Thousand Bloom Valley Sect.

The old man with gold and silver robes stepped forward again, his voice loudly projecting across the stadium. "Welcome all. It will be a pleasure to watch each of you exchange pointers on the martial stage. I must ask that you refrain from fighting in the stands."

The old man was a hypocritical ass. They knew there was fighting, but only now did they ask for it to stop. I only assumed that his sect had gotten the information they wanted by that point.

"We will start the competition. The rules are simple. The winner stays on the stage. You keep going till you win five rounds or are knocked off the stage. This is a chance to measure against your peers. You are not here to settle grudges. No weapons."

I started looking into the crowd for those I'd want to challenge, but he continued. "This is to be a training exercise for our younger generation. There will be no weapons used. Please do your best not to permanently injure each other. But alas, fist and feet do not have eyes. Please gather down on the stage for the first round."

Celina scoffed, "Don't hurt anyone, but oh, accidents happen. Speaking out of the same hole he shits."

"I take it you don't care much for the Sun and Moon Hall?"

She set her jaw and breathed heavily for a moment before answering. "No, you could say I don't." Celina then turned to me. "You don't have any interest in them, do you?" Her tone was harsh, but I saw a plea in her face as well.

I waved off the beautiful poison mage. "No. They took a friend of mine back to their sect already. I've since then learned they can't be trusted."

Celina visibly relaxed at hearing that. "They do far worse things than poison mages."

Michelle put a hand on Celina. "We would love to help you get your pound of flesh from them if you want. Eventually, we'd like to try and pull our friend out of there."

Celina shook her head. "If they took her that quickly, she must be important. No way we could pull her out of that den of vipers without someone at least possessing an immortal body."

"That's the second time you've mentioned immortal body. What is it?"

She paused, surprised at my question, before settling in to explain. "To break through from the third ring to the fourth, you need to form your immortal body. Don't worry about it too much for now. You have a ways to go before you get there."

I had never heard of an immortal body, but Locksprings did not have any mage above the third ring. I wondered if this was why.

The first group gathered down on the martial stage, and I turned to pay attention.

"Looks like there are some scary people down there." I pointed out a few of the people on stage who had claimed a corner of the martial stage, while everyone else was congregating in the center.

"Those two are at the cusp of their second ring." Celina nodded towards them. One wore the gray robes of the Ferrymen and another had the Sun and Moon Hall's robes.

"Starting off with a bang," I said as the stage was covered in a fire spell from the Sun and Moon mage. I could feel the heat all the way up in the stands.

When the fire cleared, the Ferryman hadn't moved an inch and didn't seem bothered by the spell.

These were powerful mages. I wasn't sure that I could stand amid that fire without flinching.

"He lost," Celina said from my side.

I took another look, and sure enough, the Ferrymen disciple was pressing the Sun and Moon Hall disciple to the corner of the stage without using any spells, just martial arts.

"Are all the Ferrymen so strong?" I asked.

"They possess the highest individual potential, but the sect remains small. They are actually the closest sect to my own." She didn't take her eyes off the stage while she said it, like she was trying to memorize his moves.

Members of the sects continued to show off on the stage, each challenging one another and using the opportunity to show off their spells.

241

It wasn't long before they started calling on the locals to join them. I recognized Jonny as he climbed into it. He looked nervous. "There's Jonny." I pointed him out to Michelle.

"Think he will step off when it starts? I don't know if he's really cut out for this if the previous rounds were any indication of the intensity."

"I'm not sure he has a choice. That guy from the diner looks pissed" Celina said.

I found Hank on the stage, glaring daggers at Jonny. I hoped Jonny would be able to hold his own.

"You don't think they'd take it too far?" I asked Celina.

"I don't know how deep this enmity of yours goes, but to pick on your weaker friend only makes his Earth Flame Sect weak in everyone's eyes."

I gripped the seat tightly and watched the fight below. When Jonny turned to the edge of the stage at the start, I let out a sigh of relief. He had decided to forfeit.

But apparently that didn't work for Hank, who grabbed Jonny before he could forfeit and pulled him back onto the stage.

The crowd gasped. It wasn't exactly subtle, but the elders didn't react to the brutal beating that ensued on Jonny.

I ground my teeth. It would be against the rules to interfere.

But I couldn't sit still and watch Jonny get beaten like this.

I was about to jump down there and deal with it myself when a thin figure flashed onto the edge of the stage.

Jonny was still down there on the stage being beaten black and blue by Hank while the thin figure watched. The newcomer wore unrecognizable robes, and calling them robes was being generous. The thin figure was wearing mud colored rags and a necklace of wooden beads.

Before Hank took it too far, the figure was there, and his mere presence seemed to pin Hank in place. The elders of the sects seemed to be pretending to ignore the interruption in the competition.

I could only watch. It looked like the thin man was speaking to Jonny. By the way Hank looked nearby, I was guessing it didn't favor him.

When they finished, the man in rags pulled Jonny up and had him meditate to the side of the stage while he watched over him.

"Who's that?" I asked Celina.

"Looks like an Ascetic from the Daoist Monastery. They are terrifying mages, but no one actually wants to join them."

Michelle's interest was piqued. "Ascetic, as in giving up all pleasures? Oh shit, did Jonny just become celibate?"

"Yes, they practice giving up all pleasures of the body to pursue purity of the mind and soul. Like I said, terrifying mages. But what's the point of cultivation without some enjoyment?"

Michelle and I exchanged a look before we burst into laughter. "Jonny... giving up all physical pleasures... I wonder if he even knows what he just signed up for."

My laughter was cut short when I looked up and saw Hank glaring at me from the stage, as if his previous hits on Jonny were meant as a warning.

"Why don't we get closer. Probably about time to represent the locals, Michelle?"

Heading down to the stage, I passed Jonny and gave him a thumbs up, holding back a laugh. Celina came with us, but she put on an act of aloof arrogance as we got down to the stage.

She followed me to a corner of the martial stage. As we neared the stage, the other contestants moved swiftly to the side, cowering from Celina and hiding their faces.

An elder held up a gong and rang it for the start of the next fight, and I watched another set of fighters start and end quickly. In the end, both stepped down from the stage.

Grant landed on the stage and fixed me with a challenging glare.

"You don't have to accept," Celina said from my side.

"No, I do. We said we'd settle it here." I stepped up on the stage.

The elder led us through bowing to the opponent before we separated to our sides.

I had half-expected Grant to throw a few haughty insults my way. Instead, he stood across from me looking determined and serious. He'd lost the attitude he'd had the other day.

"Fight." The elder clapped his hands.

Grant wasted no time. "Pierce," he said, shoving his hands forward. Several sharp rocks made of earth mana appeared, stabbing towards me.

I batted them aside, circulating my own mana to protect me before charging across the stage.

"Do you have no spells?" Grant said, an earthen hue casting over his body as he met my charge.

"Nope," I lied. I didn't want to use Aurora's spell here. It had been too much when I had used it before, and it would be giving it away to the entire crowd of people.

"Good!" Grant cheered as our fists rang like gongs.

We met punch for punch as we both circulated our mana to supplement our bodies.

Unlike before where I was able to use my raw strength to overpower Grant, this time, his spells made up the difference.

It felt like I'd just punched a rock.

Grant grinned. He felt his advantage and followed up with a high kick.

I ducked low and went for his back leg, but again, my attack barely made any impact.

Rolling away from his next attack, I centered myself. My bloodline wasn't going to be enough. I needed to draw on the savage aspect of life mana.

My body had recovered, but my meridians weren't recovered yet. Life mana flooded me from head to toe as I lashed out in an explosive use of mana.

This time, Grant went stumbling back. Even enhanced with a spell, he wasn't a match for my strength when I used the more powerful side of my mana.

I flowed through his hasty guard and caught him in the chest, sending him airborne just enough. I grabbed him mid-air and slammed the large mage on his back.

Letting go of my mana, it flooded through my system without meridians. I could feel the strain; my body felt like it was about to burst with raw energy.

Grant groaned before rolling to the side and back to his feet. He wheezed air back into his lungs as he got back into a loose fighting stance.

The spell he had used to boost his fighting was gone. It had shattered when I'd hit him against the ground and disrupted his mana.

"I'm not done," Grant growled before taking an aggressive step forward. When his foot slapped the stage, a spike of earth mana shot out of the ground towards me.

I side stepped the spell, but more of them continued coming at me.

Grant looked tired but determined. He sent spike after spike at me trying to keep me from coming close.

Blocking and dodging, I managed to still get near him. The large mage was pale and out of breath. His mana was exhausted.

I held my punch, hitting him just enough to break his concentration and topple him over.

He stumbled and fell hard on the stage.

I waited a moment, but he seemed down for the count this time.

The elder agreed and called the fight.

"Good fight," I said, giving Grant a hand up as two others from his sect came to help him off the stage.

"Do my pride a favor and don't lose so easily going forward." Grant gave me a weak smile while his eyes contained a hint of respect.

"Deal," I said, handing him off to his fellow disciples. Oddly enough, it felt like I may have somehow just made a friend. I was still coming to grips with the world of sects, but it was clear that strength was the best way to get through anything.

With Grant out, I was suddenly aware that I was standing alone on the stage.

I was breathing heavy from the fight with Grant, but I felt great. My life mana still ran chaotically through my body. I did my best to calm myself and return it to a flow that I could use for this next fight.

Looking out, I saw a number of eager faces in the crowd itching for a fight.

The crowd churned as a plain looking girl from the Earth Flame Sect stepped up on the stage with a cocky grin.

Chapter 22

I recognized her from Hank's group. As she stepped forward, she gave me a come-hither gesture, raising her eyebrow in challenge.

The elder presiding over the stage instructed us to bow to each other and step to separate sides.

"You're gonna eat shit," she whispered as we bowed.

"Doubt it," I said, turning back towards my side of the stage.

As soon as we were in place, the elder announced the start.

I kicked off the stage and hurled myself at the member of the Earth Flame Sect. I crossed the distance in a heartbeat. She managed to block my fist but hadn't expected the force behind it. She stumbled back, a look of surprise flashing across her face before she refocused.

The woman came back at me with a spell, kicking her leg and a wave of flame roaring out at me.

The proper way to deal with spells was to respond in kind and neutralize them, but I still hadn't learned any besides Aurora's. So instead, I used brute force to neutralize the attack.

I met the fire with a punch that scattered the technique, punching straight through to her. Even with the strength reduced, I still caught her hard enough to send her reeling.

But she had enough experience to throw a blast of fire to cover herself.

Unable to follow through to take her down, I dodged back, avoiding the flames.

By the time I recovered, she came bursting through her own fire, using it to cover her attack. Her face was ferocious.

My blood pumped furiously in my veins, and my mana circulation matched it. I felt myself swell with the strength of both my cultivation and bloodline. I threw my fist and met her attack.

Our fists connected and her arm gave with a sickening crunch, before we separated.

She muffled a scream as she backed away, cradling her arm. A vicious glint shot through her eyes before she breathed another larger wall of fire.

I sighed. She was going to use the same trick twice? It clearly hadn't worked well last time.

She came from my right, swinging with the arm I'd already injured.

That caught my attention. I blocked it, looking for the follow-up.

It came with a dagger in hand.

The moment paused in my mind as suddenly this became a lethal fight.

I should step down; this wasn't part of the competition.

But she came with such intensity I didn't have time to think.

I could feel the savage aspect of life rushing through my body, and I reacted with a right hook to her face. The full power of my bloodline and aspect of my mana were infused in the hit.

The roar of fire swept past me as I heard her neck snap, and I watched as her limp body rolled backwards.

It was like the whole world slowed, and her death was the only thing in focus.

I hadn't intended to kill her, but that didn't matter now. She was dead by my hand.

She wasn't the first person I'd ever killed, but the others had been in heated battles out in the wilderness.

This was almost cold-blooded as I killed her in a competition that had no right to spill blood.

Yet here I was, I had the power to kill and had used it.

Pressure unlike I'd ever felt slammed down on me, and a red-robed elder was before me, like an executioner ready to serve my final sentence.

I realized the whole crowd had gone silent. A mix of fear and excitement shone in their eyes as they anticipated my impending death.

"You insolent whelp. You dare kill one of our disciples!" He had a sword suddenly in his raised hand, ready to cut me in two without judge or jury. He was an executioner.

247

Another man was suddenly on the stage. His gray Ferrymen robes rippled behind him. "I think this little junior was fair in his killing of the girl. She drew a deadly weapon first. Sadly, we all know your Earth Flame Sect is blind to justice." There was killing intent in his voice that chilled me to the bone.

Somehow, the element in his voice crawled across my skin. Raw emotion filled me; it was as if I had descended into a bloody hell filled with corpses.

The Earth Flame Sect elder must have felt it too, because he nearly dropped his sword and stepped back. His eyes were wide, like he was watching a blade descend on his neck.

But the elder from the Ferrymen hadn't even moved. To contain killing intent that could be this deep and complex—how many people must he have killed? It was unlike anything I'd felt before.

Suddenly, another elder took the stage. She was a beautiful woman in a gauzy green dress the same color of Celina's. She was beautiful beyond comparison, like an immortal fairy had just arrived from heaven. When she smiled, the tension on the stage evaporated.

"We shouldn't interrupt the juniors, should we?" she said in a voice that was soft, but carried through the whole stadium. It hadn't felt like much of a question, but her words carried power. She tilted her head and made eye contact with each of the other elders, awaiting their compliance.

The red-robed elder bowed to the woman. "Apologies, but that child killed. He should suffer the repercussions."

The woman nodded. "Agreed, he should."

I suddenly felt very exposed. If any of these three wanted me dead, I would be before I even saw the blade.

But she continued. "I also believe that your sect should be punished for drawing a weapon and escalating the situation. All of your disciples should be executed, along with your present elders."

"Unreasonable!" he shouted, but he made no move to do anything.

A voice came from off the stage. "Elder, our disciple has shamed our sect. Our Earth Flame Sect is a righteous upholder of justice, and I will not stand for her to tarnish our name."

Hank was in the front row. He turned, projecting his voice to the audience. "It's commendable that our Elder cares so much for a disciple, but our Earth Flame Sect will uphold justice in its highest regard!" He turned back to the stage.

"Elder, please burn her body. She has no right to represent our sect."

The attacker was dead, and her body wasn't even cold yet. Yet here was Hank, reading the direction of the moment and deciding to sacrifice her to pompously orate his sect's merits to the crowd. His underling's life was so cheap that she was only a prop to recruit.

Then I realized her life had likely been forfeit before she'd even stepped on the stage. If she had managed to kill me, it would have been a similar scene.

My stomach churned. I hadn't had a lot of respect for Hank before, but how little he cared for those who dedicated themselves to him was unacceptable.

I couldn't even fathom it. A leader protects their followers in exchange for loyalty. I could never cross the same line as Hank had. To use those loyal to you for their death was worse than spitting on their corpse.

"Do all your juniors interrupt their elders and make demands?" the woman said, her smile gone. "It seems your Earth Flame Sect needs new instructors."

The red-robed man staggered back. I didn't see anything, but his neck rapidly darkened as purple veins crawled up his face. He fell to his knees.

"Stop!" The old man from the Sun and Moon Hall was on the stage, blocking whatever the woman from the Thousand Bloom Valley had done and fed the red-robed elder a pill.

"It is unseemly for us to fight in front of children. Let us discuss this elsewhere." His amicable smile made it feel like insects were crawling inside of me.

Celina stepped up next to me. She must have made her way over during the back and forth with the elders. She seemed apprehensive but offered support.

The Thousand Bloom Valley elder turned to Celina. Celina immediately dropped into a bow. "Law enforcement elder. Congratulations on forming your immortal body. I hadn't realized you had come out of seclusion."

The elder nodded. "Let us talk somewhere less open." She turned and led the way off the stage.

The elder from the Ferrymen clapped me on the shoulder, and I felt a rush of mana scan me for injuries. "Good show. I was worried there wouldn't be blood spilled here, and we'd be left with a boring day. Come along. That old hag likes you." He pulled me along to follow Celina and her elder.

The elder turned and gave the Ferrymen elder a sharp glare. "Senile fool, open your eyes. I still have many years to live."

They were using harsh words but didn't seem to have any hostilities between them. It was like supercharged banter.

"There's a Treasure Hall in town, yes?" the elder asked Celina.

"Yes, it's not far," Celina answered as we left the stadium. Michelle was waiting for us when we exited. A worried look evaporated into a grin when she saw me walking with the elders. As we passed her, I snatched her hand and pulled her along.

The Ferrymen elder only gave her a passing glance before continuing without comment.

I stepped up to the Treasure Hall, leading this small group. The guards took one look at the elders and pointedly ignored us.

Emera saw me come in and gave me a welcoming smile. When she saw the elders, she went into a low bow. "Welcome to the Treasure Hall, how may I help you?"

"Tea for five in a private room," the Ferrymen elder said.

There was no asking for proof that they needed it. Apparently, everyone could tell that these two were not to be trifled with.

Emera quickly led us up to a private room on the third floor, where she performed a ritual tea service. Mixing and pouring tea in a dance that left both elders smiling.

I watched with interest. It was a gracefully timed routine that almost seemed sensual. After the tea was prepared, she left.

Just as soon as the doors closed, the Ferrymen elder roared in laughter. "You put on a good show, boy. And you even got the interest of one of the Thousand Blooms." He pointed at Celina with his chin before sipping his tea.

Trying to appear casual, I picked up my own tea and took a sip. It was nice, but I wasn't an expert on tea. The tea service had made it seem expensive, and I felt like somebody who would appreciate it more should be enjoying it.

Just as I put the cup back down, I felt my mana spin wildly, absorbing mana as it diffused from my core. This tea was actually a cultivation resource.

"Ha! Kid, you have a lot to learn. Yes, drink the tea, but do it slowly to let your body absorb it completely and not waste any."

"Manners." The green-dressed elder glared over her teacup.

The older man waved her comment away. "Who needs manners when we have a boy here that kills members of the Rhys family? In front of their own elders no less! Ah, you let me vent a belly full of anger…" He paused and assessed me.

"I should probably stop calling you boy. I'm Elder Shaw from the Ferrymen. The old hag is Elder Gu." He extended his hand, while nodding towards the other elder with his head.

I shook it. "I'm Isaac, and this is Michelle. We grew up in this town… it's been interesting the last few days."

"To think there was such a quaint place hidden up here and a heaven-grade formation hiding you all. Pity it was destroyed; I'd have loved to examine such a thing," the green-dressed woman said.

I paused. I wasn't sure if I could trust these elders, but I needed at least some allies. I decided to take the gamble and offer a bit of information to see how they took it.

"The thing is… I was the one who broke the seal… so I know where it is."

"Once that light beam went into the sky, someone found it and took it away. It won't still be there."

I grinned and waved my hand, releasing the broken stone pillar from my spatial ring.

"Oh. Oh!" She was before it in an instant staring into the pattern, even though it was broken. She seemed mesmerized for a moment before shaking her head and looking back at me. "I would love to take this away and study it further. Would you consider selling it to me?"

I looked over at Michelle, who nodded as she caught my eyes. She agreed we needed to solidify some alliances. And they had saved my life.

"Yes. Without both of you, I'm sure I'd be dead on the martial stage." It didn't seem like a bad use of it to make friends with someone who was a fourth-ring mage.

She nodded, looking truly gleeful. She was still sitting next to it, slowly tracing some of the patterns with her finger. She paused to motion in the air before returning to her study. A thin wooden case had appeared.

"This is a hundred poison needle." She reached over and slid back the lid to show a single needle glimmering with a rainbow sheen, like fresh oil.

"Oh, that's not bad." Elder Shaw leaned forward, looking at it. "You should take it, boy."

I accepted the case carefully and put it away in my spatial ring.

"That can kill a third-ring mage," Celina noted. "Since you just made some enemies, it would be a prudent gift."

"Isn't it dishonorable for a third-ring mage to attack him directly?" Michelle spoke up, concern in her voice.

"Yeah, but the shameless bastards would do it anyways. Rules like that only matter if you have any honor in the first place. Though, they'd try to do it when you were alone." Elder Shaw tipped his tea back and downed the whole cup before letting out a light belch.

I looked down. I had barely managed to drink a quarter of it. Refining the mana from it was slow going.

"Listen, I like you, and not just because you killed some Rhys bitch." Elder Shaw brought out a thin book, no thicker than twenty pages. "I'd like to formally invite you to the Ferrymen."

"I..." I shot a look over to Michelle for her input, but Elder Shaw took it differently.

"The girl can come too." He produced a second thin book and put it in front of her. "I knew you two were a package deal."

I didn't pick it up immediately. First, I needed to know a bit more about what I was signing up for. "Can you tell me a bit about the Ferrymen?"

Elder Shaw looked confused.

"They haven't been outside this village in their lives. They don't know about the Ferrymen," the Thousand Bloom Valley elder reminded him.

252

Elder Shaw scratched the back of his head, like he was struggling for words. "Well…"

"Elder, if I may?" Celina asked. He nodded for her to continue.

"Isaac, the Ferrymen are mercenaries."

"We are not mercenaries. We simply make paying tasks available to our disciples, just like any other sect."

Celina ignored Elder Shaw's insertion and directly continued. "Other sects give minor missions, like harvest a type of beast or collect herbs, to keep their stocks full and provide monthly resources to their members. The Ferrymen also offer missions to kill other mages."

"Many of whom are mad men and are wanted for killing non-mages." Elder Shaw crossed his arms, clearly not loving the direction of the conversation. "The Elders vet the missions; we don't put out missions for just anyone."

So they were assassins… with a moral code.

Elder Gu must have seen my hesitation. "They aren't bad people. In fact, our Thousand Bloom Valley shares a friendship with them. They just cultivate their disciples with a wealth of combat rather than other less brutal means."

"Nothing teaches you to dodge faster than a hatchet wielding mass murderer." Elder Shaw nodded sagely.

I didn't hate the idea. I needed a strong sect with all the enemies I had made, and out of the elders I'd met, I liked him the best. I knew Michelle would likely follow me, but I wanted to give her the last chance to back out. Glancing over, she just nodded, conviction in her eyes.

"Deal. We will join the Ferrymen." I picked up the cultivation technique. It was Seven Hells Meridians. "This name…"

"Consider it your entry trial. Start upon this technique today, and I'll find you a pair of disciple robes." Elder Shaw had a wicked grin on his face.

Elder Gu sighed. "While that cultivation technique is… unique, all cultivation comes at a cost. Our disciples must inject and resist dozens of types of poison to step into our cultivation. No path is easy."

I looked back at the technique in my hands. A domineering name like Seven Hells Meridians wasn't enough to stop me. After what my father had put me through, I felt more than ready to take this one on.

"Many thanks, seniors." I cupped my hands and bowed to both of them.

"Such a good disciple already." Elder Shaw smiled. "Alright, I have other business to attend to. I'll see you all before you head into the dungeon. Hopefully, you are ready for your robes."

The Elder Shaw stood up and made his way out past Emera. She looked like she had been waiting at attention outside the room the whole time.

She chased after him as the doors closed.

"Now that he's gone, do be careful when practicing that technique. It is strong among first-ring cultivation methods. Celina," she finished with a knowing look at her disciple, "don't do anything rash."

Celina's cheeks flushed and she looked down. "Disciple knows."

"Good. I wish you all the best of luck tomorrow. We'll be watching. Try not to require our aid again though; it will hinder your cultivation to receive too much help."

With that, Elder Gu left with a radiant smile, leaving the three of us alone to finish our now cold tea. The effects had lessened with the tea cooling, but we each savored every drop.

"You should each take a moment to memorize the technique and cultivate the first layer. This room won't be disturbed, and you'll get a chance to lay a steady foundation," Celina said.

"Do you know much about this technique?" I asked.

She looked hesitant. "Most of the techniques to form your meridians are similar, but yes, as our sects work together often, I've seen the results of the cultivation."

"That sounded grim." Michelle eyed the book with a moment of trepidation. "Our teacher taught us that forming your meridians wouldn't be that bad. Just tedious."

"I believe the techniques that you use here are... tame compared to those that we use in the sects; they are merciful to yourself which is no mercy at all. I've sensed the strength of many of your guards in town that are two-ring mages. They barely meet the qualifications of the sect students to form their second ring."

Given how isolated we had been for so long, it came as no surprise that everyone else had advanced their abilities to cultivate past our understanding.

I grabbed my tea and went to sit close to Michelle. She was clearly anxious. She snuggled into me, taking the comfort.

I leaned down, talking quietly to her. "We need to become stronger. Even if this technique is painful, what could it compare to all the hours of hard work we've already put in to get this far? We can do this." I squeezed her shoulder and leaned over, picking up the book and skimming through it.

The Seven Hells Meridians had seven parts, each with its own cultivation sutra and method of circulating your mana within your body. Leaving the other six parts aside, I focused on the first part, which was contained within only two pages.

Ten minutes later, I put it down, feeling like I had the sutra memorized. "I'll start first."

Celina and Michelle nodded. "We'll watch over you."

Closing my eyes, I settled down into a cross-legged position that the book referred to as the lotus position, with my hands cupped and facing upwards.

Evening my breath, I started the sutra. I ran through it twice without circulating my mana to make sure I had it fixed in my mind.

When I was ready, I started channeling my mana in a new fashion, with swirls and loops. As I continued, I carved the first hell's meridians into my body. I felt distant, like it was someone else's body that I was doing this to.

The pattern reminded me of the swirls and loops I had seen on the formation in the abandoned dungeon. It was like I was carving an enchantment into my very body.

Numbness to the entire process started to pass through me. I struggled to feel any purpose behind what I was doing. The sweet release of death called to me as I settled the patterns into this body.

I could feel my soul giving up, letting my body wither as I embraced the apathy and the freedom from the struggle of life.

But then my blood surged. I could clearly feel the blood beast within my bloodline raging in my body. Like a child throwing a tantrum, it seemed offended by the newly formed meridians.

Pain shot through my body, and I could feel a spurt of blood leave me. My bloodline continued to rampage, modifying the meridians. It was still the first hell of the technique, but loops were rounded, and edges became sharper as my bloodline did what I could only describe as perfecting the technique.

Who was my mother to have a whole family of this bloodline? It already had made me supernaturally strong within my cultivation. Now, with a mind of its own, it refused anything less than perfection with my meridians.

I hadn't noticed it at first, but the feeling of apathy had subsided as I watched my own bloodline with interest. I shook off the feeling and felt a cold sweat on my body. I had expected the technique to be painful, harsh in some physical way.

The technique had nearly made me give up on life and cause my soul to flee straight to hell. This was absolutely terrifying. And the worst part was that there was an entire sect full of people who practiced like this.

I felt the technique solidify and pull on my soul once more, like hell itself was trying to drag me down into it. If I had been in my previous state, that might have been the end for me. But I had regained my consciousness and shrugged off the final pull as the first layer of meridians settled within me.

Breathing out a heavy breath that contained a part of the old me, I felt more in tune with the world. My body glowed with the rich gold lines of the cultivation technique.

"Heavens, gold meridians," Celina gasped.

I opened my eyes to the beautiful poison mage staring at those glowing gold lines with awe.

"What are gold meridians?" I asked before growing quiet and looking over at Michelle who had already started cultivation. I was on my feet and beside her in an instant.

"Don't worry, she has held strong. Her conviction seems to be stronger than yours."

But I wasn't worried about her giving up. The Michelle I knew was too stubborn to die. No, I wanted to impart the perfected meridian style to Michelle as well.

It was incredibly rude to barge into someone's internal space, but I doubted Michelle would mind given how much of her body she had already shared with me.

I suppressed a grin at the memories and focused on sensing her meridians as they were forming. They weren't solid yet, and she still seemed to be actively focusing on them.

I pushed my mana through her, helping form the meridians while being careful not to cause a deviation in her cultivation. I was able to push and pull the forming meridians into the shape that my bloodline had done for me.

She could sense me, and her mana accepted mine as she modified her meridians in pattern with what I had shown her.

I withdrew and let out a breath. Good thing she hadn't solidified them too much and could still make changes.

"That was incredibly dangerous." Celina was glaring at me as I came back to myself. "But, seeing that she didn't even reject your mana naturally while cultivating, she must truly trust you." Her eyes held barely concealed envy.

"I wanted her to form meridians like my own. But I'm not sure if the changes made them golden as you called them."

She looked at me like an idiot. "You can't just make golden meridians. That is heavenly luck to create golden meridians. They are the top tier of meridians, and only those who are either blessed by luck or cultivating geniuses can form them."

As if to prove her wrong, Michelle's body lit up with golden lines. Not as bright as mine, but certainly what Celina would consider golden meridians.

"That's not possible, you can't just... wait let me back up. If someone could just help someone form golden meridians, then the elders would all be doing that to improve their sects. It can't be possible."

Michelle opened her eyes. "So I did good? What are gold meridians?"

Celina sighed. "Most of the people here have clear or white meridians. Those are the lowest level and essentially junk. They might be able to form their second ring, but the foundation is too weak to progress much past that."

"Then there are the ones capable of progressing to third ring. They have bronze, silver and gold meridians."

"Can bronze not make it to the fourth ring?" I wondered. If that was the case, even among first-ring mages, they already striated into different tiers of mages.

"Not exactly. Silver and bronze are still talented mages. Just not monsters like gold-meridian mages." She gave me and Michelle an odd look before continuing.

"Gold meridians can handle more mana, so you can cultivate faster and will be stronger in combat. To say a bronze-meridian mage can't reach the fourth ring would be false... but it will be much harder.

"You can change your meridians... it is just wildly expensive, and no sect is going to spend that money on a first-ring or even a second-ring mage. But it isn't unheard of for third-ring mages to cleanse and enhance their meridians before making their immortal body."

I gave her a big smile. "Then we just need to get you to the third ring, then we can cleanse your meridians and you'll have gold meridians like us."

Celina's mouth opened and closed several times without making a sound.

"I think you broke her," Michelle joked from the side, looking quite cheerful that she had kept up with me in terms of talent.

"You both are treating this like it happens every day. I have silver meridians and my sect threw a grand party when I formed them. I suspect they even sent Elder Gu, the third strongest elder in our sect, to look after me."

I just shrugged.

"I can't believe you don't realize what a big deal this is! We spend our entire lives waiting to see what color our meridians are. Our family reputations sometimes even depend on it. I can't believe this." Celina seemed to lose her patience with us.

But we both just laughed. "Want to come to dinner with us?" Michelle asked. "I think we cultivated for a while, right?"

My stomach growled at the thought of food. "Come join us. We are having dinner with Michelle's family. You'll get to watch her mothers embarrass the crap out of her, and probably me."

Celina shook her head at how we were taking the news of our gold meridians, but in the end, she followed us out of the Treasure Hall.

I didn't see Emera to say goodbye, but she was probably off assisting the elders.

Chapter 23

The booklet describing the Seven Hells Meridians explicitly said to take a break and recover your mana between each step of the cultivation.

It lined up well with taking a break for dinner with Michelle's family. But as we walked, I realized there was no doubt they'd ask questions about our relationship. We hadn't really discussed any specific labels.

I wasn't quite sure where we were now on that front. She had essentially promised to run away with me, and now we were destined for the same sect. So... girlfriend with some serious commitments? Michelle also didn't fully understand about Aurora yet, and it felt weird to get too far without letting them meet. While I was serious about Michelle, Aurora was literally a part of me.

Thoughts still scattered, I realized we had arrived at her parents' place. I guess I'd be winging it a bit.

Michelle's mother opened the door with a broad grin, which only got bigger when she saw Celina with us. "Welcome, welcome. And you might be?" She looked over at me and wiggled her eyebrows. I tried not to blush.

"Celina." She nodded respectfully. "It's nice to meet you. You must be Michelle's mom?"

"I'm Megan, Michelle's biological mother, although we are all 'mom'. No need to separate based on which of us she came out of! Although the girl did put up quite a fight. It was some rough sex that conceived her; I've always wondered if that played a part. You know, the type of sex that..."

Michelle groaned. "They get the picture, mom." She pushed past her mom, pulling me with her.

Celina stayed back. She cupped her hands and bowed her head at Megan. "A pleasure to meet you." She stuttered a bit, clearly flustered. It was cute.

"So formal. Come come, let us take care of you tonight." Megan ushered her in behind us.

Michelle shook her head. "I almost feel left out. But a part of me is happy I won't be the only one at dinner getting questions about our sex lives. I can't wait to watch her face as they launch into tips on the best way for multiple women to please a man." She chuckled, and we both looked back to see her mom whispering and making hand gestures, while Celina lit up like a light.

"Honestly, it's a bit of a relief for me. Your moms are so relaxed; I don't feel judged at all. They're so welcoming." It was a refreshing change of pace from the brutal world of mages.

"Well, since we are alone for a moment. How are you doing with everything today?" She tilted her head, and I could tell based on the look in her eyes that she was trying to ask something specific. The problem was I had no idea what it was she was asking.

I went broad. "I'm good with joining the Ferrymen, and Celina seems great?"

She paused, waiting for me to continue. Clearly hadn't gotten it yet.

"Uhm, glad to be in the same sect with you and our future together?"

Michelle started cracking up. "I'm not looking for some deep proclamation of love." She nudged me in the side. "But seriously, Issac. You just killed someone in front of a thousand people! Ring a bell?"

I opened my mouth to argue, then closed it. In everything that happened, I hadn't had the time to reflect on that. It wasn't the first time I had killed, but the Rhys scion and the guy who fell into the dungeon with me were tense situations. This one really wasn't so much of a killing as an accidental survival.

But in the arena today, I'd killed that woman in defense, in front of hundreds if not a thousand people.

A sigh rushed out of me before I realized it. "I don't know, Michelle. I certainly don't regret it. After what they did to Jonny, part of me was just so worried they'd do something like that to you."

I paused, running my hand through my hair. "You don't think I'm a—"

She put a hand over my mouth, stopping me from finishing that statement, while rolling her eyes. "No, I don't see you any differently. If anything, it was kinda hot." She blushed before a bit of ferocity entered her eyes. "Given the chance, I would have killed them then too. It's just... I wanted to make sure you were okay."

"I am... I probably shouldn't be okay with killing them. But I am. Do you think this is what all mages become like?"

She shook her head. "I don't know, but we will find out together." She grabbed my hand, and even though I knew it was in my head, a warmth spread from her touch.

"Awe."

My head snapped to the side and Brenda peeking around the corner, watching us. "Don't stop on my account, you two are just too cute. Although far too dressed after that touching moment."

Michelle snapped her hand back and glared at her mother. "Is it time for dinner?"

"Yes, I was just coming to get you two; you had lingered so long. I thought that—"

"Alright, mom, lead on. We shouldn't make people wait on us."

"But if you need a moment more—"

Michelle directly pulled me down the hall knowing the way herself and not wanting to start whatever conversation her mother had in mind.

Her house was nice from the small amount that blurred past us as Michelle practically raced to their dining room.

When we got there, Celina saw us, and her eyes lit up with rays of pleading hope. Oh god, what had Michelle's mothers done to her?

We sat down. I was positioned with Celina on one side, Michelle on the other. She was clearly buffering me from her family, while Celina seemed to want to cling to me for safety.

Michelle's mothers were arranged around an unassuming middle-aged man with gray hair just starting to pepper its way along his temples. He had a solemn air of strength around him, which made sense. Michelle had said he was at the peak of his second ring.

Part of me wondered what color his meridians were. With what I'd learned, maybe they were the reason he couldn't advance to his third ring.

His women were arrayed around him. Each was different, but still stunning. I took a moment to study them closer. Megan was buxom and blonde, her curves clearly on display. Brenda was mousier with petite features and brown hair. And finally, Raven was a lithe, dark-haired woman who moved with a serpentine grace that constantly drew your eyes.

Raven caught me staring and returned a polite smile. "So, you are Isaac."

"Yes, pleasure to meet you. Michelle has told me quite a bit about her family." I picked at some of the family style dishes and added them to my plate.

"Oh, I'm sure she told you all about us. Don't worry, we have seen to her full education." Megan gave me an exaggerated wink.

I had to clear my throat to not choke. "Yes, she's told me quite a bit." Looking over to Michelle for help, she seemed to be entirely focused on her food, just like Celina.

"You picked up our little Michelle so quickly. Now there is Celina, and I heard before you were with a girl named Kat? Michelle talked about her stealing you away for weeks, so it must be getting serious," Raven said plainly but I could sense a bit of accusation in her tone. "Are you satisfied with those three?" There was a twinkle in her eye as she sat back.

I swallowed a bit, trying to figure out what to say. What they didn't know was that I also had Aurora, and she planned to add more women on her own. Given Aurora's encouragement of Michelle, I was sure she'd latch onto Celina if I gave her the chance.

"I'm not sure. Really, it is just me and Michelle at this time. Kat left for a sect and Celina hasn't made any promises." I desperately kept myself from looking over at Celina. It was so awkward to hint at the possibility of something before we'd even had time to talk.

"Don't be so cruel to the poor girl. I'm sure she's already had many fantasies about licking those amazing abs of yours. She'd be a fine addition," Megan chided me. "But you should at least add a few more. A dozen or so would give us enough grandchildren to take care of." She looked at the other two for confirmation.

Brenda nodded. "At least a dozen, if not more. I want a steady stream of grandbabies. Honestly, it would be best if you knock up our Michelle and leave us a grandbaby before you leave."

I nearly choked on my food. Michelle laughed, patting my back in sympathy.

"If you need help with technique, we could help demonstrate how to keep a dozen women satisfied if that's your concern with increasing your harem," Raven added, not to be outdone.

I had to close my mouth before food fell out. Looking at Michelle's dad, he was pointedly looking down at his plate, but I caught a bit of a smirk on his face. He clearly was recalling some fond memories.

"Moms!" Michelle sighed, finally bursting. "I've only slept with him once, and we are still new. Would you stop hounding him?" Her moms let out gleeful claps, as she put her hands over her mouth, realizing the ammo she'd just given them.

I looked over her parents. Her dad had that barely concealed fury that I expected every father to have when he learned his baby girl wasn't his anymore. He got up, clearing his throat and making some excuse to go grab something from the kitchen. Her moms, however, all lit up, leaning forward with rapt interest.

"How was she?" Raven asked, leaning so far forward that I had to avert my eyes to not see down her shirt. "Was she great? How many times did she get you to orgasm? It's important to build a strong foundation even when alone, even if it becomes easier with multiple women."

This had to be a joke. I tried to call her bluff. "Four, no wait, five times. She was great."

Her moms got even more excited, and suddenly I was barraged with questions and exposed to countless topics about sex and group positions, ranging from three people to a dozen.

I had opened a set of flood gates that could not be closed. I couldn't unsee things as Raven and Megan got up after the food was done and started miming some of their comments and tips. They got to the point that there weren't even names for some of the positions. And then moved into ones that were just theories because they hadn't had enough people to experiment themselves.

It turns out, with the town opening up to the rest of the world, they were quickly trying to rope in another woman to test these theories.

Michelle's dad had returned with a bottle of alcohol and was steadily pouring himself more throughout all of it.

I must have looked completely shell shocked by the end. Michelle finally took pity on me and rescued me by telling them we needed to go test out some of these ideas. What an odd way to wrap a dinner with a girl's parents.

They let me go with several asks for grandbabies.

Finally escaping up to Michelle's room, we all breathed a sigh of relief as we closed the door. Michelle slid down to the floor, her face buried in her hands. Celina chuckled and crouched down, wrapping her arm around Michelle.

"At least he isn't running, and I mean..." Celina trailed off. There were no words for some of what was discussed at that table.

"Michelle, in fairness, you did warn me. I just... yeah... nothing could have prepared me for the..." I trailed off and realized it didn't matter.

Scooping Michelle up off the floor, I carried her over to the bed and patted a spot next to me for Celina.

She joined us, but she kept some space between me and her.

"It's just so much." Michelle peeked out between her hands. "You aren't completely disgusted with me now, are you?"

"Not in the least bit. If I'm truly honest, I'm a bit turned on from imagining us doing all they talked about. That's more embarrassing than anything."

Michelle's hand wandered into my pants to confirm that I indeed had turned into a steel rod after all of that discussion. She looked up and licked her lips.

I looked over at Celina, worried she'd be uncomfortable. But she was watching with wide, excited eyes as she slowly touched herself.

"Would you like to join us?" I said, reaching out my hand.

But she violently shook her head. "No!... I mean... Yes, but I can't. We can't."

Michelle stopped trying to undo my pants. "What do you mean?" There was a look of sympathy as she rambled on.

"We didn't know. I'd thought you were fine with this. Ugh, the dinner conversation. I'd just assumed. I'm so sorry…"

Celina chuckled and cut her off. "I want to. I just can't." She let out a frustrated grunt with a shrug of her shoulders.

"I won't poison you with a hug or a handshake, but my body is still full of toxins… during the heat of the moment… I'd… you know."

"Poison us to death. Death by snu snu?" Michelle asked, raising her eyebrows.

Celina looked at the floor. "Yeah. They tell us all to not have sex because we don't have enough control of the toxins in our body to not release it in the moment."

I felt like a jerk. We'd spent the night talking about and almost having sex in front of her, yet she had to deny herself.

She forced a smile on her face. "But, after we form our immortal bodies, we are able to experience the pleasure of flesh again. That is… if you two don't mind waiting."

Michelle spoke first. "Of course! It's not like it's all about the sex. You're great and are a great addition to our group. And we'll make sure that, when you can, it's truly special."

I cleared my throat and adjusted my pants. "I agree. A relationship is more than just physical. Let's just say we are dating. Taking the time to get to know you."

"Thanks. Dating works. Sorry to kill the mood a bit," Celina said, her smile becoming more genuine.

Michelle waved her off. "It's fine. If we want to make it all the way to forming our immortal bodies, we should focus on cultivating anyways." She pulled out the Seven Hells Meridians booklet and started reading the next section.

I checked and my mana had filled my previous formation of meridians. I should be able to cultivate the next layer of the technique.

I sat studying the next layer. The booklet talked about it in the same vague wording as the first. I tried to read between the lines and glean a fragment of what would happen for these meridians, but all I got was that you should have someone you trust with you.

I had Michelle and Celina, so that was covered. I checked the next section to see if there were any hints there, but the next one said it was imperative that you go into isolation for it.

"Celina, do you know anything about the next stage?"

"No. I know that sometimes people seem to give up and die during a number of the stages. Oh! I heard that one of them makes you go crazy and try to murder anyone around you. I hear the Ferrymen seal you in a tomb for that one."

My body burst into a sweat at that, and I had to wonder what kind of crazy people made this cultivation technique.

"So, want me to start and you can watch it Michelle, then give it a try?" I felt confidence that my bloodline would protect me and ensure it was correct. This time, Michelle would watch and copy those changes.

She shrugged casually, totally unphased, like we hadn't almost died last time.

I sat cross-legged in the lotus position on the bed. Michelle came up behind me and put her back to mine. I felt her consciousness dip into my inner world along with me.

The next pattern was to be overlaid on top of the first. But, before I started tracing it, I stirred the blood beast within my bloodline.

It woke like a grumpy animal and paced through me, agitated. I concentrated on the mantra and began creating the second layer of the Seven Hells Meridians.

The blood beast stirred and started watching the new pattern being formed. Like the first time, it started to change the pattern, looping it around the first in places and exaggerating parts.

My mind wandered as the pattern took form. Images formed, fueled by the explicit dinner conversation.

I found myself surrounded by women. Aurora with her heavenly beauty, Michelle in skintight clothes begging to be peeled off, Celina with her girl next door temptation, Kat with her fragile beauty that made you want to protect her, even others started appearing. Women of all shapes and beauties, some clearly derived from mana beasts, formed in my thoughts as the world blurred into a lust filled hedonistic paradise.

I was in the middle of enjoying a game of guess-who-this-is as a dozen lips were pleasuring me and taking turns sitting on my face when a sharp pain blossomed in my chest.

It built like a thousand angry ants fleeing from their nest as my entire body suddenly felt like it was burning up.

267

I sat up and coughed up a bloody mist as I found myself sitting back on Michelle's bed. I blinked, trying to remember what was happening.

My head spun and my manhood begged to be released. There was a fire in my veins that could only be purged through lust. I desperately needed a release. I was in a fog of lust so thick that I could barely understand my other thoughts.

"Isaac, are you okay?" A girl came into focus. She had thin brows and a delicate face, with lips that were plump. The lower one jutted out a bit extra, which made me want to suck on its delicious permanent pout.

I grabbed her head and pulled her close, sucking greedily on her lips. I couldn't wait. Spinning and tossing her on the bed, I pounced and reclaimed those lips, reveling in their sweet softness.

She struggled for a moment before her hand slammed into my chest and rocketed me across the room.

I crashed into the wall, a bit dazed but not hurt.

"Isaac, stop. You can't." She had a look of fear, but not for herself. For me. Something about the numbness in my mouth sent a sobering warning. It was enough for the haze to clear for a moment.

I felt Aurora's seal hammering for her to be released, and I did so without a thought.

Celina stared wide-eyed at Aurora as she appeared with her wings spread like an angel ready for anything.

"Get off the bed. He won't keep his senses for long," Aurora shooed Celina, who scrambled away falling onto the floor and got out of my line of sight as Aurora pressed herself against me.

I took the offered body and wrapped my arm around her hips, pulling her into me as I tasted her neck, working my way down to suckle her chest.

Her dress slid down in time for me to reach her breasts and take a nipple into my mouth, rolling it with my tongue. She pulled us both back to the bed, and I pulled off her dress as I continued to make my way south to the real prize.

Her legs opened for me like jade gates, and I lifted her by her hips as I explored the succulent flesh between her legs.

I wanted nothing more than to satisfy my own urges, but the breathy moans and gasps brought a satisfaction to me that only made my swelling member grow like it was going to burst free.

When she screamed and wet my face, I couldn't hold back and rose up on her like a beast.

I slid in all the way to the hilt as her silken heat accepted me completely. I stayed there for a moment, savoring it.

She wrapped her legs around my waist and let out another sigh of pleasure that once again sparked my lust.

I lost myself into her pleasure as we rutted like animals. I took her on her back as she screamed my name. Then I picked her hips up so her torso was perpendicular to the bed and began ramming her into the bed. Her muffled orgasmic screams drove me to be harder and faster as I raced again and again to fill her with my seed.

I wasn't sure how many times I had released inside of her when a pair of hands wrapped around my back, and I turned to see a glassy-eyed Michelle panting on me.

There was enough sense in me at this point that I could tell Michelle was far worse than me. My haze of lust had cleared significantly.

I looked for Celina, and she looked shocked when our eyes met. Hers were glazed with satisfaction as she sprawled naked on a chair in the corner. Her thighs and the seat soaked with her juices while her hand kept going.

Michelle didn't like my distraction and pulled me out of Aurora and onto my back. Then she mounted me, throwing her head back like a beast in heat.

Somehow, after all of this, I was still hard and ready to go. I grabbed her hips and held her down.

She bucked trying to create friction for herself, but I held on, keeping her hips plastered to mine until she calmed down.

In an agonizingly slow motion, I pulled my hips back before thrusting deep inside of her again. Each time I sheathed myself into her, she writhed and gasped in pleasure clawing my chest.

When I let go of her hips, she threw herself back down on me unable to patiently enjoy this.

It wasn't long before her first orgasm soaked my thighs and she lost some of that wild edge.

Aurora joined after that, massaging Michelle's breasts while her hands wandered down to where we were joined.

I was so done being on bottom. Flipping them both on the bed, I enjoyed the sight of Michelle underneath Aurora, their breasts pressed together.

Lining myself up, I entered Aurora and pumped for a minute before entering Michelle, switching off between the two while they made out.

"So close," Aurora begged as I pulled out of her again.

I went back in and drove myself into her till she screamed in ecstasy with Michelle clamped onto her breasts, tweaking her nipples.

Aurora rolled off of Michelle, her wings hanging off the side of the bed as she melted into what appeared to be a sex induced coma.

Michelle pulled me back into her, and I could see clarity in her eyes as we made love one more time before passing out.

***

I woke up the next morning to a three way stare off. Michelle and Celina were staring at Aurora, who was using me like a bunker wall, peeking out over my shoulder.

"Morning, Master," Aurora said, looking happy that I was awake.

"Morning, what's going on?" I asked the room rather than just Aurora.

Michelle was the first to speak. "She's a mana beast. An angel mana beast. Stud, she can speak! Do you realize how amazing that is?"

I rubbed the morning grit out of my eyes. "No, really? Aurora did you know that you were amazing."

She smirked. "You have said it a few times."

Celina inched closer. "You are a fourth-rank mana beast, aren't you? No, you've got to be higher than that." She stared at Aurora like that would unlock more of her secrets.

"What does it matter? She's my first ring and that's that." I hadn't had the conversation with Aurora about what rank she was, but I wasn't going to squeeze it out of her now. I wasn't stupid enough to believe that she was a low-ranked mana beast. I also was smart enough to let her tell me on her own terms.

Michelle blinked at me defending Aurora. "Of course, you knew. How could you not. And you two...?"

"Yes, Aurora is my woman too. We were planning to tell you. Just with everything, there hadn't been a chance yet. And we are trying to keep her secret," I said.

Michelle turned back to Celina. "Is this an issue?"

Celina looked a bit afraid. "No one can know, Isaac. If she has a human form, she is at least a rank four mana beast. Which means that your body is a valuable resource for anyone wanting to form their own immortal body. You are essentially a very rare resource to a third-ring mage that knows you have Aurora."

I started to wave it away and received an even sterner look.

"Like, put you in a cauldron and refine you into a pill kind of resource," Celina clarified.

"That doesn't sound good, Master." Aurora shook her head. "I didn't know I caused that much trouble for you."

I shrugged. Without Aurora, I would have already died. And, at this point, I wouldn't trade her for any other mana beast.

"We just need to keep her secret. I trust both of you, and no one else knows."

"Can she fight a third-ring mage if one comes?" Michelle asked hopefully.

Aurora shook her head. "This form is constrained by how much mana Master can utilize. I can't use more mana than he has access to."

"You could use it better than he could, though," Celina added.

"Correct. While I might be able to kill a second-ring mage, I wouldn't be able to kill a third-ring. Not until Master advances."

I thought about it, but I really didn't want Aurora to try and close the gap to a higher-level mage. If something went wrong and she died, that would cripple my cultivation, and then I would be as easy as picking a herb for a high-ranked pill. I needed to grow stronger myself.

"Worrying won't help this. What happens, happens. Right now, we just need to grow stronger."

Opening up the Seven Hells Meridians, I found the next section. There was a requirement for a place with concentrated mana.

Flipping the page again, I saw that the fourth stage had a requirement for five thousand beast cores to cultivate. I sucked in a breath seeing that. This cultivation technique was insane.

I didn't have that many beast cores, but that wasn't a problem for now. I first needed to find a place with rich mana. Maybe Elder Shaw would be able to help.

"What do you need, Master?" Aurora peeked over my shoulder at the book.

"We need a place with concentrated mana for the next stage. Then we need ten thousand mana beast cores for the fourth stage," I said, looking at Celina.

"The beast cores won't actually be that bad. A half a year of work at the sect could probably net you that... What?"

My face fell. A half a year. How long was this technique going to take?

"A half a year is a long time for just one stage of this..." I looked at the book regretfully, but now that I had started on this, I needed to finish the technique. It was a recipe for disaster to try and mix cultivation techniques like that.

"It took me three years to reach the peak of the first ring. It's not like turning over your hand. Cultivation takes years," Celina huffed at my eagerness to gain my second ring.

"We can kill people for the cores. I'm sure some of the disciples will wander around town," Aurora offered.

"You can't just go around killing mages for their spatial rings. That's how you get the Ferryman sent after you," Celina sighed and rubbed her face.

"What if we only went after people like the Rhys family and the Sun and Moon Hall?" I asked. Those assholes deserved to die.

"Be very careful of the Sun and Moon Hall. They are far more dangerous than they appear. You don't end up as the top sect in an area for nothing, even if they are only a branch. Here in the Eastern Region, they are king. As for the Rhys family... yeah, you could probably get away with using them as a whet stone. They will eventually send someone higher for you," Celina said.

"Alright, I'll play nice. For now, we still have the trip to the dungeon to take care of." So much had changed in such little time. I needed to grow faster than the world changed, or I'd be left behind.

Michelle and Aurora had separated from us and I realized they had been conversing in whispers while I had been talking to Celina. They both had friendly smiles on, and I realized my budding harem was going to be just fine.

"You two good to get going? We have a dungeon to dive. But if you need a moment more to discuss my amazing skills in bed, I'm happy to wait a few minutes," I teased the two girls.

Chapter 24

"Aurora, you coming… or?" I left the option open.

But she shook her head. "Some of the cultivators from the sect will undoubtedly be able to tell what I am. That would only put you at more risk, Master. It would be best if I returned to my ring."

I pulled Aurora up and gave her a kiss before she returned to her ring. I touched the spot on my chest, marveling at the near quarter of a ring that had grown since last night.

Aurora was quite literally the engine that drove my mana. Without her, I'd be a normal person. "We should get something for Aurora while we are out," I said to Michelle.

"That's a great idea. We'll have to keep an eye out." Michelle clapped her hands.

We waved goodbye to Michelle's mother on our way out. She gave me a saucy wink and a motion that seemed to indicate a good job.

I could feel my face burn at the thought of her listening to last night.

When we got to Jonny's family restaurant, his mother looked at me like I was her savior. "Please, Isaac, talk some sense into my boy."

"What's wrong?" I asked. She looked even worse than when she found out Jonny had been spending all of his money on porn.

"My baby isn't my baby anymore."

"Mrs. H, we are all going off to a sect, but we'll be okay. Jonny is going to be at the Daoist Monastery, no one will hurt him there."

"No, you don't understand. If that boy leaves, I just know I'll never see him again." The dam broke and tears started.

"It's okay. Stud will go talk some sense into your son. Won't you?" Michelle looked at me as she consoled Jonny's mother.

I gave her a thumbs up. "Of course." I hurried up the stairs to Jonny's room.

It was far cleaner than I had ever remembered. His bed was even made. Jonny sat on a worn reed mat in the center in meditation.

More than anything, the shine of his freshly shaved head caught my eye.

"Hey, Jonny. Wow, you really cleaned up." I whistled at the room.

Jonny opened his eyes slowly before half-bowing to me with his palms pressed together. "Morning, brother. It is a pleasant day, is it not?"

I gave my friend a blank stare. This really felt like I was talking to someone else. Knowing how the Sun and Moon Hall seemed great on the surface but was controlling members behind the scenes, I grew more concerned.

Was the Daoist Monastery doing something similar to Jonny?

I saw a corner of paper sticking out from his pillow and grinned. I reached and pulled the lewd image of a cat girl wearing what could barely even be called a bikini out. I paused for a moment. She was actually pretty hot.

But the paper was snatched out of my hand, and Jonny flicked his wrist. The image disappeared.

Coughing into his hands, he tried to regain his image. "I must have missed that one in cleaning," he said without meeting my eyes.

"Sure, buddy. So why the act? Your mom is worried sick." I crossed my arms.

Jonny got back on the prayer mat. "Dude, these guys are super strict. When the elder saw the posters in my room he took them all! Then he shaved my head." Jonny looked on the verge of tears.

I couldn't help it. I laughed.

Finally calming down. "Phew, I thought we lost you, Jonny. Don't worry, I'll see if I can't find you a few replacements before we leave."

"Yeah?" I could practically see his eyes shine before they dimmed again. "But I'm going to become an ascetic... that means no sex ever again."

Celina had clued me in on who the old man that recruited Jonny was—an ascetic from the Daoist Monastery. Apparently, they were among the strongest cultivators.

"Jonny, you are going to become the disciple of the strongest mages out there. In a few years, who the fuck is going to tell you what to do? Just make up an excuse, like doing it for the necessity of keeping your family line."

That dimming spark in his eyes grew back to a raging fire. "Yes." He pumped his fist.

"And, to make it even better, if you are that strong, think of how many beauties will throw themselves at you?"

Jonny nodded like I had just opened the pathway to the knowledge of heaven.

"But hey, I need to tell you some things." I sat down with a more serious expression and started going over joining the Ferrymen and what I'd seen at the brothel.

Jonny nodded along, keeping a calm face until I mentioned my fears that were growing about the Sun and Moon Hall in regard to the town.

"I think it would be a good idea to talk to the Monastery about sheltering your parents. Maybe tell them that you don't want them to be used against you and shatter your resolve? Or that worrying about them will affect your cultivation?"

"I get it. These guys are super strict, but they might just go for it. As for everything else in town... I'm pretty sure the Monastery already knows or guesses. They want me to leave as soon as possible." Jonny blew out his cheeks.

"That's... why don't they do anything?"

"The Monastery is neutral. They are more concerned with maintaining balance and focusing on cultivating than getting involved in what my teacher called 'petty squabbles of ants'."

"That's cold—"

Jonny cut me off before I could say more. "They take separation from the world pretty literally. Also, it's why the monastery is so powerful. But I think if a large-scale battle ever did break out, they would show up."

I guess they couldn't really stay out of it if a war really started on the scale of all of the sects versus the corrupt mages. That meant, if nothing else, the Monastery was a balancing point in all of this.

"So, want to grab a bite to eat? Find Steve and have one last hurrah in the dungeon before the Daoist Monks steal you away?"

"Like a bachelor party! Only I'm getting married to a cold lonely cave. Don't suppose you'll invite some strippers?" Jonny said, the boyish smile back on his face.

"No strippers. What would the monks do if they found you with those? I bet they would—" I mimed scissors with my hand and Jonny gulped turning pale.

"I was just joking. Let's go talk to your mom and tell her the plan. Then we can track down Steve."

Jonny went downstairs and had a private conversation with his mother in the kitchen while I hung out with Michelle. Maaria looked far better after they both came out. I hoped it worked well for Jonny and they let his parents follow him to the Monastery.

We tried to go grab Steve, but Maaria wouldn't let us go until we had a few skewers of meat each.

"You know these would be great to have in our spatial rings," Michelle said as we walked.

I looked over to Jonny. "If you guys end up packing up early, I'll buy you out of all your meat."

"Deal."

The three of us walked over to Steve's place. It was at the edge of the town; Steve's father owned a farm out here.

But we were only a block away when we heard the noise. Crashes and the sound of wood snapping were loud enough that we all put on a burst of speed and raced to Steve's house.

The place was normally steeped in quiet that was only broken by the occasional livestock noise. But Steve's ranch-style home was looking worse for wear. The railing at the front of the house was smashed, and there was a standoff in front of one of the livestock pens.

Steve and his father were facing off against two disciples in Sun and Moon Hall clothes and one in Earth Flame Sect garb. There was a hole in the fence behind them as they used their bodies to patch it.

I immediately recognized one of them as the disciple I had seen fighting yesterday in the competition. But, this time, the idiot had a knife twirling in his hand as he threatened my friend.

"Hey, it's no big deal. Just want to buy all your livestock," the knife twirler said.

Steve's dad harrumphed and spat at him. "Offering to buy them for pennies on the dollar isn't buying. It certainly ain't buying if you have to use a knife to bargain."

I turned to Jonny. "What's the point of having all our strength if we don't get a chance to use it now and then?"

"My thoughts exactly," Jonny said with a smirk.

The three of us exploded forward, each taking a different target. I took on the knife twirler as Jonny and Steve found their own opponents.

I was there at his back in a flash, sending a strike to his head.

Steve's eyes went wide and gave me away. The knife wielder managed to twist away with a slash of his dagger that kept me from connecting the blow.

I darted to his side for another attack, this time sending out a clawed strike.

The Sun and Moon disciple tried to use his movement technique to escape but realized it was too late. He cut a sharp slash through the air that became a ghost of a dagger, cutting off my attack.

Our two attacks canceled out, but it was enough to send the Sun and Moon disciple stumbling back. He looked worn. His cultivation was clearly disturbed from the exchange.

I had no love for the Sun and Moon Hall, and even less for bullies that went after my friends.

"'Bout time you showed up." Sun and Moon disciple dusted off his robe like this had been his plan the whole time. "I thought I'd have to start killing here soon."

"You did this to draw me out?" I said, realization seeping into me.

He didn't answer, just vanished from his spot.

I dodged back and drew a sword. With us both back on the same level, I was able to block his stab and kick him in the chest, sending him flying back.

His dagger had an oily sheen. The bastard wasn't playing around. This wasn't simply wanting to compare notes. The Sun and Moon disciple intended to kill me.

I had no doubt that the poison would take my life. Stepping forward in a flash, I attacked.

The Sun and Moon disciple dodged and tried to come in for my side. He was a slippery opponent with a movement technique. But I was better.

Speeding up my slash, I turned it into a wide sweep to my side. The Sun and Moon disciple was forced to block with his dagger.

Luckily, sword beats dagger. The Sun and Moon disciple learned that as my wide swing knocked him back and to one knee.

I was on him in an instant, not letting him have a moment to recover. My overhead swing forced him to lock himself in a block.

The Sun and Moon disciple knelt before me in a stalemate, only his dagger was keeping my sword from descending.

Lashing out with a kick, I sent him tumbling to the ground. There was a hot desire to finish him right here, but some instinct stopped me from finishing him.

"Get lost," I shouted loud enough that I hoped to attract a crowd.

Looking over, both Michelle and Jonny had finished their fights. A big golden bell sat over their opponents, trapping them.

"Let them out," I told Jonny.

The bell disappeared and they scrambled to reform their ranks. The Sun and Moon disciple held his dagger like he was ready for round two. "Come on, let's finish this," he said, still not making a move.

I felt like my suspicions were only confirmed by that. They had someone else here. Someone who couldn't outright kill me publicly. That meant there was an elder from one of their sects here waiting for me to kill them.

"I said scram dog, unless you want to kowtow to my friend here for disturbing his family." I took an aggressive step forward.

I could practically see the lackeys starting to shake. They were scared; I just needed to push them away.

"They more than deserve it," Jonny said through clenched teeth.

"I'll explain later." I put a hand up to stop him or Michelle from taking action. That would just play into their hand.

The trio of dogs seemed to be indecisive on their next action. The Sun and Moon disciple looked over behind a building, like he was looking for direction.

Now I was absolutely sure that this was all bait to justify killing me. "Okay, since you aren't leaving, please beg for forgiveness to my friend here." I waved back at Steve and his father.

There was some noise as people started arriving to witness the fight, and the Sun and Moon disciple was looking nervous.

"You got lucky this time!" he shouted and put away his dagger before turning and fleeing away before this could become a spectacle.

I could feel a pressure I hadn't even realized was there disappear along with the Sun and Moon disciple. I blew out a heavy breath. That had been closer than I cared to admit.

"We should have just killed them," Jonny sighed.

"No, I'm guessing there was someone else?" Michelle asked. She had full confidence in me.

"Yep. Pretty sure there was a second- or third-ring in the wings ready to kill us if we gave them justification." I turned my back to the crowd that looked disappointed that it didn't get to see a fight.

"Thanks." Steve came up and gave me a friendly pat on the shoulder. His father was quickly trying to make sure to block the hole in the fence.

Jonny wrapped Steve in a hug that clearly made the quiet man slightly uncomfortable.

Steve gave Michelle a once over before giving both of us a solid nod.

Now that I had a moment, I noticed Steve was wearing sect robes of a sect I didn't recognize.

"You got into a sect," I said.

Steve snorted, "Don't sound so surprised." Steve separated from Jonny and put himself on display. His robes were more ornate than some of the others. It was a burnt orange with a trim of animal silhouettes.

Jonny recognized it first. "Thousand Beast Sect. They tame mana beasts! That's like perfect for you, Steve."

It really was quite perfect for him. He had always had a way with animals. Though we joked, we were pretty sure he would rather spend time with a mare than a woman.

"Congrats, Steve." Michelle gave him her best cheery smile.

"Thanks." He ducked his head. "But they want to get out of town. Seems like once you put all the sects together, it is too hard for them to play nice." He rolled his eyes. "Worse than two cocks in a coop."

"Sticking around for the dungeon today?" I asked.

"I think so." He stared up at the clouds like they held the answer. "Weather looks nice. I don't see a storm coming yet."

"The weather doesn't indicate any omen, Steve," I said, patting him on the back.

He just shook his head.

"You got what you need?" I asked.

"One moment."

Steve and his father shared a stern handshake and a rough hug before Steve rejoined us. "All done. These rings come in handy." He pointed to his spatial ring with a grin.

We walked away and Michelle slipped her hand in mine. Jonny didn't miss the exchange.

"So cute. They finally figured it out, Steve."

Steve just nodded at the two of us. "About time."

Michelle gripped my hand tighter, and I turned to see a blush dust her cheeks.

A perky voice saved us from having to talk about this more as Celina waved us down and joined us on our way to the meetup spot for the dungeon. "Hi."

Celina had done her hair in an elaborate bun and put on makeup that highlighted her bright eyes and pouty lips.

She looked at me with a red face, probably remembering last night.

"Hi, I'm Jonny." Jonny was suddenly in front of Celina, smiling like a prince charming.

"Hi, I'm Celina, and I'm with both of them." She pointed to us as she tried to circle Jonny.

I could see him droop a bit as she saddled up to Michelle and started chatting.

"It's the bald head, isn't it?" Jonny asked me and Steve in a hushed voice.

"No. The two of them have just hit it off. Also…" I leaned in so the girls wouldn't overhear. "Thousand Blossom Valley girls cultivate poison—it would kill you to sleep with one."

Jonny sighed, "What a way to go. But I'm going to become celibate, so maybe a girl like that would work for me."

I stifled a laugh. "We'll ask if she has any friends." I pulled away from him, getting closer to the girls again.

"So, Celina, any news on the dungeon?" I pulled the two groups back into the same conversation. The five of us would be working together in the dungeon, after all.

"Not so much specific news about the dungeon, but some of the smaller sects are pulling out of town. They've gotten a disciple or two and are leaving. With how little mana you all were exposed to growing up, you are a treasure to some of the smaller sects."

As we arrived at the town gates, I saw what she was talking about. The sea of colorful robes had dimmed in variety.

Sun and Moon Hall was present, along with the Ferrymen and some of the larger sects. But the difference was noticeable.

Rigel leapt to the top of the city gates to get everyone's attention. "I thank everyone for joining us today. A reminder: together we are all mages. Inside the dungeon, I expect you to work together."

His eyes roamed the crowd as he exerted the pressure of his three rings.

"If only they'd stick to that," Celina whispered.

I turned, raising my brow in question.

Celina had a hard look on her face. "Elders always say that, but one of the first rules of going into a dungeon is that no one is to be held accountable for what happens inside. It is all a competition. Every resource in there must be fought for."

I thought about the note that Narissa had given me. I was certainly heading into the dungeon to promote my cultivation, but I also wanted to save her.

"—if you'll all follow me," Rigel finished. I hadn't been listening, distracted by thoughts of the future.

A warm sense enveloped all of the disciples as the elders released their auras and headed out of the city.

The dungeon wasn't far. In an hour, I was face-to-face with the first dungeon portal I'd ever seen.

The crackling blue swirl of mana seemed to engulf the surrounding area. It was as large as a house as it spun in on itself. The portal rumbled with rushing wind that had stripped the nearby trees of leaves.

"Woah," Jonny whispered as we finally saw it.

It felt so oppressive standing in front of the giant portal. I knew inside would be like a small world unto itself.

The ground was cracked where the portal met it, and the entire atmosphere was crackling with mana as some of it bled out of the dungeon portal.

Mana made the world what it was—it made mana beasts and mages. These portals had torn down the old world and created the era of mages.

These dungeons had changed the world. Standing before one, I could almost feel the pressure of the dungeon changing me.

"Have you been in one before?" I asked Celina as we all stared at it.

"No. If it was so easy to find one appropriate for early cultivators, the sects wouldn't have stuck around this small town," she said, determination flashing across her features. "This is an opportunity."

The dungeon portal continued to swirl as everyone gathered before it.

I repeated what she'd said to myself. It was an opportunity. Dungeons were filled with mana beasts and mana in its purest form. Even just hunting in one was a boon. But dungeons had a deep history. That much was clear.

Inside, there would be remnants of a civilization, even if just in the form of tattered equipment. Mana seeped into anything left behind, from weapons to small trinkets. Even plants and minerals would be changed.

Natural enchantments would form, creating items of power. The type of items that mana beasts were drawn to.

I knew there would be tough fights ahead, but there would be plenty of rewards as well.

"A little late, aren't they?" Michelle was watching the Sun and Moon Hall along with the Earth Flame Sect stroll into the clearing and take up a spot closest to the dungeon portal.

Leading the group was a man so pretty it made me uncomfortable. It was like he was a porcelain doll rather than a person.

I hadn't seen him before, and his robes were different from the rest. They were more ornate, with detailed trimmings and a deep embroidery around his collar.

"Inner Court disciple," Celina answered the question we all had.

Jonny looked confused, so Celina continued, "Sects are often divided up into outer, inner and core disciples. It's all enforced by a competition system so that only the strongest disciples move up and obtain more resources."

I looked again at the mage in question and caught the attention of Aiden, who was following behind him.

He whispered something to the pretty boy, who turned our way as well.

"What would be the position of the Sect Head's son? Would he be an inner disciple?" I asked Celina as I met the gaze of the pretty boy.

"Unlikely. He'd be a core disciple, or maybe even a special case above them." I nodded. I felt both disappointed and relieved that this man wasn't likely the one Aiden had said Kat was destined for.

Our stare off was broken when a bald man in tattered robes approached us, homing in on Jonny.

"Monk," Jonny greeted him with a respectful bow.

The elder just played with a strand of wooden beads as he stared at Jonny. "You were to leave today. We have already collected your family."

"I'm sorry elder, but what kind of mage would I be if I abandoned my friends at this point?" Jonny kept his head bowed as he answered.

The monk seemed to consider his words. "Then you have made your choice. Lucky for you, the Monastery is willing to invest in you."

A small stone tablet appeared in the monk's hands, and I could see the extravagant enchantment pattern. "An insurance policy," he said, touching it to Jonny's forehead and breaking off a small chunk cleanly in a way that made the pattern shift.

The monk stepped back, looking satisfied.

"What was that?" Jonny asked.

"A very expensive enchantment meant to teleport you back to him if he feels you are in danger," Celina said, looking at Jonny in a new light. "They must highly value you if they are going to that trouble."

He shrugged. "They are certainly intense. I don't know how that differs from their other disciples."

Celina gave him another once over, not finding what she was looking for.

I clapped Jonny on the shoulder. "That's great! If they are going to this much trouble, we can all rest easy for your safety."

Jonny nodded thoughtfully. "Will this help the rest of you?"

"It won't save us, but look around," Celina said.

We had caught some extra stares after being visited by the monk.

"That monk just marked you as important, and you can be sure more than a few people will be scared of offending him by doing too much to you."

More and more people gathered around the dungeon entrance as elders said their last words to their disciples.

The first to head in was the group from the Sun and Moon Hall. They disappeared into the vortex, and that started a trend of groups forming up and walking through.

"We all ready?" I asked the group, not looking away from the maelstrom of mana. I felt a warm glow as Aurora signaled she was ready. The others nodded, and I took a deep breath.

Chapter 25

Stepping through the portal was an experience. A suffocating pressure of mana enveloped me with that first step. It was as if my body was going through something too tight to fit, yet I was being stretched along through the tunnel to come out the other side.

There was nothing to compare the feeling of going from one world to another. In just an instant, everything around me changed.

Sticky heat blasted my face, an abrupt change from the temperate forest I'd just left. I looked around, finding myself in a wild jungle dense with vegetation.

The area around the portal had been cleared, likely from the first investigation of the dungeon.

I breathed in the air and felt my mana stir. I smiled, it seemed like even taking a breath here would further my cultivation.

"Beautiful," Michelle said as she took in the tropic flowers that colored the landscape.

The previous groups had already hurried ahead of us, and we were alone for a moment before another group would head through.

"Come on. We can take in the sights when we aren't right next to the portal." I headed off in a random direction.

I wasn't worried about finding our way back. With the mana draining from here into our world, all you had to do was follow the wind to make it back to the portal.

Celina was the first to stop and pluck a flower from the growth around us.

"Is that important?" I asked.

"Nothing great, but I was sensitive to its poisonous properties. It caught my attention. If nothing else, it will continue to grow back at the sect." She shrugged as the flower vanished into her spatial ring.

I saw movement out of the corner of my eye and didn't have time to say anything before I tackled Celina to the ground.

Sharp pain lanced through my shoulder as the snake managed to alter its target.

Michelle and Steve were on the rank one beast in an instant, knocking it off me and keeping it from fleeing.

Celina's eyes went from confusion to determination in the instant we landed on the ground together.

Pushing me off her, she got on her hands and knees to inspect the wound. Even as she looked, I knew that the snake had poisoned me.

Numbness started to spread down my arm from the bite.

"It's poison," she confirmed for me after she probed the wound with her mana. "Shit, I'm sorry."

"Not your fault, and I'll heal right up." I started to cycle my life mana before Celina shook me.

"Poison doesn't always work that way. Let me see if I can help." She pulled out a vial from her spatial ring.

"Are you a doctor too?" I teased, but she looked determined.

"Oftentimes the only difference between medicine and poison is dosage." She wrapped her lips around my shoulder and started drawing the poison out, spitting it into the vial.

I watched as the others wrapped up what looked like a harder fight than I would have expected for three against a rank one mana beast.

The serpent moved gracefully and almost flowed around their attacks. They played it cautiously, given my current state, but it was Jonny who finished it with the spell that formed a golden bell, dropping it on the snake with a crunch.

"That thing was tough," Jonny said, looking like he was going to be sick and turned away from the crushed snake. Steve dug out its core, a muddy yellow. It was nothing more than a variant of earth mana.

"We knew mana beasts would be tougher in a dungeon. Just like it's dangerous for us, it is for them too. Only the strong survive," I quoted Professor Locke.

"Bring me the snake?" Celina asked Michelle, who hurried to comply.

"This will make things easier," she said, pumping venom from its dead jaws like she'd done it a hundred times. She started mixing it with a vial she'd pulled out of her spatial ring, while we all watched with fascination.

When she finished and looked up, her face flushed red. "What? We work with poison and the mana beasts that make it all the time. Of course I'd be prepared to deal with a snake bite."

She ignored them and handed me her finished concoction. "Drink that. It'll counteract the paralysis. Luckily, this is a pretty simple poison."

"Thanks. Glad to have you." We all agreed with nods.

"No, I screwed up. I stopped next to a plant that contained elemental mana. I should have known that there would be a mana beast nearby." She wrung her hands.

"I lived, and you made it right," I said, downing the potion. It was bitter and soapy, but I did my best to swallow without tasting it. "We lived and we learned."

Getting up, we stored away the corpse and continued to wander through the jungle.

My arm felt a bit stiff, and I stretched it as we walked, circulating my mana to heal the puncture wound.

We traveled for hours. The humid jungle was filled with small but deadly beasts, but we knew there would be larger predators here.

The snakes and sharp-beaked birds were just fodder for the dungeon. All around us, the dungeon was filled with mana-infused life fighting for survival. Even the trees fought for sunlight, blanketing the jungle in a green canopy.

I spotted gray stone through the trees. "There's a building." I pointed towards the overgrown structure before slowing down and approaching slowly with the group close behind me.

"So strange to see something built by humans in a dungeon," Michelle whispered. "That means once upon a time there were people, or at least something close to them in the dungeons."

The thought set off strange alarm bells in my mind. Where did dungeons come from?

I didn't have time to reflect as metal on metal sounded up ahead.

"Get down," I hissed as we crept up to a worn-down portion of what I now realized was a wall.

Inside, there was a stone building just as overgrown as the wall, but the fight inside really caught my attention.

The mustard yellow robes of the Earthen Bull Sect stood out as Grant fought alongside two of his fellows against five figures wrapped in black clothes that hid their face.

"Bastards," Michelle hissed, catching up and seeing the same scene.

I was fairly certain she meant the mages dressed like thieves, but Celina spoke up first.

"It's not uncommon. Our elder all gave us clothes like that. If you need to fight, sometimes it is easier to not risk retaliation."

There was a large mana beast corpse on the ground and likely something in the structure. From the way Grant's group looked worn down, and the mystery cultivators fighting with full energy, it was clear they were here to poach from Grant.

I grunted in acknowledgment and stood, stepping over the wall.

"What are you doing?" Jonny hissed. But the others were following right behind me.

"Making friends." I smirked before I drew my sword and attacked one of the masked mages.

My sword drew a clean arc through the air that sprayed blood as the masked mage barely reacted in time to prevent their arm from being severed.

"Ambush!" he yelled as he clutched his arm and darted away.

The others turned, and I caught a look of hopelessness flash through Grant's expression when he saw who it was.

"Michelle, guard Jonny. Jonny, patch up our friends. Steve, Celina, with me," I shouted, rushing the next thief.

There was no hesitation as the group split up to their tasks.

Blades of wind shot at me as another thief charged me with a sword.

I tapped into the savage aspect of my mana and slashed through the wind blades before lashing out with a kick and knocking the sword off course.

Unbalanced from striking in two directions, I fumbled on my follow-up hit, and the two mages recovered.

They came at me fast, with the speed only two wind mages could have.

I shifted from trying to win to trying to stall. It was five on three at present, but if Jonny could get Grant's group on their feet, we would quickly outnumber them. All I needed to do was stall.

Blocking another strike, I felt the danger as one of them cast a wind blade again.

Gathering mana to my hand, I punched it out while I blocked another sword.

This was getting uncomfortably close for me. I switched back to a two-handed grip, but my fist that had blocked the wind blade was hurt.

Celina appeared before one of the thieves and blew out a cloud of green smoke with a spell.

The thief screamed as their body rapidly decayed.

"Retreat!" a deep voice of one of the thieves screamed and two others fled with him.

"Celina, Steve, don't chase," I shouted.

Steve had already pinned the thief whose arm I had cut. He wasn't going anywhere, and it looked like he might not last very long.

"Take his mask off and figure out who we are dealing with," I said before turning to Grant, who was back on his feet.

"Not who I'd expect to come to my rescue," Grant said, meeting my eyes.

Now that I got a better look at him, I realized he had been nearly dead on his feet. Tracks of bright red claw marks dotted his arms, and he was looking far paler than last I'd seen him. But after a round of Jonny's healing, the wounds were already fading to an angry pink.

I held out my hand. "Forgiven and forgotten. Pretty sure we left any past grudges on the fighting stage."

Grant just shook his head in disbelief before grabbing my hand for a shake. "I'd certainly rather a friend than an enemy right now. Take what you want from here as thanks."

"Grant you can't—" one of his sect mates shouted before Grant cut them off.

"They just saved your lives. Shut it."

Showing up as the hero and taking everything from them didn't sit right with me.

"I'll take the rings off your would-be thieves. You take what you want from that mana beast, and we'll both take what we can from the keep," I said.

He smiled savagely. "Take what you kill. Sounds more than fair. If that second-rank mana beast hadn't worn us out, we'd have been fine with those vultures."

I gave the steely blue tiger another look. It was as big as a horse. One look made it clear that it was a fight of attrition rather than a simple kill. Numerous shallow wounds covered the beast, and the ground was covered with its blood.

It was deserving of being a second-rank mana beast. The fact that Grant and his group of three had managed to take it down was a show of their strength.

"Any other mana beasts inside?" I asked, eyeing the building.

"Nothing yet, but we haven't explored the building," Grant said as his two men started on the tiger corpse.

It was getting late even though the sky hadn't shifted in the dungeon. I wasn't sure it was going to, or at least, not at the rate we were used to.

We had some time left in the day, but why waste such an opportunity.

"We'll camp in the building. Explore it before we settle in for the night," I said loud enough for everyone to hear.

Nods were followed by a pitiful scream of the remaining thief as Steve finished him.

I stepped up to the building. It was large enough to be called a mansion back in Locksprings. Built with stone and with its surrounding walls, it really did seem like a keep or defensive outpost.

"I'll take a look with you." Michelle came up to my side as I approached the entrance.

The door was long gone, and the entrance widened large enough for... I looked back at the tiger corpse. That looked about right.

"If that thing lived here, it's not likely there is something else here. Well, except for treasure." I leaned around the entrance to see inside.

"Or something like a mate," Michelle said.

I froze and looked back at her to follow her line of sight. She was staring into the door with me. I realized she was just guessing; she hadn't seen anything.

"Don't scare me like that," I said, letting out a sigh. She was just asking for something bad to happen.

Inside was a mess of scattered bones. It looked like the tiger had dragged numerous meals home.

We were soon joined by the rest of the team after we finished scouting, and we set up camp before digging through the place for treasure.

When we found what appeared to be the tiger's resting spot, we knew we had hit the jackpot. It was a half-dug hole in the floor of the keep, filled with dry bones and dried up vines, like a nest of something that occupied this building before the tiger.

Michelle fished out a round shield that radiated mana. "This is nice." She tested it as it glowed a faint purple. "Really nice!" She gave it a good thump.

Grant and his group were there, but they held back. When I pulled a large warhammer from the nest, I looked over to see one of his men practically drooling.

"Here, this doesn't fit any of our fighting styles." I handed the weapon to Grant.

He shook his head in disbelief. "It's times like this that make me remember our true purpose. Not to fight each other, but instead to unite against the corrupt mages. I feel like too many have forgotten that."

"Remember, we are from the boonies. I've never seen a corrupt mage and I feel our elders didn't go into detail on purpose," I said pulling more debris out of the hole.

"That's right. So easy to forget with how well you all fight. The corrupt mages are those who've perverted cultivation." Grant tossed a find in his spatial ring.

"Can you explain that better? What's wrong with their cultivation?" Michelle asked.

"You cultivate by absorbing the ambient mana in the world and with beast cores, correct?" Grant led with a question.

"Of course." Michelle shrugged. "That's how you cultivate."

"Well, there are other methods."

I couldn't help thinking of the dual cultivation method I'd heard in the brothel, and my face flushed.

"Not all of them are bad; some can even be quite enjoyable." One of his men chuckled at that.

"But some are considered too dangerous or too vile. There is a corrupt sect that captures people and harvests them for their blood and organs. They will feed the person countless herbs and mana cores until they die from being overloaded. Their blood and organs are then consumed to boost their disciples."

"That's terrible! Why go to all the trouble when you could just hunt mana beasts?" Michelle looked disgusted.

"Because it is effective," Celina cut in. "Corrupt mages are very powerful, and that sect is entirely cannibals. What do you think happens when they win a fight?"

"Oh god." Michelle looked even sicker. "They eat them, don't they?"

"Yes, and worse." Celina's eyes burned with fury of a personal grudge. "But the core of it all is that corrupt mages harm other humans to cultivate."

That sounded a bit too familiar; my stomach turned. I looked over at Jonny as I asked, "Like controlling someone?"

Celina scowled and shifted. "Yeah, that certainly fits."

"There used to be corrupt mages that did that. We have them in our records because they liked to hunt physically stronger mages." Grant beat his chest.

I almost didn't want to ask. "What happened to them?"

If Grant picked up on my discomfort, he didn't show it. "There was a decisive battle between them and the Sun and Moon Hall. Afterwards, they were wiped out. The Puppet Sect was considered one of the strongest corrupt sects and were the rivals of the Sun and Moon Hall. Since they've been gone, the Sun and Moon Hall has been a behemoth, continuing to grow."

"Good thing too," one of the other Earthen Bull disciples said. "Puppets are terrifying. They feel no pain and often are enhanced in ways you couldn't do to a typical mage, like casting metal around their bodies. Worst part is that supposedly the person's soul is still in the puppet. That's how they still have their fighting skills."

"You could create an army like that," I said, suddenly feeling like the ground had disappeared below me. "You'd just need a source of low-level mages, right?"

I swallowed a thick lump in my throat as I thought of Kat and every other young mage that had been recruited to the Sun and Moon Hall.

"Exactly. Good thing the Sun and Moon Hall got rid of them," Grant said, pulling more out of the hole.

But I'd stopped, thinking of Narissa and all the low-ranked people who had joined them. What if the Sun and Moon Hall hadn't won? What if they were now one giant puppet?

I couldn't help but feel a ball of terror grow in my gut.

"What's wrong?" Michelle whispered.

I thought about talking it out right there, but I wasn't sure if Grant would believe me. I sounded insane to myself.

"Later. I'll tell you later, Michelle. Now let's see what's at the bottom of this pile."

I tried to push it out of my mind and focus on the matter at hand. While something needed to be done, it was going to take a lot to overthrow the Sect.

Pulling on a large chunk of the nest, I ripped it up and over my shoulder. A few things fell out and some loot was still in the nest, but all of our eyes locked on what was under it.

"Are those all mana crystals?" Jonny asked, jumping down into the hole.

Under the nesting was a small cave glittering with blue crystals that peeked through the smooth surface of the wall.

The rest of the nest lifted with everyone working together, wanting to get a better look at the prize.

Jonny already had a pick out and was swinging at the wall to uncover one of the mana crystals.

But as soon as he struck, his pick bounced off, nearly hitting himself in the face.

"What?" Jonny flexed his hands from the strike before trying again and finding the same result. The stone was too hard for him to break through.

"Sam, go try," Grant said to one of his partners.

The large man jumped down into the hole, crowding Jonny, but he didn't seem to mind as he pulled out his own pick and slammed it into the wall with just as much effect as Jonny.

"Might be able to get one out, boss, but it would take all day."

Grant clicked his tongue. "Useless mana crystals. And it looks like either the tiger or something else sheared them all back to the wall."

He said that, but I could feel the rich mana in the cave and had other ideas. "Can I cultivate in the cave?"

Grant shrugged. "Sure, it'll help, but there's already so much ambient mana in the air."

I didn't explain the peculiarity of the Seven Hells Meridians as I grinned inwardly. This would save me hundreds if not thousands of beast cores if I was able to pull from the mana crystals in the wall.

Cultivating with such pure mana in mana crystals was a luxury I was sure almost no one performed this technique with.

"There might be more treasure, but this was the big haul. Call everything else fair game and rest for the night?" I said to my group before setting up my tent and bedroll by the cave.

Looks went between Celina and Michelle as they together eyed my tent. Michelle seemed to agree to something, followed by them crowding into it with me as everyone settled down.

"I need a bigger tent," I grumbled. It was crowded, but at present, I wanted it for its wards.

"What was wrong earlier?" Michelle asked.

I looked at the enchantment on the tent to make sure it was still powered before I spoke. I started off with the story of going to the brothel. The girls listened patiently with confused faces until I got to the confused woman and the note that she'd given me. That, along with the conversation with Grant, started to connect the dots.

It was quiet in the tent after I finished. "So, you think the Sun and Moon Hall is practicing corrupt techniques, and there is a girl who is evidence of it here in the dungeon?"

"That about sums it up. I want to try and save her if what Grant said is true. And I believe it by how she acted—her soul is still there."

"But if you save her, you'll be hunted for uncovering what is likely their darkest secret." Celina's gaze held something I couldn't quite put my finger on. She wasn't telling me something.

I shook my head back at her. "It might cause more trouble, but I can't look away. I've seen the callousness in the sects, but I reject it. I can't ignore something like this."

My mind was made up. I had seen the attitude of the sect disciples in constant pursuit of greater cultivation and ignoring what inconvenienced them. I wasn't going to be that type of mage.

Celina nodded slowly. "Okay, we'll save her, but we need to wait until we have the advantage"

I gave her a big grin, and then shared my plan to cultivate in the cave to replace the high cost of the next layer of our meridian cultivation.

"That… that just might work," she said once I was finished with the plan.

"Can you keep watch while we both try and break through the next layer?"

"Of course," Celina said with a grin as we climbed out of the tent. We wouldn't be using it tonight.

She posted up outside the cave, cross-legged and practicing her own cultivation while I climbed down with Michelle.

Michelle gave me a quick kiss before sitting down. "Isaac, good luck. I feel like this technique is dangerous. Don't leave me."

There was vulnerability painted on her face.

"Don't worry. I'm too stubborn to let a cultivation technique tear me down." I kissed her on the forehead and sat down close enough to her such that our knees touched, then settled in to try to break through the next layer.

Chapter 26

I settled my mind as I sat in the cave. The mana crystals gave off a soft glow in the dark, slightly sparkling, making it feel even more otherworldly.

I took deep breaths and started to clear my mind. I pressed the worries for the Sun and Moon Hall away. I breathed through worries for my family and my future as a mage. I sank deeper into my meditation and slowly looked around my inner world once again.

The mantra for the third layer of the Seven Hells Meridians floated from my mind out my mouth. My mana synced up with the words and began to flow in the elaborate script that would become another layer of reinforced pathways for my mana to flow.

Not long after I started, I could feel a raw hunger set deep within me. Everywhere my meridians brushed the surface of my body, dozens of hungry vortexes formed, draining the mana from my environment.

I could feel the air thin with mana before one of the vortexes locked onto a mana crystal and drained it dry.

For a brief moment, I felt full. Then a deeper gnawing hunger for mana overtook me, and I actively adjusted to draw mana from another mana crystal.

I drank mana crystal after mana crystal before it felt like I tapped into one that was too large for me to handle.

But it didn't matter. My meridians kept draining the mana as they began to swell. Yet the hunger never decreased. If anything, it grew.

In the center of my heart, my bloodline stirred. The blood beast that had been dormant awoke, like it sensed a challenge.

The representation of my bloodline opened its maw and consumed my mana faster than I could drain it from the mana crystals around me. One by one, each of my vortexes found a mana crystal until it felt like I was drowning in mana.

Inch by inch, a gold pattern grew on my bloodline until its whole body was alight in a pattern the same as on the hilt of my mother's sword.

When it finished, I felt a connection snap into place with Aurora. A great pressure released from my body, as mana fed into Aurora's ring. It came back out as a released stream. Somehow, in the deep hunger, I had failed to cycle my mana and continued to try and pack foreign mana into my meridians.

Now, with the help of Aurora once again, mana flowed through my meridians swiftly and orderly. But I was still absorbing mana from the cave at an alarming rate. Slowly but surely, my meridians at each level of the technique flexed to accommodate.

I wasn't sure how long it had taken, but when my meridians finally became satisfied, the draw of mana slowed.

My ability to pull mana rapidly into my body was still there, something I apparently had gained from this layer of the technique. But it was under my control now. I could see in my inner world that a new pattern overlaid the first two, connecting my meridians to the exterior of my body in a way that would let me draw ambient mana from the world more efficiently.

Opening my eyes and breathing out, I felt like even my breath was rich in mana.

I heard a sigh next to me and saw Michelle already awake.

"I wasn't sure how much longer you'd take. Had me scared," she said as a loud crack resounded in the cave.

Grabbing Michelle and moving with a speed I didn't even know I had, I leapt from the cave as it collapsed in on itself.

The ground shuddered as the building groaned and the floor sank into the cave.

I stared at the mess where we had just been. The loss of mana crystals must have destabilized it.

Celina was by our side in a heartbeat. "Did that interrupt you during the process?"

I felt great and Michelle, even though she was covered in a sheen of sweat, never looked more vibrant.

"No, lucky us, the cave decided to wait for me." I shot her a cocky grin, not wanting to show unease and make her anxious. That could have been the end of me if I hadn't come out of meditation when I did.

Dragging them both back to the tent, I settled down to get what sleep I could. Celina cast more than a few worried looks but settled in when she picked up that all I wanted to do was sleep.

***

I felt something tickle my nose as I woke. A vision of green feathers filled my sight.

With Michelle and Celina to my side and Aurora on top of me, the tent was packed to the brim. I was sure we were stretching the side walls.

It was really time for me to get a larger tent.

Wiggling and clearing my throat, I hoped to wake one of them so I could dislodge myself. But they were either content or sleeping like the dead.

I blew in Aurora's ear until she stirred and looked at me sleepily.

"Morning. Getting up," I whispered.

She blinked her groggy eyes before turning into a stream of light and entering her ring.

With Aurora off me, I managed to escape the tangle of limbs.

As I stepped out of the tent, I saw Grant and his two friends packing up the last of their things.

"Leaving already?" I asked light heartedly. He owed me nothing, and while it was more dangerous moving in a small group, there were fewer people to split rewards across.

He looked like he'd been caught red-handed. "Morning, Isaac. We didn't want to disturb you all. It sounded like you were up late last night."

Grant looked at the cave that had collapsed in on itself.

I waved off the unasked question. "It was a pleasure to work with someone rather than fighting off every other sect."

Grant grinned. "As it should be. Though I set us off on the wrong foot, I'm glad we left it all back on the competition stage."

He pulled a scroll out of his spatial ring. "One of my guys found this last night. That you are up saves me time writing a note."

Taking the scroll, I could tell it was a spell and looked at Grant with a raised brow.

"When we fought, you said you didn't have any spells. I know life mana focuses on healing and doesn't have many offensive abilities, but I think this'll help."

"Thanks. You didn't have to, so it means extra. Maybe I'll get to use it when we fight together again." I grinned, hoping that if a fight with the Sun and Moon Hall came, other sects would join. I was sure that the Ferrymen would take the opportunity to fight. I just wasn't sure about the other sects.

"Deal." Grant stuck out a hand, and I shook it.

They headed out not long after, and I sat at the entrance to the building with my new spell in one hand and jerky in the other.

The scroll detailed the life of a self-proclaimed wandering healer. It went into his life as he traveled the world and eventually his need to defend himself.

Though life mana is not offensive in nature, he created a spell of concentrated life mana in the form of needles to protect himself when needed.

Pulling down the last segment of the scroll revealed the Golden Needle spell. The scroll stated it was an altered form of a spell intended to provide acupuncture.

I memorized the mana patterns for casting the spell and circulated my mana in those patterns as I watched the morning sun rise.

Feeling like I had the hang of it, I cast the spell for real and a golden beam shot out of my hand, making a hole in a nearby tree.

It was fast. Incredibly fast.

Jumping up to examine the tree, I saw that it had made a clean hole about the size of my finger.

The world in the dungeon was infused with an incredible amount of mana, which meant this tree was strong. For the spell to make such a clean hole meant that, not only was it fast, it was sharp.

I paused to take stock of my mana. I had only lost about a tenth of my reserves, and they were quickly recovering with the aid of the latest layer of Seven Hells Meridians.

Noise sounded behind me, taking me out of my contemplation.

"Morning, Isaac." A sleepy Jonny half-yawned before he looked around and noticed Grant was gone.

"They left at the crack of dawn," I answered before he could ask the question. "But they shared this before they left."

I handed Jonny the spell. He also had a life mana beast for his first ring.

"No need. The Ascetic already gave me some spells. I need to keep practicing those," Jonny said before he turned quickly to me. "But I wasn't holding those from you. He said that others wouldn't be able to practice them."

I shrugged it off. "They are your sect's spells. You probably shouldn't share them around anyways."

"The old man kept saying that I had the heart of Budda and that's why he wanted me, and why I can use these spells." Jonny looked down at his hands as he said it.

"That bell is pretty awesome. Offense and defense in one."

Jonny's eyes shined. "It really is. It's just pure overwhelming force. You can trap people in it, and boom, done."

Steve came out next looking far more put together than Jonny. And finally, both girls came out together. They looked like they'd spent some time getting ready and were dressed ready to move out. They must have packed everything too.

Michelle had just a hint of makeup that made her blue eyes catch and hold my vision. She was gorgeous.

She caught me looking and gave me a smirk.

I felt a swell of pride at having such a beautiful woman, and while things were a bit undefined with Celina, I was looking forward to seeing where things went.

"Grant already left. I'm thinking we head out and find more opportunities in this dungeon." I flashed everyone a grin before heading off into the dense jungle of the dungeon.

With my newest layer of meridians, I could feel the mana in the air of the dungeon. A sense of it ebbed and flowed through the air.

"Michelle, can you sense the mana better?" I asked the beautiful blonde.

She paused a moment, closing her eyes. "Yes, and it's thicker that way." She pointed off to the right.

I looked at the rest of the group for their opinions.

"Thicker mana would be more likely to have resources, but also stronger opponents. But probably the best shot we have," Steve said, and I agreed.

Following the mana, we continued through the jungle with a few findings along our way. But as the mana in the air grew richer, the jungle grew quieter.

I held up my hand to slow the group before carefully moving forward.

There, right up against a cliff face, was a small, lone fruit tree.

"Those are Meridian Cleansing Fruit," Celina whispered in awe.

I looked at the fragile little tree and noticed the ground was bare of even a single blade of grass around it. I wanted these fruits for our group; they would help Jonny and Steve soar ahead in their own sects.

But something was wrong. I had a gut feeling that something was guarding this little tree. "Isn't it a bit suspicious that the jungle is so quiet? That nothing has gone near that tree? Beasts should be drawn to it like that snake we saw earlier."

Celina cursed. "Yeah, you're right, good call. There's no way this isn't guarded. But I really want those fruits."

We were all looking around, trying to find what might be guarding it, but there was absolutely nothing but the little tree against the cliff.

"Maybe it's not here right now?" Jonny suggested with hope in his voice.

I looked around again, not seeing anything. "Okay, I'll go snag the fruits. You are all on watch. If you see anything, yell. Or better yet, take it down." I gave Michelle a squeeze before darting off before she could stop me.

Without a doubt, Michelle was glaring at me right now for endangering myself, but I wasn't going to turn and look.

I ignored the bushes and vines and darted to the tree, hoping to get this over quickly.

Up close, the Meridian Cleaning Fruit looked so fragile. The fruit's rind was almost transparent, and you could see golden threads of mana coursing inside of them.

This was the first time I'd actually seen such a treasure. It made me pause just a bit longer than I should have, but my urgency prevailed and I reached to start harvesting them.

As soon as I reached for the first one, there were audible gasps from my group.

I didn't have time to worry. They weren't shouting, so I grabbed the fruit with the haste only a mage had.

"Run!" Michelle said suddenly by my side, casting her shield spell between me and the cliff face.

I didn't understand why until I saw the cliff... move?

It rose up on four short legs, and I realized it certainly was not a cliff face. No, the mana beast was a massive rocky-scaled flood dragon.

Its eye locked onto me, and I knew in that moment it was a terrifying body of power. This had to be a peak second-rank mana beast if it hadn't already passed into the third rank.

"Run," I echoed Michelle, grabbing her hand and rushing away from the waking giant.

I had managed to pick the tree clean of ripe fruit before it had stirred, storing the eight fruits away in my spatial ring.

But that wouldn't matter if I didn't live to use them.

The flood dragon lifted its head and roared with a voice that echoed for miles before it slammed its long tail around, leveling the surrounding trees.

I looked back, hoping to see Jonny and the others fleeing to safety. They weren't in sight.

"We need to worry about ourselves. They'll be fine," Michelle yelled over the sound of devastation as dozens of trees crashed to the ground.

The flood dragon was looking right at us, with its slit golden eyes staring down its maw of a mouth.

It didn't look fast, which might save us. It was clearly growing to be like a dragon, but it lacked flight and its legs were small compared to its body.

Unfortunately, it was going to do what it could with what it had to protect the tree. It abandoned the pretext of using its legs and started slithering across the ground, closing the gap between us quickly.

Pouring on the speed, I tapped into as much mana as I could handle, bursting through the jungle floor and pulling Michelle along.

The flood dragon practically swam through the forest as the trees tore away from its path. I couldn't so much see it as see the massive devastation it was leaving in its wake as it cut through the jungle.

We burst through to a clearing, where several mages were fighting a mana beast. Both sides paused in surprise, but we kept pushing forward.

Screams from both mages and mana beasts came from behind us as they realized the greater danger of the flood dragon.

"Stud, it can't see us. Let's. Cut. Right." Michelle was gasping for breath.

Taking the turn in stride, we made a sharp right, hoping to lose the flood dragon to the dense forest.

It certainly couldn't see us through the jungle, but it wasn't dumb.

Not long after we'd switched directions, an eruption of water came from the flood dragon like a tsunami. The wave of water stripped the forest bare for a mile around the flood dragon. This thing really liked scorched earth policy when hunting.

"Isaac. Duck." Michelle pulled us down behind a large tree and threw up her shield to cover us.

The tree flexed and groaned as the wave tried to rip it out by the roots.

I was afraid it was going to wrench free, until the top half of the tree splintered and was swept away in the flood dragons attack, taking the pressure away.

The roots resettled, and we hunkered down as the flood dragon continued to send tidal wave after wave out, wrecking the surrounding jungle.

I looked around, and what was left was like the jungle had suffered a natural disaster. This rank three mana beast was a force of nature.

The flood dragon stood amid the leveled forest, looking back and forth for the thief that stole its fruit.

I could feel dozens of eyes scanning the forest. There was no way this level of destruction didn't pull the attention of everyone in the dungeon.

Every mage in the dungeon in the vicinity was watching this scene.

"Should we make a run for it?" Michelle asked.

I shook my head. "We do not want to be the first to pop back up and make a run for it. The flood dragon is on a warpath."

Digging at the roots of the tree, I tried to make a better position to last.

"What are you doing?"

"Digging in. It is going to keep watch until it finds something to chase. It might even start spewing those waves again." I kept digging, not afraid to get my hands dirty.

As my hands touched the soil, I felt a draw to the earth. I couldn't explain it. I worked life mana—earth shouldn't be pulling me.

"This is ridiculous," Michelle grumbled as she joined me to help. "Why is there something so strong in this dungeon?"

"The flood dragon is probably the king of this dungeon. And even though the dungeon portal wasn't stable enough for second-rings to enter, it doesn't mean the dungeon would be tuned to a first-ring mage's strength."

As if in agreement, the flood dragon let out another frustrated roar before huge waves of water began hammering the surroundings again.

"Isaac!" Michelle hissed happily as she cleared away dirt to reveal the lip of a stone hatch. "I swear, we are far too lucky."

Looking at the hatch, I paused. The draw and the hatch made me hesitant, but we didn't have many options. Plus, it just felt right.

Hurrying to help her clear away more of the dirt, we found a metal ring still attached and slipped inside the hatch.

I could feel cold stone steps below me and pulled a ball of life mana into my hand for some light. We still couldn't see much further than a few feet with the light it gave off.

Michelle already had out a torch and was working to light it.

The torch came to life, and the stone room lit up. It wasn't some ancient tomb, or a cavern full of danger. Instead, it seemed like a simple cellar. Like one that might have belonged to a building long gone on the surface.

The contents of the cellar had turned to dust, at least most of them. In the center of the cellar was a stone pillar etched with an enchantment. It looked very familiar.

"Stud, are you okay?" Michelle asked. Aurora pulsed in her ring.

Letting Aurora out, she joined Michelle's concern before looking at the pillar again. "I think you should try to put your blood on it."

"What do you mean?" Michelle looked back and forth between us until I explained why I was so startled. That pillar looked surprisingly like the one I had retrieved my mother's sword out of.

It had the same patterning—the mana beast that seemed to flow from one type to another.

I cut my palm and pressed it against the stone.

Unlike before, there was no big flash. Instead, my blood seeped into the channels of the enchantment, and it shifted, unlocking a portion.

A soft blue beam came out and standing before me was my mother, smiling with crinkling corners of her eyes.

"It's been a while my baby boy!" my mother squealed, her arms spread wide for a hug. I stood dumbstruck.

Chapter 27

My mother stood before me with wide open arms and an excitement that was impossible to miss.

But how was this possible? There's no way my mother could be here, now.

I stepped back, looking around the room for some ambush or other trick to this. Could this have pulled my memory of her from my blood?

The excitement in her eyes dimmed as she pouted. "My baby boy won't hug me. I'm sorry, Isaac. I had to leave."

Hearing her plea felt like someone stabbing me in the heart. "If you're really my mother, I'm going to need you to prove it."

She rolled her eyes before sighing again. "Well technically, I'm not really your mother. I'm a fragment of her soul, left here, where so many of your threads of fate converged. It was a near certainty you'd end up in this little cellar for one reason or another. And it was a safe place for me to leave a message."

"Strings of fate? I don't understand." I lost some of my caution, my curiosity taking over.

"Bothersome things my—our family spend far too much time on. We are naturally lucky, but no, that wasn't enough. We had to start manipulating our luck until we touched fate itself." My mother shrugged then opened her arms again with a hopeful expression.

"Should we give it another go?" She transitioned straight from speaking factually to ebbing with energy.

I didn't really understand, but a part of me wanted this to really be my mother. Honestly, a part of me felt this was really her.

Taking a chance, I stepped forward into her embrace. She wrapped her arms around me in a fierce hug that only a mother could have.

Tears stung at the edge of my eyes, but I took a deep breath and returned the hug with all my might. This was my mother. I could feel it.

"My baby boy," she whispered over and over as she hugged me, like she was trying to make up for thirteen years.

When she finally calmed down, she put me at arm's length and looked me over before she looked at Aurora and Michelle with a judgment that could only come from a mother.

"You are not who I expected." She gave Michelle a tilt of her head. "His strings of fate were tied so tightly with that little girl, Kat." Then she looked back at me, but it felt like she was looking through me to something else.

"Still are actually," she said, her forehead wrinkling. It was like she was looking through me.

My brain spun as I tried to process finding a bit of my mother, that wasn't my full mother, but was able to see aspects of fate?

"Mother, where are you?" I asked.

She focused back on me. "I don't know. When I'm done here, this piece of my soul and our meeting will go back to my body. But since this fragment was left here, I don't know what's happened. I've probably long since returned to the clan. They will probably put me in isolation for a very long time as punishment for running around. I'm probably super bored."

"Clan—where's that?"

My mother just shook her head. "I don't want you to be found by our clan. Not yet." I went to press her, but she just held up a hand and silenced me with a look only a mother knows how to give.

I was frustrated, but I had expected it on some level. Aurora had been quiet, and I pulled her close. The moment I touched her, I realized she was shaking.

"Aurora?" I asked, turning to her as she stood still watching my mother, full of caution.

"Oh yes, this little one."

Aurora stiffened as my mother focused on her again. My mother tilted her head, studying her closer. Aurora's shaking picked up.

"You did very very well with your first ring, Isaac. Though, I might have bumped a few strings of fate before I left, seeing if we could spice things up." She winked.

"You forced—" I started, but Aurora cut me off with an intensity I never expected.

"You will not think that my choosing you was forced. It doesn't work that way, and damnit, Master, we are not going back to you being rocks-up-your-nose stupid!"

Laughter filled the cellar as I struggled to come up with words.

"Feisty. I approve of you and my son, Aurora." My mother scooped her up in a hug that destroyed Aurora intensity.

Aurora grumbled something to my mother that I couldn't hear.

"It's okay. I'll set him right if that's what's needed. But first, don't I have a second daughter-in-law to meet?" My mother turned to Michelle.

"Hi... mother?" Michelle said after a moment. I certainly wasn't expecting to meet my mother, and I doubt Michelle was ready for the meet-the-mother-in-law moment here.

"So cute." My mother pulled Michelle into the hug with Aurora.

Free from my mother's attention for the moment, I couldn't help but come to grips with just how crazy this all was.

My mother, or rather a piece of her soul, was here. Here because she could read fate and this spot was the best place to ensure I was here.

And now I had a clan somewhere, which is apparently strong enough to imprison a woman whose soul fragment terrifies my strong mana beast.

I sighed with the sudden realization at just how far I had to go and how much I still needed to learn.

My mother turned to study me. "Good, it's good that you understand." She nodded to herself.

"That flood dragon is going to be throwing a hissy fit for at least a day, probably two. Which means two days with your mother!" She giggled to herself, like she'd planned this all along.

Part of me wondered if she hadn't actually planned this in some way or had nudged it into reality.

"Two days with my mother." I smiled, feeling a sense of warmth.

"Now, if you are to survive what comes after this, we need to work fast. Isaac, Michelle, your cultivation technique is okay. These next few days you'll be safe and not want for resources. You need to hurry up and finish your meridians."

"But the next stage says we should seal ourselves in a cave alone," Michelle protested, earning herself a sharp look from my mother.

"Each of your stages is testing and forging your soul so you have a solid foundation for forming your nascent soul during your second ring. You will fight the urges that present themselves, or you aren't good enough for my son." My mother finished her statement with a stern face. Gone was the bubbly mother and out was coming tough love.

Michelle looked like she'd been slapped. My girl never took a challenge lightly. "Fine. Let's do this." She raised her chin, moving to a side of the cellar and sitting down, immediately getting to work on meditating.

"She's a keeper. Just have to motivate her," my mother said, winking. "As for your lovely mana beast, I'll work with her while you form your meridians. The pillar will be concentrating mana from the dungeon for you to use. Just focus on cultivating."

Aurora rapidly looked between me and my mother.

"Aurora, it'll be okay. She only has your best interests at heart." I looked to my mother. "Right, mom?"

"Of course. Aurora, you are my daughter-in-law and quite literally inseparable from my son. I'd never do anything to make him hate me."

I gave Aurora a kiss before stepping off to my own corner to cultivate. My mother was a bit odd for sure, but I didn't doubt Aurora's safety with her for a moment.

If the flood dragon would be active above ground for the next two days, then I'd take this opportunity to use the cellar to cultivate.

After we left here, there wouldn't be much time left in the dungeon. And I had no doubt we'd need every bit of strength we had.

Settling down, I calmed myself, putting all of the problems out of my mind and finding my center.

Armed with the knowledge that each of these layers was a test, I focused on my will as I began the next layer of the Seven Hells Meridians.

The warning about locking oneself in a cave was a hint. I'd be a harm to others.

I steeled myself as I concentrated on the mantra and the pattern that began to unfold in my inner world.

The layer of meridians was becoming a sharp, abrupt design like an angry mana beast. It was so filled with aggression that my own blood became hot with the urge for violence.

I felt the mantra swell in my voice, with barely contained violence as a haze of bloodlust gathered in my mind.

My bloodline was oddly quiet this time. Was it because of my mother's presence?

Just the thought of someone else being present with me filled my head with murderous thoughts that I recognized as a test against my will.

Breathing deep, I let those urges into my will and smothered them. I could almost feel it, like an unused muscle stretching for the first time.

I continued letting in the attacks on my soul and suppressing them in turn. It didn't take long for exhaustion to touch me as I continued to exercise my soul in resisting the effects of this layer of the Seven Hells Meridians.

Without a sense of time, I fell into a rhythm, taking in the bloodlust and suppressing it, unsure if there was going to be another.

I could feel my resistance growing weaker every time I let in the foreign emotions, but the flashes of things I'd do to Michelle and Aurora should I lose the war in my soul only made me steel myself and dig deeper.

And then, like a passing breeze, it was over.

I slumped to the floor, gasping for breath. I was sticky, covered in sweat as Aurora came to my side and helped me sit against the wall.

My beautiful mana beast looked paler than I remembered. "Aurora, are you okay?"

"I'll be fine. Your mother helped me regain something, but it wasn't easy." Aurora kissed my forehead and wrinkled her nose. "You stink."

"Good. Good. You were able to fight it and exercise your soul," my mother said, watching both of us.

"I need to be stronger. If I'm ever to find your clan—"

"Our clan. If they do find you, they will accept you. But they are quite adamant about not letting any of our bloodline wander free."

I heard her but was distracted when I saw Michelle.

She was still meditating in the corner, but it looked like something was wrong. A black pattern was spreading on her forehead, like a disease.

"Mich—" I started to get up, but Aurora held me down and my mother shook her head.

"Don't disturb her. I'm helping her. No daughter-in-law of mine can be ordinary."

"What are you doing to her?" I asked, watching the pattern grow like it was taking over Michelle's body.

"Helping her keep up with you. She has a bloodline of her own, terribly weak as it is. I have given her something to help bring it out and elevate it."

"Does she know?" I felt a surge of protectiveness at my mother doing things to Michelle without her consent.

"Yes. She exited cultivation hours before you. She begged me to help her keep up with you." My mother gave me a smile that turned her eyes into half-moons. "I'm very pleased with my first daughter-in-law. She has set a high bar for all of the many others now."

All the others? I mean, she could see into the future right? That meant there would be more, much more by the sound of it.

"Don't look at me like that. It's natural for our clan to have many spouses, usually at least a dozen per clansmen. I expect many grandchildren. After these memories return to my main body, I half-expect I'll start building a few nurseries."

"Mother," I chided. She was getting ahead of herself.

She just chuckled at my embarrassment. "What? This old woman would love all over them." I stayed silent, so she continued on.

"Anyways, Aurora, do you want to give it to him?"

Aurora looked a little sheepish before pulling out a vial that contained a swirling sphere of gold and green, like a droplet of liquid suspended in air.

"What is it?" I asked, feeling a large desire towards the droplet.

"Your mother explained that your bloodline is incomplete because of your father. That you need the blood of powerful mana beasts to help complete it." She looked at me with a smile on her pale face.

"You hurt yourself to make this," I said, realizing it.

Her smile only grew. "Yes, I did. But it will help you tremendously, and to me that is worth the price. I'll recover this drop of essence blood eventually."

I pulled back from the vial that represented her pain, but I was against a wall and didn't have anywhere to go.

"Oh no. You will take it. I didn't make this for nothing." She opened the vial and the bead slid out to my chest.

The pull I felt towards it intensified and my bloodline awoke in a crazy frenzy that felt like it would reach out of my body to grab this drop of blood.

I cradled the drop to my chest. "Thank you, Aurora. I'll make your efforts worth it."

As soon as the bead touched my chest, it was sucked into my heart where the bloodline beast devoured the drop of essence blood.

It shivered and expanded before contracting several times. Each time it did so, golden streaks would appear both within it and within my body. It left my heart and swam through my bones, changing my marrow.

Pain ripped through my body as my bloodline sought to change the core of my being. But the pain was short lived.

Gold streaks appeared in my marrow, and slowly, all the blood throughout my body started to match with its own gold streak.

When my bloodline beast finally settled back down in my heart, it felt content.

Returning from observing my inner world, Aurora looked at me expectantly.

"Did it work?"

"Yes, I think so," I said, feeling my body bursting with explosive energy.

She leaned in and nuzzled my neck. She took deep inhales, like she was trying to remember my scent.

I gave my mother a puzzled look, wondering if she had an explanation.

"It's our bloodline. It is very attractive to mana beasts."

"Care to share more?"

"I can't say. It will only cause you trouble," she said, sounding serious, but a little twinkle of mirth hid in her eyes.

"Really?" I glared at my mother.

"You can't be found lying about it if you really don't know. People will ask when they see your strength. It is better to let them assume than tell them what it really is."

I let out a sigh. If she wasn't going to tell me, I'd just have to figure it out later.

I paused, trying to figure out what to do next. It was still going to be a while before the flood dragon calmed down.

I decided to rest and recover. I'd exhausted my soul with the most recent layer of the Seven Hells Meridians. I also needed to give my body time. It was continuing to adjust to the drop of Aurora's essence blood.

"Alright. The plan is to eat, rest, and keep cultivating." I said, to no one in particular.

Mages often entered secluded cultivation to force themselves to grow quickly. That's how I'd treat time in this cellar.

***

"It's time," my mother said, waking both Michelle and I from our meditation.

She looked at me with an expression of sadness. "Even if you know the time is going to end, it doesn't make facing it any easier when the time comes. Give me another hug?"

It was the most vulnerable I'd seen my mother look. Over the last two days, I had started to get an understanding about just how unfathomable her cultivation was. To think there were mages with cultivations this deep was a startling realization.

"Of course." I gave the fragment of my mother's soul a tight hug that I hoped would transfer my love back to her when she returned to her main body.

314

"I love you, my baby boy." She kissed my forehead, and a brilliant warmth spread into my soul as it swelled.

I felt her touch disappear, and for a moment, I didn't want to open my eyes.

With her parting moment, I knew she gave me some strength that entered my soul. Over the last two days, I'd trained to the sixth layer of the Seven Hells Meridians. And with each one, I'd flexed and could feel my budding soul grow in strength.

I felt ten times stronger. I was confident I could resist the last layer of meridians.

Taking a deep breath, I opened my eyes. She was gone. I smiled, knowing that her body had received the piece of her soul back, and she knew of our time together.

Aurora gave me a solemn smile. "I haven't heard the flood dragon in hours. It's time to finish the dungeon."

I kissed my lovely mana beast. "I bet you could trounce it if you weren't in my ring, right?"

She blushed scarlet. "Maybe."

I laughed. After experiencing her blood when I had used it to enhance my bloodline, I no longer had any doubt. She was on the level of a mythical beast.

Michelle gave me a hug filled with emotions, knowing my mother's departure was tough for me. "I know she was a little odd, but my mother-in-law seems amazing."

"Yes, she is. I'm still dealing with just how different she is than what five-year-old me remembers."

"She left us one last gift though." Michelle went over to the enchanted pillar in the center of the cellar.

"Do you know how to use that?" I looked at the network of complicated enchantments.

"Sorta. She showed me how she used it to draw out my bloodline. At a minimum, it's my responsibility as the start of your budding harem to make sure the rest are capable."

Michelle started tracing lines in a way that definitely seemed like she knew more than just how to awaken a bloodline with it.

"Can we not just awaken the bloodlines of everyone back in town?" I asked, looking at the device.

Michelle shook her head. "Nope, she used essence blood from a mana beast. A powerful one aligned with my path in cultivation."

The pillar cracked and unfused from the ground with Michelle's final flourish before she stored it in her spatial ring.

I knew we needed to head out. "Love you, Aurora." I gave her a peck on the head before she disappeared into the ring on my chest.

Her mana pulsed warmly within me.

Knowing Michelle would be following me, I headed out of the cellar for the first time in two days.

The light of the dungeon made me squint as I took in what had been a jungle two days ago.

It was now flat earth. We had dug a few feet into the ground to find the cellar hatch; now it was even with the surface.

The flood dragon had scoured over two feet of earth in a ten-mile circle trying to get to us.

I shivered at the sheer power of a rank three mana beast. With the forest cleared, I could see the mana beast curled into a ball around what I assumed was the Meridian Cleansing Tree.

The rise and fall of its gargantuan frame made me think it was slumbering after exhausting itself.

Giving Michelle a hand out of the hatch, she looked around with the same awe that must have been on my face a moment ago.

"It wiped out the whole jungle."

"It didn't run rampage over the whole dungeon though. This was only maybe a fifth of the whole. I wonder if there are other beasts here that it didn't want to tangle with."

Michelle slugged me in the shoulder. "Do not jinx us."

I rubbed the spot. With her training, she hit harder than she did before.

"There's little left here for us. Let's get out of here." I set off away from the sleeping flood dragon.

"I still can't believe this was the result of a single mana beast," Michelle said as we made our way across the flat muddy plain.

Grabbing Michelle, I tumbled to the side as a snake shot out of the mud to strike where she'd just been.

She let out a startled squeak, throwing up her shield spell in the same instant.

Instead of the previous blue, her shield was now black as the bloodline mark appeared on her forehead.

The snake recovered quickly, curling back in a striking pose as I drew my sword, watching for the slightest movement from the snake.

Now that I got a good look at it, it was probably twelve-feet long and as thick as my thigh. But it had moved with such speed that its size didn't seem to hinder it.

Michelle, however, was not in a patient mood.

"Ha!" she yelled as she shoved her shield forward, using it as a blunt weapon.

The snake tried to move out of the way, but Michelle picked it up on the edge of her spell and slammed it into the ground, then she pulled her mace free and started battering the mana beast into the ground.

Heaving, she finished it off, pulling out its beast core.

"What did it do to you?" I chuckled. She wasn't the only one feeling pent up from being in that hatch.

"I'm all muddy now. These were my favorite leather pants." She frowned as she tried to rub off the mud from her form-fitting pants.

"Maybe I'll keep my eyes open a bit better to avoid having to roll in the mud."

Chapter 28

We picked our way through the forest, which was full of mana beasts.

Mana beasts that looked like they belonged in the jungle continued to be present as the terrain shifted to a hilly forest.

"These must all have been displaced from the flood dragon's territory," I said, pulling out the core of our most recent kill.

At least all of these mana beasts kept me from being able to get stuck in my head and worry too much.

After parting from the intense training with my mother, I was worried about the rest of our group.

Did they make it out of the area before the flood dragon went mad? And how were they doing in the dungeon?

Especially given the hatred that I'd garnered from the Earth Flame Sect and the corruption I now believed was in the Sun and Moon Hall, the last thing I wanted was for my friends to come to harm for my actions.

And I couldn't help but feel some guilt over Kat. I now knew the monsters that she was trapped with, and I hadn't been able to do much of anything about it. We may not be in a romantic relationship now, but I'd always care for Kat, and I still hoped for a future with her.

"I can't stand leaving Kat with those monsters much longer. We need to take them down. Maybe that's what my mother meant about our destinies? Saving Kat?" I looked over to gauge Michelle's expression.

Michelle took a deep breath before answering. "I know you have a deep need to protect us all, but I don't think there is much we can do right now. Your mother gave her something too. I think she'll be alright for the short term."

"My mother?" I cocked a brow.

"Yeah, she gave Kat a bloodline as strong as the one she gave me, and she wasn't weak before that. She can handle herself for now." Michelle paused, tilting her head to listen.

I stopped the conversation and listened as well.

It was faint, but a sound like tiny pin drops echoed through the forest. Somewhere ahead, metal was meeting metal.

"That way." I pointed towards the sound of mages battling and hurried.

It could be anything, but on the chance that it was the rest of our group, I needed to get there quickly.

I plunged through the forest, giving up any ideas of stealth.

Michelle kept pace with me as we jumped into the middle of the fight.

Our arrival didn't even turn a head; the two sides were clearly going at each other with their full focus. It was a fight for their lives.

I recognized one of the closest defenders as one of the guys who'd been with Grant. Fighting him was a mage in black robes. There wasn't a sect that had been wearing black robes.

Trusting my gut, I cast Golden Needle at the first mage with black robes.

It caught him off guard, and though he reacted at the last second, the incredibly deadly spell tore right through his abdomen.

I winced. It was a fatal wound, but a slow one.

To my surprise, the wounded mage didn't even falter. Instead, he let out a crazed laugh and cast a spell. Like a red balloon, his chest began to inflate as his eyes filled with manic glee.

Grant's friend noticed us and shouted, "Run." Then he dove to the ground and threw a wall of earth over himself.

The black robed mage continued to swell until he exploded in blades of blood.

Michelle cast her shield, and the razor-like streams of blood hammered her shield.

Its black tiles shifted and sunk, as if they were going to collapse until the blood was spent. Finally, Michelle let go of her shield.

The enemy mage was no more than a smear of blood across the ground. Grant's friend was releasing his protection, but his shield hadn't been as good as Michelle's.

He was torn up in a dozen places where his shield hadn't held.

The finale to that fight had finally drawn the others' attention to Michelle and me.

There were seven on five remaining, with one black robed mage dead and Grant's fellow disciple too injured to fight.

Grant and a slim woman in teal robes had been holding back two of the black robed mages together.

Having a moment to take it all in and seeing that spell, I now understood. These were corrupt mages.

"Isaac?" Grant shouted, realizing who I was.

"Hey, buddy. Looks like you continue to have all the fun without me. Some friend you are." I swung my sword in lazy circles as I started flowing my mana throughout my limbs. Looked like it would be time to test out my new strength.

I continued swinging, taking in the scene and planning my attack. "Thanks for that spell. Came in handy." I nodded towards what remained of the exploding mage.

Grant kept his eyes on the corrupt mages but tilted his head in acknowledgement. "No problem. Looks like you might be able to use it a bit more. Although I gotta tell you, I'm starting to think you may be my bad luck charm."

"Me? I'm as lucky as they get. What better lesson in corrupt mages than to kill a few? Where did these guys come from anyway?" I thought back to the elders of each sect, who should still be guarding the entrance to the dungeon.

"I'll tell you my theory later. All you need to know is that the sects always band together to take them down. So it's your lucky day. You get to fight alongside me again." Grant positioned himself, preparing to attack.

The corrupt mages didn't seem phased, despite one of their group having just turned himself into an exploding balloon. They simply stood there taking in our exchange.

A bad feeling trickled up the back of my neck. If all of the sects were fighting the corrupt mages, what were the Sun and Moon Hall up to? From what I knew so far, they may be helping each other. But there were more immediate problems I needed to solve.

Three of the remaining corrupt mages had their hoods down, showing off their pales faces and blood red eyes. The other four had their faces hidden deep in their hooded robes.

Without warning, all of the corrupt mages threw themselves at one of the teal-robed mages.

I was on them as fast as I could, forcing them back.

Michelle put herself in a position to protect the downed mage.

All of us worked together to square up a fight with the corrupt mages, but the blood mages ignored the others, with three coming straight for me.

I didn't have time to worry about the mage they had just attacked as a flurry of blood spells sought to empty my veins.

Their spells were sharp, but there was minimal volume to them. Like lines of bloody barbed wire, they were effective but would take a long time to cause extreme damage.

"Hold him down," the woman among the blood mages hissed.

I blocked one attack to the right and kicked out to the left, only to feel a blade sink into my calf.

Twisting, I used the blade in my calf to pull the attacking mage closer as I let loose my full power, smashing a fist hard enough to cave in his skull.

Staggering away, I managed to stumble through blocking another hit as the other blood mage came at me.

He rounded on me, coming from my right side in a flurry of blows.

With my left leg still injured, I struggled to redirect the attacks.

Out of options, I cast my Golden Needle spell to force him off me.

"Bet that leg is feeling pretty heavy about now," He laughed, anticipating his impending victory.

I knew that he was only buying time for the female blood mage. Looking over, I saw her channeling some spell that I was sure I didn't want to finish. But I cringed further after seeing a six-armed, three-headed monstrosity that had appeared beyond her and was fighting the rest of the mages.

The tattered black robes on the beast indicated that it had been one of the other corrupt mages. That was a new one.

That fight looked close. I needed to finish this and help them. I took quick inventory. My left leg was going numb even with my life mana doing its best to mend the wound. Whatever poison they used was doing its job.

Digging deep, I felt the aspect of life mana that Aurora had taught me. I felt my body burn brightly, and it felt like my forehead was ablaze.

The blood mage paused in excitement. "Ha! I knew you had powerful blood. Time to bleed!" The blood mage came at me again.

I swung hard enough to force him off balance and moved quicker than he expected.

His eyes were wide with surprise as he realized I was inside his guard. His chest expanded, and he spat out a dagger made of blood.

I cast Golden Needle at point blank range to intercept it.

It cut right through the dagger and took out a chunk of the blood mage's throat.

Jumping back, I was wary he'd try another trick, but he clutched at his throat and gurgled blood as he slumped to the floor, looking over my shoulder with a smile.

I turned back to the female blood mage who floated slightly in the air, her hair whipping every which direction.

Blood from those who had died was already streaming towards her.

I readied myself for whatever spell this was, and in the back of my mind, I was readying the spell Aurora had taught me to counter this one.

But the spell she used wasn't what I was expecting. Rather than form something in front of her, the blood dived to her body as it changed.

She bulked up as blood built upon her, sheathing her like a second body. Large blood red arms and legs formed over her own, ending in claws as she transformed into a demonic blood creature.

The change was so rapid, so jarring, that I didn't even get a chance to attack.

Her eyes lost all humanity, as she screamed like some demon rising from hell rather than a human woman.

I was on her before she lowered her head from the scream. I could end this here and now. I had a feeling this transformation would be on par with the six-armed creature fighting the others.

The blood devil whipped its arm, catching my blade in a stalemate for a moment. Then it pushed and sent me flying back.

I landed on my feet, but the blood devil was already upon me. Its entire body was covered in protrusions, turning its entire surface into a weapon.

It slashed, and I jumped out of range as I cast my Golden Needle spell once again.

The sharp spell tore a hole in its arm. I smirked at the damage done.

But my smirk didn't last long as blood welled up and reformed where I'd done the damage.

"Shit," I cursed as the blood devil pressed on, barely pausing from the damage.

There had to be a better way to deal with this thing. I realized that the entire body was a spell, but there should still be the female mage underneath. If I could kill her, maybe the spell would end.

She leapt into the air, howling as she flew at me like a meteor.

I dodged to the side, getting a face full of dirt spray as the ground erupted.

This spell was on another level from what I'd seen. The only thing like it would be Aurora's.

But if I used that, I wasn't sure I'd have mana to help the rest of them with the creature. A glance over at their fight showed they were still being suppressed by the six-armed monstrosity.

The blood devil screamed at my lack of attention and threw a hasty fist at me.

I summoned the strength of my bloodline and the aspect of my mana to meet it fist for fist. Looked like I'd truly get a chance to test my new strength.

The air rippled as we both were forced back by the attack. I steadied myself after about eight steps. The blood devil had only taken three. We were closely matched, but I'd need to be creative to pull out a win.

It snarled and narrowed its eyes, like it only now saw me as a threat.

I was sure the mage who had cast this spell was in there, but I didn't think she was in control. Which gave me an idea…

The blood devil roared again before throwing itself into another charge. It was powerful, amazingly so, but I wasn't fighting a mage. I was fighting a beast.

I took a gamble and put away my sword, readying myself.

The crazed monster saw my gesture as giving up, abandoning all pretense of defense, already savoring victory.

But at the last moment, I summoned a spear from my spatial ring, bracing it against the ground.

The blood devil realized the move too late. It tried to throw its body to the side but wasn't able to move far enough. It staked itself to the ground by its shoulder.

I was prepared for that, and in the blood devil's moment of surprise, I was already behind it. I pulled out two more long swords and staked its exposed legs to the ground.

It flailed, trying to pull itself free of the spear in its chest and the swords in its legs. I knew it would be free in seconds, not minutes.

So I moved quickly. Placing my hand against its back, I cast three golden needles in rapid succession down its back, hoping to strike through to the blood mage.

I wasn't sure exactly where her vitals were, but each one of the spells put a hole completely through the blood devil. I could see that I had hit the blood mage underneath.

The blood devil began to bubble and boil. Afraid of a repeat of the first blood mage, I dodged back and watched as the false body formed by the spell melted away, leaving the female blood mage.

She was actually quite pretty behind all of the spooky makeup. Unfortunately, she had three fist-sized holes in her chest. By how fast she was fading, I must have hit her heart.

"Lucky shot." She coughed up a mouthful of blood.

"Maybe you should kill fewer people in your next life if you're given the chance." I really did hope that she got a chance to make things right. I couldn't imagine the horrors she'd done to gain the spell she'd used.

She chuckled. "Of course someone from a sect would see us as evil."

"We—" The blood mage started a coughing fit that ended in eerie silence.

I sighed. I wasn't sure where she was going with that, but I didn't have time to dwell.

Turning back toward the group, Michelle seemed to finally have the six-armed monstrosity backpedaling.

The other three corrupt cultivators were pinned down by the rest of the group.

I was sad to see there were only three of them still in the fight.

Michelle saw me coming. "Kill the two cultivators. I'll keep this thing distracted."

I blinked and looked at the monstrosity. Only now did I realize it was stitched together, like it was made. It was a puppet.

That meant one of the other three was controlling it.

Grant and the other two still fighting were looking worn out. If I let this drag on, it would only become worse for our side. Fast and intense it was.

Drawing on my mana, I began to cast the giant talon spell. It would only take a few seconds, but in a battle with mages, seconds were precious.

One of the corrupt mages sensed my spell and dashed around his opponent to stop me.

I smirked as I let loose the gigantic spell. I could feel my bloodline surge from the drop of Aurora's blood as the spell finished.

A massive golden claw stretched open as it raced towards the corrupt mages.

The corrupt mage that had come at me was first up.

He exploded with dark mana, but his resistance only lasted a second before the claw pushed forward, destroying his defenses and carrying him with it.

The force of the spell caused his robes to explode, showing yet another puppet.

The other two had a moment to brace but couldn't do much as the spell crashed into them and destroyed their defenses outright. One of them was immediately crushed, leaving the other weakly coughing on their knees.

The girl in teal robes moved like the wind and was there, cutting both of their heads free of their shoulders.

I looked back and saw Michelle's fight was over as well. The six-armed puppet had collapsed to the ground.

I released a deep sigh, taking an equally deep breath as I re-centered. "So, now can you tell me what's happening?"

Grant sank to a knee, breathing heavy and struggling to form words between deep gulps of air.

I looked to the other leader in the group. The girl in teal robes had her hair dyed purple, and it was shaved on one side, leaving the other side to fall down to her chin. I was sure it normally looked better than the wind-whipped and muddy mess it did now.

She stood taller as I observed her. But she was small to begin with, probably not much over five foot. What skin I could see was covered in corded muscle. She was almost more handsome than pretty.

She stepped forward, taking the opportunity to greet me. "I'm Zee. We appreciate the hand but let me see to my fellow disciples before we talk. And I wouldn't turn down some additional help if you are willing to give it."

She gave me a stiff nod before moving onto helping her sect mates.

Michelle was already dragging one of Grant's friends free from the dirt and working to patch his wounds.

I went over to Grant. I really needed to learn how to heal others. I decided to give it a shot anyway. He was pretty badly injured, and it might be his best bet.

Putting my palm to Grant's back, I was surprised as my life mana began pouring into his body, searching for wounds and nourishing them with mana like my own self-healing. I smiled.

His breathing settled down quickly, and I felt my mana concentrate on his ribs. He'd been fighting on with four broken ribs. This had been a true life and death battle.

"Thanks," Grant wheezed as he stood straighter. "I'll last. Can you help him?"

Grant had nodded to his other sect mate, who was lying still on the ground.

I feared he was already dead, but on touching him, I found he still breathed. Pouring more life mana into him, I managed to stabilize him, but he still didn't rise.

After helping all we could, five of the six were back on their feet. But nobody was looking ready for another fight, besides Zee, who always looked like she was ready to punch someone in the face.

We moved away from the scene of battle and made camp. The wounded were quick to lay down for rest.

"The Windswept Mountain owes you a debt," Zee said stiffly as we settled down, everyone pitching in to make some stew.

I waved off the favor. "I just need to understand what happened."

"Your friends have been looking for you. Given how long it had been, we feared you were dead," Grant said.

I winced at the thought of Celina thinking we were dead. She'd for sure do something stupid. "No, we were near the flood dragon and dug in, literally, to wait it out."

"Ah." A bit of enlightenment showed in Grant's eyes.

"You were lucky then. Many died from the flood dragon," Zee said, stirring the pot.

"Given what we saw when we came out, I doubt many survived if they were in the area. But I'm glad to hear our friends managed to escape," Michelle said.

Grant looked at Zee before continuing. "Maybe it would have been better if they bunkered down like you. The dungeon has gotten far more dangerous."

I stared at Grant hard, waiting for the next bit. Corrupt mages shouldn't be here, and if there were puppets again… I feared the Sun and Moon Hall had betrayed the other sects.

"You saw the corrupt mages. We've been fighting them since just before the flood dragon went crazy." Grant reached towards the pot, only for Zee to slap his hand away with a reproachful look.

Grant looked like a chagrined husband as he pulled back his hand with another look at the pot.

"What of the other sects?" I brought him back to the conversation at hand, ignoring his and Zee's flirtation.

"We are all fighting the corrupt mages. But I don't know how they got in here."

"There are ways to enter dungeons without going through the portal, and some dungeons do present two portals." Zee didn't look up from the stew.

"What about the portal we came in? Can we not leave?" I asked.

"It is our duty to remove corrupt mages when we find them," Grant said with a hard face, starting to stand.

I held up my hands palms out. "Not saying we should run. I'm just wondering what the situation is."

"Sorry," Grant said, sitting back down. "After what they've done here, I am feeling a bit hot-headed."

"As for the portal we came in, the Sun and Moon Hall is protecting it for just the reason you were concerned. They're guarding in case we need to retreat." Grant looked over, watching intently as Zee pulled out a very large bowl half-filled with rice.

She poured the stew over it before handing Grant his steaming dinner.

He accepted it happily and started to dig in.

I on the other hand had gone stiff with the news. If the Sun and Moon Hall was protecting the dungeon portal, that meant we were trapped. Worse, those outside the portal would be fresh if we managed to clear out the corrupt mages.

"Is the Sun and Moon Hall not helping clear the corrupt mages?" Michelle asked, disapproval clear in her voice.

"Guarding the dungeon portal is important," Zee said, as if it was natural.

"But aren't they supposed to be the top sect? Shame that they sit by while the rest of us fight," I argued.

Grant and Zee shared a look before shrugging.

"That's the way of it. If our escape route was cut off, they could turn this whole dungeon into a death trap. The Sun and Moon Hall even sent in their new Saintess."

"Saintess?" Michelle asked.

"Haven't seen her face because she wears a veil, but I hear she's a breathtaking beauty. But more than that, they say she has the bloodline of a vermillion bird and possesses its five-colored flame." Grant shook his head.

"Heaven-born genius. She's not on a level we can compare to."

328

Zee looked at Michelle. "I saw you both expressed a bloodline as well. Is your whole town full of talents like you?"

Michelle looked a bit panicked at the complement. "No, it's just a weak mana beast bloodline that runs in the family."

Zee gave her a look that said she didn't quite believe her, but she left it at that.

I didn't think there was anything special in town besides my mother. She was the source of both mine and Michelle's bloodlines.

"Anyways, shouldn't this Saintess be showing an example and destroying the corrupt mages along with the rest of us? Feels like they are lording over the rest of us." I turned the conversation back to the Sun and Moon Hall.

Zee answered for Grant. "We respect strength. They have the strength to lead."

I couldn't help it. A heavy sigh escaped from me.

"Got an issue with the Sun and Moon Hall? I thought they ran your town." Grant asked.

They certainly did run Locksprings, though it took me a while to realize it. I wanted to tell Grant and Zee everything, but I decided to start small and see how it went.

"Sun and Moon Hall recruits from Locksprings, but we never see them again," I said, starting into the conversation.

"Sects do keep people busy, Isaac. I haven't been back home since I joined. That's not unusual. Sects are also quite dangerous. Some of them probably have died." Grant gave me a look like I should know better.

"It's not that simple. They recruit mostly the pretty girls, who never come back home. Sometimes the recruitment is a bit... forceful." Michelle stepped in, locking eyes with Zee when she said it.

"I can see how that might look bad, but they do practice Dual Cultivation. Dual, they both must actively participate," Zee said, explaining away the insinuation.

We couldn't undo years, maybe even decades, of their beliefs with one conversation. They had answers to all our issues with Sun and Moon Hall. Half of them even started to convince me, but I had my own conviction after seeing Narissa.

"Just keep an eye out for yourselves. Okay?" I said at the end.

I could feel the distance between me and Grant growing with my attempt to warn them of the impending threat that Sun and Moon Hall represented.

Wanting a change of direction, I asked after my friends and Grant's last meeting with them.

I was relieved to hear that Jonny and Steve were still together, but news of Celina was that she'd gone off on her own after Michelle and I disappeared.

With heavy topics on my mind, I settled down for sleep with Michelle in our tent. Aurora joined us, raising our spirits as we enjoyed each other's warmth.

Chapter 29

The next morning, I found myself up early, stirring a pot of oatmeal.

As soon as I woke up, I was filled with an eager restlessness to find Celina, Jonny and Steve.

Celina was strong. I had to have faith that she could take care of herself. But I'd also seen the fury in her eyes when she talked about the Sun and Moon Hall.

I was more worried about her doing something stupid than being overpowered by the mana beasts in the dungeon.

She wanted to help Narissa as much as I did. I just hoped we could figure out a way to pull it off.

I looked over at the rest of the group's tents. Everyone was still resting off yesterday's injuries. If Michelle and I left them, it would leave two able-bodied fighters to defend the group of six.

It felt like I was leaving them to die if I headed off with Michelle.

I compromised and made breakfast, hoping to speed up their recovery, so we could move on.

If only we could gather a large group from all the sects, we could protect each other. I was also hoping that if such a large group exited the dungeon together, it would force Sun and Moon Hall to play nice.

They couldn't do anything underhanded if there were enough people; they wouldn't be able to silence everybody.

The oatmeal looked a little bland, so I focused on adding some dried fruit I had taken from home.

I needed to keep my mind off all the worries and focus on what I could do here and now. The best move I saw was to hustle everyone out of camp to group up with more of the sects.

Michelle came over, sitting next to me as I worked on breakfast.

"You didn't sleep well. Was the tent too cramped?" She leaned over, giving me a peck on the cheek as a good morning.

I shook my head as I stirred. "I'm worried about Celina and the others." Grabbing a ladle, I scooped out some oatmeal and handed her a bowl.

"I am too, but we need to keep our strength up, so we can bail her out of whatever mess she's gotten herself into." Michelle smirked, avoiding my eyes as she took the bowl.

"You're so sure she's going to be in a mess?" I asked, trying to get her to look at me.

"Yep. Mmm, this is good. I like the strawberries." I did not miss the change in subjects, but Michelle was stubborn. She clearly wasn't going to voice whatever she knew.

I continued to stir the oatmeal to keep it from burning, looking over at our fellows' tents.

"Stud, it's okay. We'll head out soon." She rested a hand on my leg, settling it. I hadn't even realized I'd been bouncing it.

"Michelle—" I cut off as our friends started rustling in their tents.

"Morning! I made breakfast," I yelled, loud enough to reach those still in their tents.

Zee came out, giving me a curt nod and joining us, followed by Grant and their teams. Each moved their tent into a spatial ring on their way over.

"You look ready to get going." Grant nodded thanks as he took a bowl of oatmeal.

"Unfortunately, we can't continue on," Zee interrupted. "We need to get our teams back through the dungeon portal. We're not going to make it much longer here; it's time to retreat to safety." She eyed me, waiting to see if I'd push on why the Sun and Moon Hall was guarding it again, but I'd already seen it was going to be hard to sway them.

"So, we head to the exit together? We send them through for medical, and then the four of us continue," I said, waiting to see if they'd join us further.

Grant looked at Zee, and she nodded. "Sounds like a plan, Isaac. You'll get a chance to see the Sun and Moon Hall in action outside your town. I'm sure they'll be different than you imagined."

I just smiled and packed away camp, ready to go as soon as everyone was done with their meal.

"It'll be a whole day's journey back to the portal," Grant said, looking over his shoulder as we got underway.

I focused to feel the direction that all the mana in the dungeon was flowing. "If there are two portals, would we potentially follow the mana flow to the wrong one?"

"I haven't felt a second flow to indicate another portal." Zee shrugged. "There might be another, but I'm fairly sure the one we used is the only portal drawing this much mana."

"So, you two an item?" Michelle asked as we walked slowly so the injured could keep up.

Grant froze and went beet red. "U-uh."

Zee gave him a glare that shut him up. "Yes. But it's complicated being in a different sect."

Michelle saddled up to Zee and started talking in hushed voices that I did my best to not overhear.

My beautiful woman sliced right through the tense atmosphere that had settled since our disagreement last night, as both the girls began talking in the rapid back and forth that only girls gossiping could mimic.

Something caught my attention, and I stopped. The rest of the group paused only seconds after me.

I scanned the surroundings, but that feeling of unease spread as I looked back through the trees, trying to figure out what caught my attention.

"What is it?" Grant asked.

"Something isn't right," I said, trying to take in all of my senses at once. Feeling the mana flow, I listened to the forest as I scanned our path.

Grant started to object, but Michelle cut him off. "Isaac has great instincts and is generally quite lucky." She gave me a wink.

I wasn't in a joking mood. Everything was so peaceful around us. Then it hit me. That was it, wasn't it? I didn't sense any mana beasts, nor small woodland critters.

There was absolutely nothing, like there had been a fight near here recently. But there was no sign of a fight, and a mana beast wouldn't cover their tracks.

"I think there is an ambush up ahead."

Grant frowned and looked around like he'd missed something. "How do you suppose that?"

"It's too quiet," Zee agreed before checking her sword. "Best be cautious. I will not gamble with my fellows' lives."

After she finished speaking, Zee blurred as she shot forward.

I lost sight of her, unsure if it was some sort of wind spell or if she really was that fast. "Damn."

"She's incredibly fast and finishes most of her fights in her first sword stroke," Grant said with a proud grin.

She'd make an incredible assassin, but from what I saw of the fight yesterday, she struggled with the drawn-out engagement. The Puppet Sect's reinforced puppets were also likely her greatest weakness.

Zee appeared before us again. "Isaac's luck holds out. Four corrupt disciples are ahead, lying in ambush. One of them appears to be injured."

"So, we aren't their first prey," I sighed, knowing that meant another group had fallen prey to them.

"But we will be their last," she said.

Time to ambush the ambushers.

"Zee, Grant, Michelle, with me. Michelle, you're going to spring the ambush. Stay safe, keep your shield ready. Zee, take out anyone you can when the fight starts. Grant, stay close to me. Let's take out anyone who hangs back from the initial engagement."

Nods were shared all round and we separated from the injured mages to spring the trap.

Michelle went straight forward, while Zee led us around to the side.

"Are you not worried about your wife?" Grant asked.

"She won't go down from an ambush. We just need to act fast." I had every confidence in Michelle. And I found it actually made me happy that Grant had thought she was my wife.

"Quiet. We are getting close," Zee shushed us.

Ahead through the trees, I caught sight of the ambushers. I could see three mages in black robes waiting among the branches. They were right in the path we'd been walking.

If they were that ready, then the corrupt mages must have already scouted us. That made me look over my shoulder for the fourth.

"There." Zee patted my shoulder and pointed to a second tree, where the last mage was leaning heavily, like his leg was injured.

I didn't have time to worry about anything else. Michelle was about to spring the trap.

She walked under the tree where they were lying in wait. They patiently waited until she was well within the trap before the three jumped down, casting spells.

Michelle ducked into a roll, throwing up her black shield around her.

The spells were followed by weapons, and I could hear cursing as more than one of them felt the sting of hitting a solid wall.

Zee was already gone, dashing towards the injured man in the tree.

I let her deal with him as I leapt out, casting golden needles as fast as I could at the three ambushers, who were recovering from their failed attacks.

The first caught him square in the neck, and he slumped down dead.

The other two managed to react, one gaining an injured shoulder and the other dodging it entirely.

Grant was near me and was there to distract the one who avoided injury. Michelle came out of her spell swinging at the one with the arm injury.

I felt like we had cleaned this one up when I felt danger from behind me.

Falling into a roll, I felt the air ripple where my head had been.

Popping back up with my sword ready, there was a fifth corrupt mage pulling his sword around into another swing.

I blocked his sword and kicked him in the chest with a snap kick to make some space.

He just grinned and stabbed far short of me, but his sword bridged the gap and I jumped back.

It had been like his sword stroke bent space. I then realized what it was; he practiced void mana and was able to warp space.

I shot a golden needle at him and checked on the rest of my group. The other three had converged on the remaining corrupt mage. This would be over soon.

Looking back, I saw his body ripple around my spell as he calmly strode forward.

It was then that I noticed that his mouth had been sewn shut. The skin long scarred over, it had happened to him years ago.

He wasn't in a hurry as he pulled a pouch off his belt and opened it up to show me it contained dozens of spatial rings.

The silent mage jangled the bag happily, showing off his trophies.

"You're sick, you know that?" I slashed out in anger.

He stepped back further than he should have and put away his bag with a tilt of his head, like he was asking me a question in turn.

I didn't have time for games. Letting my mana flood my body, I rushed him with a flurry of my sword.

He saw the move and manipulated space to stay out of my range while he stretched his thrusts into my guard.

It was a frustrating fight, like trying to hit a ghost.

When I saw Zee in the corner of my eye, I schooled my expression to not give her away.

She came at his side, and for the first time, I saw his mocking expression disappear, replaced with worry.

He managed to pull away, but now with a deep wound in his side. He glared at both of us and took in the fact that the rest of his team was dead.

With a shrug, the silent mage tried to escape.

I chased after him before Zee stopped me. "Don't. You won't catch him. And we need to go check on the others."

Her expression was grim, and I felt my throat go dry when I thought about all the spatial rings he'd been taunting me with.

I set off as fast as I could to where we had left our four injured compatriots.

They were laying with deathly stillness that made my heart plummet.

Four clean cuts to the throat. They hadn't even put up a fight.

"Fuck." I lashed out at a nearby tree.

The others were right behind me, and I heard their own sounds of grieving as I was lost in my own.

"Who—what—was that?" I asked.

"I forget you don't know that much about the world," Grant started. "That was a Specter. A very small sect within the corrupt mages. They sew their mouths closed as infants and train them from birth to be assassins."

"They don't do dungeons though. They cultivate by killing and consuming the soul of their victims. If one of them is here, it means this is a full-blown attack." Zee didn't take her eyes off her fallen comrades.

"Should we bury them?" I asked, not wanting to leave them to nature.

"We'll take them back to the sect. They died as heroes," Grant said.

"They fought valiantly. Giving their lives for a purpose greater than their own. Let your sects do them the proper honors as such," I said, bowing my head in a moment of silence.

Grant and Zee took their bodies into their own spatial rings.

I turned and saw Michelle crying silently.

"Come here." I hugged her and kissed her tears.

She calmed down after a moment, and I felt Aurora pulse sympathetically in my chest.

"Thanks," Michelle said, pulling away and wiping away the last of her tears. "They were just the first, you know?"

The first friends that had died in a war we'd just stepped into merely by cultivating a certain way.

None of us had known that, outside our small town, there was a war on this level. This loss was just our first taste that we'd likely have of this war.

I felt anger and the wrongness of it build in me until it galvanized to a firm resolve. This needed to end.

"Change of plans," I said to the group. They all turned their heads.

"We respect their deaths by preventing others. We'll head towards the portal and clear out the woods around them. I doubt this is the only ambush setup on the way to our exit. We clear the way for other injured."

"Perfect." Zee grinned with revenge in her eyes.

***

We had killed two other ambush parties. Neither of them gave us as much trouble as the Specter had.

We all fought with a zeal and passion unlike anything I'd felt before.

I wasn't fighting; I was killing those who would kill my friends. Each ambush destroyed, was lives saved.

When we came upon the fifth group, we were messy and splattered with blood. I knew I certainly didn't look like a 'good guy'.

I looked like a serial killer after a bender and I felt powerful, like I was growing with each kill.

The sounds of battle caught our attention as we stalked through the forest, looking for another ambush site.

At this point, we didn't need to talk. We knew each of our roles.

With a glance, we all set off in that direction. Zee and I were in the lead; Michelle and Grant were bringing in the rear.

We'd used the tactic of Michelle springing the trap before, but for this active fight, myself and Zee would surprise them. Michelle and Grant would come barreling into the fight after.

Darting through the woods, I felt faster, sleeker than before.

The sudden influx of combat had let me tap into my potential as a mage. I was more accustomed to my mana. Each of these fights was quickening my cultivation towards completing my second ring.

The fight came into view, but this one was more like a battle than an ambush. I split from Zee to spread out our opening move.

Corrupt mages were everywhere as they swarmed a large group of sect disciples with many injured among them. It almost looked like this was all of the surviving disciples making a final push to the portal.

The injured disciples had formed a ring to protect themselves and those unable to even hold a weapon.

I set my sights on a cluster of corrupt mages fighting them.

In a flash, I was behind one of the corrupt mages, skewering through his back before whipping my blade out to decapitate another before they realized what was happening.

They all turned to me, and one swung with all his strength.

I blocked and jumped, letting his attack carry me back out of range of the rest and what I knew was about to happen.

Like a wrecking ball, Michelle came in from the side with her shield spell up, barreling straight through the bunch of corrupt mages.

I picked off those that fell or stumbled my way in their disorientation.

Michelle had already stopped her spell and took the chance to crack a few skulls.

Our arrival was met with cheers as the injured disciples advanced, taking their own kills.

Cheers turned into vigor as the desperate disciples exploded with mana, pushing back their corrupt counterparts.

Zee and Grant had made a similar explosive entrance, freeing up more of the able-bodied disciples to roam the battlefield.

I lost myself as Michelle and I danced together in battle. My vision became covered in red as I slew corrupt mage after mage.

When I lifted my blade but saw no corrupt mage for me to swing at, it all came to a screeching halt. I sagged suddenly, feeling unsteady on my feet.

My mana was down to dregs, flowing slowly through my meridians.

I looked over at my partner, and Michelle was just as worn as I was.

"Come here," I said, pulling Michelle to my side as we both leaned against each other for support.

Michelle blew out a heavy breath. "We almost lost all of them."

I looked at the injured disciples, and to my surprise, I saw Jonny running between the injured, applying as much of his healing as he could to keep them stable.

"Jonny," I tried to call out, but it came out as a croak.

Michelle got the idea, and we carried each other over to our friend.

When he looked up, there was no recognition in his eyes, only exhaustion as he spotted another two mages in need of healing.

"Jonny," I said again with as much excitement as I could muster.

Recognition flashed in his eyes. "Holy— Isaac! Michelle!" He was suddenly filled with energy as he gave us both a big hug.

I took a moment to really see my friend. It had been less than a week, but in that time, he'd lost so much weight. His face no longer held that childish grin. It was replaced by a resoluteness that made him seem so much more a man.

"Damn. I barely recognized you two." He gave me a once over, and I imagined I'd gone through a transformation not that different from his own.

I was like a blade, tempered for years in Locksprings. In this dungeon, I was finally quenched in blood and came out forged.

"I'm so glad you're okay. Where are Steve and Celina?"

Jonny sighed. "Celina ran off not long after we were separated. She said her goodbye, like it was final."

I knew she had a deep grudge with the Sun and Moon Hall, but I didn't think she'd go off on her own to take care of it herself.

"What about Steve?" I asked, feeling a sense of dread that Jonny hadn't mentioned him.

"Among the injured," Jonny said, leading us back to the hastily setup infirmary tent.

The whole group likely numbered almost two hundred. Quicker than I could imagine, a sea of tents was set up, and a group started patrolling the parameter like a small army.

Tents formed a tight square, only broken by a few large trees like we were huddling together for safety.

"You are all well-organized," I noticed, watching as the army camp sprang to being.

"It's only been a few days, but it was a necessity to stick together. The corrupt mages have been coming in larger and larger numbers. Hopefully, tomorrow we'll reach the portal and can get out of here." Jonny pulled aside a tent flap and led us inside.

Steve was laid out on a cot. When he saw Jonny enter, he smiled, but when I and Michelle joined him, his grin looked like it was about to split his face in half.

He whistled at us. "Damnit Isaac. You didn't need to go swimming in blood. We all know you're ferocious." He winked at Michelle.

I smiled at my friend's good humor, but coming from my typically reserved friend, it seemed forced. "You're not looking too bad yourself."

In truth, he had some new heavy scars across him, but it was nothing that would put him in a ward and not back in battle.

Steve pulled back the sheets covering him and wiggled a stump at me where his leg should have been. "At least I still got my looks."

I sucked in a deep breath. "There are miracle medicines out there that could restore that."

Steve shrugged. "And lose out on an excuse to just ride everywhere? Nah." He cast about, looking for something. When he didn't find it, he whistled loudly, and something snorted behind the tent. I could hear whatever it was moving to enter.

A shadow that looked like a horse's frame stepped around to the tent flap and poked the front of its body inside to look at Steve.

I looked closer. It actually didn't look anything like a horse. Large fangs stuck out of its jaw, and its body was covered in heavy scales. Each leg ended in massive definitely-not-herbivore claws.

It still had blood dripping from its mouth, like it had participated in the fight.

"Meet my first tame. Once Doctor Worrywart here clears me, I'm riding that beautiful beast all day long." He smiled at his own double entendre, which we all hoped was just a joke.

"Glad to see you're handling it well," Michelle said, walking over to the mana beast. "Can I pet her?"

"Sure," Steve said, looking surprised. "Glad to see someone else sees the beauty and not the beast."

We talked about other things like old friends and showed off our rings to each other.

"Woah. You are almost at your second ring!" Jonny said as I showed mine.

I did a double take. It really was almost complete, and I still had one more layer to set in my meridians. A panic almost set on me as I realized I needed to complete the Seven Hells Meridians before I became a second-ring mage.

But I pulled myself back out of my thoughts to focus on my friend. "Yeah, damn time really does fly when you are fighting for your life."

They both gave nods to that. Both of their second rings were over half-formed, which meant that each of them had seen plenty of combat during the dungeon.

The tent flap opened, and Zee hurried in. "Isaac, a woman has come to the camp all on her own. We are worried about corrupt mages trying to sneak into camp, but she says she knows you."

Three faces flashed through my mind. Kat, Narissa and Celina. Maybe the first two escaped the Sun and Moon Hall or were here to warn me. Celina wouldn't be back unless she finished what she set off to do. But a part of me still hoped that it was her, back safe and sound.

I raised my brow, unsure what I'd find. "Lead on. Let's see who it is."

Chapter 30

Heading out of the tent, Zee led the way east through camp.

I was confronted with the reality of our situation. This small army of mages was more injured than it was healthy.

Those going about tasks in the camp were bandaged up, but given the degree of their injury, many should be resting in the infirmary. They pushed on, but their bodies were still far from recovering.

One mage near me was supporting another, more injured, mage. They were slowly making their way to the nearby food, but both were clearly struggling. I went towards them, ducking under the injured mage's free arm and taking the brunt of his weight. They nodded in appreciation, too exhausted to speak. Once they were settled with a bowl of stew, I jogged to catch back up with Zee and the others.

I hoped that, once they returned to their sects, they could recover. While Jonny was a decent healer, he was still a first-ring mage. There was only so much he could do for them at this point and so many for him to help. Under the care of their elders, they would recover far quicker.

"Think we can make the final push to the portal tomorrow?" I asked Zee.

"That is our hope. If nothing else, we should be able to connect with the Sun and Moon Hall. Once we do that, the journey will become far safer."

I smothered the sigh that threatened to spoil any hopes of conversation. I hoped Zee was right and the Sun and Moon Hall would be our saviors, but everything I had learned made that a long shot. I'd seen for myself their slavery of an innocent woman, so it was easy to extend that to even greater evils. But Zee needed to put it together herself. Her hope in them was too deep to sway her without evidence.

"Let's hope it all works out," I said, seeing the edge of camp and looking around until I saw the gathering of mages that must have been on guard duty.

I smiled. This was something I could do to contribute to the group right now. I picked up the pace and strode over to the circle of guards.

The air was tense, and a number of the mages had their weapons drawn.

When I looked at what had them spooked, I understood.

First, I recognized Narissa, who was wearing the black robes of the corrupted mages. But she was glassy eyed and in the arms of Celina, who looked like she'd been through hell. Her hair was covered in mud and twigs while her eyes drooped with exhaustion.

"Put your weapons away," I growled as I pushed through to embrace Celina.

She melted into me, with the comatose Narissa sandwiched between us. Then the tears started.

I had questions, but they could wait. "It's okay," I repeated as I rubbed her back.

The display settled the guards a bit, and about half of them put away their weapons. The others eased up a bit, but still looked wary. All but one gave us space, milling about, but still keeping an eye on us. The one that stayed waited patiently while I soothed Celina.

"Shh. It's okay." I made eye contact with the remaining guard and he stepped forward.

He looked down, clearly feeling awkward as he pulled out a set of cuffs. "We need to detain the corrupt mage."

I felt Celina tense as she did a complete one eighty, her energy surging. She was suddenly like a cobra with its hood up in warning. "You will not touch my sister!" The fierceness in her eyes made the guard take a hesitant step back.

Well, that answered a few questions. Looking more closely now, I could see the similarities.

"I'm sorry, but she is a second-ring mage and a corrupt mage. We need to take everyone's safety into account." The guard looked to Zee for help.

344

I hadn't realized Zee had taken on some leadership among the camp, but she stepped forward to try to mediate.

"Isaac, can you introduce us?" she asked in an overly calm tone people used on cornered animals.

Celina looked like she was ready to fight. I pulled her back into an embrace, but she remained stiff.

"This is Celina. We entered the dungeon together and fought together before we were split up."

"Hello, Celina, can you tell me about the corrupt mage in your arms?" Zee eased forward.

Celina choked on tears as she tried to talk. "It's my sister. She was—"

"—taken by corrupt mages," I finished for her, knowing saying it was Sun and Moon Hall wasn't going to make the conversation any better.

"They controlled her. She isn't really a corrupt mage." Celina curled over Narissa defensively.

"How did you capture her?" Zee continued her questions.

"I killed the one controlling her," Celina said, a vicious smile creeping across her face before she looked down at her sister, her smile drooping.

"But she's been like... like this since."

My heart went out to her, and I gave her a squeeze.

"I'm happy you found your sister, but I'm sure that, when she wakes up, she'll be incredibly confused. It would be best if we did what we could to prevent accidents." Zee moved slowly, taking the cuffs from the guard.

"To wake up cuffed!" Celina recoiled into me, looking for help.

I wanted to support Celina, but in a camp full of injured mages, it made sense. Even if Narissa didn't mean to harm anyone, she was a second-ring mage. A tantrum in the middle of camp could lead to an unacceptable loss of life.

"Celina, we'll be there for her when she wakes. She'll be scared, but think how bad she'll be if she kills someone in that moment. We need to save her from that guilt," I said.

"She'd never hurt me." Celina teared up again, but she let up her vice grip on her sister.

"But we need to keep everyone else safe." I took the cuffs from Zee and softly clasp them on Narissa.

Celina let out one last sob as they clicked closed.

I put away the key in my ring. I'd rather not have someone else hold on to it.

"Come on. Michelle and the others will be excited to see you." I pulled Celina along with me and shot Zee a mouthed 'Thank you' as we went back through camp.

Celina only looked around briefly before wincing and focusing back on her sister. "We aren't doing so well, are we?"

"No, but we are a day out from the portal."

"Which is guarded by those assholes. There is no way they won't fight me for my sister."

I knew there was a risk, but we were out of options. "These injured mages have no better option. Besides, with this many of us, they will have to keep their nice guy routine going."

Celina clicked her tongue. "Even when they are pretending to be good, they still act like asses." She scowled in annoyance.

"Come on, let's get you some rest. Jonny can look after your sister." I opened the infirmary tent where I'd left the rest of the group.

They looked nervous, but when Celina showed up, they all jumped to their feet and welcomed her warmly.

When we sat down, Jonny took Narissa and did an examination.

Celina refused to leave her side, so we all sat around Narissa's bed.

"So what happened after you left?" Steve asked.

"I headed off on my own, looking for answers. I... I hunted some Sun and Moon Hall disciples. I left one alive for questioning, and I found out my sister was here with them. From then on, it was a game of hunting and gathering information until I found her."

I could tell she left a lot unsaid. By how bloodshot her eyes were, she'd barely slept and had exhausted herself in pursuit of her sister. And she was covered in blood, some dry and some still relatively fresh. Not that I could talk.

"What about the rest of you?" She turned to me.

I told her the story of hiding in the cellar, but I left out the part about my mother. I described how we had trained for several days before leaving, and then went into our time with Grant and Zee. I wrapped it up with the loss of our injured and finding this group of mages heading for the portal.

When Jonny and Steve told their story, it wasn't that different from my own. But when they got to the part about Steve losing his leg, Celina sank in on herself.

I knew she was beating herself up for it, thinking that if she had stayed maybe things would have ended differently. I tried to change the subject.

"I think it's about time we washed up and got some rest. Tomorrow will be a big day." I gave Narissa another look.

"She will not wake up on her own," Jonny said, finishing his inspection. "Something is suppressing her soul from interacting with her body. She's alive and well, and she's inside there. But she can't control her own body right now."

"Can she hear me?" Celina asked, putting herself in Narissa's line of sight.

"I think so," Jonny said, stepping back to give the sisters space.

Celina was whispering encouragement to her sister as I left to get cleaned up.

By the time I'd gotten clean, Michelle found me and led me off to a large tent.

"Turns out, with all the spatial rings, we've collected quite the fortune. And a bigger tent," she explained, stepping inside.

I chuckled as I ducked in and saw Celina as well as Narissa laid down in the corner. I laughed. Cleaned up, it was even easier to see the resemblance. I was kicking myself for not seeing it before.

Celina was tucked away in the corner with her sister. I could feel a distance starting to yawn between us. She was recoiling into herself after everything that had happened.

But I wasn't about to let that happen.

I came over and tilted back her head, letting our lips meet. I kissed her deeply until she returned it with growing fervor.

She leaned back with a satisfied sigh. "I thought that, after everything, you'd be done with me. I am causing you too much work."

"A relationship takes work. Anyone who thinks otherwise is a fool," I said with a smile.

My lips had gone numb from her kiss, and I had to remind myself that we couldn't go too far as I cycled my mana to speed up my recovery.

Michelle had come over, and she wrapped herself around Celina. "No way. I'm dead set on keeping you."

Michelle locked eyes with me as my beautiful woman started kissing along Celina's neck, trailing up to her jaw line.

Celina let out a slow moan as she leaned back into Michelle.

I became hard in an instant.

Aurora begged to be free, and I summoned her from her ring. She came out and pounced on the other two.

The three women devolved into a full exploration of each other's bodies.

"He really likes this. Look at him, Celina." Aurora turned Celina's head to me.

I could feel a bit of heat rise in my cheek, but I didn't look away. "I really do," I said, my voice coming out rough. My eyes locked with Celina's.

She blushed from ear to chest as she let the other two girls pull her down and smother her with affection.

"Hmm. I think we've neglected, Master."

The way Aurora purred her name for me made my cock twitch with anticipation.

I cleared my throat, trying to also clear my head. But my blood was not rushing to my brain at the moment. I took a deep breath, using all the willpower I had to make the right choice. "We will definitely find time to continue this, but it will have to be later."

Michelle cocked a brow at me, clearly thinking now was the perfect time.

I sighed. "I'm at the edge of my second ring, and I need to complete the Seven Hells Meridians before we potentially fight again tomorrow." I hoped the women would accept it; my willpower was running thin.

The girls nodded at my reasoning, but Michelle still looked unwilling. I needed to get her thoughts elsewhere.

"We still haven't consumed the Meridian Cleaning Fruit." I pulled out three of the fruits. I had given two away to Jonny and Steve. With these three, I'd be down to three left. While they were a treasure that would make me rich, it would be better for us to focus on strengthening ourselves for the upcoming battle.

The reminder of the fruits sent both of the mage girls into excitement as they plucked their fruit and sat down together to cultivate.

I knew the fruit would have the best effects during our first ring, and even though me and Michelle had formed golden meridians, there was no end to the progress of cultivation as a mage. I knew we would benefit.

As I sat down cross-legged, Aurora rested her head against my knee.

Once I was centered in my meditative state, I consumed the fruit in just a few bites, feeling the rush of mana pour into me from it. The mana was so pure it flushed impurities from my meridians as it went.

I thought my meridians were at their peak based on what Celina had said, but the medicinal fruit proved us all wrong. It strove to perfect my meridians.

To help the process, I began cultivation through the Seven Hells Meridians.

Lesson learned, I prepared myself for the attack on my soul that came with each layer. I breathed deeply, pushing away the anxieties of the past few days. I knew I had gotten blood on my hands, but it was part of the life I had chosen. A mage's cultivation was built upon a pile of corpses.

There was a reason that my town had taught us mental strength and balance.

As my mind wandered, the world I was in started to shift. The sky became red, and I found myself standing in a field of the dead. Vultures circled overhead and had already started picking apart the carrion I'd left on the field.

I was pure power. I instinctively knew I had done all of this. I had killed all these people in the pursuit of power.

Blank faces of corrupt mages and disciples of the sects stared up at me in accusation. I wondered just how far I'd go to reach the top, to become the most powerful mage. Powerful enough that I could enforce my will upon the world.

For the first time, I noticed a beautiful woman kneeling before me. Her red hair caught in the wind as her stunning face stared up at me. It was Kat. She knelt in the blood as it soaked her skirt and climbed slowly up the cloth. She smiled brilliantly and drew me in with her beauty.

"Kill me, and nothing will stop you," she said with all the fervor and passion Kat had always had. She had always wanted to change things, and in this moment, she could. By letting me grow stronger, she was determined to change everything.

"Kill me and change the world for the better." Her smile became fanatical.

I could feel it. I was on the precipice of power that would help me lord over the world. The choice became clear to me. I'd have to give up love of all those who were close to me, sever myself from those that would distract me.

Become unfeeling and above the world. To become transcendent in power, would be to leave behind my humanity.

I could touch upon that power, taste it upon my lips. Power to change everything.

The ecstasy of that power was so sweet that I nearly forgot myself.

I could change it all. It would just cost me everyone.

A shiver from my soul shook off that taste of power that had turned bitter and metallic like blood.

That wasn't what I wanted. It wasn't a life worth living. Taking a deep breath, I dropped my sword. "If I killed those I loved for power, what use would it be?"

I felt the world shudder as the illusionary Kat shattered.

The cracks spread, and the world around me shifted again. Destruction gave way to peace. I was now resting with countless beauties, feeling confident in my ability to protect and care for them. I drew power from each one of them as they drew power from me in a harmony that sang to my soul.

I breathed in deep, starting to emerge from the haze. As I opened my eyes, I felt each layer of the meridians smooth together and form one giant pattern that encompassed all the benefits of the previous layered technique and so much more.

My soul, now tempered once again, opened me up to an entirely new world. Everything was clearer and crisper than it had been before. I felt an enlightenment that had eased something inside of me.

Looking at my ring, it even looked complete. But I knew that there was a thread so small it was barely visible.

Michelle, Celina and Aurora were all staring at me, giant smiles spread across their faces.

"I think we've all learned that we should enjoy those we love. Thoroughly." I paused, making eye contact with each of them and waiting as they understood my full meaning. Aurora licked her lips. "What would you guys say if we picked back up where you'd left off earlier?" I reached over, grabbing Aurora around her waist and pulling her into my lap.

My gorgeous mana beast pushed back, forcing me to pin her arms to her side to keep her in place.

"You're so feisty." Michelle said, leaning in and kissing a trail up Aurora's neck. Aurora leaned into the kisses and let out a throaty moan, her struggle weakening.

Animal instincts drove Aurora. She demanded to be overpowered, but clearly Michelle had enough strength to make it past Aurora's defenses. I felt Aurora grind against my rapidly growing length as the kisses continued.

Gripping her supple thighs tight, I felt my fingers sink satisfyingly into her curves. Taking control, I pulled and pushed her, causing her to grind against me.

"Master." Aurora gasped, leaning back and letting Michelle assault her neck and nibble down to her cleavage.

Another set of hands came from behind me and slipped into my robes, giving soft sensual touches that slowly opened my robe.

I leaned back for a kiss from Celina, Aurora still pressed against my chest. The petite brunette had her robe slipping off her shoulders as she stared into my eyes.

Our tongues slipped past each other as I explored her warm mouth, sticky with traces of poison. My mouth tingled. Before my tongue could go numb, Aurora pulled me back to her, and I shared the taste of Celina's mouth.

Warm life mana passed between us as I held her still. The soft passionate kiss washed away the tingle of Celina's poison.

"Fuck." I groaned, bucking between the women's soft bodies.

"Yeah Stud? Who did you want to fuck first?" Michelle pulled Aurora's breasts free of her dress and kneaded them in my face. Aurora gasped as Michelle leaned down and bit one of her nipples, causing her to gyrate even harder against me.

"Aurora, lose the clothes." I growled, needing to be inside of her. I lifted her off my lap long enough for Celina to pull free the last of my robe.

Her clothes exploded in green light as she stopped holding the mana construct. Aurora was beautiful. Her gold spun hair was free and draped over her breasts like a shy maiden. But her naked body betrayed her anticipation. It was flush and the moisture was obvious between her legs, like a juicy peach ready for me to devour. Her nipples were perky, still firm after Michelle's playing.

I grabbed her hips and pulled her sex to my lips.

"Master." She squeaked, falling backwards into Michelle's lap as I gently lapped my first taste between her folds. She tasted earthy and sweet as I dove my tongue further into her warm slit.

"Have you been a good little mana beast?" I asked, flicking her clit at the end of my stroke.

"Yes, I've been very good, Master." She said gasping, abruptly cutting off as Celina and Michelle started trading her mouth while they mauled her breasts. I kept my eyes up, watching the two girls play with them while I slowly continued my licking.

"If you were fantastic, you'd help your sister wife get ready for me."

Aurora leaned forward, making sure not to lose contact with my mouth as she clawed at Michelle's dress until it came free. Then she reached and pulled Michelle forward to sit on her face.

"Such a good girl." Michelle said, as she started rocking her hips into Aurora, moaning and increasing the speed.

I looked over, noticing Celina's hesitation. She was the only one still dressed.

"Only take it off if you are comfortable." I said, pausing between Aurora's moans. My mana beast grabbed my face and pulled it back against her slit. I laughed and enjoyed her rumble at the vibrations the laugh caused.

"Touch me with my clothes on?" Celina whispered, taking a small step forward.

Michelle grabbed her and pulled her close, and I watched my warrior woman's hands dive into Celina's skirt. "Watch our Stud while I do this."

I kept eye contact with Celina, not letting up on Aurora's slit, which was flooding. If Michelle's face was any indication, Aurora was not going easy on her either.

"There you go. Imagine my hand is his tongue, and he's between your legs right now." Michelle breathed on Celina's ear. Pulling her hand out to lick it slick, she put it back down Celina's skirt. I could see her hand keeping pace with my tongue.

"Yes." Celina arched back into Michelle as we kept our eyes locked.

"You're so swollen." I flicked Aurora's pearl, and all three girls let out gasps as each of them mimicked my tongue. It seemed Aurora had even joined this game.

"More!" Celina gasped.

I buried my face in Aurora's sex, licking her from top to bottom and lavishing her clit. She was so close to her peak. Her sex squeezed my tongue, and her juices coated my face.

Each of the girls came undone. Celina popped off like a firecracker, screaming with her release as she fell to the side. She took over with her own hand, stretching out her own orgasm.

Michelle whistled at the wanton display. "She really needed that."

Aurora free tackled me to the ground and rubbed herself against my hard length. "Please, Master."

I grinned at my needy mana beast and knew what she needed. Flipping her over, I lifted her butt into the air and lined myself up. I had become hard like steel throughout the exchange. "Michelle, pin her arms."

She turned from watching Celina, grabbing Aurora's wrists and handing them to me. "This'll be better."

I grabbed both of Aurora's wrists in one hand and pulled her up on her knees with her back arched before I sank into her silken vice. "Fuck. You're so tight."

"Master, I'm ready. Please don't hold back." She was already struggling against me. Her soft wings were beating against my face as she squirmed.

I had to remember she was a beast and her instincts told her to fight this no matter how much she wanted it. She needed me to prove I was strong enough to deserve her.

353

My slow, teasing strokes only made her fight more. She bucked back against me, panting with need. "Harder."

Michelle grabbed a fist full of Aurora's hair and lifted the feisty mana beast to her own sex. "I don't think you've earned your finish yet."

I took that as my cue to pound into Aurora. Her sticky juices were already soaking down my legs. I held her wrists and used them to pull her into each of my thrusts.

She felt glorious. Her sex was sheathing my cock just tight enough to not be painful.

I was already painfully hard from watching Celina, who was still rolling on the floor recovering from her own explosive pleasure. It didn't take long in Aurora for me to feel my own finish coming.

"Aurora, I'm getting close." Her sex tightened like a silken vice, determined to milk me. That was all I could take. I drove myself deep and pulled her back against me.

I exploded into her and could feel our mixed juices coating my balls.

Her own orgasm came as I filled her, and her sex rippled like she was trying to suck me dry.

Aurora went limp and slid off my cock, recovering from her own aftershocks as she twitched on the ground with a cheerful smile.

Michelle stepped around the blissful mana beast. "Hope you still have some energy, Stud." She sank to her knees and cradled my still hard member.

"I think it needs a little resuscitation."

She smiled and licked me from balls to tip, savoring Aurora and my combined juices. "Delicious."

I didn't have the patience for her games, so I grabbed her by the hair and sank myself into her throat.

Michelle hummed as she bathed my cock with her tongue. As my head pressed into her throat, I felt myself revive rapidly between her ministrations and my own life mana.

She came off with a wet pop and licked her lips. "Get on your back."

I laid down on a blanket and tucked my arms behind my head, as Michelle straddled my hips and started tracing the muscles on my chest. She reached behind her and pushed my cock between her ass cheeks.

Her tight athletic body rippled with barely contained muscle. She clenched my cock in place and started swaying her hips.

It was not the skin on skin friction I expected. "You oiled up back there?" I cocked a brow as she wiggled, coating my member with oil.

Michelle bit her lip and played coy. "We still have one hole of mine you haven't taken." She leaned back. My member was at full mast, and it pushed against her ass. "Just. Stud, you're big. Let me take this easy."

She took a deep breath, and I could feel her thighs relax as she pressed her ass back into me. "Oh fuck." She cried as she opened up and let me in. Putting her weight on her hand, she braced and slowly wiggled me deeper.

"You sure you're okay?" I fought the urge to thrust. She felt so damn good.

"Yeah. Just don't move for a moment. Let me stretch."

Her slit was still open before me, so I sank two fingers into her and started stroking a come hither gesture. I could feel her relax into the pleasure of my fingers.

Celina had recovered, stepping up behind Michelle. She began kissing her neck and nibbling on her ear, trying to take her attention off the tightness.

Michelle closed her eyes and started rocking steadily, my cock still buried in her ass. She escalated to bouncing as her breathing turned into pants. Her moans built louder and louder.

When she came all over my fingers, her ass squeezed my cock with a tightness I'd never felt before. It was almost too much. My cock was locked in place.

"Celina, grab her legs." I pushed her legs back, folding her in half as I sat up.

"Oh, Stud. I don't know if I bend quite that way." Michelle groaned out. But Celina folded her, leading to her ass sticking up in the air while I got my legs under me.

Grabbing her hips, I pushed deep, bottoming out into her. She cried out in new bliss, as I started pumping into her tight asshole.

I kissed Celina over Michelle, tangling our tongues in a torrid pyramid as Michelle moaned below us, lost in her own bliss.

"Imagine that's my tight hole you are working." Celina said, as she broke the kiss and started down my jaw line. "Unload into me, baby."

Michelle rolled into another orgasm and squeezed me, ripping out my own pleasure into her ass before I pulled out. I leaned back, watching my seed dripping from her ass as she lay there zoned out.

"You three are going to kill me." I laughed between deep breaths.

All three of them broke into laughs. "We can't let that happen. I'm not sure we are going to find another monster like that." Celina pointed to my still hard member.

I grabbed her and finished with a breathy kiss that left my throat numb.

Settling in to rest for the next day, the last thoughts on my mind were Kat. I couldn't figure out why she was the one that had tested my soul. While I did care for her, my relationship with the three beauties around me were growing so much deeper.

In the end, I decided that I really did still have feelings for her, and that was okay. I would be a heartless monster if I could kill a once lover.

***

I woke up the next morning to three smiling girls. "What's got you all so happy?"

"Check your meridians." Michelle grinned.

I did. They were still gold in color, but instead of having a luster like ore, they were crystalline like a gem.

"What does that mean?"

"No idea. I've never heard of something like this. Maybe it's your bloodline?" Celina shrugged.

Well, at least it seemed like a good thing. I added it to my list of things to figure out later.

For now, we needed to get all the injured disciples out of the dungeon. The death trap that it had become needed to be broken.

I started getting ready. "How's your sister?" I asked.

"The same." Celina looked over in the corner where her sister rested.

I paused. I'd accessed my soul before. Normally, it took a second-ring mage to do it, but since I'd already touched on the power, I might be able to sense something from Narissa.

Walking over, I laid my hand on her and probed out with my soul. I could feel her soul, active and stirring at my presence. But there was a gap. It didn't connect to the rest of her body.

Finding the gap, I slipped a thread of my soul into it. Her soul flooded that thread and pulled it tightly into place.

I heard gasps and crying outside of my body, but I was still lost in Narissa's inner world. Her soul was pulling hard enough that it felt like she was going to drag mine from my body.

She was there, her soul contained an image of a stone house. Her sense of self locked away in what had become her prison.

There was a gap in the construct, a key needed for her to step outside her small stone house and affect the world.

I could feel the urge to completely fill the gap between her soul and her body. But my gut told me that would end with my complete control over her. The thread of my soul would be a gate between her body and mind.

I shivered at how terrifying that was. It would be complete dominance over her.

I recoiled, pulling back my soul, and I heard more gasps from the women around me and the thud of Narissa hitting her mat again.

Celina's face was in mine when I opened my eyes again. "What did you do? She was back just for a moment. Please, Isaac, do it again."

I felt faint. Tussling souls with Narissa had worn me out. If she'd been more in control of her own soul, I wasn't sure I'd still be alive.

"Give him room." Michelle hovered over me, shoving in front of Celina.

"I'm fine. It just took a lot out of me." I waved off Michelle's protectiveness.

"Can you do it again?" Celina asked, worry etched on her face. We were about to leave the dungeon, but she wanted to see her sister again.

"I wasn't waking her up, Celina. I was enslaving her. If I had finished, she'd be…"

Celina stopped me. "She'd be awake, and I know you wouldn't treat her poorly." Her eyes begged me to bring her sister back to her.

I turned my focus to the once again comatose Narissa. "I know you can hear me. I will try again. This time, give me a sign if you want me to complete it or if you want me to stop. Regardless, we'll take you back to the Ferrymen and try and solve this, giving you back control."

Once again, I bundled up a piece of my soul and stuck it into her. This time, I went slow, waiting for the response from her soul.

When I touched upon the connection, her soul flooded mine and happily dragged it into place.

I had no doubt that this was her will. This time, the process was much less taxing, and I opened my eyes again to see hers flutter open like sleeping beauty.

She sat up and looked at me. "Thank you."

Celina tackled her with a hug, but I was still stunned at just how drawn I was to her. She was beautiful, and from the time at the brothel, I knew she had some sort of seduction technique. But being connected to her soul had brought it to an entirely different level.

I heard the tent flap pull aside as Zee poked her head in and took us all in. "I'm glad your sister is awake, but camp is starting to move. We need those able bodied to be ready and helping."

She didn't react to Aurora, but my mana beast dove into her ring before another person could spot her.

"If we are going, I need a change of clothes. Black is not my color." Narissa picked at the robes she was wearing.

"Michelle, do you have something for her?" I asked, knowing that Celina's clothes wouldn't fit her sister. Michelle's clothes might even be too tight in the chest.

"Here." Michelle tossed out a dress in the Ferrymen's colors.

Narissa stripped right there in the tent, and I had to look away to keep myself focused on preparing to head out.

Michelle joined me, a knowing smirk on her face as I started pulling everything into my spatial ring. "So, you almost did that at the brothel? I really can't blame you."

"Yes, well, I have to apologize for that. It's part of how I've cultivated. I radiate charm as part of it," Narissa jumped in, clearly having heard Michelle.

"Shit, sorry. I don't mean to make this harder for you." Michelle lost her teasing smile.

"Speaking of which, aren't you taking this a bit too much in stride?" I pulled the tent in my spatial ring, suddenly exposed to the hubbub of the camp breaking down to move.

"Probably? Honestly, I think you are subconsciously suppressing a lot of it." Narissa shrugged, stepping into stride with the rest of us.

I cursed under my breath. I didn't want to be exerting that much control over her.

But she laughed. "It's okay. We'll deal with my shit later. Honestly, it's probably for the best. I'm likely either going into an extreme rage or depression when my emotions catch up. Probably a mix of both."

I noticed men around the camp doing double takes as she walked past, followed by some glares my way. I pictured what we must look like, one guy walking with three beautiful females. My mother would be so proud.

"Do you know what we are we up against?" I asked, knowing it was likely going to be our small group against everyone. The disciples trusted the Sun and Moon Hall far too much, so we'd need to be the ones ready to take them on.

"The sect's new Saintess showed up a few months ago. She has the bloodline of the Vermilion Bird, and she skyrocketed in cultivation after she joined, breaking into the second ring within a month. Her soul power is on a completely different level. If you think my presence is charming, it is nothing compared to her. She literally has the entire body of disciples eating out of the palm of her hand."

"If she's here, and as powerful as you say, could they do what was done to you to the rest of the disciples here?" I asked, realizing what we were walking into.

She grimaced. "Yeah, I think that is their plan. They move slowly, sending people they control into the rest of the sects and using them to further manipulate the rest of the sects. They won't even know they have been taken over till it is too late."

"If we stop them, we'll be starting a war." Even given the potential consequences, I knew in my bones it was the right thing to do. There was no way I could sit by and watch the corrupt mages take over every sect.

"Moving out!" a shout came, and everyone echoed it down the line. We all started moving together toward the portal. I reached out, holding hands with Michelle and Celina as we walked. We were going into battle, but I'd do all I could to come out the other side with them.

Chapter 31

"It's easier now, isn't it?" I quietly asked Michelle.

"Huh?" She tilted her head.

"Knowing that we are going into a fight. There's not the same anxiety as waiting, not knowing if you'll be attacked. Somehow, knowing what's to come makes it easier."

I knew we were going to end up fighting the Sun and Moon Hall, and chances were, the corrupt mages would be there too.

Michelle gave a long pause. "I guess it does feel different. We are the ones making the choices versus waiting for someone else to make the first move. We both know I don't mind hitting first and hitting hard." She gave me a wicked grin.

I laughed, thinking back to when we had trained at the academy. The woman could definitely hit you like a train when she wanted to.

I looked over at Narissa, seeing her watching our exchange and smiling to herself. "What are you thinking you'll do after we get out of here?"

"I guess that depends. What are you going to do?" Narissa smiled, both her and Celina joining the conversation.

"First, we need to get to the Ferrymen's floating mountain. Once there, we should be able to fill our second rings. I want to expedite our training any way we can."

The girls all nodded. It really was our best shot at this point.

I went to continue on, but cries came up around the convoy, cutting me off.

It was time. I shifted into a fighting stance and took in the situation around us.

"With me." I drew my sword and went for the closest flank.

Black-robed mages swarmed the side of the army. I could feel their cultivation levels as they came near. None were even halfway through their first ring. This was purely a tactic to drain us.

Narissa was with me and waved her hands. Everywhere she pointed, the ground rumbled, sending corrupt mages staggering.

In turn, the disciples cut the unsteady mages down with ease. It was a bloodbath.

She fell into sync behind me, and I could feel her coordinate through the soul bond we had.

Michelle was there too, covering our backs while Celina darted out, dealing swift death to those that rushed our formation.

I suddenly felt like a rock in a stream as the corrupt mages continued to pour out of the trees. This wasn't a battle; it was a slaughter.

When the first blood mage exploded, taking out a nearby group, Narissa threw up a stone wall to keep the line.

Disciples paused, looking at the size and speed of the spell with awe. They quickly rallied behind our group, realizing we had a second-ring mage, as we pushed through the corrupt mages.

I continued killing every black-robed mage I saw like harvesting wheat, when I recognized one of them mid-stroke.

It was the same girl Aiden had recruited back in Locksprings, the one that had led to Aiden's fight with Jonny and me.

My swing had slowed, but the momentum was too much. I watched in horror as I cut her head clean from her black robes.

I froze. She'd been turned into something disposable, as if her life meant nothing. Anger and revulsion churned through my gut as I came to grips with what I'd just done.

Michelle bumped me as she knocked out a few mages I'd let get too close. She continued focusing on the enemy as she yelled at me to fight.

I blinked and refocused. My survival instincts kicked back in, and I pushed it all aside to deal with another time.

Fires erupted along the line of corrupt mages, consuming dozens at a time. Cheers broke out in the army of disciples.

I didn't understand who had saved us until I heard cheering for the Sun and Moon Hall.

They swept in as heroes, burning their way through the corrupt mages with the intensity.

"Sun and Moon Hall!" Cheers went up all around me as the corrupt mages were routed, and the pressure eased off the front line of disciples.

A huge five-colored fire flared at the front of the line, and I knew that was the Saintess. The five-colored flame must be the vermilion bird.

"It looks like it's time," Narissa said, looking at the flames warily.

I nodded. "Everyone ready?" I asked the other two girls, who joined in nodding. "When we have an opportunity, we rush through the portal and get the elders involved."

I took stock of the army around us. The disciples were looking even more ragged than they had the day before. But their spirits were high as we all gathered and pushed forward. They were lining up to greet the Sun and Moon Hall.

The portal to the dungeon loomed about half a mile behind them. We were so close.

"Everyone!" a call to gather was shouted. The disciples pressed forward to a hill as the Sun and Moon Hall representatives mounted the top of the hill, looking down upon the rest of the sects.

The Earth Flame Sect hung close to them, taking up a perimeter around the hill.

"Everyone! We fought valiantly, and we prevailed!" a Sun and Moon Hall disciple shouted from the top of the hill, echoed with a roar from the army below.

"We've honored our ancestors and avenged our friends. Best yet, we've saved many lives to come by fighting the corrupt mages together."

More cheers echoed the sentiment.

"But now it is time to enter a new era. One of unity. One of peace."

Confused murmurs began emerging around us. A few cheers started, but they fell off as they realized something was wrong.

The Saintess ascended the hill like she was flowing instead of walking. Everyone's attention was riveted to her as the wind swept her flame red locks back in the picturesque definition of otherworldly beauty.

I felt myself drawn to her. My sense of dread was immediately smothered and replaced with a sense of deep loyalty as my soul fell under her influence. My mental defenses completely short circuited watching her.

She wore a veil, but I could imagine what she looked like underneath.

Her sinuous body rippled with provocation as she crested the hill. Five colors of fire burst from behind her, rippling hypnotically.

You could hear a pin drop at that point as the crowd was enraptured by her. I wasn't sure if anyone was even breathing.

"We are entering a new era. One where you all have the opportunity to be seeds of change. Together, we will issue in an era of peace in this slice of the world."

I found myself nodding.

"You are all so injured. Let us take care of you before you head home."

A sea of heads bobbed as we agreed to be seen by the Sun and Moon Hall.

I even felt like my leg was suddenly causing a limp. It all made perfect sense. We'd go see the healers before we leave the dungeon.

Glancing to the side to look for the healers, I saw they had glassy looks in their eyes. Nagging doubts entered my mind about how prepared they were.

"Do not worry. Our healers are ready and waiting. Please, step forward." Her voice soothed my concerns.

When I looked back at her, even though she was wearing a veil, I felt like we'd made eye contact.

Our eyes locked and it was just the two of us in the world for a moment as my heart ached for her.

She beckoned me to her, and I stepped through the crowd that had parted for me.

As I walked up the hill, I got a closer look. Pinning the veil in place was an opalescent vermilion bird clip. It was the very same one I'd gotten Kat on our first date.

I walked before her and turned her away from the crowd.

"Isaac," Kat said in a lilting voice.

She pulled back the veil, and I was struck by how much she'd changed. Kat had always been a beautiful woman, but in the short time we'd been apart, her entire aura had changed. She was more confident, and with that, she radiated power and appeal. Her hair billowed out behind her like flames of passion.

Kat's eyes had become a kaleidoscope, her five-colored flame shining through them as I was lost in her eyes.

Her eyes were lidded with sensual pleasure as they crinkled with her smile. "I've missed you, Isaac. But now we can finally be together again! No one will fight me if I bring you into the Sect. I can give you everything we have talked about."

I drew her closer, wanting nothing more than to take her up on everything she offered.

If I claimed those plump red lips, I knew she'd give me everything I ever wanted.

But all I would want from that moment on was her.

As I leaned into her, I felt a pressure build in my head.

The pressure became a distraction and I frowned, like it was stopping me from kissing the woman I loved so dearly.

She was right there, all I had to do was lean another few inches.

Kat pursed her lips and her arms snaked around my shoulders to draw me in closer. "Everything, Isaac."

I pushed forward as the pressure continued to build until something in my mind shattered.

The final wall in my cultivation crumbled from the pressure of Kat's trance.

And for the first time, I knew what it was like to be a second-ring mage.

With the sudden expansion of my soul, I snapped out of the charm Kat had me in and held her at arm's length.

Fully in control of myself I walled out her influence.

"What are you doing?" I let outrage bleed into my tone.

Kat's eyebrows jumped up before she smothered her surprise. "I'm both delighted and disappointed that you broke the charm. But who am I kidding? I wouldn't love you if you weren't extraordinary." She started leaning back into me, but I held her firmly away.

I looked around, taking in the situation with a clear head. The army of disciples were moving like zombies, lining up for the Sun and Moon Hall to do whatever it was they did to people.

Even the mages of the Sun and Moon Hall wore glazed expressions under Kat's influence.

"Why?" It was the most important question.

"Isaac, we always talked about what we'd do if we had the power to change the world. We'd use mages to heal the sick and provide for the poor. Towns like Locksprings would flourish under the guard of a few disciples of a sect. With the disciples here brainwashed to follow me in the future, they will be the seeds that turn over all the sects. If I do this enough, I can reshape the world of mages to better the world."

I nearly stumbled back. I could tell she meant what she was saying, but I didn't understand how she could believe it. "What good is changing it if you are enslaving everyone? Do you know what the Sun and Moon Hall uses this technique for?"

She sighed, clearly not feeling understood.

Kat's eyes were like glowing flames. "It's not enslavement. I'm just forcing behavior changes of one generation to make the world better for years! It is a worthy goal, and we need radical steps to make a change! The world of sects and mages is not going to change on its own."

"Kat, please listen to me. This technique. The Sun and Moon Hall uses it for horrible things." I felt for Narissa in the crowd and used my soul to call her to us.

"I trust you, Isaac, but you just don't understand. They aren't enslaving people." She looked at me earnestly. "It's just behavior modification. Yes, it's drastic, but we need the sects to come together. We need an era of peace." She was quietly pleading by the end.

There were still glimpses of the Kat I used to know in her speech. Her mannerisms, her expressions, they were all Kat. But the look in her eyes and the way she spoke was different, much more fervent. I kept feeling like I was looking at Kat and talking to a stranger. But I knew she was in there somewhere. I needed something to cut through her confusion.

"If you trust me, then listen to me."

My fiery-haired love turned to Narissa as she approached. "Who's this?"

"This is a woman I found in our town, in the brothel that the Sun and Moon Hall owns."

Kat scoffed, dismissing Narissa. "The traitors to the Sect are the ones who are sent there."

"Narissa, tell your story," I said.

She described how she'd started out like how most disciples of the Sect did, being picked from a small town. But hers was far larger and more connected to the rest of the world than Locksprings.

The man Narissa had followed to the Sect courted her, and one night, when her guard was down, he performed the technique that turned her into his love slave.

He used her for dual cultivation, and she was scared, but she still had most of her free will.

It was later when another girl who had just joined the Sect caught his eyes that it all changed. It started as little asks, getting Narissa to help lure the new disciple in. Then it turned deeper, using Narissa to start to turn the new girl into a slave as well.

Eventually, he lost interest in Narissa and had her work menial jobs for money. Finally, that escalated into prostitution when he wasn't satisfied with the amount of money she was bringing him.

By the time Narissa finished her story, Kat's haughty air was gone, and she looked confused. I could tell she was piecing together this new information with all she'd seen in the Sect. We stood in silence for a moment.

I thought my Kat had returned for a moment before she sighed. "There's always a cost to power Isaac. We both knew power to do what we wanted wouldn't be free. I can't change the past, but I can stop it going forward."

I smiled. It was about damn time she came to her senses.

She turned to me. "A war is going to start. This was only the opening move. None of us can stop what's going to happen. Only shape it, and Isaac, you are on the wrong side to do that."

I was wrong, my Kat wasn't back. "No, Kat, we don't give up."

Kat's voice became shrill in frustration. "Who's giving up? I'm saving the damned world. All I asked was to keep my love. But you won't join me, will you?"

"Kat, can't you see what they've done to you. They've changed you. Come with me now, we can make this right." I realized in that moment that Kat had been offered the same choice I had. And she'd chosen power.

"I'm fine—I was fine as long as I had you." Tears of blood started dripping down her face.

The emotional turmoil had unsteadied her soul and now she was straining to keep control of the mass of young mages.

I pulled her close. "Kat. Sun and Moon Hall changed you, drastically. I can tell you are back now, but if you leave, I'm not sure I'll ever see you again."

She choked a laugh in my arms. "You made your choice and I made mine, love. You want to be the hero so bad? Then I love you enough to be your villain."

I didn't have a chance to react when she laid a searing kiss on my cheek.

It was like someone had stabbed hot pokers straight into my soul.

I could see her soul as it touched mine. The beautiful Kat I always knew was wreathed in flames of five colors. Her soul dwarfed mine in that moment, I could see so much of her soul focusing on keeping the disciples under control. There were other marks, inky black tethers hooked into her soul.

"Kat, we can fix this."

"I don't need fixing. I need your love—it's what held me together through everything."

"Kat, I love you. But I can't love what you are becoming."

Tears leaked from her eyes. "You finally said it."

Kat's personification of her soul reached into her chest and ripped out the very core of her soul. It gleamed, completely free of the taint that had touched the edges of her soul.

"I love you too." She thrust the piece of her soul deep within mine.

My soul felt like it was burning up from the inside and I fell to my knees back on the hill in the dungeon.

The pull towards her grew, before it all of a sudden vanished. She wilted as it vanished, and a wave crashed across all the disciples. Kat began coughing up blood.

"Kat!" I grabbed her before she could completely fall to the ground.

"You only have a small head start. Use it." She smiled, the blood blending in with her ruby red lips.

"Saintess!" Members of the Sun and Moon Hall rushed to her aid.

I tried to pull Kat back, but I was mobbed by the mages. Looking at one, I realized their eyes were once again clear. The enchantment was gone.

The entire hill burst with confused and angry murmurs, which quickly grew into open complaint and hostility. The sects started to remember what had just happened to them.

That was when the screaming started, and I knew I was running out of time.

Kat had disappeared into a sea of Sun and Moon Hall disciples. They were turning their focus to the rest of the sects.

I wanted to go after Kat, but I had to choose. And I couldn't make her effort be for nothing. The decision was already made, but I didn't like it.

"Damnit," I roared, pulling my blade on the first Sun and Moon Hall mage to catch my eye. At least I had some opponents to take my frustration out on.

The silver and gold robes were gaudy, but at least they were easy to find. With one swing, I cleaved him in two.

"To the portal!" I yelled to the sect disciples, trying to get them moving.

At first, only a few started moving, but it quickly became a larger and larger stream. Soon, it turned into a stampede of people carrying or dragging their friends forward. I caught sight of Steve riding his new mount, which had Jonny in its jaws, leading the pack. I relaxed a smidge, a few of my friends accounted for and moving towards safety.

I held the hill that separated the Sun and Moon Hall from the rest of the sects, but the Sun and Moon Hall was reforming.

I cut a horizontal slash at the mages who were advancing on me.

They backed up, but it seemed to wake them out of the fog even more, giving them a place to focus.

"He defeated the Saintess," a cry came up from the back of the crowd. More murmuring and gasps came from the Sun and Moon Hall.

"He injured her!" a pained cry came out as if they'd been personally wounded.

The cries galvanized the Sun and Moon Hall as they pressed forward.

I blocked and parried, hoping to buy time for more to flee. Using the height advantage, it wasn't so hard at first. But it didn't take long before they began to cover the hill, and I was beating back swords from too many angles.

One sword caught my leg, and I hissed with pain, jumping back. I wouldn't be able to hold the hill for much longer.

Drawing on the strength of my second ring, I cast Aurora's spell.

The giant claw materialized behind me, only now it was far more distinct. Green and gold scales trailed along the top of the claw as the spell crashed down among the Sun and Moon Hall.

Dozens of mages gathered together to repel the spell, but even then, they just barely managed it.

Once again, I was stunned by the power of Aurora's spell.

With only a moment of concentration, my mana was back to flowing normally. I smiled at the progress, then breathed deeply and prepared for round two.

Looking over my shoulder in the brief respite, I saw the other sects were starting to disappear through the portal.

Bracing myself, I caught another attack and parried it off, stepping away. I needed to start retreating towards the portal.

One mage lunged deep with his thrust, and I spun to the side with a stroke meant to take his leg.

Unfortunately, another sword came from the side and I had to pivot. I made a gash in his leg before I needed to pull my sword back for a block.

I caught his blade awkwardly, and my momentum was stalled as we locked swords.

That was all it took for several probing attacks to turn into cuts.

Wincing, I stepped back and poured my life mana through my body. I was severely outnumbered. The Sun and Moon Hall poured over me like an angry ant hill.

Hitting a breaking point, I knew it was time to make a final stand. I didn't love my chances, but not many options were left.

I exploded with the strength of my bloodline, the aspect of my mana, and the full strength of my second ring.

The next disciple blocked me, but I didn't care.

I overpowered his block, tearing and scoring deeply enough along his collar for a fatal wound.

A charging attack was met with my bone crunching fist to his chest.

I descended into fighting like a wild beast. I fought for every other disciple here. I fought for the future of the sects. It was a fight of survival, but more than just mine. I was fighting for survival and freedom of the masses.

Scores, large and small stacked up on me as I fought like a berserker.

"Isaac!" A scream tore through the air right beside me as Michelle came crashing into the pile. "Run. I got your back."

I knew she was lying. Michelle was about to throw herself away for my chance to escape, the same as I'd been trying to do for her. I was not going to let her ruin it.

"Damnit! What is with my women?" I grabbed her and threw her over my shoulder.

"Isaa—"

"Shield. Now."

Michelle cast her black shield, and I was already running, plowing through the Sun and Moon Hall.

"You and I are going to have a conversation when we are done here. If I weren't busy right now, I'd be spanking your round ass," I yelled, my blood pumping furiously as I pushed free with a clear sight to the portal.

Narissa and Celina were there at the portal, waiting for us and protecting our exit.

"Stall them," I called, as Michelle and I blew past them.

I could feel both of them pour all of their mana they had left into an attack before darting behind us through the portal.

A field of spikes and a cloud of poison erupted behind us as we escaped the dungeon at last.

I came up short as we exited, taking in the scene and wondering if the dungeon hadn't been safer than the outside.

We had the eyes of everybody around. Disciples of sects were running to their leaders, and startled whispers were escalating in volume as I carried Michelle away from the portal, looking for Elder Shaw.

I needed to get the full story out before all hell broke loose. I noticed that the sects were physically divided.

Sun and Moon Hall, Earth Flame Sect and one other I wasn't familiar with stood to one side. The rest were all to the other.

The tension in the air was so thick I was afraid it would snap with a moment's notice, launching into a full-scale battle among the elders.

"Isaac," Elder Shaw called. He already had several disciples whispering quickly.

I hurried over. "Elder, we need to go."

"Our disciples are saying that some sects were engaging in corrupt techniques." He looked at Sun and Moon Hall's side as he said it.

"Yes. And we need to go. Now."

I was garnering more attention, and I could hear words like Hero and Saintess being thrown about. I knew I was about to get far more attention than I'd like, or needed, at the moment.

Soon, the confusion would combust as they determined a target.

"We need to clear the field," I said loudly, feeling hundreds of eyes turn to me, sizing me up and looking to the elder for guidance.

But all of the young mages followed my orders. They'd seen enough inside the portal to trust me.

"Young man!" an elder yelled in outrage.

But I didn't have time to argue. Once those Sun and Moon Hall disciples came out, this was going to turn into ground zero for the next war between the sects and corrupt mages.

As the field started slowly clearing, the first mage from the Sun and Moon Hall came screaming out of the portal. "Elder! We failed to control them. Someone defeated the Saintess!"

Silence ensued and I braced. I was out of time.

The world turned on its head as elders from the sects collided. Meteors, hundred-foot tall waves, earthquakes. It was like a dozen natural disasters merged together as a fight broke out among the elders of the sects.

I stumbled and watched as a number of disciples I'd just saved were blown back. Some at the back were twisted like rag dolls.

The Sun and Moon Hall didn't hold back. They had less to lose; their disciples were still protected in the dungeon.

The scene was cut off from us, as a massive stone wall soared into the sky to protect us. Several old men were working together at its base.

"Get the disciples out of here," yelled the same old man who had scolded me earlier.

I nodded.

"Move it!" I shouted, pulling those close to me to their feet as the sentiment rippled through the crowd and we rushed away. Michelle, Celina, and Narissa helped me herd the disciples.

But we hadn't gotten very far before a red-robed elder appeared in front of us. I recognized him as the one that had tried to kill me in the competition.

The Earth Flame Sect elder held one of his disciples by their neck. "Is that the one?" He pointed to me.

"Yes, Yes." The disciple nodded. "He's the one that injured the Saintess and ruined the plan."

I felt the pressure of his cultivation slam me to a full stop.

Others started to stop with me, but I knew that would only get them killed. "Keep going. Get clear. Return to your sects!" I shouted, and they continued on.

This man was powerful, and his anger was currently pointed towards me. There wasn't much these disciples could do to protect me from him; it would be suicide.

I did a quick inventory of my body. I was at the ragged edge of my rope. The wounds from holding back the Sun and Moon Hall had taken their toll, and my mana was nothing more than a slow trickle.

Michelle, Celina and Narissa had stayed with me, and I could feel Aurora pounding in her ring.

With little to lose, I summoned Aurora, catching surprise on the elder's face as he tilted his head.

"Ah." Understanding seemed to dawn on him. "That's why you were so formidable. To have such a mana beast as your first ring..." He tisked.

Aurora held my hand, and for the first time, I felt her soul.

It was so large, I felt like a grain of sand on the beach when our souls touched.

Isaac. We have one shot. Together, we attack. Then I'll take us out of here.

Through our souls, she spoke to me. I was so shocked; my face must have reflected it.

"What? Do you not even know what your mana beast is?" The elder laughed. "Well this should be even easier than I thought."

I gathered the rest of my mana.

"Now. Now why must the *heroes* always fight? I'll actually leave a corpse for your family to bury if you make this easy."

Aurora and I cast the giant claw spell, together.

The elder's laugh cut off. His eyebrows popped up at the strength we were able to unleash. He threw up a hasty shield of mana, but he was pinned under the combined weight of our spells.

"Get on my back!" Aurora pulled me away as she started to change.

The change was fast. At first, standing before me was Aurora. Then, a bus-sized mana beast was there. And she continued to grow past the size of a house, then further.

I grabbed onto her back as she continued to grow, stunned with what I was seeing.

She was glorious. Two familiar talons bit into the earth as her upper body stretched. A long flowing tail sprouted from her tailbone, and her wings yawned open to cover the sky.

Her underside was all green and gold scales, which bled seamlessly into feathers until her top, covered in soft downy feathers. She now had three sets of wings and a long, fish-like tail finned with feathers.

Aurora had fully transformed into one of the auspicious beasts. The Kunpeng. She let out a cry that was half bird and half something far deeper and dangerous than any bird.

Aurora grabbed Michelle, Narissa, and Celina into her talons gently.

A massive rush of air slammed me to her back as we were suddenly hundreds of feet into the air. My brain was still reeling.

I could hear the elder cursing below, but he was cut out by the sound of wind rushing in my ears.

Aurora didn't quite so much fly as swim through the sky.

Below us, I could see the disciples dispersing through the wilderness. I knew some of them would be hunted down, but word of what happened would get out.

The elders at the dungeon paused, and I swore I could see a few of them looking up at Aurora as we disappeared into the sky, mixtures of concern and awe in their faces.

She slowed down once we were clear of any danger, and I looked around myself in awe. The world quite literally opened up before me.

"What's that ahead?" I called out, looking at a large looming shape in the distance.

"Sun and Moon Hall," Narissa answered from below.

The sects were each located on a floating mountain, and for the first time, I realized just how massive of an entity a sect was. I looked in awe, knowing that, given the distance, that mountain was larger than anything I could imagine.

Aurora, are you okay?

Tired, master. Do you still love me?

Of course, now more than ever. You're a total badass.

"Where to?" Michelle called.

"Where we were always headed. It's time to join a sect."

Celina directed us towards where the Ferrymen's own floating mountain would be, and Aurora pivoted, heading in that direction

The world flew by below us, and I took a moment to breathe in the cold, crisp air. So much had changed. The war had begun, and we'd all have a role to play. The corrupt mages had to be stopped, and the balance of power was still in their favor.

It felt daunting, but I had an amazing team by my side, and an ally within the enemy. I hoped that one day I'd be able to save Kat.

Author's Note

That's a wrap folks. I absolutely loved writing this book. It has been a dream of mine to write a Xianxia, and I'm excited it's getting popular for western readers. I learned a ton from people who read and reviewed LR1&2. I feel like I was able to flex some of those learnings in this book.

I wanted to take a moment to thank everyone who's given me a review. I can't express as an author how empowering it is to read those reviews when I'm tired and want to put the pen down. I thank you all for cheering me on. Know this and future books only come out faster with your continued encouragement.

That said, I have to ask you to review once again. Reviews are the lifeblood of the Amazon system. Each review is a health potion before the Zon boss strikes a killing blow and buries your book in the deep recesses of the 100th page of recommendations.

Please, if you enjoyed the book, leave a review, you can even just click the stars now and not leave a written review. Anything helps.

Made in the USA
Monee, IL
12 January 2024